PRAISE FOR DIANE ARMSTRONG

'Diane Armstrong's novel is a nuanced rendition of the moral conundrums individuals face in extremis. She concludes that "perhaps no sin is unforgivable, if you can understand the sinner". Among survivors, forgiveness and understanding are highly charged and hotly contested notions. Armstrong's novel is a sincere contribution to that fraught discussion.'
—Louise Adler, *The Australian* on *The Collaborator*

'Both moving and evocative, *The Collaborator* will appeal equally to lovers of historical fiction, romance, legal drama or family mystery. With six historic works behind her, Armstrong (herself a child Holocaust survivor) knows well how to develop full characters and to cleverly plot multiple story strands with deftness and finesse.'
—Scott Whitmont, Lindfield Bookshop on
The Collaborator

'Guaranteed to hook you with its powerful and emotive journey back into a turbulent history, *The Collaborator* is a superb and compelling novel that comes highly recommended.'
—*Canberra Weekly* on *The Collaborator*

'This is a very remarkable story and Armstrong retells it well. Certainly, she had a lot of reference material at her disposal, but she has assembled it skilfully and coherently. Armstrong brings out the hothouse atmosphere of both wartime Budapest and the new Jewish State very convincingly and is particularly good in conveying the precarious uncertainties of those times.'

Geoffrey Zygier—*J-Wire* on *The Collaborator*

'Just as she did so successfully in [*Mosaic*], in *The Collaborator* Armstrong fills in the gaps history cannot describe, and fictionalises the true story — bringing elements of it into 21st-century Australia, Budapest and Israel.'

—*Daily Telegraph* on *The Collaborator*

'A stunning blend of the past, the present and the promise of the future. Annika's determination to find out both the story of her grandmother and that of Miklos Nagy is inspiring…Diane Armstrong seamlessly intertwines these beautiful and heart-wrenching stories…*The Collaborator* is evocative and moving; a fantastically written gem that you won't want to put down.'

—*Better Reading* on *The Collaborator*

'This is most certainly a fascinating tale of courage and compassion during dire circumstances. Tied in neatly to the present day with the search for not only the truth but also personal answers, this is a book I would highly recommend to history lovers.'

—*Great Reads and Tea Leaves* on *The Collaborator*

'By skilfully passing us between time zones and geographies, Diane Armstrong manages to keep the novel pacey without losing either story detail or a necessary focus on character.

—*Living Arts Canberra*

'a well-researched, interesting and thought provoking novel…relevant and educational as well as deeply moving, and recommend[ed] to all lovers of the genre.'
—*But Books Are Better* on *The Collaborator*

'*Mosaic* flows like a novel, which once started is hard to put down. It is a compelling family history of extraordinary people against some of the most frightening events of our century. The depth of emotions evoked is stunning. I was thrilled and deeply moved.'
—Joseph Heller, author of *Catch 22* on *Mosaic*

'Diane Armstrong's book is a source of delight to the reader. Written with fervour and talent, it will capture your attention and retain it to the last page.'
—Nobel Prizewinner Elie Wiesel on *Mosaic*

'A most remarkable book about one family's experience…a rich and compelling history…Just as AB Facey's *A Fortunate Life* and Sally Morgan's *My Place* have become part of the national literary heritage, so too has *Mosaic* earned its place in our social dialogue as part of our cultural tapestry.'
—*Daily Telegraph* on *Mosaic*

'I found myself replaying the scenes in the book like a film reel in my mind…*Nocturne* is one of those novels that will leave you reading into the night and will stay with you, like the notes of an unforgettable melody, long after you've read the last line.'
—*Australian Jewish News* on *Nocturne*

'A moving and poignant celebration of survival…'
—*Booklist* on *Mosaic*

'A consummate writer at the top of her form…remarkable for her narrative dexterity and emotional resonance. A bold adventure of a novel…a fine fictional debut from a writer who's already made her mark.'
—Sara Dowse, *The Canberra Times* on *Winter Journey*

'A cleverly crafted mystery…a good story, well told. Armstrong's skill in weaving an elaborate fabric out of her characters and subject matter stand her in good stead…the bleak wintry landscapes of the Polish countryside are vividly captured.'
—Andrew Riemer, *The Sydney Morning Herald* on *Winter Journey*

'A complex and often heart-and-gut-wrenching novel. The book intelligently explores the need to confront and acknowledge evil before it can be exorcised. Armstrong's supremely confronting basic material is crucial to our understanding of ourselves as "warped timber" humanity.'
—Katharine England, *Adelaide Advertiser* on *Winter Journey*

'The best and worst of the human spirit are dredged up in this profoundly moving, compelling and superbly written story.'
—Carol George, *Australian Women's Weekly* on *Winter Journey*

'Like Geraldine Brooks, Diane Armstrong's historical research is expertly woven into the fabric of a fictional tale, providing an engrossing "action" of heroism and resilience

which will appeal to both fans of fictional dramatic/romantic sagas, as well as lovers of insightful history'
—*Australian Bookseller & Publisher* on *Nocturne*

'Easy reading, racy...Diane Armstrong's *Nocturne* is in the category of blockbuster with extra heart. The stories of the role played by young women in the Warsaw revolt are extraordinary...Armstrong keeps us turning the pages and may well introduce a new readership to a story that must keep on being told.'
—*The Age* on *Nocturne*

'A gallant and gut-wrenching story. The accounts of the two uprisings...are dramatic and heart-breaking...superb reading.'
—*Australian Book Review* on *Nocturne*

'*Nocturne* had me captured from its opening chapters...it is an inspirational account of how ordinary people are forced to find strength and courage within themselves when the world around them falls apart.'
—*Vibewire* on *Nocturne*

'Compulsive reading, thanks in no small part to Armstrong's ability to bring each character to life.'
—*The Bulletin* on *Mosaic*

'A stirring and powerful tapestry into which she has masterfully interwoven the story of her family with the enormity of the Holocaust, commuting fluently between the individual and the historical, the particular and the universal.'
—*Australian Jewish News* on *Mosaic*

© Jonathan Armstrong

Diane Armstrong is a child Holocaust survivor who arrived in Australia from Poland in 1948. An award-winning journalist and bestselling author, she has written five previous books.

Her family memoir *Mosaic: A chronicle of five generations,* was published in 1998 and was shortlisted for the Victorian Premier's Literary Award for Non-Fiction as well as the National Biography Award. It was published in the United States and Canada, and was selected as one of the year's best memoirs by Amazon.com. In 2000, *The Voyage of Their Life: The story of the SS* Derna *and its passengers,* was shortlisted in the New South Wales Premier's Literary Award for Non-Fiction.

Her first novel, *Winter Journey,* was published in 2004 and shortlisted for the 2006 Commonwealth Writers' Prize. It has been published in the US, UK, Poland and Israel. Her second novel, *Nocturne,* was published in 2008 and won the Society of Women Writers Fiction Award. It was also nominated for a major literary award in Poland. *Empire Day*, a novel set in post-war Sydney, was published in 2011.

Diane has a son and daughter and three granddaughters. She lives in Sydney.

Also by Diane Armstrong

Non-fiction

Mosaic: A chronicle of five generations

*The Voyage of Their Life: the story of
the SS* Derna *and its passengers*

Fiction

Winter Journey

Nocturne

Empire Day

Diane Armstrong

THE COLLABORATOR

First Published 2019
This Paperback Edition published 2020
ISBN 9781867202394

THE COLLABORATOR
© 2019 by Diane Armstrong
Australian Copyright 2019
New Zealand Copyright 2019

Published by
HQ Fiction
An imprint of Harlequin Enterprises (Australia) Pty Limited (ABN 47 001 180 918), a subsidiary of HarperCollins Publishers Australia Pty Limited (ABN 36 009 913 517)
Level 13, 201 Elizabeth St
SYDNEY NSW 2000
AUSTRALIA

A catalogue record for this book is available from the National Library of Australia
www.librariesaustralia.nla.gov.au

To Bert
For all that you are

PROLOGUE

Tel Aviv, 1952

Isaiah Fleischmann presses his nose against the grimy window pane of his rented room, wipes the steam off the glass with his handkerchief, and stands very still. Soft white flakes are floating through the air. Snow in Tel Aviv! Who could have imagined such a thing? The sky is the colour of tarnished brass, and as he watches, the grey street is transformed by a fine layer of snow, pure, silent and untouched.

He has forgotten he is still holding his pen until it drops from his numb fingers and he bends down with a groan to pick it up. He is about to resume writing, but the snow distracts him. It crosses his mind that such a rare phenomenon could be a portent of something momentous, but he shrugs that off. *Bube mayseh, superstitious nonsense,* that's what his mother would have said. The silence is now broken by children who have run outside, squealing at their first sight of snow, gathering handfuls which melt as soon as they try to shape them into balls. Some splatter against his window and slide down, leaving a watery trail.

He shuffles back to his rickety wooden table and pulls a blanket around his bony shoulders, determined to start writing, but snow is still falling, and he rises again and peers through the window. It's a seductive sight, watching flakes drifting from the sky onto the ground, but he knows you can't trust snow any more than you can trust people. It lulls you with its beauty while it disguises reality. Beneath its plump whiteness lies poverty, squalor and misery.

Snow creates an illusion, it fools people into mistaking the appearance for the substance. Every winter, it used to transform the huddle of overcrowded cottages back in Kolostór into a wintry wonderland scene like those in fairy tales.

But inside their hut his father was bent over his worktable, mending shoes with chilblained hands, his mother added water to the soup to make it go further, and he and his little sister Malka shivered as they huddled together in bed to keep warm.

Most people were too stupid, too complacent, or too trusting to detect the reality concealed beneath the beguiling surface, behind false smiles and lying words, but whether they liked it or not, he intended to continue exposing dishonesty wherever he saw it. Courage and conviction were what mattered, not approval or acclaim.

He knows that people laugh at him, and ridicule the pamphlets he writes. They call him a *nebbish*, a loser, a curmudgeon with a bee in his bonnet, a crank with a grudge against the whole world, but their mockery has never deterred him and it never would. Those who reveal uncomfortable truths usually face derision, so he doesn't expect praise when he hands out his smudged, closely written leaflets that expose corrupt politicians and public servants who serve only their own interests. He has turned survival into a mission.

He rubs his stiff fingers and picks up his pen. One day they would realise he had been right. As his mother used to say, you can't be a prophet in your own kingdom. She was a wise woman with a proverb for every situation, but he wonders if she ever realised the irony of naming him Isaiah.

So he keeps handing out his pamphlets to passers-by on the corner of Dizengoff Street, the busiest thoroughfare in the city. Most people quicken their pace when they see him standing there and avert their gaze, the women staring at the pavement, pulling their dogs and toddlers away, and the men finding a sudden reason to cross the road. Occasionally someone takes a pamphlet, probably out of pity for the thin, unshaven fellow in a shabby overcoat and worn-out shoes who thinks he can put the world to rights. He suspects that when he isn't looking they throw the thin sheets into the garbage bins or use them to wipe their behinds, since toilet paper, like so many other things here, is an expensive commodity.

That brings his mind back to his current hobbyhorse. He unwraps the crinkly packet of tobacco, places a pinch onto a sheet of cigarette paper, rolls it carefully so not a single shred will fall out, and licks the edges of the paper to glue them together. He takes a comforting puff and continues writing. This time his target is the Rationing and Supply department which he likes to refer to, in capital letters, underlined and asterisked, as the *RATIONALISING* Department. Because that's what they did. They kept making excuses for their mismanagement.

Every day he passes long queues of women lining up to buy essential food for their families. This is supposed to be the land of milk and honey but you often can't buy milk, let alone honey. How are mothers supposed to look after their families when they spend hours every day queuing up for basic food which is either unavailable or sold out? His neighbour Fruma who has two kids under five often comes home in tears because when she finally reaches the counter, the grocer spreads his hands in a helpless gesture and says he has run out of milk. 'But the newspaper says there is milk!' she complained the day before. The grocer shrugged. 'So put your newspaper in the saucepan and boil it!'

By now Isaiah has worked himself up into a fury and his pen flies fast over the sheets of lined paper. This time he decides to address the women. Have you ever seen Ben-Gurion's wife waiting in line? Do you think Moshe Yosef's children miss out on bananas? Do Moshe Sharrett's kids exist on two eggs a week? Moshe Yosef, the minister of our *RATIONALISING* department keeps telling you to be patient, because we are a young country, and our population is growing. He thinks austerity is good for your soul, but he and the other politicians live in towers of plenty, they have no idea what ordinary women like you are going through every day, trying to feed your families with the pathetic coupons they issue.

He pauses, checks what he has written and nods agreement with his words. Week after week he writes the truth about the deceptions and lies of the government but no-one seems to be listening. He reaches for the latest issue of *Ma'ariv* just as the light globe flickers and plunges the room into darkness. Another blackout. Everything here is a *balagan*, a mess, all due to inefficiency and mismanagement. Cursing, he fumbles for the candle he keeps on the table just in case. He smokes his cigarette down until the butt burns his nicotine-stained fingers, places his small saucepan on the primus stove and a few minutes later he is sipping scalding tea through a lump of sugar he sucks between his teeth.

Squinting at the small newsprint, he shakes his head in disbelief. He is reading about the war in Korea. 'So now we are worrying about Korea, as if we don't have enough *tsures* of our own,' he mutters. From the moment he arrived in 1948, they'd had to cope with Arab attacks, war, inflation, rationing, recession, unemployment, severe housing shortages and endless discussions about who should be allowed to enter the new nation and in what numbers.

The Jews were God's chosen people all right — chosen for perpetual suffering, persecution and endless arguments. As for believing in some divine being who ordained every event on earth and directed human lives like some kind of celestial traffic warden, that was just absurd.

He turns, startled to hear a man's voice in the room, not realising it is his own. They say that a man who defends himself in court has a fool for a client, so what do they call one who talks to himself? He chuckles, and reads on. It seems that the Korean War does affect them after all, because as a result of it, America has now reduced its donations of powdered milk and other food to Israel. More *tsures*.

He arrived in 1948, a reluctant immigrant to the Promised Land. He had come via Auschwitz and Bergen-Belsen, hellholes he tries to blot from his memory. He came with a battered suitcase held together with a leather strap, and a heart full of hate. He loathed the Nazis and the camp guards, but most of all he hated that upstart from Budapest who had refused to save his mother and his sister. Miklós Nagy also came from Kolostór, but Nagy's family had lived in a villa in the best part of town, not in a cobbler's hut, and ate chicken every day, not just on holy days. After Nagy left town, he became a big shot in the capital, and they hadn't seen him for dust. Until that day in 1944, a day that is branded on his memory as clearly as the number tattooed on his arm.

For several weeks, they had heard rumours that the Germans were lying, that the Jews being rounded up and interned at the local brickworks would eventually be deported, not to some town where they would find work, as the Germans claimed, but probably to a concentration camp somewhere in the East. It was a story most people found incredible. It didn't make any sense, and besides, they trusted the Hungarian government would protect them because Jews were patriotic Hungarians. After all, they had been in the forefront of the fight for Hungarian independence after the Great War, so what did they have to fear?

But when they discovered that the Hungarian government colluded in the Nazis' anti-Semitic agenda, stripped the Jews of all their rights, and facilitated the deportations, people started to panic. No-one wanted to be forcibly taken to some unknown destination. And that's when Miklós Nagy appeared in town, like some sort of knight in shining armour. It was supposed to be a secret, but word soon got out that he was organising a train to take some of the towns- folk away from Hungary and the Nazi Occupation to a neu- tral country on the way to Palestine. There was apparently a list of people who would be included on the rescue train. Desperation reached fever pitch. What did they have to do to be included?

For some reason — and Isaiah reckons he now knows the reason — although Miklós Nagy was a Jew, he had the power to save some people in Nazi-occupied Hungary. No doubt he'd put his own friends and relatives on that list, as well as some wealthy people, but maybe there was room on the train for a few more. Isaiah was among the villagers who crowded outside the Nagy villa like feudal supplicants at the manor gate, all beside themselves in their anxiety to get away. But Miklós Nagy flung open the door and pushed past them, not looking right or left or making eye contact with anyone. Isaiah, who was at the back of the throng, stepped forward and blocked his path, begging him to add his mother and sister to the list, but Nagy had looked through him and walked on, as if he was a worm on the ground, not even worth a glance.

Of course, if they'd had money to buy a place on the train, it would have been a different story, but they didn't, so his poor mother and little Malka ended up in the chimneys of Auschwitz instead, and their ashes were scattered over some godforsaken part of the Polish countryside. He remembers seeing the smoke over the camp that day, and some days he thinks he can still smell its nauseating odour. It's a memory that haunts him. One day he might forgive the Germans, but he knows he will never forgive one of their own for his perfidy.

Unlike the ardent Zionists who couldn't wait to get to Palestine, as it was called back then, he had wanted to migrate to the United States, where he had a cousin, but

America hadn't given him a visa and Israel did. He wasn't in a position to pick and choose, but he refused to be grateful.

A caption on page two of *Ma'ariv* catches his eye. *War hero accepts position as spokesman in the Department of Rationing and Supply.* Isaiah chuckles. That department was always at war with the community, so no wonder they chose a man who had proved his mettle in armed conflict. He'll probably wish he was back on the front line when he finds out what kind of job he's taken on.

A moment later he stops laughing. His heart is hammering so fast that he is afraid it will jump through his chest. His breath comes in short gasps. He knows this war hero who is being praised for saving thousands of Jews in Hungary. They might describe Miklós Nagy as a hero, but Isaiah knows him as a *mamser*, a bastard, duplicitous and corrupt.

Isaiah leaps from his chair, then sits down again. He is trembling with excitement. This is the story he has been waiting for. Now he will shake them up, now they'll sit up and take notice. They won't make fun of him when he exposes their so-called hero as a swine with blood on his hands, a quisling who collaborated with the Nazis and helped them achieve the biggest mass murder in human history.

Elated by the prospect of unmasking the fake hero, Isaiah can't sit still. Perhaps there was a god after all. This wasn't vengeance, it was poetic justice. Fate had chosen him to debunk the myth of Nagy's heroism and expose his secret. He would do it for his mother and his sister, and for all the other innocents who paid the price for Nagy's crime.

Outside, large snowflakes are still falling from the leaden sky. They melt as soon as they touch the ground and form grey puddles on the broken asphalt. Soon no trace of snow would remain, the street would revert to its usual greyness, and the snowfall would be a distant memory. Perhaps it is his mother's voice prompting his thoughts, but he can't help wondering whether it is really only a coincidence that such a phenomenon has occurred just as he is about to publish his most sensational revelation.

He sits down at the table, picks up his pen and writes for several hours. He doesn't stop to change a single word. He knows his moment has come at last.

SYDNEY

CHAPTER ONE

2005

The morning sun has been blazing through the windows of Annika Barnett's apartment for several hours, and the last currawong stopped its gargling call and retreated to the coolness of the stringybark across the road long ago, but she's in no hurry to get out of bed. For the first time in years there's no office to go to, nowhere she needs to be. It's almost a month since she resigned from her job, and time has coagulated into a shapeless conglomeration of days punctuated by the television programs that represent the virtual reality she now inhabits.

At times she suspects that she has replaced meaningless work with meaningless idleness. No job, no man, no purpose. No-one waiting for her to light up their life or to promote their business. All her friends are working, and she feels isolated and disconnected from everything and everyone, alternating between hope that this feeling will pass, and dread in case it doesn't. Ever since she was small, her mother and grandmother had told her she was a bright and capable girl who could achieve anything she wanted, but she no longer knows what she wants, only that she doesn't want to continue doing work that feels dishonest. But how can you be almost forty and not know what you want to be?

With a sigh she rolls out of bed and pulls on the loose grey T-shirt and baggy pants she bought in Target when the ones with the Trent Nathan label had grown too tight. She glances in the mirror and catches sight of the square jawline that a friend once compared to Grace Kelly's. Sadly the resemblance ended there. Instead of sleek blonde hair, she has an unruly mass of copper-coloured curls that defy all her efforts to straighten them.

On her way to the kitchen, she averts her gaze from the empty chocolate box lying on the bedside table on top of a recent translation of Aeschylus's play *Prometheus Bound*. Since resigning, she has begun reading the plays of the ancient Greeks and become engrossed in the tragedies and the sufferings of their flawed characters at the hands of the merciless gods. Ever since finishing the play, she cannot get the fate of Prometheus out of her mind, indignant at the injustice meted out to the man whose heroic deed in bringing fire to humanity resulted not in praise, but horrific martyrdom.

Perched on the stool in the kitchen nook in front of the microwave and the tiny sink, she spoons toasted muesli into her mouth and switches on the television for the midday news. It's the usual mixture of triumphs and disasters. In Jordan, a suicide bomber killed over sixty people, in Louisiana people were still struggling with the deadly effects of

Hurricane Katrina, in England Prince Charles had made a public appearance with his unpopular new wife Camilla, and in Australia Keith Urban had won a country music award. She can imagine how her magazine would go to town on that last item. Soon stories would appear about the imminent break-up of his marriage to Nicole, based on the gossip of some anonymous friend. To back up the claim, photographs would be edited to show them either not looking at each other, or looking at someone else. Annika lets out a sigh of relief. Thank God she was out of that factory of fallacious rumours and fake headlines.

The next segment on the program is introduced by the iconic black-and-white image of a small Jewish boy walking with his arms raised in front of a Nazi soldier whose rifle is aimed at him. In the studio, the presenter introduces David Freeman, an American executive who has arrived in Australia to encourage Holocaust survivors to record their experiences for the Shoah Foundation. He explains that this project was initiated and funded by Steven Spielberg to create a worldwide archive of testimonies of those who survived.

'It's essential to record these stories while there is still time,' he says, 'because each year there are fewer survivors left, so the window of opportunity for videotaping their testimonies is becoming narrower all the time.'

The presenter now introduces two men and three women who have recently recorded their stories. Transfixed, Annika turns up the volume, anxious not to miss a word. One man recalls his terror and pain at being subjected to Mengele's sadistic experiments; the woman tells how, as a prisoner in the Stuttgart concentration camp, she gave birth to a baby girl who the guards tossed against a wall. All agree that it has been liberating to finally get rid of the crushing burden of wartime guilt, shame, pain and humiliation that they have kept to themselves for over fifty years, and how much their disclosure has meant to their families.

Annika's thoughts turn to her grandmother. She knows that Marika Horvath lived in Hungary during the war, but that's all she knows. Like so many Holocaust survivors, Marika has never talked about her experiences either. She is forbiddingly private, and when Annika thinks back, she realises that her grandmother has always side-stepped personal questions by changing the subject. Marika's past is a locked door to which she has hidden the key.

Not that she herself has probed her grandmother's past. She has always been too busy or too preoccupied with her own life to think about Marika's wartime experiences. But it's obvious that unlike so many survivors of horrific events she has read about in the newspapers, her grandmother hasn't suffered from post-traumatic stress disorder. Without resorting to alcohol, drugs or psychiatrists, she has rebuilt her life in Australia and made a success of it, Annika reflects with admiration. According to psychologists, it was unhealthy to suppress traumatic experiences, but Marika was clearly an exception.

Suddenly she yells, '*Shit!*' She jumps off the stool and rummages under the pile of newspapers for her mobile. She scrolls down her calendar reminders and groans. She had arranged to have dinner with Marika at six that evening, not realising that she had arranged to meet Emma, one of her former colleagues, at a popular watering hole near the magazine where she used to work. Now that she was free of office politics and the pressure of deadlines, she looked forward to catching up with the latest gossip and finding out how her replacement was getting on. She would prefer to put her grandmother off, but knows she isn't brave enough. Breaking an arrangement with Marika was unthinkable. Without a word of reproach, she could make her feel guilty and incompetent with just a flash of her dark eyes.

*

Driving through peak-hour traffic to her grandmother's home that evening, she inserts her Leonard Cohen CD into the stereo. 'I'm your man,' he sings, and she sighs at the sensuality of the voice that always draws her in with its revelations of the ache of unrequited love and the glory of sexual ecstasy. The CD ends, and without thinking, she clicks to restart it.

As she weaves in and out of a line of cars that creeps a metre at a time along the congested road that winds towards her grandmother's home in Bellevue Hill, Annika reflects that she admires her grandmother but doesn't love her. So much sentimental drivel has been written about families. It occurs to her that those closest to you understand you the least. Perhaps that's why it's so much easier to sympathise with other families than to forgive your own. Her grandmother doesn't understand her or her life, but the power of her rigid standards makes Annika feel that she has let her down, that she hasn't lived up to her hopes and expectations.

Bracing herself for the argument she knows will ensue when Marika hears that she has resigned from her job, Annika climbs the four steps that lead to her grandmother's

Art Deco apartment block and presses the buzzer, relieved that she's only twenty-five minutes late. The large foyer is decorated with huge potted philodendrons whose thick leathery leaves have attached themselves to the walls, where they have left brown traces. They remind her of triffids, and she can't resist the feeling that one day they will creep up and twine themselves around her neck and strangle her.

'It's wonderful to see you, *édesem*,' Marika says, using the Hungarian endearment. She envelops Annika in a hug, and a moment later Annika feels her grandmother's glance sweeping over her, from the messy curls falling across her face, to her baggy pants. Looking at her elegant grand-mother with her immaculately coiled white hair and expen-sive silk blouse — probably Italian — Annika regrets not making more of an effort with her appearance.

Marika has a designer boutique in Double Bay, and her customers — who include actresses, diplomats' wives and society matrons — come as much for the owner's charming personality as for the exclusive imported clothes. Marika has the gift of creating a sense of intimacy and friendship with total strangers who enjoy her company, admire her taste, and trust her advice. They wouldn't dream of choosing an outfit for any gala function at the racecourse, Government House or the opera without Marika's advice. She never lies or flatters, but in her silken manner she points out their best features and suggests clothes that will make them look younger, slimmer and more alluring.

'It's so long since I've seen you. Sit down and tell me what you've been doing, darling,' Marika murmurs as they sit in the lounge she has furnished exactly as if she still lived in Budapest before the war: Persian rugs, carved walnut sideboard, and plump settees upholstered in cream brocade. 'How is work?'

Annika takes a deep breath. 'Actually I've resigned.'

Marika is frowning. 'Resigned? What do you mean? What happened? You were doing so well as editor.'

Annika can feel her muscles tensing. 'No I wasn't. It was phony. All they wanted was stories about actors and actresses who are gaining weight, losing weight, screwing around or splitting up, and anyway half the stories were based on gossip or made up. I hated having to publish before and after photos of celebrities to show they'd lost weight, because it sent the wrong message to young girls, but whenever I didn't have a diet story on the cover, the circulation went down, so they pressured me to keep running them. I couldn't hack it any more. I can't spend my life doing things I don't believe in.'

From Marika's expression, Annika is aware that her grandmother is disappointed by her decision, but refrains from saying so. Instead, she takes Annika's hand, and with a sympathetic smile, she says, 'This probably isn't a good time to resign, *édesem,* but there are so many magazines, and with your experience, you'll soon find a better job. What do you have in mind?''

'I really don't know what I want to do,' Annika says slowly.

Marika raises her eyebrows. Sensing her disapproval, Annika can't conceal her irritation. At least her mother, who had also been dismayed by her decision, had shrugged and said, *I suppose you know what you're doing.* But it hurt that neither of them had acknowledged that she had chosen to walk away from a well-paid, high-profile job on account of her principles. Now, watching Marika, she supposes her grandmother is shocked that she has thrown in her job without having another offer, and that, at nearly forty, she is still wondering what to do with her life.

Marika goes into the kitchen, and returns a few minutes later, holding a Rosenthal tureen decorated with nymphs, shepherds, and aristocratic ladies in crinolines on the fine glaze, and places it on a white tablecloth embroidered with scarlet cross-stitch depicting figures in folk costume. When she raises the lid, it releases the tantalising aroma of Annika's favourite dish.

Annika praises the goulash, but for once she can't finish the food on her plate. The air is still heavy with unresolved tension, which Marika tries to diffuse by telling her anecdotes about her clients and their latest gossip. After the goulash, she brings out her pièce de resistance, a *dobos* torte. Annika knows that she has baked this festive cake especially for her, but after a few mouthfuls of the seven layers of sponge cake layered with chocolate cream and topped with crisp toffee, she pushes away the plate.

In the uneasy silence that follows, she remembers the television program she watched earlier.

'Grandmamma, did you ever think about recording your story for that Spielberg project?'

Marika shakes her head. 'Definitely not. Someone called me about it a few years ago, but I said no.'

'But why? It would be so good to have your story on tape, not just for us, but for people who don't know much about the Holocaust.'

'I have better things to do with my life than dwell on the past. That's good for people who have nothing in their lives.'

Annika sits forward on the settee and tries to control her frustration. 'I think survivors have a duty to tell what happened.'

For the first time, Marika raises her voice. 'The only duty of survivors is to survive and try to lead normal lives. Darling, let's drop the subject. You won't convince me. Let's just agree to differ.'

*

Visits to her grandmother always leave Annika feeling flat, and that night, when the cloying scent of jasmine wafts through the warm air, she tosses in bed, unsettled by the thoughts that drift into her mind. She wonders what became of the successful life and happy relationships she had always assumed she would have. But she has published enough self-help articles to be aware that her own choices were responsible. The men were never good enough, and the jobs never fulfilling enough.

Unable to sleep, she picks up her volume of Sophocles, but feels depressed by his vision of a world where humans stumble through life understanding nothing, incapable of recognising the truth. Too restless to continue reading, she replaces the book on the bedside table and goes to the window. A young girl and a guy are jogging side by side along the darkened street and, out of breath, they stop under a street lamp and fall into a passionate embrace. Watching them, Annika sighs. It must be intoxicating to be loved by a man you love in return, but it has never happened to her, and she wonders if her problem with relationships stems from the fact that when she was growing up, there were no men in the family.

From her mother Eva she knew that her grandmother was widowed soon after Eva was born, and she never remarried, so she had no grandfather. Marika had probably put all her energy into bringing up her daughter on her own, and rebuilding her life in a new country. Annika's father, whom she adored, hadn't been an exemplary role model. He was a gambler who took up with his nineteen-year-old secretary and deserted her mother when Annika was ten, leaving her mother with debts and lifelong bitterness. Annika was devastated when her father abandoned them, and couldn't rid herself of the conviction that she had somehow been to blame for his desertion and her mother's unhappiness.

Her thoughts turn to her frustrating conversation with her grandmother about the Spielberg project. She longs to know what Marika had gone through during the Holocaust, and how those experiences have shaped her life, but most of all, she wishes that her grandmother felt close enough to entrust her with her story.

Tired now, she goes back to bed, but a moment later she sits up. She doesn't need to rely on Marika to find out more about the Holocaust. Now that she has time on her hands, she can do some research on her own to gain an insight into her grandmother's story. And suddenly she knows what her first step will be.

CHAPTER TWO

2005

An ambulance streaks past, siren blaring, and Annika jumps aside. She watches it turn sharp right towards St Vincent's Hospital, almost colliding with an oncoming car that fails to stop, and she hopes that the unfortunate soul inside will make it in time. She is crossing Forbes Street, near the sandstone buildings that once formed the old Darlinghurst jail, but now houses an art school.

Annika is reflecting on what life would have been like for the prisoners there a hundred years ago when she reaches the Sydney Jewish Museum on the corner of Darlinghurst Road, and steps into the foyer. After a perfunctory glance inside her Kate Spade handbag, a remnant of her editorial days when having a designer bag was almost as important as having a laptop, the security guard waves her through. Past the honour roll of Jews who died in two world wars, she enters the hall and looks around. This is her first visit, but that's not surprising: religion has never played a large part in her life. Her parents didn't belong to a synagogue, and as a child she didn't go to Sunday school. From conversations she overheard while growing up, she suspected that for years after arriving in Australia, her grandmother had pretended she wasn't Jewish, and she had enrolled Annika's mother in Church of England scripture classes at school. Even after Eva discovered that her mother was Jewish, which meant that she was Jewish as well, she sent Annika to an Anglican private school, and encouraged her to cultivate Christian friends. It seemed that being Jewish was something you needed to conceal.

Annika had never missed having a religious upbringing, but now, standing in front of a display of a family sitting around a Passover table with its white cloth, matzos and candelabra, she is acutely aware of her ignorance. She knows nothing of the rituals and beliefs that have sustained Jews for thousands of years, and is disconnected from her heritage. In the small museum shop across the hall, she surveys the books on the shelves, the hand-painted Passover plates, silver candelabra and Star of David pendants. A tiny woman with a hunched back and frizzy red hair comes towards her with a smile.

'My name is Kitty. I'm a volunteer guide. This is your first visit?'

Annika nods, and Kitty goes on, 'I think for most people it feels a bit strange to be here for the first time,' she says. 'They often say they have intended to come for a long time, but sometimes I can see they are wishing they had not come. It is understandable. This place can be confronting, and some of the exhibits are upsetting, so they feel uncomfortable and do not know how to react. They wonder if it is okay to ask questions, and if they are expected to feel responsible in some way for what happened.'

Annika has an urge to say that she is Jewish, but feels ashamed that she probably knows less about the history and traditions of the Jews than even the non-Jewish visitors. She remains silent, and when she looks down, she is shocked to see the numbers tattooed on Kitty's forearm. Kitty follows her gaze.

'This is why I became a guide here,' she says. 'When I was liberated, I was so desperate to remove those numbers that if I had had a razor blade, I would have cut them out. I could not bear to look at them. Physical pain would have been a relief from the rage I felt whenever I looked at that reminder of the past they stamped on my body. When we were liberated, I weighed 35 kilos, I had no hair and no teeth, but I still had that loathsome tattoo. The nun who nursed me in the hospital said, "Don't think of it as a stigma, but as stigmata. It's not a sign of victimhood, but a sign of victory." That made me even more angry. What did she know? How could she possibly understand?'

Annika is overwhelmed by the woman's story and by her candour. This is the first time she has met a Holocaust survivor who has told her such a personal experience.

'For my first few years in Australia, I wore long sleeves so no-one would see the numbers,' Kitty continues. 'But when I heard that the Jewish Museum was looking for Holocaust survivors to become volunteer guides, I remembered what the nun told me, and I decided it was time to get over my embarrassment and use the tattoo to show people what prejudice and racism can lead to.'

'Was it hard for you to show the tattoo?' Annika asks.

'At first it was very hard. You see, I was only fifteen when I was liberated, but in time I realised that the numbers were superficial. I could cover them up and never see them, but what was carved on my memory was far more indelible.'

Annika gazes at the older woman with admiration. 'Do you have time to guide me around the museum?' she asks.

'I would like to,' Kitty replies.

They pause beside the list of Jewish convicts transported to the new colony. Annika is surprised to learn that there were several Jews on the First Fleet. One was there for stealing a handkerchief, another for stealing a loaf of bread. One sounded like Dickens's character Fagin. After surveying the recreation of a street from 1840s Sydney Town, with sound effects of horse carriages rumbling over cobblestones, they move on to the replica of a traditional Sabbath table, complete with prayer book, candles and sacramental wine, and again Annika feels a stab of regret for the closeness and connection she has missed.

They are about to go upstairs to see the Holocaust exhibits when a clatter of school shoes and the hubbub of young voices resounds through the museum.

'Our first school group of the day,' Kitty says, and gives a mischievous smile. 'I'm glad it's Ervin's turn this morning.'

'Do you find it hard to talk about your experiences?' Annika asks.

Kitty reflects for a moment. 'You know, I've been a guide here for fifteen years, but I still get churned up whenever I face a new group. You never know what they've been told or what their attitudes are. I worry in case they won't believe me, or say the Holocaust never happened.' She glances in the direction of the students. 'Shall we go and listen to Ervin's story?'

They stand at the back of the group while the chattering students throw their backpacks on the floor and rifle through them for notepads and pens. The sound of their voices grows louder, and their teacher, a harassed-looking young woman, repeatedly urges them to show respect in a voice that doesn't expect to be obeyed.

It's Ervin's stillness that eventually gains their attention. A tall man with thin strands of grey hair combed carefully across his skull, he introduces himself in a soft voice that reminds Annika of Peter Lorre's hoarse whisper in *Casablanca*. She watches as he unrolls a map of Europe and points to the city where he was born.

Kitty whispers, 'Most of them have probably never heard of Hungary, let alone Budapest. Some have probably never heard of the Holocaust. Thank God for teachers who bring their pupils here.'

Ervin has a friendly manner. He doesn't talk down to the students or lecture them, but draws them in with humorous stories about his childhood pranks. Annika listens with growing interest to his account of life in pre-war Hungary, and wonders if her grandmother's experiences were similar. When he asks, 'Do any of you have a pet?' almost all the students nod and wave their hands in the air.

He tells them about his little dog Lili, which did clever tricks and followed him everywhere, even to school. Then they stop smiling when he describes the day he was forced to leave Lili behind, and he and his parents were moved to a horrible place where hundreds of other families were crowded into a filthy space without food or water, simply because they were Jews.

'I had to leave Lili all alone in our flat, and I could still hear her crying while we were being herded along the street,' he says.

The students are very quiet now, and some of the girls are wiping their eyes.

'I was the same age as you when we were in the ghetto,' he says. In a hushed voice he tells them about the terrible day when his parents and little brother were taken away. 'I never saw them again,' he says, and his eyes glisten with tears. Then he describes brutal labour camps and concentration camps, where taking care of others helped him to keep going. But he doesn't dwell on the horror, the hunger or the suffering.

Annika wonders if her grandmother went through a similar experience, and reflects that she will probably never know.

'But whatever happened, I never gave up hope,' Ervin is saying. 'And in the end I survived because one man in Budapest risked his life to save me and hundreds of others.'

Annika thinks he's about to tell them about Raoul Wallenberg, the Swedish diplomat she has read about, but to her surprise he names someone she has never heard of: a Jew called Miklós Nagy who, during the Nazi bloodbath that almost killed the last remaining Jewish community in Europe, by some miracle managed to organise a train that took about fifteen hundred Hungarian Jews to Switzerland and safety under the noses of the Nazis.

'Miklós Nagy didn't just save one thousand five hundred people, he saved over a hundred thousand lives, and he saves many more every year.'

The students look puzzled, they look at each other, and a boy with hair that flops over his forehead calls out, 'How come?' Another calls out, 'That doesn't even make sense.'

Ervin nods. 'You're right, so I'll explain. If it wasn't for Miklós Nagy I wouldn't be here, and my children and grandchildren wouldn't be here, and in future years, their children and grandchildren, and that goes for every one of the people he saved. I'm not very good at maths, but I think that would eventually add up to over a hundred thousand people. And all because one man had the courage to do something that seemed impossible. So never give up hope, look after each other, and never forget that even one person can make a huge difference.'

The students applaud Ervin but when he asks if they have any questions, they are silent. He is the first person they have ever met who has lived through an event that they have heard about in their history lessons and they are over-whelmed, as much by his story as by his positive personality.

Annika marvels at his attitude and willingness to reopen his wounds by sharing his story, and compares them to her grandmother's silence, which she no longer regards as an indication of strength. She is musing about that when a freckled girl with one thick plait down her back asks, 'Do you hate the Germans for what they did?'

'That's a very good question,' Ervin says. 'I don't hate the Germans, but I do hate what some of them did during the Holocaust.'

Now they all have a question to ask. Did he ever find his little dog? What happened to his little brother? Were the cruel Nazis in charge of the camps ever tried for war crimes? The teacher keeps urging them to collect their things so they can leave, but she can't tear them away.

'We have an interesting new exhibition, perhaps you'd like to see it,' Kitty says, and asks Ervin if he has seen it. He looks pale and drained after his session. 'First I will go to the cafeteria and have my daily indulgence, a strong cappuccino,' he says. 'Then I will join you.'

Upstairs, Annika is looking at *Liberation 1945*, a collection of photographs that covers the walls of the exhibition space. She shudders at the images of skeletal bodies that no longer look human, heaped together in grotesque piles on the site of the Bergen-Belsen camp. The caption underneath states that the photographer, who entered the camp with the British army, became famous, and was later called the Frank Hurley of the Second World War. But he paid a high price for his fame.

'These images were to haunt him day and night for the rest of his life,' Kitty says. Annika can feel her stomach folding in on itself, and fears that they will haunt her too.

Other images depict celebratory scenes in Paris, Amsterdam and Prague, but Annika is surprised to see several photos that were taken in a Swiss town she has never heard of, St Margarethen.

She frowns. 'Wasn't Switzerland neutral during the war?'

Before Kitty can reply, she hears a hoarse whisper behind her.

'I can explain this to our visitor,' Ervin says.

He taps lightly on one of the photographs taken in Switzerland. 'In December 1944, a large group of Hungarian Jews, including me, arrived in Switzerland thanks to the man I mentioned in my talk, Miklós Nagy.'

He points to a middle-aged man with wavy brown hair brushed back from a broad forehead, and an expression that suggests steely determination. 'That's him.'

'What happened to him?' Annika asks.

Ervin sighs. 'That was a real tragedy. But you know what they say, no good deed goes unpunished.'

She has never heard this adage before, and is about to ask him what he means when his phone rings, and excusing himself, he walks away. She continues looking at the photographs when one of them catches her attention. In a group of people looking at the camera, one face makes her stare. She moves closer and examines it to make sure. The photo is grainy and slightly blurred, but there's no mistaking that heart-shaped face or the deep-set dark eyes and dimpled smile.

For once she can't wait to talk to her grandmother. At last they will have a subject they can share and discuss, one that might inspire Marika to loosen up and talk about the past.

*

'Grandmamma, you won't believe this,' Annika begins when she phones Marika that evening. Her grandmother laughs happily. 'So tell me, what happened? Do you have a job?'

Annika swallows the retort that rises to her lips. 'I was in the Jewish Museum today and I saw your photo!'

'My photo? Impossible. I did not give them my photo.'

'Not a photo you gave them, a photo that was taken of you in Switzerland in 1944.'

'You must be mistaken,' Marika says, and her voice is cold.

'Grandmamma, I don't know why you're arguing. It's definitely a photo of you and it was taken with the group that arrived on that train. Surely you can't have forgotten.'

'I'm telling you it must be someone else.'

There are a thousand questions Annika wants to ask, but her grandmother's words are a wall too high to scale, and she fights the feeling of powerlessness she always feels in the face of Marika's determination.

'Grandmamma, I'm not a child,' she protests. 'Why don't you tell me something about that man, Miklós Nagy?'

There's a tense pause before Marika snaps, 'Annika, I want you to drop the subject. Listen to me. I don't want you to mention that man's name again. Ever.'

Annika sits by the window but she is too preoccupied to see the cobalt water of Coogee beach in the distance, or hear the fruit bats squeaking among the trees across the road. Her grandmother's strange words keep running through her mind. She wonders if her mother knows anything about this, and decides to call her.

But as soon as she hears Eva's soft voice, she wonders why she bothered. Over the years, Annika could not recall one instance when her mother sided with her against a decision her grandmother had made, a course of action she espoused, or an opinion she expressed.

Eva has always lived in her mother's shadow. When a girl has a powerful mother, she has two choices: submit or rebel. Reflecting on her own personality, and that of her mother, Annika decides that rebellion has skipped one generation.

'Grandmamma's reaction was so bizarre,' she tells her mother. 'I can't believe what she said to me. She won't even talk about the man who got her out of Hungary. It doesn't make sense. I know I saw her photo with a group who were on that train, but she denies it was her. Has she ever talked to you about it?'

'No, but it's probably because she has decided not to dwell on the past. She's always wanted to look forward.'

Annika's voice rises. 'But don't you want to know what happened to her?'

'Of course I do,' Eva counters. 'I can't even imagine what she went through. But why would she want to relive it? She's not unique, you know. Lots of Holocaust survivors find it painful to talk about the past.'

'Well, I've just spent the morning at the Jewish Museum, and I've met Holocaust survivors who share their stories, not just with their families, but with strangers.' Annika speaks vehemently, irritated by her mother's passivity.

There's a moment's silence, and then Eva says, 'Well, that's their choice. Grandmamma must have her reasons, and whatever happened in the past, it's her life.'

'But now that I've told you about that photograph, aren't you curious to know what happened, and why she is so angry? You'll ask her about it, won't you?'

But even before her mother replies, Annika knows what her answer will be.

'You're a journalist, so it's your job to ask questions no matter how they may upset people. You think you're entitled to know everything, and it seems to me that sometimes your curiosity gets the better of your empathy. I think your grandmother is entitled to her privacy and you should respect that.'

Stung by Eva's retort, Annika thinks about the dysfunctional triangle in which they are enmeshed. The one with unequal sides, with her grandmother at the apex, and she on the smallest side.

Fuming, she hangs up, but she knows that she won't let the matter of Miklós Nagy rest. For once her grandmother won't succeed in imposing her will.

BUDAPEST

CHAPTER THREE

May 1944

Miklós Nagy is walking slowly along the Danube embankment, past the fanciful neo-gothic facade of Parliament House and the gigantic statues in Hero Square, but his mind is not on Budapest's impressive monuments. He is back in Kolostór, the country town where he was born forty years before. He can see the spreading mulberry trees in front of his family home, the purple mess on the unpaved street that the crows made of the fallen fruit every summer. Along that street, which ran down to the wheat fields, old women in headscarves led their cows to pasture in the mornings and brought them back again at night. He smiles at the memory of the town crier who was usually followed by a ragtag group of rowdy urchins as he beat his drum along Main Street, shouting the latest news. Everyone stopped whatever they were doing to listen, and later discussed the day's events, arguing back and forth as they puzzled over them. It strikes him now that it was probably the excitement of the townsfolk at hearing the news that had inspired him to become a journalist.

Lost in thought, he crosses Erzsébet Avenue and comes to the Astoria Hotel, another relic of the grand days of the Hapsburg Empire, now the headquarters of the Gestapo. That jolts his mind to the bleak present. The skies over Budapest have darkened ever since that Sunday barely two months ago. It was on the nineteenth of March, a day he will never forget. That day he watched hundreds of jackbooted Germans on motorcycles with sidecars roar into the city along Andrássy Avenue ahead of a motorcade of tanks and beige Mercedes Benz automobiles carrying the SS officers. Miklós had taken the measure of the complacent faces inside those cars, the Death's Head insignia on their peaked caps, and the pitiless gaze that conveyed the chilling conviction that they were Aryan supermen destined to rule the world.

He crosses the Chain Bridge and steps into the shiny red *Sikló* cable car which sways up Swabian Hill on the other side of the river, clenching his fists to stop his hands from trembling. He has to keep his wits about him for the meeting ahead. He must appear calm and in control, but the thought of the man he is about to confront brings beads of sweat to his forehead. A cruel wind is blowing, and even though it's May, spring feels a long way off. He takes off his grey fedora and wipes the perspiration from his brow.

An avenue of old oaks and beeches cuts through the terraced gardens that surround the Hotel Majestic at the top of the hill. Armed guards at several posts along the avenue order him to halt in guttural German voices and demand to inspect his papers. The sight of armed German soldiers in their helmets and stiff uniforms all over the city always churns his stomach, especially as the ever-increasing anti-Semitic laws have included a ban on Jews using public transport, holding any public office, swimming in public baths, or even shopping for many basic food items. But from the perfunctory way the guards check his papers, he knows they have been informed about this meeting. With a peremptory gesture, they motion for him to enter the hotel.

Miklós waits in the marble foyer while the guard hands his papers to the official behind the counter, a Hungarian flunkey whose smug expression indicates that he relishes his new role. The guard shrugs, and gestures several times towards Miklós, who looks around. The last time he was here, it was on a very different mission. This hotel used to be ideal for secret rendezvous, with its discreet reception staff and well-trained waiters who never seemed to notice the languid presence of a woman in a black lace negligee reclining on a velvet settee.

He sighs as he recalls delicious afternoons spent with lovers in the intimate boudoirs upstairs. With its gold-framed mirrors, crimson velvet couches and Bohemian chandeliers, this hotel is another of Budapest's famous Austro-Hungarian extravaganzas, but now, as he looks towards the ornate reception desk with its gilded arabesques, the gaze of the reception staff is a grim reminder that this hotel is no longer a pleasure palace but the headquarters of the most feared man in the city.

The guard strides across the foyer and escorts him up the curved staircase to the second floor. When they come to a double door with moulded panelling trimmed with gold leaf, his escort knocks with the deference that hotel staff once displayed when these apartments were occupied by princes, diplomats, and their mistresses.

Miklós takes a deep breath and straightens his shoulders. Under his woollen coat, he can feel sweat pooling in his armpits and knows it's not the heat. An angry voice from inside the room orders them to enter.

'The Obersturmbannführer will see you now,' the guard says in the self-important voice of those who are convinced that the power of their superiors has rubbed off on them. With exaggerated deference, he opens the door. The moment Miklós has dreaded has finally arrived.

The man inside the large room is sitting at a carved walnut desk, smoking a cigarette that fills the room with the sweet aroma of Turkish tobacco. He is smaller than Miklós had imagined, quite insignificant-looking really, with a narrow face, pale eyes and a sardonic curve in his thin lips. His grey-green SS jacket fits him so well it looks as if he was born wearing it. The four stars on his epaulettes indicate his rank: lieutenant-colonel. His pistol lies on the desk in front of him in a brown leather holster. He glances at Miklós without interest and doesn't ask him to sit down.

There are chandeliers on the frescoed ceiling, sconces on the walls, and silk Persian rugs on the marble floor, but the man behind the desk doesn't appear to be awed by the palatial setting. And that's not surprising. After all, Miklós reflects, he wields more power than the hotel's illustrious residents ever did.

The tasselled burgundy velvet drapes on either side of the window frame the best view in Budapest, one that has inspired painters for centuries, the wooded slope of Buda rolling down to the Danube, and the filigree spires of

Parliament House on the opposite bank of the river, but Miklós notes that the man sits with his back to the window, arrogantly indifferent to the view. He wasn't sent to Budapest to admire the scenery.

In any case, it's clear that the beauty of this city holds no interest for him. From what Miklós has heard about his single-minded devotion to his task in other countries, he knows that the man is not simply obeying orders: he is carrying out what he considers to be his sacred mission.

Finally he looks up from his papers and surveys Miklós with an expression that suggests that this is Judgement Day and the sentence will not be merciful. He doesn't offer him a chair. Tamping out his half-smoked Turkish cigarette with short jabs, he immediately lights another, stands up, and pushes his armchair back so violently that it topples over and crashes to the floor. Miklós supposes this is meant to intimidate him and put him off guard. He watches the Nazi lieutenant-colonel pacing up and down the Persian carpet in jackboots whose sheen reflects the light from the crystal chandelier. With each step he winds himself up into an uncontrollable fury.

'I'll soon rid Budapest of you vermin! You Jews are the scum of the earth! The sooner the world is free of you, the better. Even your Hungarian leaders agree. In fact they can't wait to get rid of you. We've never encountered such enthusiastic co-operation. If it was up to your government, we'd be getting rid of you even faster.'

With a scornful glance he plants himself in front of Miklós and yells, 'Do you know who I am?'

Miklós is drowning in fear but he looks straight into the granite eyes without flinching. He knows only too well that he is confronting Adolf Eichmann, who has been sent to Budapest to destroy the last surviving Jewish community in Europe.

Like a snowflake floating inexorably towards the flames of hell, Miklós knows that this moment could be his last, and he must make it count.

How he, a Jewish journalist, has come to confront the most terrifying man in Hungary at a time when being a Jew in Budapest means being deprived of every civil right, being rounded up into a ghetto and then forced onto a train for a journey to an unknown destination, is a source of wonder even to himself. His father often said that you only discover what you're made of in times of war. Miklós has never asked his father what he discovered about himself during the Great War, in which he fought for Emperor Franz Jozef and the Austro-Hungarian Empire, and now he wonders what he is about to discover about himself.

He knows he's no hero. Was it courage, foolhardiness or sheer stupidity that has lured him to this audience with the Devil? Vanity, perhaps? Defiance? Or hubris? Was it the unspoken, unacknowledged longing for prominence and praise, the desire to become the Moses of his people at a moment when their extinction seemed certain that has pushed him towards this hopeless encounter? He is astonished that Eichmann has agreed to this meeting, but he knows that no matter what happens, he must push his advantage to the limit. Doing nothing would be tantamount to colluding in the destruction of his people.

But right now, in Eichmann's terrifying presence, he doesn't have time to analyse or philosophise. Time is running out, and he must summon all his energy, all his guile and strength, to focus on his aim. He must find some way of negotiating with the arbiter of death for the lives of the remaining Jews of Hungary.

There is one other person in the room, a younger SS officer, and Miklós wonders about the tall blond Nazi with a smooth round face and the eager expression of a child about to receive a longed-for gift. While Eichmann has been ranting and pacing, this young man has moved towards the window and gazes impassively at the river, as if to distance himself from their conversation.

Eichmann is finally still, and he sits down again. When he speaks, his voice is surprisingly quiet. There is a mocking smile on his lips, and his eyes have the triumphant gleam of a wolf that has cornered its prey.

'Are you a Zionist, Nagy?'

Before Miklós can reply, Eichmann says, 'I believe in Zionism.'

Taken aback by this extraordinary statement, Miklós doesn't know what to say. Is Eichmann baiting him, trying to put him off balance? Or is he making some kind of macabre joke?

But Eichmann doesn't expect an answer. He leans over, picks up a book from the far corner of the desk and holds it out. *The Jewish State*. 'This Herzl had a point,' he says. 'All you Jews should be in Palestine, instead of contaminating Europe. It would have been easier and cheaper for us to deport you all there, but the Grand Mufti wouldn't allow it, and he's our ally, so we had to abandon that idea and find some other way to get rid of you.'

He sounds like a businessman discussing the need to dispose of unwanted waste. Pausing to light yet another cigarette, he inhales, gazing at Miklós with narrowed eyes. Miklós is wondering how long this harangue will continue, and whether he can believe any of it, when Eichmann points to the book.

'I read it so I could understand you Jews. It's important to know your enemy, especially when he controls world finance and politics.'

Miklós suppresses a bitter laugh. He wishes he could point out how ludicrous this statement is. How can Eichmann believe in the world domination of the people that he and his fellow Nazis have almost wiped off the face of Europe? Only the Jews of Hungary now stand between him and his goal of total annihilation.

'You see, Nagy? I can be as devious as you people, but I'm not as good at making money.' He chuckles and looks at Miklós, as if expecting him to appreciate his joke.

While Eichmann is still in full flight about the wealth and power of the Jews, it strikes Miklós that Eichmann's fantasy about a powerful World Jewry might make him receptive to the offer that he has come here to make. When he pauses, Miklós takes a deep breath. He doesn't know if he has the authority to speak on behalf of international Jewish organisations, but he has to sound as if he has some powerful body behind him because the situation is so desperate. There's no time to lose. His mouth is so dry that he rasps the words in a hoarse voice he hardly recognises.

'Every day, you deport thousands of Jewish men, women and children to concentration camps. I'm here on behalf of the Jewish World Congress to make you an offer. We are willing to raise a large sum of money if you stop the deportations.'

At the mention of a ransom, Miklós notices that the young SS officer at the window, who until now has been motionless and apparently detached, turns slightly and inclines his head towards the speakers. He figures that money is the button that switches on this Nazi's attention.

Eichmann slams his fist on the desk and screams, 'How dare you! Are you trying to bribe me, Nagy?'

He plants himself in front of Miklós, so close that he can smell the tobacco on the Nazi's breath. 'You are offering me Jews for sale!' He spits out the words. 'Don't take me for a fool!'

Miklós stares back at Eichmann with what he hopes looks like cool indifference but his heart is pounding and his legs are about to buckle. He clasps his hands to conceal their trembling. He can't allow any twitch, tremor or flicker to betray his terror. He is playing a lethal game of Russian roulette with the murderer who holds his future, and that of the remaining Jews of Hungary, in his hands.

Eichmann has stopped yelling once again. He returns to his desk and this time he motions Miklós to sit down. 'I'll tell you what, Nagy. Get me ten thousand trucks and I'll let a million of your people go.'

Miklós looks straight into Eichmann's face and tries to regain his equanimity as he wonders how to respond to this preposterous offer. Is this Eichmann's idea of a joke, or is it a trap of some kind? It can't possibly be genuine. Even if the Allies wanted to save Jews — and the fact that they have refused to bomb the railway line carrying trains full of Jews to their deaths in Auschwitz makes him wonder if they do — no western government would supply the Germans with ten thousand trucks during the war knowing that they would be used against them.

As if he can read Miklós's thoughts, Eichmann adds, 'We would only use the trucks on the Eastern front.'

Miklós has to think quickly. The tables have unexpectedly turned, and instead of considering his offer, Eichmann has made a counter-offer, an outrageous demand that he must know will not be taken seriously. Britain and America would never agree to supply *matériel* for Germany's war effort.

As for the Jewish organisations in Istanbul and Switzerland, they wouldn't agree to making any deal with the Nazis, and in any case he doubts if they have the necessary funds. But he knows he can't risk an outright refusal. The lives of hundreds of thousands of people, as well as his own, hang in the balance.

Eichmann is still talking. 'If your rich Jews agree in principle, as a sign of goodwill, to prove that my offer is genuine, I am willing to let six hundred Jews leave Hungary. You can compile a list of six hundred names of those with visas for Palestine, and give it to me. In the meantime, I will send your colleague Gábor Weisz to Turkey so he can pass on my offer to the Western Allies and the Jewish Agency in Istanbul.'

Miklós's mind is racing. There is no chance Eichmann's plan will succeed, and when it fails, the fate of the remaining Jews of Hungary will be sealed. Sending Gábor to Istanbul is pointless. And yet their only hope is to stall for time, to delay the deportations. The Germans have suffered defeats all over Europe, and the Russians were advancing towards Poland. Surely the war would end soon. And then there was the matter of the visas. The Jewish Agency's Palestine office has issued some permits but there weren't enough, and they didn't have official stamps and application forms to forge more of them. But somehow they would have to overcome that problem. There was too much at stake.

Miklos manages to keep his voice steady as he says, 'We will pass on your offer.'

As he leaves the Hotel Majestic, he can hardly stand up. He feels exhausted and drained, as if all his marrow has been sucked away, leaving his bones desiccated and brittle. He walks slowly towards the Chain Bridge, hardly seeing the Danube or the buildings on the Pest side of the city as he struggles to make sense of this surreal proposal. Somehow he will have to present his colleagues with a coherent version of the conversation, create more permits for Palestine, and decide on a strategy to keep Eichmann dangling in the hope of receiving his trucks.

He wonders if he is equal to the task that he has taken upon himself, and his father's words resound in his head, accusing him of falling short. It feels as if he has lived a lifetime of anxiety, tension and terror in the past hour, and now Eichmann has chosen Gábor to go to Istanbul. He knows that he himself is a much better negotiator than Gábor, and he is convinced that he should be the one to go on that vital mission.

He has almost reached his rooms when he feels a sudden surge of guilty joy. With Gábor holed up in Istanbul, his wife Ilonka will be left in Budapest. Alone.

CHAPTER FOUR

May 1944

Miklós is about to enter the Europa Café when he feels someone tapping his shoulder. He turns and is alarmed to see the Slovakian couple for whom he has recently found shelter and false documents.

'You are our saviour,' the man is saying. 'I don't know how to thank you. You saved our lives.'

While he is talking, his wife has grabbed Miklós's hand and tries to kiss it. Miklós pulls his hand away, glancing around to make sure no-one has overheard their reckless expression of gratitude. They should be lying low instead of exposing themselves and endangering him.

'You're welcome,' he mutters, and quickly pushes open the heavy glass doors of the coffee house. As soon as he steps inside, he breathes in the aroma of freshly roasted coffee and the scent of vanilla and chocolate, smells that evoke the carefree pre-war world of Budapest café life that he yearns for.

Heading to the rear of the café, he makes his way past the three-piece band in their embroidered vests and baggy trousers, who are playing nostalgic *czárdás* melodies on their gypsy violins. He moves through the thick smoke of Havana cigars and Turkish cigarettes to the table in the far corner where Gábor usually holds court, makes deals, and arranges assignations. Watching him, cigar in one hand and apricot *pálinka* brandy in the other, leaning back in the high-backed Empire-style chair, you'd never guess he had a care in the world. Miklós envies Gábor's ability to blot out future problems while enjoying present pleasures, whether it's eating, drinking or womanising. He knows that his own sangfroid, the controlled voice and calm face that reassures others, is only a mask, a layer of ice no thicker than an eggshell that covers red-hot lava ready to erupt.

For the past year, he and Gábor, along with the other members of their Rescue Committee, have helped thousands of destitute refugees flooding into Budapest from Poland and Slovakia. He and Gábor make a good team: he has been the front man, talking to influential groups to arrange shelter and raise money, as well as sending parcels to Jews deported to forced labour camps, while Gábor and the others have been in charge of forging and printing false identity papers and finding accommodation.

He gazes appreciatively at Gábor. His friend is an affable bon vivant and a good poker player, but he is hopeless at chess because he's incapable of thinking several moves ahead, and that's why Miklós is convinced that he's the wrong man to go to Istanbul. He can feel his blood pressure rising at the prospect of such a delicate and crucial matter being left in Gábor's clumsy hands. Only a skilled negotiator should be in charge, but Eichmann has made his decision and it is irrevocable.

Miklós sits down, glances around to make sure that the Slovakian couple haven't followed him inside, and orders black coffee from the pretty young waitress in a crisp white apron who is hovering around Gábor, enjoying his admiring glances.

'Another apricot *pálinka* for me, Zsuzsi,' Gábor says, and Miklós wonders whether the alcohol is an attempt to calm his nerves or to keep the girl in attendance.

He looks around the café. There is a war on, and in the past five years millions of people have been killed, but inside the Europa Café life goes on as it always has. The tables are covered with starched white linen cloths, there are rosebuds in vases of Venetian glass, and the patrons eat off fine Zsolnay porcelain with silver cutlery and drink from glasses of Bohemian crystal. In the background, the band is playing Hungarian melodies that make everyone feel patriotic and secure in the conviction that they and their beautiful city will survive.

'When are you leaving for Istanbul?' Miklós asks.

'As soon as Eichmann organises our visas.'

'What do you mean, "our" visas?'

Gábor sits forward and lowers his voice. 'Didn't you know? Eichmann has ordered Zoltán Klein to go with me.'

'Zolly Klein? Are you serious? Why?'

Gábor shrugs. 'No idea. That's what he said: *Herr Klein will go to Istanbul also.*'

Miklós shakes his head. He can't make any sense of this. Klein is a small-time crook with a shady past and an unprepossessing appearance. Small, skinny, with buck teeth and small eyes, he resembles a weasel, and his manner is oily and ingratiating. Everyone suspects him of being a spy, though no-one is sure who he is spying for. Some people think he is a double agent with a foot in both camps. Either way, he is the least trustworthy person Miklós knows, and he is shocked that Eichmann wants him to accompany Gábor on this sensitive mission.

They fall silent as the waitress sashays towards them, hips swinging. She beams her charming smile at Gábor as she sets down the coffee and brandy. Miklós waits until she has gone before asking again, 'Why on earth is he sending Klein?'

'He says he's going to deliver messages and some cash.'

Miklós gives Gábor a shrewd look. It's more likely that Eichmann wants Klein to spy on him and on the diplomats and Jewish leaders he will contact in Istanbul, but he is sure that this has not occurred to his friend.

Miklós takes out his monogrammed silver cigarette case, lights a cigarette, and leans towards Gábor. 'Listen, your only hope is to stall. There is no way they're going to agree to this outrageous offer, but if you even hint to Eichmann that they've refused, that will be the end. We'll have nothing to bargain with, and he'll go on with the deportations until not a single Jew is left in Hungary or anywhere else in Europe.' He can hear himself speaking faster than usual, but he can't slow down. He feels he is a bowstring about to snap.

'You must make them understand that they have to make it look as if they're genuinely considering his offer,' he continues. 'That's our only hope, to keep stalling Eichmann.'

Gábor's usually cheerful face looks glum. Knowing his friend so well, Miklós can imagine what is going through his mind. He didn't volunteer for this mission, and its magnitude is weighing him down. The price of failure will be catastrophic, and he will be held responsible. He lets out a loud sigh. 'How long can we go on stalling him?'

'As long as necessary. The war must end soon. They've been defeated in Russia, North Africa and Italy. It can't go on much longer. But they're not going to stop murdering Jews until the last moment even if it means deploying all their soldiers, trains and ammunition. That's how fanatical the Nazis are. They'd rather kill Jews than enemy soldiers. That goes for Eichmann too.'

He isn't usually so voluble, but he is too worked up to stop, and he is looking at Gábor with such intensity it's as if he has grabbed him by the collar. 'So don't forget, it's up to you to string this out, whichever way you can, make him believe they're eventually going to supply his bloody trucks.'

Gábor shifts in his chair and looks into his friend's eyes. 'You've been coaching me what to say and what to do from the moment we found out I was being sent to Istanbul. Don't you think I know how much hinges on this mission? Is it because you think I'm stupid, or not up to the task? Maybe you think you're the smart one who should be going to Istanbul instead of me?'

Miklós shakes his head, embarrassed that Gábor has seen through his advice. Gábor rarely takes offence, but no doubt the enormity of the task was making him unusually anxious. No wonder.

'It's just that knowing what an uphill task you'll have trying to convince the leaders of the Jewish Agency, the American Joint Distribution Committee and the British Embassy how drastic the situation is, puts me on edge,' he replies.

'None of them have lived in Nazi-occupied countries, so they won't be able to grasp how drastic our situation is in Budapest. How can they, when even most of the Jews of Budapest don't realise that their lives are hanging by a thread?'

He doesn't need to remind Gábor what Eichmann has already gloated over, that Baky and Endre, the Hungarian leaders, have needed no persuasion to enact the Nazis' anti-Semitic laws, and that Ferenczy, the Hungarian police chief, has even offered to speed up the process by providing his own men to deport the Jews.

He glances at his friend's gloomy face and feels contrite. 'This whole business is driving me crazy,' he says. 'Of course I have faith in you.' He hopes he sounds sincere.

Gábor finishes his brandy and looks into his empty balloon, obviously contemplating a top-up. 'Eichmann said that my wife has to stay in Budapest as a hostage in case I don't come back. What will happen to Ilonka if something happens while I'm in Istanbul and I can't get back?'

At the mention of Ilonka, Miklós can feel his heart beating faster. He is sure the blood has rushed to his face, and he studies the menu so that Gábor can't see his expression.

'Why should something happen to you? You'll be back in Budapest before you know it,' he says, speaking to the tablecloth.

Gábor looks dubious. 'Will you make sure she's all right until I get back?'

Suddenly everyone stops talking and looks at the door. Three SS men have walked into the café, and one of them, a tall blond officer with a round pink face, surveys the restaurant and approaches Miklós.

It's Kurt Becher, the SS officer who was in Eichmann's office the previous week, and he greets Miklós with a friendly smile.

'*Guten tag*, Herr Nagy,' he says, and clicks his heels. 'The coffee here is *sehr gut, nicht war?*'

By now the other patrons are turning to stare at Miklós and whispering. He doesn't have to hear what they are saying to know they are wondering how a Jew has come to be on such good terms with one of Eichmann's top Nazis.

After exchanging a few pleasantries, Becher rejoins his colleagues, and Miklós says in a low voice, 'This fellow might be useful to us. I've heard he's in charge of appropriating Jewish paintings, jewellery and cash. They say he's been amassing a fortune all over Europe, wagons full of stuff. I heard he's Himmler's protégé, but I don't think he's a fanatical anti-Semite like the rest of them. He might be able to help us if we can wave enough cash in front of him.'

Gábor doesn't reply. He is fiddling with his glass and looks preoccupied, and Miklós realises that he is still thinking about Ilonka.

'Don't worry, of course I'll make sure she is all right,' he says and tries to sound matter-of-fact despite the twinge of guilt he feels. After all, this situation isn't his fault. He hasn't manoeuvred for Gábor to be sent away. He has never believed in fate, only in the power of the individual, but it does seem as if fate has conspired to throw him and Ilonka together. He prefers not to acknowledge that what fate promises, it can also take away.

He knows he should behave honourably and resist the temptation, but he suspects that his passion for Ilonka may triumph over loyalty to his friend.

He looks at the Doxa watch his father-in-law gave him when he and Judit became engaged, and pushes away his coffee cup. 'I'd better go home,' he says. 'Judit is expecting me for dinner.'

He leaves a few pengos on the plate for the waitress, picks up his hat and coat, and pushes open the glass doors of the café. Outside the air is cold and damp, and the Danube looks grey. As he walks home along the embankment, he wonders what will happen in Istanbul and what stories he will have to invent to keep Eichmann on the hook while Gábor is away.

His thoughts turn to Ilonka, and fantasies quicken his pulse. As he turns the key in his apartment door, he is already calculating when he will be able to visit her. As the door closes behind him, he hears Judit's voice, and he wonders if somewhere, sometime, there will be a price to pay for this.

CHAPTER FIVE

May 1944

A week later, Miklós is pacing up and down in front of Ilonka's building in Király Street, flowers in hand, like a nervous suitor. He bought the posy of lilies-of-the-valley from a woman sitting on the street corner bundled up in a brown shawl and a headscarf tied low over her forehead, like the village women back home. Thinking of his village evokes thoughts he has tried to push from his mind on this bright spring day. Already Jews in some of the provinces have been rounded up and placed in ghettos prior to being deported, and a rumour from a sympathetic Hungarian politician has warned him that the Nazis were planning to create a ghetto in Budapest. The situation was growing desperate and he knows he will have to talk to Eichmann again about the Jews he has promised to release, but here he is, bringing flowers for the woman he can't get out of his mind.

Already the dark green spear-shaped leaves have lost their sheen and the exquisitely scented miniature white bells are drooping on their short stems, probably from the heat in his hand. Several times as he nears the entrance, he is about to press the buzzer but continues walking. He has waited so long for this opportunity to be alone with her, but now that the moment is approaching, he is wracked by doubts. What if he has misread the signs and she is offended or shocked? What if she rebuffs him?

Despite his anxiety, he can see the black humour of the situation. At the age of 40, with Allied bombs now falling on Budapest, and the entire Jewish community of Hungary threatened with destruction, he is behaving like a smitten schoolboy. His heart is thumping, his palms are sweating and his mind is churning with hopes, doubts and erotic fantasies.

He has had affairs in the past. For as long as he can remember, women have thrown themselves at him. But when he looks in the mirror, he sees a man of middle height with broad shoulders, a head of wavy brown hair, and a level gaze. Nothing remarkable.

Women are drawn to you because you are strong. They like powerful men, his mother once told him. *You see the world with your own eyes and you seem indifferent to their charms. Women like a challenge.*

Women obviously did see something that eluded him because they continued to make themselves available. On the dance floor, they pressed their soft bodies against him so that he could feel every curve. In the salons, they sat close to him, their lips parted, their low-cut dresses falling open as they leaned forward, flaunting their full white breasts. Some made risqué jokes about men's sexual prowess and gave knowing smiles to indicate they were experts on the subject. He didn't love them but he enjoyed the game. He would appear noncommittal and aloof until the very last moment. And when the chase came to its inevitable conclusion, they played the ingénue, pouted and accused him of being a heartless seducer while they were rolling down their stockings, unfastening their corsets and unbuttoning their blouses. The interludes were pleasurable but brief. There was no conquest and no elation.

But this was different. Ilonka wasn't one of those empty-headed coquettes, and she has never flirted with him. What's more, she was married to his friend, although from the openness with which Gábor carried on with other women, and the matter-of-fact manner in which he and Ilonka conversed, Miklós suspects that their marriage is based on friendship and familiarity rather than passion. Hovering near her front door, he hopes he is right.

If he was to sum up his own marriage, he would describe it as amicable and comfortable. His life with Judit is smooth and easy, and what he feels for her is affection and respect. Admiration, too. She was an accomplished pianist when they met, a dainty blonde with a rose-petal complexion who turned heads in the street. She had turned his as well, but his ardour wilted soon after they married. Her fear of becoming pregnant suppressed her enjoyment of sex, and the nightly effort of trying to evoke a spark of desire or a sensual response eventually stifled his own lust.

She told him from the beginning that she didn't want to have children, and his efforts to change her mind had been futile. War was coming, she argued, hardly the right time to bring children into the world. Besides, children and music didn't mix, and she didn't want babies to interfere with her career.

Disappointed and frustrated, over the years he found the physical release he needed with other women, and if Judit was aware of his liaisons, she ignored them. He supposed that, like many married women, she accepted the fact that husbands played around. He recalls a conversation he once overheard between his mother and her friend who was complaining about her husband's philandering. 'Don't worry,' his mother had said. 'It's not made of soap, it won't wear out.'

Miklós has watched Ilonka with growing admiration ever since he and Gábor Weisz formed their committee to help the destitute Polish and Slovak refugees flooding into Budapest the previous year. While they arranged shelter, raised money and forged documents, Ilonka had donated some of her own clothes and household linen.

When that was gone, she had importuned all her friends and acquaintances for clothes and bedding for the refugees. When she had exhausted all her contacts, she got hold of a sewing machine and set up a workshop in their apartment making shirts, blouses and dresses. She discovered a flair for converting the used clothes she was given into new styles, and her designs were so original that word soon spread and women from all over Budapest came to buy clothes from her. Her business grew, and before long she was able to employ some of the female refugees to hem and stitch the clothes.

'I'll never be out of business because war or no war, the women of Budapest are the vainest in the world. They'll go without food rather than go without new clothes,' she told Miklós once as he watched her cutting up used garments on her dining-room table. He liked listening to her low, musical voice, admired her resourcefulness and generosity, and always left in better spirits than before. Being in Ilonka's company was like walking into a sunlit room after spending hours in a damp, dark basement.

He knows the exact day, the exact hour, when his admiration flared into desire. Three months before, he had come to talk to Gábor about a problem they were having with the forged documents. Ilonka was sitting at her sewing machine on the other side of the room when he saw her looking at him. There was no mistaking that glance. It wasn't demure or casual but it wasn't flirtatious either. She was looking at him with a deliberate, intense gaze, and their eyes locked like magnets, neither willing to disengage. Then she looked away and continued sewing, and he continued talking to Gábor, and the moment passed, but in that instant he knew his world would never be the same again. It felt as if a secret declaration had been made, an unspoken promise now hanging in the air between them. The memory of that shared glance thrilled and tantalised him and he was convinced that one day she would be his.

But now, standing at her door with his confidence wilting along with the flowers, he wonders whether his overheated imagination has exaggerated the significance of that moment. He takes a deep breath to steady his nerves and presses the buzzer. Whatever happens, he has to know if she shares his feelings.

As soon as he sees her, his doubts evaporate. She smiles at him with that slow, sensual smile he finds so alluring, and her dark eyes linger on his. As soon as she closes the door behind him, he takes her hand. It's firm and strong, unlike the soft, boneless hands of other women he knows, and he bends over to press his lips to it as he breathes in the spicy scent of her perfume.

She releases her hand when she notices the lilies-of-the-valley, leaves the room, and returns a moment later with a vase. As she arranges the flowers, she says in a voice that is low and husky, 'I wondered when you'd come.'

Without replying, he pulls her down onto the couch beside him, and kisses her for a long time. Her lips are warm and yielding, and he feels them parting against his as he explores her mouth.

'I've wanted you ever since the day we looked at each other across this room,' he whispers. 'I've relived that moment a hundred times.'

He starts to undo the little covered buttons on her cream blouse but he is too impatient and under his clumsy fingers one of them snaps off. Laughing, she takes his hand and leads him to the bedroom. With quick, deft movements she unfastens her blouse, pulls off her silk camisole and unpins her thick dark hair which spills over her naked shoulders. He strokes her slender body and covers her face and neck with kisses. 'I wake up every morning aching for you,' he whispers.

Later, as they lie in each other's arms, she traces his lips with the tip of her finger. 'I've often wondered what it would be like to make love with you,' she says. 'Now I know. It feels as if we were meant for each other.'

He nods and holds her tightly. 'Gábor is a lucky man. I wish I'd been your first lover.'

She smiles that slow, sensual smile as she caresses his body with her fingertips, making him shiver with pleasure.

He wants to tell her that when she drew him deep inside her and they were locked together, he felt a rapture he had never experienced before. Despite death looming around them, he is suddenly aware of the dazzling beauty of life and its meaning. He's not religious but the joy he felt when they made love was almost spiritual. He had never imagined that such bliss existed on earth. At that moment, even the existence of God was a possibility. But he just holds her closer and doesn't speak. Putting his feelings into words would ruin this moment of perfect communion.

For two miraculous hours he has forgotten the war, the occupation, and their predicament, but the fall from heaven to earth is swift and sudden when he recalls the deal he has made. Eichmann has offered to release six hundred Jews from Hungary to a neutral nation as down payment for the trucks he hopes to receive from the Allies, and he has ordered Miklós to compile a list of names for his approval.

His initial elation at the possibility of snatching several hundred Jews from the fate awaiting them in Hungary has now given way to more anxiety. He never wanted to play God. How was he to select six hundred from half a million? Who should he include, and who would he exclude? He knows that in Poland, a German called Oskar Schindler was saving some Jews by employing them in his factory in Krakow. He met Schindler the previous year when he arrived in Budapest to ask Miklós and his committee for money so that he could continue supporting his Jews.

Miklós admired what Schindler was doing but he didn't trust the man. He suspected him of hobnobbing with the Nazis to provide himself with a labour force. A collaborator masquerading as a humanitarian. Still, for whatever reason, there was no doubt that he was saving Jewish lives, and Miklós approved a donation to help him continue his rescue efforts.

But now that the Germans had occupied Hungary, the task of rescuing Hungarian Jews had fallen on his shoulders, and he no longer knew whether he had sought that burden or whether fate had chosen him. The deal Eichmann had proposed was impossible, but the stakes were high and he knew he would have to string out this game as long as possible even though the prospect of having to confront Eichmann again made him feel sick. Eichmann was unpredictable and fanatical, and couldn't be trusted to keep his word. And unless he heard from Gábor in Istanbul very soon, he would have nothing to bargain with.

Looking at Ilonka as she sits slowly brushing her hair in front of the mirror in her camisole and silk culottes, he is distracted from his dark thoughts. His body is stirring with excitement, and he longs to pull her onto the bed and make love to her again, but with an effort he looks away. He has arranged to meet Egon Friedlander, Rezsö Kadar and Lajos Kis, some of the members of the Rescue Committee, to update them about Gábor's progress. They were all dedicated, hard-working men, but he wonders if they have the resourcefulness and strength needed to deal with the Nazi Satan.

Ilonka turns from the mirror to watch him. 'Are you thinking about what you'll say to Eichmann?'

He nods. 'You have no idea how terrifying it is to stand in front of him.'

'I'll find out tomorrow,' she says quietly. 'He has ordered me to come to his headquarters. I suppose it's about Gábor.'

He takes her hand, turns it over and presses his lips into her palm. He can't bear the thought of her confronting the monster by herself. 'I won't let you go alone, my darling,' he whispers. 'I'll go with you.'

*

The following morning, on their way to the Hotel Majestic, Miklós and Ilonka walk in silence. She takes his arm and squeezes it, and occasionally they look at each other and smile the complicit smile of secret lovers. The old woman is sitting on the corner of Andor Boulevard again beside her small wicker basket of lilies-of-the-valley. Faded signs in Hungarian advertise the workshops of the Jewish tailors, cobblers and jewellers who live in the maze of alleys in the Jewish quarter behind the boulevard. In Dohány Utca, they pass the synagogue with its two towers topped by oriental cupolas. Miklos knows that at its inauguration in the nineteenth century, a time when the Jewish community felt secure within the realm of the Austro-Hungarian Empire, Franz Liszt had played the 5000-pipe organ. The erection of the Dohány synagogue represented a vote of confidence in the future. It was a sobering reminder that unless he succeeded in getting Eichmann to honour his promise, that synagogue would soon become a memorial to an extinguished community.

Inside the Sikló cable car ascending Swabian Hill, Ilonka points to the obsidian waters below. 'I don't know why Johann Strauss ever thought the Danube was blue,' she says, and he knows she is trying to defuse the tension with light-hearted chatter.

He notices that she has worn high-heeled shoes with ankle straps, a smart jacket over her floral dress, and tilted her felt hat at a jaunty angle over her hair, which falls to her shoulders. She looks fetching, but he knows that if she is hoping to charm Eichmann, she is wasting her time.

The cable car shudders to a halt at the top of Swabian Hill. Ilonka straightens her shoulders and lifts her chin. 'No matter what he says, Miki, we have to keep calm and sound firm. People like him only respect strength, they despise weaklings. Bullies are all the same, the only difference is the amount of power they have.'

He looks at her composed expression and wonders if she is as fearless as she sounds, and whether she realises that she is Eichmann's hostage and what that could mean. But he knows that it is strength and pride, not ignorance, that dictates her words. She is too smart not to be aware of the peril she is in.

If the security checks at the German guard posts on the hillside leading to the hotel make her nervous, she gives no sign of being affected by them. On the contrary, she gives the impression of being accustomed to this procedure, and reacts with polite disdain.

Miklós is going over in his mind what he will say to Eichmann, even though he realises it's a useless exercise. It was impossible to anticipate his questions or gauge his reactions.

Escorted by a cocky young guard who barks orders at them, they mount the curved staircase to Eichmann's head-quarters in silence. Eichmann is seated at his desk, his pistol in front of him as before to remind them of his power to dispense instant death. He doesn't ask them to sit down, ignores Miklós, and looks at Ilonka with an expression that reminds Miklós of a basilisk, the mythical serpent whose glance turned people to stone.

He leans forward with a cruel, lopsided smile. 'Ah so, Frau Weisz,' he says. 'I have still not heard from your husband. I think he will never return to Budapest.' He lowers his voice to a hiss. 'If he does not return, you will be joining the other Jews in Auschwitz.'

CHAPTER SIX

2005

From the back of the hire car, Annika sees a succession of dilapidated warehouses, pockmarked industrial buildings, and apartment blocks that don't seem to have had a coat of paint or fresh plaster for at least a hundred years. The awnings above the small shops are rusted, the wooden window frames are splintered, and the people walking along the streets look as weary and rundown as the buildings. Apart from an occasional tree covered in new spring foliage, there is little greenery to lift the greyness of the outer suburbs of Budapest.

There are few people in the streets, but they seem downcast, and no-one is smiling. Perhaps her perception is coloured by irritation, because when she entered the arrival hall of Ferihegy International Airport, the driver who was supposed to pick her up wasn't there. After waiting for almost half an hour, she was about to give up and find a taxi when he appeared, grabbed her suitcase without an apology, and rushed ahead of her so fast that she had to run along the uneven paving to keep up with him.

A grey sky hangs low over the city, and as they drive along her attempts to brighten the atmosphere by engaging him in even the most basic conversation prove futile. Her questions about the traffic in Budapest and the cost of living meet with shrugs and monosyllabic answers. His mobile rings every few minutes, and he answers it in an argumentative tone. In between, he glares and swears at other drivers. Although she can't speak Hungarian, she can recognise curses in any language.

Forty minutes later, they emerge from the depressing industrial area, and approach the centre of the city. At her first sight of the river she feels a surge of excitement. 'The Danube?' she asks.

He shrugs. 'Yes, of course Danube,' he says in a tone that makes her wish she had kept her thoughts to herself.

In an avenue lined with plane trees, they pass an impressive colonnaded building with ornamental brickwork and two tall towers, each topped by an oriental-looking onion dome. She winds down the window for a closer look. 'What's that?' she asks.

'*Zsidó zsinagóga,*' he says.

'*Zsinagóga,*' she repeats slowly. Then it dawns on her. 'Jewish synagogue, yes?'

'*Zsidó zsinagóga,*' he repeats with a nod. 'On Dohány Street. Most big in Europe.'

It's the first bit of information he has volunteered, and it encourages her to pursue the subject. 'We have synagogues in Australia, but not as big as that. Are there many Jews in Budapest?'

He is looking at her in his rear-view mirror. 'Today not. But before, many.'

He rifles in his glove box, muttering in Hungarian, until he finds what he is looking for, and turns around to hand her a plain white card. *Jancsi Kovács, Budapest Tours.* There's a telephone number.

'My friend very good guide,' the driver says. 'Say him Tamás sent you. He take you to Dohány Zsinagóga.'

Annika thanks him and puts the card in the pocket of the black leather jacket she bought in Florence ten years ago. It's tight now, and she can't button it up, but she likes the casual style and the feel of the soft leather. She says she will contact his friend. There's no point telling him that she had already arranged a city tour on the internet before leaving Sydney.

He pulls up in front of a multi-storey international hotel near the embankment. As soon as the bellboy ushers her into her room on the fourth floor, she goes to the window. The clouds have dispersed, and the iron bridge that spans the Danube seems polished by the spring sunlight.

The bellboy points to the other side of the river which rises steeply from the water. 'Buda,' he says. 'Swabian Hill.' A statue of a heroic figure on horseback faces basilicas with gilded cupolas, and terraces with ornamental turrets. At the summit, surrounded by oaks and beeches, a palatial building dominates the hillside. 'Hotel Majestic,' he says.

Annika stands at the window for a long time, delighted by the view. Her grandmother had never mentioned how beautiful this city was. In fact, Marika said very little when Annika told her she had booked a trip to Hungary, apart from asking dryly why, of all places, she wanted to go there. The question had taken her by surprise. *Because that's where you came from,* she replied. *You know, roots.* Marika had broken all links with Hungary and had no desire to reconnect with her birthplace. The past, as an English novelist once noted, was a different country, and it was obviously one Marika had no wish to revisit, but as Annika was at a loose end, this was a perfect opportunity to visit the country where her family originated.

There was another reason, too. Intrigued by Marika's reaction at the mention of Miklós Nagy, Annika had searched for him on the internet, but the items she had read intrigued her even more. Nagy was apparently a controversial figure who evoked strong and contradictory emotions. Some people hailed him as a hero, and described his fate as a Greek tragedy, while others described him as a scoundrel, a Machiavellian schemer, without explaining why. Perhaps her grandmother shared that opinion, although why she would regard her rescuer in that light was a mystery. It was one that Annika hoped to unravel.

Her mother hadn't been enthusiastic about her plan to visit Budapest either. 'Why don't you go to Italy or France instead?' she suggested. 'Those Eastern European countries are so depressing.' She could imagine her mother commenting to her friends at the bridge club that Annika could always be counted on to be contrary.

For the first time since resigning from her job, she was embarking on something that felt right. 'I need to get away,' she told her friend Cassie. 'My mother and grandmother are driving me crazy about finding a job, but I can afford to take some time off, and there's nothing at the moment to tie me down, so I might as well take advantage of my freedom and travel. I've never been to any of the countries in Eastern Europe, and I want to see where my family came from.'

'So you're escaping, right?' Cassie commented in her blunt way, before adding, 'I don't blame you. You've been a bit depressed lately, and going away will do you good.' Annika is thinking about Cassie's comment as she enters the hotel dining room the next morning. Perhaps there was some truth in her words, and a change of scenery might be just what she needed to sort herself out. She refrained from mentioning her fascination with Miklós Nagy, not wanting to provoke Cassie's scepticism about a wild goose chase.

After a buffet breakfast that includes peppery csabai sausage, paprika-flavoured cheeses and grilled red and green capsicums, she goes down to the lobby to meet her guide. It is busy with tourists milling about, mostly Americans, whose demanding voices and assertive tones resound throughout the foyer. Her tour was booked for nine o'clock but by nine-thirty the guide still hasn't appeared, and she asks the concierge to call the tour company. From his frequent glances in her direction, and his subdued voice, she realises there's a problem. He hangs up and turns to her.

'Unfortunately, madame, there is a mistake about the date,' he explains. It seems they had her booked in for the previous day. Would she like them to send a guide tomorrow instead?

Annika shakes her head. I'm not going to book with that incompetent lot again, she decides. Standing at the door of the lobby, she sees a cloudless blue sky, and whenever the door opens, a refreshing breeze ruffles her hair. It's a perfect spring day, ideal for sightseeing. She takes the lift to her room and searches for her Lonely Planet guidebook. Then she remembers the guide's card in her pocket.

Jancsi Kovács runs into the lobby twenty minutes later, panting. He has driven across the city, and the back of his pale blue T-shirt is patched with sweat. He wipes his forehead as he comes towards her with a smile.

He has the trim figure of a young man, and she thinks he's about thirty, but when he removes his New York Yankees baseball cap, she sees grey hairs on his temples and realises that he is probably older.

'*Kezét csókolom*,' he greets her, and raises her hand to his lips. 'Hungarian custom, kissing lady's hand,' he explains. Annika is taken aback by a man in today's Budapest practising what she sees as a sexist old-world ritual, but he is already asking where she would like to go. 'My friend Tamás said you are interested in Jewish places, yes?'

'This is my first time in Budapest, so perhaps an overview of the main sights to start with?'

Waving his arm in the direction of bridge, he says, 'The Danube divides Budapest into two parts, Buda and Pest. We begin here, in Pest, okay madame?'

'Sounds good.'

As they head off along the embankment, he says, 'I will start with short history. So I can say to you that Hungary has been on wrong side of every major war. Our history is invasions, wars, occupations and defeats. Mongols, Turks, Russians, Austrians, Germans and again Russians. In World War I we are on side of Kaiser. Bad choice. We lose war and we lose peace. Treaty of Trianon in 1920 takes away most of our population and our land. World War II, bad choice again. We fight with Hitler. Germans occupy us. We lose that war two times — after Nazis, Communists come.'

History has never been Annika's strong point, and as she listens to his sardonic account of his country's past, she realises how ignorant she is about Hungary. It also strikes her that peace treaties seem to create unforeseen and catastrophic situations not only for the defeated but for the victors as well. The words of Sophocles spring into her mind: no-one is exempt from the wounds of war.

Past the impressive Hapsburg building that houses the parliament, they continue their riverside stroll until they come to a row of oddly assorted shoes spread along part of the promenade. When they come closer, she sees that they are bronze installations, bolted to the cement path. There are little children's shoes, women's high-heeled pumps, work boots and men's lace-up shoes. Some are lying on their side, as if they had been carelessly kicked off, while others are neatly lined up as if in a wardrobe.

She looks at him questioningly.

'This is in memory of another event in our unhappy history. In 1945, Hungarian fascist militia, Arrow Cross, brought thousands of Jewish people to this place. They forced them to take off all clothes, tied hands behind backs, and shot them. To save bullets, sometimes they tied families together and shot person in front so all fell into Danube and drowned.'

Annika's mouth is so dry she can't speak. Although the sun is warm on her shoulders, she shivers. What a horrible way to die. In her mind she sees the crowd of people herded along this embankment at gunpoint, husbands and wives perhaps, and mothers and children, hears them crying, screaming or pleading. Did they suspect what was to befall them? Did they hope, even at that moment, to be rescued? Did they realise that this river beside which they used to play as children, where they wheeled their own children in prams, strolled with their sweethearts, or dreamed about the future, would become their tomb? She thinks about her grandmother. Thank God Marika escaped such a terrible fate.

As she stands there, lost in thought, a car screeches to a halt and two young men lean out of the window, yell something at them, and speed away. Jancsi raises his middle finger and yells something back. When he turns towards her, his face is white and hard.

'What was that about? What did they say?' she asks.

He hesitates before saying, 'They called us dirty Jews.'

To have racist abuse hurled at her beside this memorial to the victims of race hate infuriates her. She wants to yell something back but it's too late, and besides they wouldn't understand her. She feels sick, and flops onto a nearby bench, staring at the shoes.

'Does this happen often?' she asks.

'Too often,' Jancsi replies. 'We have not many Jews but much anti-Semitism. If Hitler came back today, ultra-nationalist Jobbik party would do like Arrow Cross. We have fascists in government.'

She wonders if he is Jewish, but he is already standing up. 'Tamás said you are interested in Dohány Tsinagoga. We go now.'

Half an hour later, standing in the doorway of the synagogue, she is struck by the opulent decor, the enormous organ, the frescoed ceiling, the pulpit to one side, and three richly decorated aisles. 'This is amazing,' she whispers. 'It reminds me of a cathedral or a mosque.'

Jancsi is watching her with a smile, obviously pleased at her reaction. 'It's a potpourri of architecture,' he says. 'They called it Israelite cathedral but it's a mix of Byzantine, Gothic,

Moorish, Christian and Jewish, with rose stained-glass window, five-thousand-pipe organ inside and onion domes outside.'

'I didn't know synagogues had organs,' Annika says.

'This one is unique. Franz Liszt played it when synagogue opened in 1859. The Jewish community was big then, it could seat about three thousand people. I suppose you know what happened to most of them. Not many left today.'

She is silent. After a pause, he says, 'It's unique for another reason as well. Come outside and I'll show you.'

At the back of the synagogue, they stand in a paved courtyard.

'This is cemetery,' he tells her. 'In 1944, Eichmann made this area into ghetto and relocated over seventy thousand Jews in here from provinces. Thousands died of hunger and cold and were buried here, that's why we have cemetery next to synagogue. You don't see that anywhere else.'

Wandering around the sunlit courtyard, she comes to the Raoul Wallenberg *Emlekpark* with a memorial in the centre to the Hungarian Jewish martyrs. The memorial resembles a silver weeping willow whose delicate leaves are engraved with the names and tattoo numbers of the dead.

'Is called Tree of Life,' Jancsi says. As she gazes at the thousands of silver leaves, a breeze stirs them and they make a haunting sound, like the tinkling of tiny bells outside a Buddhist temple.

She stands very still. It seems as if the souls of the dead are whispering all around her, trying to tell their stories, and although she can't understand what they are saying, she strains to listen, and suddenly everything blurs.

Jancsi looks at her with concern. 'You are upset, I think so. We will go from here.'

She shakes her head. 'I'm all right. It's just, so much emotion in one morning.' She blows her nose and straightens her shoulders. 'This is a beautiful memorial.'

'You heard of Tony Curtis, Hollywood actor? He was born Bernard Schwartz, in Hungary. He paid sculptor to design it,' he said. 'And Madame Lauder, cosmetics lady, she paid for renovation of synagogue after war.'

On the other side of the courtyard, Annika stops beside a plaque commemorating Raoul Wallenberg. She has heard of the Swedish diplomat who rescued thousands of Jews during the Holocaust, but plaques nearby honour people she has never heard of: the Swiss Vice-Consul Carl Lutz, Angelo Rotta the Apostolic Nuncio to the Pope, and various Spanish and Portuguese diplomats.

Standing beside her, Jancsi says, 'One name is not here. Nagy Miklós.'

'Miklós Nagy,' she repeats, astonished to hear him say the name. 'Do you know anything about him?'

'He saved my father and my grandparents,' Jancsi replies.

CHAPTER SEVEN

2005

Inside the Europa Café there's a buzz of conversation and a clatter of plates as waitresses in starched white aprons with sweet smiles and soft twittery voices run around serving coffee and pastries. As they make their way to the only free table, Annika and Jancsi pass the curved glass counter displaying cheesecakes, raspberry tarts, swirled walnut pastries, poppyseed twists and chocolate hazelnut gateaux. As soon as Annika spots the *dobos* torte she exclaims, 'My grandmother's speciality!'

From their table in the far corner, she gazes at the tasselled velvet curtains, silver and gold wallpaper and crystal chandeliers. 'I've never seen such an ornate café,' she says.

'Is oldest in Budapest. Politicians and diplomats came here in Hapsburg days. They say Houdini came too.'

She raises her eyebrows, and he shrugs. 'Maybe not Houdini, but he was born near here.'

A moment later a group of musicians enters the café and begins to serenade the customers with gypsy melodies, their shrewd eyes searching for female tourists. Hearing their rhythmic melodies, Annika closes her eyes and sways in time to the seductive beat. It feels as if the music is embedded in her soul.

Jancsi leans forward. 'You like *czárdás*, madame?'

She grimaces. 'Please don't call me madame. My name is Annika.'

The musicians move towards their table, and the leader, a burly man with a big black moustache and a stomach that swells his embroidered vest, says something to Jancsi while looking at Annika.

'He wants to play for you,' Jancsi translates. 'He asks what you like.'

Taken by surprise, she can't think of any tune that these musicians would know. 'You choose,' she whispers.

She doesn't recognise the song, but she loves its sensual rhythm, and the way the violinist plays it, not taking his smouldering black eyes from her face. She looks away. It feels as if he can see into the secret crevices of her life.

The song ends, and Jancsi takes a few forints from his pocket and hands them to the violinist who bows and moves to the next table. 'That was Hungarian love song, Annika, about man who loves woman but he knows she will never love him.'

It's the first time he has said her name, elongating it so that it sounded like Aanikaa. Was there something intimate in the way he said it, and the way he looked at her as he talked about the song, or did she imagine it? The blood rushes to her cheeks, and she looks down at the menu, feigning sudden interest in the selection of pastries and deserts.

'They all sound tempting, but I have to try the *dobos* torte. My grandmother always makes it for me.'

Jancsi is still looking at her.

'You are telling about grandmother but nothing about you,' he says. He glances at her hands and she wonders if he is looking for a wedding ring. 'In Sydney you have boyfriend, yes?'

Annika controls the urge to retort that she doesn't feel disposed to discuss her private life with a stranger who is probably hitting on her. She has heard too many stories about gullible tourists getting involved with predatory guides. And they weren't naive, stupid women either. Just the previous year her friend Ella, the headmistress of a girls' school in Melbourne, had fallen for her guide in Cairo. He had sworn she was the love of his life and promised to follow her to Australia and marry her, but she found out too late that he was married and had five children. On her return to Melbourne she had to have an abortion. Annika had been incredulous. How could a smart, educated woman of forty-three be so stupid? 'But he was so handsome and so passionate, and he looked like Omar Sharif,' Ella had sobbed. 'He made me feel like a teenager again.'

Not that she herself has been a good judge of men. The ones she has fallen for, who all seemed perfect at the beginning, turned out to be more devoted to their mothers, their footy mates, or their self-indulgent lives than to her. One talked incessantly about his first wife while another wanted her to give up her career. She had been appalled. She was a magazine editor, not a docile homemaker from the 1950s. She has always been convinced that her identity was enmeshed with her career, an idea that makes her smile bitterly when she thinks about it now. So if she wasn't an editor, who was she?

Finding the right man has always seemed impossible. The men who worked on the magazine were more feminine than the women, so she had taken Cassie's advice and tried the internet dating sites. In the photos, the guys all looked good, and each one claimed to be a sensitive new age man with a good sense of humour. They all enjoyed travel, food, and the movies, but the reality was very different. For many of them, their idea of travel was a trip to a footy match with a meat pie in one hand and a tinnie in the other, after which they tried to fumble with her clothes in the car.

Cassie had blamed her for being too picky and too impatient. She said that Annika was setting herself up to fail because she didn't really want a relationship, which meant having to compromise. That almost ended their friendship. But even Cassie agreed that she was lucky to get away from her last date in time. It turned out that he was being treated for a personality disorder, and had spent time in prison for assault. That was eighteen months ago and since then she has lost confidence in her own judgment and the hope of ever finding the right man.

But when she looks at Jancsi, she doesn't see a calculating guide who preys on female tourists. She likes the warm honey colour of his complexion and the candid expression in his dark eyes. He wasn't Hollywood handsome but there was something engaging about him. An Italian word pops into her mind: *simpatico*.

He watches her with an amused expression as she tucks into the *dobos* torte with its layers of sponge cake filled with chocolate cream, topped by a smooth layer of golden toffee.

'Is as good as grandmother's torte?'

'My grandmother's torte has seven layers,' she says, scraping up the splinters of toffee with her fork, but her mind is on something else. She leans forward. 'When we were looking at the plaques in the cemetery behind the synagogue, you mentioned that Miklós Nagy saved your father. What else do you know about him?'

'In 1944 he got many Jews out of Hungary on special train. My father was on it with his mother and father. But I don't know more.'

'So he was like Schindler and Wallenberg?'

'Yes, but Nagy was Jew. Imagine, a Jew with guts to deal with Nazis for Jewish lives!'

Annika is frowning. 'So why wasn't he included among the heroes in that memorial garden?'

'I don't know.'

She recalls some of the vituperative entries she read on the internet. 'There was a controversy about him. Do you know about that?'

'No. I didn't ask about past when I was young, and Father didn't talk about war.'

'But didn't you ask why they were on that train?'

He shakes his head. 'They are not living anymore, so now is too late.'

Annika thinks about this select group of Jews miraculously snatched from the jaws of death, a group that included his parents as well as her own grandmother. How could Marika be so angry with the man who saved her life? And why hadn't he received the recognition he deserved?

Despite the lack of information, she feels a surge of excitement she hasn't felt since she chased up leads for a scoop when she was a reporter many years ago. That shiver of recognition was familiar and tantalising, like knowing there was a seam of gold in the ground just beneath your feet and all you needed was a pick fine enough to extract it. She would keep searching.

For the next few hours, they walk along wide tree-lined avenues and wander in magnificent plazas where children chase each other around gigantic monuments. In Hero Square, in front of the colonnaded structure topped by rearing bronze horses and seven gigantic statues of ancient Magyar chiefs, Jancsi explains that seven is a significant number for Hungary on account of the seven legendary Magyar chiefs who founded the nation. They linger near a film crew photographing three teenage girls who perform intricate jumps as they skip between ropes twirled by two ponytailed guys.

'I loved jumping rope like that when I was in primary school,' she says, suddenly nostalgic about the past. 'The trouble was, my hair used to fly all over the place, and some of the girls called me Mop-Top.'

'But your hair is so beautiful!' he exclaims, and from the way his eyes rest on it, she feels he means it.

As they approach the bridge, he points out that the stone lions which guard the bridgeheads have no tongues. An omission by the stonemason. Across the river, on Swabian Hill, they wander around Fishermen's Bastion, a fairytale structure of turrets and parapets.

'A Hapsburg Disneyworld,' she quips, and he laughs.

'Seven lookout towers in honour of the original seven Magyar tribes,' he points out.

On a small stage at the top of the hill, an elderly woman in a long crimson dress is telling stories to an audience of young children. The storyteller's manner is so compelling that even though Annika can't understand a single word, she is mesmerised by her delivery.

'She is telling folk story about Magyar heroes long ago,' Jancsi explains as they move away. Then in a bitter tone he adds, 'Jobbik people believe only Magyars should live in Hungary. They say Jews are not real Magyars.'

Back on the Pest side of the city, they are walking along a square lined with pavement cafés, gelato booths, and kebab and pizza kiosks when the shriek of sirens makes her jump. Police cars speed across the city and the deafening shrill of their sirens makes conversation impossible. When they turn a corner, she is shocked to see scores of riot police lining the street. There are about eighty of them, men and women, some standing in a row, others clustered in small groups, all menacing in their black gear, with black leggings and black helmets with visors pushed back on their foreheads. She is about to dart across to ask them what was happening, when Jancsi grabs her arm and pulls her away.

'Maybe in Australia you ask police questions, here no.'

A moment later she has her explanation. Coming towards them, taking up the entire width of the avenue, are hundreds of thuggish men, with distorted, red faces, yelling slogans and waving Hungarian flags. Annika's heart is pounding. It's clear that only a spark is needed to turn this crowd's nationalistic fervour into a riot. Magyars against the foreigners.

'Big soccer match tonight, Hungarians versus Romanians,' Jancsi says. 'There will be drinking and fighting, so police are ready.'

They turn down a side street and emerge on the Corso, where a row of the touristy pavement restaurants facing the river advertise gypsy music, Hungarian specialities and pizzas. Annika is too tired to keep walking so they sit down at a table at the Panorama Terasz, whose dour waiters move like sleepwalkers.

'People in Budapest don't smile,' she says. 'Why?'

'Life is hard. Don't forget we had communist government until 1991. From 1945 to 1991, there was no God, and no religion, only communism. Suddenly, God is back, religion is back, and now we are capitalist. Too quick, too many problems. But last year we join European Union, so maybe everything will be better.'

Annika is shocked to realise that until fourteen years ago, this was a communist country, and once again she is embarrassed by her ignorance. By the time the waiter brings them *langos,* fried dough with garlic sauce, it is cold, and he has forgotten to bring *nokedli* dumplings with her chicken *paprikás.*

'This man, Nagy, I wonder how he managed to get those Jews out of Hungary. I wish I knew what happened here during the Holocaust.'

Jancsi checks his watch and pushes away his plate. 'I have tourist group now so I must go, but tomorrow I have time, so if you like, call me.' He scribbles an address on a paper serviette and hands it to her. 'If you want to know about Holocaust, go to museum.'

He says goodbye, takes her hand, and lifts it to his lips.

Once she would have dismissed the idea of a man in the twenty-first century kissing a woman's hand as absurd and patronising, but she is blushing and her heart is racing. It feels more intimate than a kiss on the cheek, or is it the way he looks into her eyes as he lingers over the kiss? She watches him walk away until he disappears among the crowd, and she feels annoyed with herself. Was she becoming one of those susceptible women she despised, the ones who fantasised about every attractive man who came their way? Perhaps Cassie was right. The only men she found interesting were the ones she couldn't have.

*

The light inside the Holocaust museum is dim and the atmosphere is sombre. Accompanying the stark black-and-white photographs of Jewish men being rounded up for labour camps at the beginning of the war, and the images of Arrow Cross fascists herding people along the Danube embankment, is the frightening soundtrack of marching feet, growing ever louder and more relentless.

She learns that in 1944 the Nazis invaded Hungary and disenfranchised the Jews with the co-operation of the government. Horrified, she tries to imagine a world where your government turns against you, where phones are disconnected, radios confiscated, car and bus travel forbidden, bank accounts frozen, and employment terminated. You wake up one day and discover that you are a despised non-person in your own country.

This was the prelude to round-ups, ghettos and mass deportations to Auschwitz. With a shock she realises that this was the world her grandmother lived through. She notices that the floor of the museum is sloping under her feet, as if she is walking in a world sliding towards destruction. She approaches the section about the death camps, and reads the heart-rending words of young girls about to be pushed into cattle trucks. One had written, *I can't believe I'm going to die before I've even lived!*

There's also a quote from Elie Wiesel:

Never shall I forget these things even if I am condemned to live as long as God himself. Never shall I forget those moments that murdered my god and turned my soul to dust.

Elie Wiesel swore never to forget what had happened. Why had her grandmother forgotten to remember?

It is almost closing time, and the young woman behind the ticket counter yawns as she flicks through her magazine. Annika wonders whether the mags in Hungary are as obsessed as Australian ones with gossip about nonentities whose only claim to fame was being written about in women's magazines.

A grey-haired attendant with a badge on his lapel identifying him as Imre looks up from the leaflets he is tidying, and asks if he can help.

'I'd like to find out something about a man called Miklós Nagy who lived in Budapest during the Holocaust. Is there anything in the museum about him?'

He surveys her for a moment in silence. 'Nagy Miklós,' he repeats. 'This is name I not hear for many years. Now I ask myself. Why does young lady from — is it America? England?'

'Australia,' Annika says.

'Why does young lady from Australia want to know about Nagy Miklós?'

She is waiting for him to answer her question when he glances at the big clock on the wall and he slaps his forehead with a wrinkled hand. 'It is late, I have to go. Is long story. Not nice story. Was scandal. And tragedy. Bad man or good man? No-one wants to talk about him.' He looks at the clock again. 'Sorry, I go now.'

She leaves the museum, frustrated and annoyed. As she makes her way back to the hotel, it strikes her that once again Miklós Nagy's fate has been described as a tragedy. Tragedy seemed to be the thread that linked her fascination with ancient Greek drama to the tantalising journey on which she had embarked.

That evening, back in her hotel room, Annika stands by the window gazing at the city below. Night has fallen, and the bridge, the castle on the hill, and Parliament House are lit up with millions of tiny lights which transform Budapest into a beguiling fairyland. But the vision is illusory, and the scintillating lights are a deceptive facade. Flowing through the dark heart of the city, dividing it into two, is the Danube, and watching the black ribbon of water threading through Budapest, she senses that this is a city divided into past and present, where ugliness lies just beneath seductive beauty, and darkness lurks in the depths of its timeless river.

CHAPTER EIGHT

June 1944

Miklós wakes with a start, the scream still vibrating in his throat. In his dream he was trudging up a mountainside, stooped under a heavy sack. Rocks scattered beneath his feet and he lost his footing several times, but he knew that no matter what happened, he had to keep going. Although the summit receded with each step, on he staggered, gasping as he forced himself upwards. Finally, just as he was about to haul himself onto the peak, he stumbled and dropped the sack. It opened, and he watched, frozen in horror, as hundreds of people tumbled from it, one after another. They plunged into the chasm below, and all he could do was scream while their terrified voices floated up, cursing him.

This is the fourth time he has had that nightmare, but waking offers no relief. No matter how he looks at it, or how often he turns it over in his mind, he is tortured by the responsibility of compiling a list of people he might manage to wrest from Eichmann's grip. Men, women or children? Young or old? Orthodox or Neolog? Rich or poor? Professionals or labourers? City-dwellers or villagers?

Was he even capable of pulling off this feat? Those who knew him would be astonished to learn that behind the confident facade, the strong voice and firm tread, he was struggling with such doubts. Ever since he arrived in Budapest from Kolostór, he has become the man everyone turns to whenever they need something done. He was the man who always knows the right people to contact, where to go, and what to do. He has to admit he enjoys the power and respect that this reputation brings him, but now for the first time he feels overwhelmed by the enormity of the task he has brought upon himself. The thrill of being able to rescue six hundred lives has now become overshadowed by the agony of deciding which six hundred to save.

To ensure that the responsibility would not be his alone, he has entrusted prominent members of the Rescue Committee with the task of selecting most of the six hundred. That way, no-one could accuse him of nepotism or favouritism. His own much shorter list contained his relatives, close friends, former work colleagues, prominent members of the Kolostór community, including several members of the Jewish Council, and some poor residents, but whenever he rereads it he is tormented by anxiety.

Judit was on his list of course, but Ilonka, the person he was most desperate to save, was still Eichmann's hostage. Her survival depended on Gábor's success in Istanbul, and there was still no news to relay to Eichmann.

Klein has sent him a peculiar coded message saying that he and Gábor had been arrested at the Turkish border as spies, but that thanks to Klein's influence with the Turks, they have been released. Deciphering his message, Miklós is worried. As he suspected all along, sending Klein has endangered Gábor's mission and the lives of those they were trying to save. In all likelihood Klein was not only a double agent but a triple agent who spied for the Germans, Hungarians and British, and was being watched by the Turkish secret police to whom he probably fed information in return for being freed. And as for Gábor, although he was sincere and well-meaning, he definitely wasn't the right man for such a tricky assignment.

In his message Klein added that Gábor was still trying to contact representatives of the Jewish Agency, who hadn't yet left Palestine despite Gábor repeatedly imploring them to meet him in Istanbul as soon as possible. It was always difficult to know to what extent Klein's own agenda was dictating his communications, but Miklós doubted that the leaders of the Jewish Agency in Palestine were deliberately delaying their arrival in Istanbul. Whatever the reason, it would be catastrophic if that information ever reached Eichmann, and Miklós knows he must keep it to himself.

The Agency's co-operation was vital, and every hour counted as cattle trucks crammed with over a thousand Jewish men, women and children continued to leave the Hungarian provinces for concentration camps every single day. Unless Eichmann believed that the representatives of the Jewish groups and the British government would make funds available to pay the Nazis a huge bribe and supply his trucks, they were all doomed.

Whenever Miklós catches sight of himself in the mirror, he is startled to see his own father. The same worried eyes, greying hair and deeply furrowed cheeks. At times like this, he wonders if God himself has become worn down with the burden of all his decisions and has decided to wash his hands of the catastrophe that has befallen the human race. The only time he relaxes is with Ilonka, but anxiety about her future is weighing him down. She is his refuge, his solace and his delight, and knowing that Eichmann wouldn't hesitate to have her deported unless Gábor produced positive news strengthens his resolve to continue bluffing.

Preoccupied with his thoughts, Miklós doesn't say much when he arrives at Ilonka's apartment that afternoon, but pulls her to him with an air of desperation that unsettles her. She takes his hand, leads him to the bedroom and, without speaking, proceeds to unbutton her demure white blouse with the navy polka dots, and steps out of her cream silk culottes, but for once the sensual movements of her body don't arouse him. He sighs as they lie on the bed side by side, his hand passive in hers.

Ilonka props herself up on her elbows and looks into his face. 'Eichmann told you to submit six hundred names,' she says slowly. 'But he didn't stipulate they had to be individuals, did he? So you could select six hundred families but submit only six hundred surnames, couldn't you? That way you'd be able to save a lot more people.'

He sits up. It's a long shot, and a risky one, but the whole enterprise is fraught with such uncertainty and danger that this ploy is worth trying. He gazes at her with admiration and pulls her against him.

'I wish I'd thought of that,' he murmurs as he kisses her eyelids and her lips. Then he stops talking. She is running her long nails delicately along his back and around his buttocks, arousing him to such erotic rapture that for one whole hour there is no Eichmann, no trucks, and no lists.

*

The following day they are summoned to Eichmann's headquarters again. He starts yelling even before they are inside his office. 'You Jews are conning me. I'll have you both shot!' Pacing up and down, he glares at Ilonka. 'And as for you, you'd better hope your husband comes through soon with those trucks!'

Ilonka doesn't flinch. 'My husband is doing all he can, but your request is so important, you must realise that he needs time,' she says quietly when he finally stops shouting and drops into his chair. He stretches his jackbooted legs out under the carved walnut desk and drums his fingers on its tooled surface, dangerously close to his pistol.

In a quiet voice, Ilonka says, 'Obersturmbannführer, if you stopped the deportations, you would prove to our people in Istanbul that you were serious, and they would be more likely to consider your offer.'

Eichmann's face contorts with rage. He springs up, and, as he takes a menacing step towards her, the bony bridge of his nose becomes more prominent, and she can smell schnapps on his breath. 'How dare you offer me suggestions, Frau Weisz. Do you take me for a fool? If I stopped the deportations, what would I have to bargain with?'

Sweating under his coat, Miklós removes his cigarette case from his pocket, lights up, and takes a long slow puff of his cigarette, hoping to steady his voice and stop the trembling of his hands. He explains that Gábor needs time for the request to reach the right people who would then have to check with their superiors. After all, surely Eichmann understands that supplying ten thousand trucks to Germany in exchange for a million Jews would require authority from the highest levels. He dreads to think what Eichmann would do if he knew that the 'right people' haven't even left Palestine to meet Gábor, and there has been no response from the British government.

Knowing that his request would never be fulfilled makes it difficult to maintain this deadly poker game, but he is buying time for the Jews of Hungary, and for Ilonka. Surely the war must end soon. The Germans must know they have already lost, yet they were still filling their trains with more Jews destined for death than with soldiers destined for the battlefield. He doubts whether in any previous war a beleaguered combatant has chosen to prosecute a campaign against civilians at the cost of wasting resources to defeat the enemy.

Although he is trembling with anxiety, Miklós manages to control his voice and sound as though he is speaking with a reasonable equal, not with a fanatic who wouldn't hesitate to press the trigger. His performance is so convincing that Eichmann calms down, and Miklós reminds him of his promise to release the six hundred Jews with visas for Palestine. He has already seen to it that members of the Jewish Agency's Palestine Office inside the Swedish Legation have stamped the permits. If his luck holds and Eichmann keeps his word, thanks to Ilonka the number of people saved will now be over fifteen hundred.

Every time Miklós leaves Eichmann's office, he feels as if his whole body has been sucked dry and only a hollow husk remains. He and Ilonka walk to her apartment, hurrying past the latest anti-Semitic regulations pasted on walls, headed with swastikas, and threatening transgressors with death.

'What makes it worse is that our own government is collaborating with the Nazis,' Ilonka sighs, and Miklós nods.

'One day they will pay for their collusion,' he mutters.

At a time when their ugly world is closing in on them, the beauty of the shimmering new foliage on the oak and chestnut trees makes his heart ache. Perhaps this will be their last spring. Ilonka glances up and sees the pain in his eyes. She squeezes his hand.

'I'm sure Gábor will send us news soon. I know he's not a diplomat, but he's no fool either, and he knows how much hinges on this. He won't give up until he convinces the people in Istanbul that they have to come up with something to keep Eichmann on the hook.'

Instead of lifting his spirits, her words plunge him deeper into gloom. She doesn't know that some of the people in whom they have invested so much hope haven't yet arrived in Istanbul, while others have ignored Gábor's entreaties.

*

It's late when he lets himself into his apartment, hoping that Judit is asleep, but he hears the strains of Liszt's *Transcendental Meditations* filling their home. This contemplative music matches his mood, and he stands at the door, watching as she plays. Her back is very straight, and her eyes are closed as she listens to the melody flowing from her slender white fingers. Until now, he has regretted that her refusal to have children. A child anchors you to the present and gives you a stake in the future. Listening to the music, he wonders if Judit regrets her decision now that the anti-Jewish decrees have put a stop to her musical career. But perhaps she was right after all. Much as he loved children, this wasn't the time to bring them into the world.

She looks up when he enters, smiles, and makes a vague comment before resuming her practice. He wonders if she has noticed that he has been coming home later than usual lately. Her composure conveys such innocence that he feels a pang of guilt as he kisses the top of her blonde head. He envies her ability to shut out reality by immersing herself so completely in her music.

'I have to travel to Kolostór tomorrow,' he says. 'I'll be gone for a day or two.'

Judit stops playing and turns to face him. 'How can you go there when Jews aren't allowed to travel?'

'Kurt Becher gave me a travel pass and a driver.'

She looks surprised. 'Really?' Then she adds, 'I've heard that Becher is Himmler's man.'

Miklós is astonished. Judit hardly ever leaves the apartment and takes no part in his activities to help the refugees or in his rescue plan. She seems to live in a universe where the only thing that exists is music, yet she has heard about Becher. He is about to ask where she had heard of him when her next question takes him off balance.

'How is Gábor's wife Ilonka managing while he's away?'

It might have been a guileless inquiry but he wonders why she has made a point of referring to Ilonka, whom she has known for several years, as Gábor's wife. She doesn't appear to notice that he hesitates before replying, and nods when he makes a noncommittal comment.

'It must be hard for her on her own, wondering what's happening over there, and when he'll be back. But in a way she has always been on her own, hasn't she? Perhaps he'll decide to stay in Istanbul. I wouldn't blame him. They'll kill him if he comes back without the news Eichmann wants. Anyway, I suppose you'll look in on her from time to time.' Then she turns back to the piano, as if dismissing him, opens the score of a Chopin *Ballade* and begins to play, transported by the music once more. He stands still, wondering how much she knows, and what lies behind her apparently innocent words.

Later, as he lies in his bed, every muscle in his body feels like a boxer's fist, and the tumult in his mind makes sleep impossible. Tormented by his recollection of the meeting with Eichmann and his fear of Gábor's failure, he dreads his impending visit to Kolostór. If only Ilonka was lying beside him. Her touch would soothe him.

He must have dozed off. In his dream she is lying beside him, and he clings to her with an urgency he has never felt before. They are locked together in an embrace he never wants to end. It is still dark when he wakes up, and he lies with his eyes closed, not wanting to break the spell of the dream, not wanting to lose the memory of her warm flesh entwined with his, her fingers stroking the most sensitive parts of his body, and her body opening up to gather him inside. The dream is so vivid that when he opens his eyes he almost expects to see her lying there.

There is a body beside him, but it isn't Ilonka. It is Judit, sleeping like a child with her fair hair fanned out on the pillow, and her lips slightly parted. He stares at her for a long time trying to make sense of what he has just experienced.

Surely it was a dream. He and Judit haven't slept in the same bed for several years, and even before that, there had been no passion between them.

Since starting his affair with Ilonka, he has regarded Judit as a platonic friend. He assumes that this suits her as she hasn't objected. He glances at her again. Perhaps she felt lonely and sought solace in his bed, and the proximity of her body inspired his erotic dream. That's what it must be. He closes his eyes. When he opens them again, light is streaming into the room and he is alone in the bed. The strains of a Schubert sonata waft from the front room, telling him Judit is already at the piano.

He kisses the top of her head as usual, and wonders if she will allude to the previous night, but without taking her eyes off the music sheet, she asks when he is leaving, and wishes him a safe journey. The question that tantalises him can't be articulated and remains unanswered.

CHAPTER NINE

June 1944

As the beige Mercedes Benz speeds through the streets of Budapest, Miklós glances through the tinted window at the river. Its dull, grey waters reflect his mood. He is on the way to Kolostór to tell the people on his list about his rescue plan, and his brain churns with possibilities, probabilities, perils and risks. For one thing, their rescue isn't guaranteed. Eichmann might not honour his promise to a Jew: he could break his agreement and instead of allowing the visa holders for Palestine to leave, he might deport them all to Poland instead. For another, he will have to be very discreet when he contacts people to let them know that he has organised a train that will take them to the safety of a neutral nation, and he'll have to swear them to secrecy, or there will be a riot when others discover that there's a list and they aren't on it.

Past the squares and monuments that made Budapest a showcase of Austro-Hungarian architecture, they drive through shabby outer suburbs whose buildings look as defeated as the people in the streets. Soon they have left the city behind. Sitting in the back seat of the official car that Kurt Becher has provided, Miklós thinks about Becher's unexpected co-operation. Although he is reluctant to admit this even to himself, in any other circumstances, he would probably have liked this man. It's gratifying to be treated like an equal by a high-ranking Nazi officer instead of as a Jew who could be deported or killed at a moment's notice, on a whim. Becher is disgustingly venal, but fortunately his desire for wealth seems stronger than his desire to murder Jews.

Miklós winds down the window. Instead of the odour of leather upholstery, he wants to breathe the fresh air of the countryside. The road is lined with poplars, birches and chestnut trees glistening in the morning light, and in the distance he hears the warble of a nightingale. The mottled white trunks of the birches gleam in the sunshine, and old bridges span streams that flow with melted snow. In the villages, they pass clusters of simple peasant huts with tall sunflowers, straggly tomatoes, and chickens pecking in the yards, and large stork nests on the roofs. It's a familiar scene from his childhood that evokes a past when life was uncomplicated, and the terrors of war were far away.

In this rural area, so close to the city, it is easy to imagine that Budapest is thousands of miles away, and the war is being waged on some distant planet. Occasionally they drive past hunched women with worn faces, thick woollen stockings, and floral kerchiefs tied around their heads, who walk along the side of the road with their cows or goats, a scene that is at once strange and beguilingly familiar. It looks as if nothing here has changed for a hundred years.

But as they approach a township, his nostalgic idyll comes to an abrupt end. Along the dusty road, groups of Jews with despair in their eyes trudge beside ox-drawn carts heaped with bedding, bundles and small children. Behind them stride Hungarian gendarmes with rifles, bayonets fixed, yelling abuse and lashing out at those who lag behind, mostly frail old people and exhausted mothers clutching babies and dragging toddlers. He knows they are being herded to a ghetto where they will be crammed in without food or toilet facilities, and he longs to leap out of the car and yell at the brutal guards who are escorting them. His driver lets out a low whistle. 'Thank God they're getting rid of the Yids for us,' he says with a grin. 'They'll all be gone soon, and good riddance. Hungary for the Magyars, I say.' Miklós clenches his fists. His plan has to succeed.

As they approach Kolostór, he feels increasingly unsettled. How much did the Jews in his home town know about the fate of those who had already been deported from the ghettos? Did they know that the Germans were deceiving them with lies about relocation to towns where they'd find work? Oskar Schindler once told him a story that made his hair stand on end. He said that over a million Polish Jews had already disappeared without a trace, and that most of them had ended up in gas chambers that had been specially constructed at Auschwitz, the most satanic machine of mass murder that had ever been invented. He warned Miklós that a similar fate awaited the Jews of Hungary. Miklós distrusted this German womaniser who fraternised with the Nazis, but his account of murder on an industrial scale was something no-one could have invented. He wouldn't have believed it had he not come face to face with Eichmann.

With a sigh he turns his mind to the present. They are almost in Kolostór, and he thinks about his impending meeting with representatives of the local Jewish Council, a prospect he dreads. As the Benz swings into the main street, he reflects on how shrewd and insidious the Germans have been in setting up these councils, ostensibly to liaise between themselves and the Jewish community to ensure that their plans ran smoothly. The Nazis assured the councils that nothing would happen to the Jews in their community as long as they followed orders and, in return, they were promised immunity from the anti-Jewish laws for themselves and their families.

It infuriated him to see how, lulled into a false sense of security, the council members had chosen to put their trust in denial and illusion, and rushed to fulfil every Nazi order, from collecting cash, blankets, valuables and furs, to furnishing lists of Jewish assets and, eventually, Jewish names, convinced that by going along with the Nazi orders they would save their families, their communities, and themselves.

Appalled by their gullibility, Miklós had argued with the council members in Budapest, urging them to stop co-operating with the Nazis. Frustrated by their inability or unwillingness to see through the deception, he shouted, 'You can't believe what they say. By colluding with them, you'll only make it easier for them to destroy our whole community.'

But they had called him arrogant and overbearing, and insisted that by following the Nazis' orders, they were protecting the community from more violence. That hadn't worked in Poland, he reminded them, referring to the fate of Adam Czerniakow, the president of the Jewish Council in Warsaw who had committed suicide the previous year when he realised that the Nazis were using the council to help them dispossess, round up and annihilate the Jews.

But his words fell on deaf ears. What happened in Poland wasn't relevant, they argued. We are loyal Hungarians, our government would never let that happen here. Miklós couldn't suppress his frustration. 'Have you forgotten that Hungary was the first country to pass anti-Jewish race laws, back in 1920? Have you forgotten that even before the Nazis occupied us, tens of thousands of Jewish men died in brutal forced labour camps run by our fellow Hungarians? Have you decided to ignore the fact that our government is enthusiastically enforcing anti-Semitic laws that deprive us of all our civil rights? And that they are colluding in the deportations?'

He sighs again. This is an argument he will never win. He knows that for most people, denying reality is preferable to confronting a disturbing truth. Fraternising, co-operating, colluding. His mood darkens. It seems that one way or another, for noble motives or base ones, or merely from self-interest and the urge to survive, war turns us all into collaborators.

They are passing the town square now, the town hall facing the huddle of small Jewish craft shops on one side and the Catholic church on the other. He wonders what the priest has said to his congregation about the deportation of Jews who have lived among them for centuries, made their shoes, sewn their clothes and ground their corn.

For the hundredth time, his mind turns to the list. To ensure that the responsibility of compiling the list would be shared among the members of the Rescue Committee, they have drawn up their lists as well, but it was his own list of the people of Kolostór that preoccupied him the most. Apart from his parents, an aunt, two uncles and five cousins, the editor who employed him after he'd graduated, and three fellow journalists and their families, he has decided to include a cross-section of Kolostór's Jewish population. Although he was an atheist, he was including representatives of the town's various religious groups, even though he knew they detested each other. The Orthodox rabbis regarded the progressive Neolog group as apostates, as if they weren't real Jews. Just the same, to be impartial, he included rabbis from both congregations.

In order to raise enough money to bribe Becher, who was demanding US$1500 per person, he had selected a number of wealthy Jews who agreed to subsidise the ones who couldn't afford to pay, as well as widows and orphans.

The list included doctors, teachers and lawyers, craftsmen, tradesmen, artisans, and couples with children. There were times when he saw himself as a modern-day Noah, sending his ark out of Hungary in the hope that this tiny part of the community might survive the Nazi inundation.

As he feared, news of his mission has leaked out after all, and as soon as the car pulls up in front of the straggly lilac bushes outside his parents' home, a crowd surges towards him. People are tugging at his coat, pulling his sleeves, demanding, shouting, pleading and begging him to include them, their parents, their cousins and their children.

Some promise to give him all their money or valuables, some threaten, others curse. With all the chaos and the shouting, no-one is listening, so it's a waste of time to try and explain why he can't include any more people on

the train. With great difficulty, he extricates himself and
strides ahead, not looking right or left or meeting anyone's
eyes in order to avoid painful confrontations and fruitless
arguments.

Finally he reaches his parents' front door, and is grateful
when it closes behind him. His mother throws her arms
around him. 'You've lost so much weight, you're not eating
properly,' she laments, and he knows she's thinking that his
wife is neglecting him, that she is too focussed on her music
to cook him decent meals. She attacks him with a barrage of
questions, most of which he cannot answer, some of which
have no answers.

He can tell them that they will be leaving on a train destined for a neutral country, but he can't reveal his negotiations with Eichmann or Gábor's mission in Istanbul. He
can't explain how this audacious plan has evolved, and he
doesn't dare say that he doesn't know when the train will
leave or where it will take them.

Watching his son's face intently, Egon Nagy urges his
wife to stop quizzing him. He makes only one comment. 'I
hope you're strong enough to deal with the anger of the ones
you haven't included.'

Miklós remembers what his father once told him. 'You
said that in times of war, people find out the truth about
themselves. So what did you discover about yourself?'

Egon rests his hand on his son's shoulder. 'In battle, you
can keep your head down or rush forward and be a hero.
But as soon as you put your head up, someone is likely to
blow it off. I found out that I didn't want to lose my head,
so I wasn't a hero.' He pauses and eyes his son speculatively.
Then he adds, 'Heroes are targets.'

Miklós is unsettled by his father's words, but he doesn't have time to dwell on them because everyone assembled in the house is clamouring to talk to him, to hear details about their departure. Of his relatives, the only one who is not overjoyed at the prospect of leaving is Vera, his cousin Peter's wife, who insists that she can't possibly leave her parents, her seven siblings or her grandparents behind.

Miklós warns them what will happen if they stay in Hungary, but she insists she will remain in Kolostór with her family and share their fate, and Peter refuses to leave without his wife and their daughter.

Miklós glances out of the window and sees that the crowd has dispersed. It's safe to venture out again. As he is unlatching the front gate, he notices a young couple and their son standing silently outside the wall. As Peter, Vera and their daughter have decided to stay, he realises that he now has three extra places, and he beckons to them. It's an impulse. The boy's bright eyes and alert expression remind him of himself as a child.

He is about to step into the waiting car when a wild-eyed man rushes out from behind the bushes and collars him. Sobbing, he grabs Miklós's coat, and begs him to save his mother and sister Malka. Cornered, Miklós explains, more brusquely than he intends, that unfortunately this is impossible.

'God will punish you!' the man shouts. 'Just wait. One day you will answer for this!'

Miklós isn't superstitious but this malediction stings. He can't wait to get away from the town, but he still has one meeting ahead of him, and he's not looking forward to it.

The Jewish Council. He feels he has to warn them about the real purpose of the deportations and their ultimate destination, but recalling the attitude of the members of the Budapest council, he wonders if they will take any notice of his warning.

There's an air of gloom in the small office of the Jewish Council. Ferenc Farkas, the council president, whose lanky build and badly trimmed moustache have always reminded Miklós of a brush at the end of a broom handle, mentions an article that has recently come to their attention.

'It's supposed to be an account of some death camp in Poland,' Ferenc says in a tone that makes it clear he does not believe a word of it. 'The writer claims that he escaped from a place called Auschwitz, but what he writes about that place is like something from one of Fritz Lang's horror movies. He must be sick in the head to invent such stories.'

'You should take his report seriously,' Miklós says, and tells them what Oskar Schindler said. His comment prompts a loud and angry argument among the councillors, most of whom scoff at the report as despicable fear-mongering designed to create a panic. When one of the members suggests that they should believe the writer, he is shouted down. 'This is the twentieth century, not the Middle Ages,' someone protests. 'Barbaric things like that can't possibly happen today. And even if they happened in Poland, they couldn't happen here. We are loyal Magyars.'

Defeated by their determination to deny reality, Miklós stops trying to convince them. He feels it's useless to remind them how tenuous that identity really is, that Jews have not been regarded as genuine Magyars for a long time, and that ever since the disastrous Treaty of Trianon at the end of World War I, they have been scapegoats for Hungary's massive loss of territory and wealth. In any case, what good would it do to insist? Where could they escape to? Perhaps they were better off deluding themselves. But despite his decision to drop the subject, he can't resist making one more attempt to warn them.

'Don't believe what the Germans tell you, and don't board the trains. They don't take people to work camps but to concentration camps,' he says.

*

Life is strange, he thinks moodily on his way back to Budapest. Instead of rejoicing in his ability to save over fifteen hundred people who would otherwise be deported and killed, he feels guilty that he can't save more. But his conscience is clear. He has tried to warn them about the situation and he can't do more than that.

CHAPTER TEN

2005

Annika was in such a deep sleep that she didn't hear the telephone the first time it rang. The grey cretonne curtains were drawn, and the hotel room was so dark that when she did hear it, she assumed it was the middle of the night. When it rings a third time, she fumbles for the receiver and drops it. Probably her mother calling at this unearthly hour to complain that she hasn't heard from her. She is about to forestall the complaint with an excuse about jetlag when she hears Jancsi's voice.

'Good morning Annika. I am ringing but you are not answering. I think maybe you are gone out.'

She sits up, rubs her eyes, and glances at the clock beside the bed. Ten o'clock. Has she forgotten an arrangement to meet him?

'Just getting ready,' she mumbles, glad that he can't see her dishevelled state.

'I have something for you, Annika. I wait in coffee shop downstairs.'

He is drinking black coffee and reading the morning paper when she comes in. As she looks at him in his blue jeans and New York baseball cap, she is struck again by his boyish appearance. On the table in front of him lies a faded manila envelope with dog-eared corners.

'Aannikaa!' he exclaims, and she feels a rush of pleasure at the way he pronounces her name. In Australia, it sounded too foreign. Her last boyfriend insisted on calling her Annie, which irritated her. No-one ever lingered over every vowel the way Jancsi does, or made it sound so intimate.

He points to the envelope. 'My father wrote this. Is about train journey.'

Perhaps it's jetlag, but she doesn't understand. 'Train journey?' she repeats.

He laughs, not unkindly. 'Annika, you are still sleeping I think so. Train journey from Hungary that Nagy Miklós arranged.'

Now she is awake. 'He wrote about that? And you've had it all this time?'

He makes a noncommittal gesture. 'Yes but also no. Was there but I did not know was there. Was in big box with father's documents. But yesterday night I look in box and find this.' He pushes the envelope towards her. 'Open, read.'

She takes out a slim sheaf of papers fastened by a paper clip which leaves a rust mark when she removes it. The paper is very thin, and in his haste to record his memories, the writer struck the typewriter keys so forcefully that they made tiny holes on the paper. She scans the first page, replaces the sheets in the envelope, and pushes them towards him.

'This is in Hungarian!'

He slaps his forehead. 'Of course, Hungarian. But I have friend, he will translate. You are here how many days more?'

'Three.' When she booked her trip, that seemed long enough to gain an impression of the city of her ancestors, before travelling on to Prague and Vienna. She hoped to discover something about the mysterious Miklós Nagy whose name had aroused such a violent reaction from her grandmother, but this unexpected connection makes her wonder if somehow fate had conspired for her to meet Jancsi. An electric spark courses through her body and she can hardly sit still.

'How long will your friend need to translate this?'

'One month, maybe two,' he says, and bursts out laughing at her dismayed expression. 'I make joke, Annika. I will ask. He is professional translator. If has time, he will do quickly. But why you leave so soon? You are in hurry to meet someone special in other country?'

When he asked her a personal question the day they met, she had bristled, but this time she says quietly, 'There isn't anyone special in my life anywhere in the world.' She tries to say it nonchalantly but the statement hangs heavily between them.

'So why you don't stay longer? Maybe you meet someone special here.' He is teasing her, looking straight into her eyes and raising his thick eyebrows.

Before she can think of a light-hearted reply, he says, 'This night, you are busy?'

Her heart is thumping. Is he about to ask her out? If she agrees, would he regard it as a date? A prelude to sex? Was she about to become a cliché like her friend Ella, a lonely female in a foreign country who believes her guide's flattery, makes a fool of herself, and then regrets it?

Jancsi was saying something but distracted by her inner conversation, she has to ask him to repeat it. 'You like music? There is concert in Rákoczy Castle tonight,' he says, and explains that he had booked this tour for a group of Americans but as one has fallen ill, he has an extra ticket.

'Will be interesting for you to see inside Hungarian castle, yes?'

'I'd love to go.'

'So come to lobby at six. I cannot go but my colleague Kati will be guide. You will enjoy. I will call her and say you will go with group.'

So he wasn't asking for a date after all, she thinks, relieved and disappointed at the same time.

*

Just before six, when Annika comes down to the lobby, she finds it crowded with Americans who are laughing, shouting and calling out to each other across the hotel foyer. Typical Yanks, brash and noisy, acting as if they owned the place. But despite her initial reaction, she warms to them. They don't seem to mind that an outsider is joining their group, and soon she becomes the centre of attention on account of her accent.

'Oh my, Australia!' one woman gasps, while another chimes in, 'I'm goin' there next year, honey. Can't wait to see your kangaroos and koala bears.'

Rákoczy Castle is a stone manor house with turrets and oriole windows, and welcoming them at the entrance is the owner, the epitome of Austro-Hungarian elegance in a long black velvet skirt and embroidered jacket. Just the kind of outfit her grandmother would stock in her boutique. If Marika knew she was attending a function at a historic villa whose owner was descended from one of the oldest Hungarian families, she would be impressed. It was something she would boast about to her clients.

Annika could almost hear her saying with a smile, *My granddaughter the magazine editor was invited to meet the great-granddaughter of the Hohenzollerns in Budapest.*

Strange how she relates everything to Marika. Her grandmother is the pebble in the shoe of her life, Annika thinks and winces at her clumsy metaphor. If one of the reporters on the magazine had written that, she would have scrawled a thick line through it.

At least on this occasion Marika would approve of her appearance. She is wearing the only smart outfit she has packed, black silk Zampatti palazzo pants which she thinks make her look slimmer, and a Scanlon & Theodore top which clings in the right places, accentuates her cleavage, and hopefully distracts attention from the rest.

She tries to concentrate on the conversation around her but she can't get involved in the ingenuous comments of her companions who seemed to travel around the world expecting to find American food and western facilities everywhere, and complained about locals who didn't speak English. 'I'm sick of paprika chicken, goulash and schnitzel, and all that fancy stuff, all I want is a big juicy T-bone steak,' one of the men is saying loudly. It's the second time she's heard him say it, and she makes an excuse and retreats to the far corner of the room.

The salon where drinks and canapés are being served evokes the atmosphere of an aristocratic hunting lodge, with enormous fireplaces, boars' heads above the fireplace, and huge framed portraits of ancestors in powdered wigs and crinolines hanging on the walls. Smiling young waitresses in white cotton gloves circulate around the room, offering flutes of champagne and tempting finger food. Annika is sipping champagne when some of the Americans gravitate towards her, firing questions about sharks, snakes and spiders in Australia. 'How do y'all cope with those dangerous creatures?' one of the women asks with a shudder. Annika is relieved when a bell summons them to dinner.

Ten round tables, set with crisp white linen cloths and silver cutlery emblazoned with the owner's initials, are arranged in a glittering hall whose walls are covered in gold-framed mirrors, reflecting an infinity of lights from the sconces and chandeliers.

A procession of waiters in white stockings and black vests, carrying plates under large silver cloches, station themselves behind each high-backed chair and, in a synchronised motion, remove the lids. On her right, a woman whispers, 'Oh my Lord, will you look at that?'

But Annika is looking at something else. A group of musicians have entered and are taking their seats on a dais. They are formally attired, the men in dinner jackets, the women in long black dresses. As they tune their instruments, the violinist on the far right turns and looks straight at her. It is Jancsi.

So he's not just a guide, she thinks.

The leader of the ensemble raises his bow, and at his signal they strike up a lively piece that she recognises. It is Mozart's *Eine Kleine Nachtmusik*, a piece she loathed as a child when she stumbled over the notes during reluctant piano lessons, but now she enjoys the familiarity of the music. As she listens, she can't stop staring at Jancsi. It isn't just that he looks so different from the casually dressed guide in jeans and a baseball cap. It's the loving way he cradles the violin against his shoulder, as if it is part of him, and the expression on his face when he plays, as if nothing else exists and nothing else matters. The concert consists of the inevitable Vivaldi *Four Seasons*, a couple of Strauss waltzes, and some favourites from *The Merry Widow* which make her table companions link arms and sway in time to the music. Some of them hum the familiar tunes, smiling appreciatively at each other. The couple on her left, who seem to be keen concertgoers, comment on the mellow sound of the cellist, the bow technique of the violinist, and the violist's euphoric expression, but she is only aware of one member of the ensemble.

The encore is a *czárdás*. It's the sensual one that the musicians played for her in the Europa Café the first day they met. While Jancsi is playing it, he looks at her with such an intense expression that she looks away in embarrassment. Then the concert is over, and the musicians bow and leave the hall while enthusiastic applause reverberates within the damask-covered walls.

As Annika follows the Americans towards the bus, she keeps looking around, hoping to catch sight of Jancsi, but the musicians have gone.

She falls asleep that night with the melodies still dancing in her head. In the morning, she pulls aside the curtains. When she glances in the mirror she is surprised to see that she is smiling. The sun is shining, the sky is an enamelled blue, and she doesn't want to waste a single moment of this perfect day. Without hesitating, she dials Jancsi's number.

'Can I speak to the violinist?' she asks as soon as he picks up.

'You sound happy today, Annika.'

An hour later, when they meet in a café near the hotel, she says, 'You gave me such a surprise last night. I had no idea you were a musician. You played beautifully. It's obvious you were meant to play the violin. How come you work as a guide?'

He shrugs. 'Is not possible to make enough money playing violin in Budapest unless you wear embroidered vest and have big gypsy moustache, so I must have other work.' He gives her a shrewd look. 'So you like violinist Jancsi better than guide Jancsi?'

She decides to ignore the implied accusation of snobbery. 'It's the same at home. Most musicians struggle to make a living.'

She wonders why she was surprised to find out he was a musician. After all, she knows nothing about him. For all she knows, he could be an axe murderer or married with five children like Ella's Cairo guide. Suddenly she has to know.

'Are you married?'

He laughs and she blushes at her own bluntness. 'Not now,' he says. 'My wife met man with money. Not musician, that's for sure! I thought she went to gym to get fit, but she was doing different exercise.'

She wishes she hadn't asked, and decides to change the subject when he takes a photograph from his wallet. 'My children. Tibor is eight and Margit is ten. They live with wife but I see them on Sundays.'

He reaches across the table and takes her hand. He is looking into her eyes and she senses that his expression is a declaration and a question. She doesn't remove her hand or look away.

'Is really necessary to leave tomorrow? There are many wonderful things to do in Budapest, Annika. And very nice people to do them with.'

This time she has no trouble coming to a decision. Prague and Vienna could wait. Budapest was turning out to be far more fascinating than she had expected.

CHAPTER ELEVEN

2005

Annika takes a Mars bar from the minibar in her room, flops into the armchair by the window, and stares at the indigo waters of the Danube below. Peeling away the crackly paper, she closes her eyes with pleasure as she bites into the chocolate, at the same time berating herself for her lack of willpower. Her doorbell rings and she jumps up, expecting to see the housemaid with her cleaning trolley, but it's the fair-haired bellboy holding out a large manila envelope.

'The man who left it, is he still downstairs?' she asks. The youngster shakes his head but continues to stand in the doorway. She doesn't know whether she is supposed to tip him, and if so, how much, so she thanks him effusively instead, hoping that this will suffice, but his expression tells her she is mistaken.

Back in her armchair, she tears open the envelope, pulls out the thin sheaf of papers, and starts reading. The first page is dated 1998 and titled *My Memoir, by István Kovács*.

Before I start, I want to say I am not a writer, and this is the first time I have tried to write about my life, so I am sorry if I am long-winded but I try to write as if I am talking, this is the only way I can do it. The funny thing is, I have never thought I had anything worth writing about. You live your life hour by hour, day by day, always looking forwards, and you don't pause to look back to examine what it all means or if it means anything at all. The clarity only comes when time starts to run out. And from what the doctor told me recently, it looks as if mine is running out.

From what I have observed, our own lives seem shapeless and elusive, a succession of incidents strung together by chance. We are too close to ourselves to understand it all. We only glimpse a little bit at a time, so it's not coherent.

But I think one day Jancsi you will want to know what happened to me when I was a boy, so I will write down whatever I can remember. And perhaps this will help me understand my life better too. I read somewhere that history is really biography, and if that is true, then maybe my story will add a small footnote to the events in Hungary in 1944.

Annika rereads that paragraph, filled with admiration and envy. If only her grandmother respected her need to know more about her, and was willing to share the details of her life. She sighs, and reads on.

But first I'll try to explain why, unlike most survivors, I returned to Hungary in 1945. You know enough about botany to know that when you cut a root, you kill the plant. Well, in spite of everything that happened here before and during the war, I felt I was rooted in Hungarian soil. I had conveniently forgotten that at the end of the nineteenth century, my grandfather, like tens of thousands of other Jews, had changed the family surname to Kovács, to sound less Jewish. Perhaps I was a dreamer, longing for the vanished world of my youth, for flirtations on the promenade and endless summers spent on Lake Balaton. I was a socialist, and deluded myself that life under communism would erase racism and fascism. But as we all know now, we had merely replaced one brutal totalitarian regime with another.

Before I describe what happened to me during the Holocaust, I have to acknowledge the vital part that Nagy Miklós played in my survival and that of my dear parents.

Annika's eyes linger on that sentence. Perhaps now she would find out the truth about the man who seems to arouse such strong emotions whenever his name is mentioned. The speed with which Jancsi's friend translated István Kovács's memoir has surprised her. So does his English. She expected a clumsy translation full of unidiomatic expressions, but to her surprise this flowed smoothly and grammatically. Once an editor always an editor, she mutters to herself as she resumes reading, drawn in by the writer's thought-provoking words and engaging style. He seemed to be talking to her, and she could almost hear his voice.

I remember June that year very clearly. It was so hot that I kept nagging my parents to take me swimming. I'm not sure how much you know about that time, Jancsi, because you never asked me and I never talked about it, so maybe you didn't know that we Jews were not allowed to use trams or go to the swimming pools. We weren't even allowed to keep pets or sit on park benches. I'm sure I don't need to explain why. Because that was the year the Nazis marched into Hungary. Their aim was to deprive us Jews of all our rights, to remove us from normal life, to isolate us from all other Hungarians, turn us into pariahs, dehumanise us and then deport us. Unfortunately our government did not resist their demands but acceded to them quite eagerly.

Now I'll tell you something ironic: being Jewish had never been important to my parents or to me in any way, but thanks to Hitler it became the most significant and defining aspect of our lives. It was something we clung to after the war to prove that he hadn't won.

Annika puts down the pages and turns towards the window but she hardly sees the view. István's memoir has evoked conflicting emotions. Why hadn't Marika clung to Judaism, but instead chosen to discard it? Why hadn't she realised that by erasing her Jewish heritage, she was letting Hitler triumph? Yet István's son Jancsi also lived a secular life, eschewing the traditions and beliefs of his parents and grandparents, just as she herself did. She stares out of the hotel window for a long time, unable to make sense of life's confusing detours.

On the pavement below, pigeons perch on top of a bronze statue depicting an artist in a dust coat and beret, standing at his easel. Looking at it, she recalls that other bronze installation spread out along the embankment a few metres away, the shoes that remind passers-by of the pogrom that took place here in 1944.

István's memoir takes her back to that year, and she reads on.

One day my father told me to pack my things, just the essential ones, because we were going on a journey and would have to carry whatever we took.

I couldn't wait. I slung my rucksack on my back as soon as I was ready, and my parents and I made our way to a railway marshalling yard in Budapest with lots of other people. I kept running ahead because I was too excited to walk slowly — I had always liked trains, and it was exciting to be going anywhere — but when we saw it, we couldn't believe our eyes. It wasn't a normal train at all.

It was made up of the kind of wagons they used to take cattle to the abattoirs. Before we climbed in, I ran along the platform and counted them. There were 35 altogether. The journey was horrible. There were too many of us crammed in there, and everyone was pushing and shoving, complaining or arguing. Young as I was, I realised that shared misfortune does not encourage mutual consideration. Quite the opposite in fact. It was everyone for themselves in those awful trucks. I don't want to go into too many details, but you can't imagine how it stank in there. There was one bucket for water and one for waste, and I was so embarrassed at having to use the bucket in front of other people, that I tried to hold it in until I thought I'd burst.

From what I gathered listening to the adults, we were being taken out of Hungary thanks to a man called Nagy Miklós who included us in his list of people to be rescued. Who he was, where we were heading, and why our names were on this list, I had no idea. Much

later my father told me that he had come face to face with Mr Nagy
just once, in the town where we lived before we moved to Budapest.
Apparently as soon as he looked at me, he just nodded, and said we
could come on his train. People talk about fate and destiny but as
you can see, my fate was decided by a chance encounter, a look and
a nod. I never found out what it was he liked about me and I don't
think my parents did either.

Annika puts down the sheaf of papers again as she tries to
grasp what happened. So Miklós Nagy had a list of people
he was about to rescue on his train. How did that come
about and how had her grandmother come to be on that
list? How was he able to organise a train to take Jews out of
Hungary? In István's case, the selection seemed arbitrary,
but perhaps he was an exception. She picks up the papers
and continues reading.

We travelled all night, and in the morning we thought we must
have come a long way but imagine our disappointment when we
realised we were still in Budapest! You see, there were air raids that
night. The Allies were bombing the city and apparently the driver
just shunted the train back and forth between stations hoping to
avoid the bombs. Of course we wanted the Allies to win the war, but
we didn't want them to kill us in the process, and there was no way
of letting them know that we were on their side. We just hoped their
bombs would miss us, and they did. Chance again.

　　When we were close to the Austrian border, the train stopped for
three whole days. It was so hot and uncomfortable inside the train
that we all camped out in the open. The Hungarian militia were
guarding us. I thought they were guarding us from the Germans

but my father said they were protecting us from the locals who hated Jews and would probably attack us if we didn't have guards. I found out later that they were ordered to guard us because we were under the special protection of Nagy Miklós.

Annika stopped reading, frustrated that the writer didn't explain things in more detail. How was it that this man, a Jew, was able to secure special protection for his group from the Hungarians and the Germans at a time when Jews were being rounded up in ghettos and deported? She needed to be patient. Perhaps he would explain it later.

All this time, no-one knew where we were going, though people kept talking about Palestine because they had permits to go there. When someone overheard that we were approaching a place called Aus-pitz, panic broke out. People thought they said Auschwitz, and they became hysterical. They said Mr Nagy had tricked us and we were being deported after all. Someone made up a black joke that did the rounds — Auspitz = Auschwitz, Cion (Zion) = Cian(cyanide.) Naturally I didn't get it at the time, but I realise now that this joke is very significant, and I will tell you why. Years later, Nagy's enemies accused him of deliberately withholding information that might have saved lots of people if only he had warned them about Auschwitz. Well from this joke, and the panic caused by the name Auspitz, it was obvious that people did know about Auschwitz, so they didn't need Nagy to spell it out. And besides, those people who blamed him later for withholding information, displayed their ignorance as well as their malice. Because even if he had warned them, what would they have done? There was nowhere they could go without being caught. You see that was Mr Nagy's triumph, and that's what his enemies ignore — he succeeded in snatching our group from the jaws of hell, whereas for the rest of the Jews in Hungary, there was no escape.

From what I remember, it took about a week to reach Linz in Austria. We were ordered off the train and taken to be disinfected and deloused. That was traumatic for all of us. We had to take off all our clothes in public which was terribly embarrassing. Strangers with rough hands and harsh voices shaved us all over and sprayed us with Lysol which stung like hell. But from what I overheard my mother telling my father, it was even more humiliating for the women. They felt violated because they were stripped, brutally shaved, and prodded all over while SS officers made lewd comments about them. I felt sorry for the girls. They were so ashamed that they tried to hide, and some of them didn't utter a word for days.

After that we were pushed back into the cattle trucks. A few days later — I remember the date, it was 9 July — the train came to a stop. The platform said Bergen-Hohne, which didn't mean anything to us. We didn't know then that we had arrived at the place which later became synonymous with the horrors of the Holocaust: Bergen-Belsen. We had to walk about seven kilometres with our belongings to reach the camp, escorted by guards with whips. In normal circumstances, seven kilometres isn't very far, but we were exhausted and terrified, not knowing what was going to happen. They were yelling and their horrible dogs were barking and straining at the leash just waiting to sink their fangs into us.

As you know, I've always liked to measure, count, and figure out distances, I suppose that's my way of feeling in control of a situation. Even now I could draw you an exact map of the camp and its baths and disinfection station, the SS quarters, the prison, kitchens, and the 80 wooden barracks. The camp was surrounded by two parallel barbed-wire fences, with a watchtower looming in between, and past the perimeter there was a pine forest with trees that seemed to touch the sky. I can still remember the clean, fresh smell of those trees.

But enough statistics. You can look them up in a history book. What you won't find there is my story which is really your story too. I didn't know, and neither did most of the adults, that at the time Bergen-Belsen was basically a transit camp where many prisoners were kept as hostages, to be exchanged for German prisoners or, in our case, ransomed for money. Anyway I'm not going to go into details about the overcrowding, the hunger, the cruel guards, and the hours we had to stand in the rain or freezing cold at the rollcalls called zahlappells that went on for hours and made our legs ache so much we could hardly stand. What we didn't realise at the time was that we were much better treated than the prisoners in the other compounds because the Germans didn't starve and beat us. They regarded us as a potentially valuable resource.

What I do want to say is that while we were in the camp, I discovered something about human nature that I never forgot. We all have a glorified image of ourselves that enables us to deceive ourselves most of the time, but our true selves only emerge in situations like this. Young as I was, I noticed that most people were totally engrossed in their own problems. Most of them manipulated, manoeuvred, pushed, and didn't care about anyone else, but there were a few who tried to comfort and help others, and even shared their meagre rations. I must confess I did a lot of whining myself, so I suppose that said something about me. I was hungry, cold and bored, although my parents did their best to cheer me up and often gave me some of their food.

One awful memory from that time just came back to me — I slept on the top bunk, and one night I spilled the jar in which I used to urinate. It drenched the man in the bunk below me. He was so furious, he yelled at me and wanted to wring my neck. My father told him off, but looking back on it, I can't say I blame him.

To distract myself from the hunger and boredom, I made a list of all the people in our group but as time went on, I was too hungry and miserable to bother with lists. Our rations gradually decreased and the bread they gave us tasted like mud mixed with sawdust. I found out how debilitating hunger is. It made everyone lethargic, and took away our interest in everything except food.

Most of the adults talked about the meals they'd eaten and the food they had wasted, which now they wished they had. The women exchanged recipes for hours which I thought was stupid, but just talking about food made them feel better. Sometimes people came to blows waiting in line for food, and I'll never forget how horrified I was when I saw one of the adults with a bloodied nose as a result of one such scuffle. I can tell you this much: hunger is a great equaliser.

For the adults, the uncertainty was demoralising. Weeks passed, and we had no idea why we were being detained in Bergen-Belsen, how long we were going to languish in there, or if we would ever get out and reach some neutral country where we were supposed to be going en route for Palestine.

Whenever we passed the other compounds and saw the gaunt, yellow-skinned hollow-eyed inmates who looked like walking corpses, we wondered if we'd end up looking like them. We didn't know that behind the scenes, Nagy Miklós was desperately trying to raise funds and negotiate our release. What I did know was that whenever people cursed him, and accused him of dishonesty, trickery and fraud, one of the women in my barracks always spoke out in his defence.

Whenever she said anything about him, I noticed people exchanging looks, and some of the women whispered behind their hands. She was very pretty, with thick hair and eyes like black velvet. She often told us children stories, and played games with us, even though she wasn't very well herself. I knew that because sometimes I saw her rushing out of the barracks with her hand over her mouth, and a few moments later I heard her vomiting. I liked her, and I couldn't figure out why the other women were always talking about her behind her back.

Once when I asked my mother about it, she said I was too young to understand these matters, which made me even more determined to find out more. Whenever I noticed the women glancing in her direction and gossiping, I would sidle over, but the words I over-heard didn't make much sense to me. I couldn't understand why they referred to her as a mistress, but when I asked my mother if it meant she was a teacher, she gave me a sharp look and told me to play with the other boys instead of eavesdropping on things that didn't concern me. I didn't find out until much later who she was.

Annika turns the page eagerly, but to her dismay István's story ends there. No wonder Jancsi's friend translated it so fast. Impatient to know more, she calls him.

'I've just finished reading the part of your father's memoir that was in the envelope, but where's the rest of it?' She blurts it out, forgetting that she meant to begin by thanking him for having the memoir translated.

'There isn't more. My father had heart attack and died soon after he wrote that.'

'So that's it?'

'That's it. Now I wish I had asked him about his life when he was still alive.'

'But you're lucky at least he wrote that much. Most people never write their memoirs, or even talk about their wartime experiences.'

Like her grandmother, who has slammed the door on her past. Annika had hoped that István's story would provide the key to that secret door, but the trail has run cold.

CHAPTER TWELVE

2005

The vapour rising from the Danube gives the river an opalescent sheen, swathing the Pest embankment in muted tones and softening the facades of Parliament House and the Hero Monument. It is as if Budapest's assertive voice has lowered to a seductive whisper. At least that's how it seems to Annika as she walks along the embankment, and she slackens her pace to enjoy the city's misty palette.

She had woken up with the thought of returning to the Holocaust Memorial Center, even though her first visit had been so unsatisfactory. The guide Imre had answered her questions with riddles, but they intrigued her. Perhaps he was about to go home, and hadn't wanted to prolong his day answering awkward questions. Or maybe his comments simply concealed ignorance, but something in the way his eyes flickered away from her, the way he hesitated before answering, made her suspect that he knew more than he was letting on. And then there was the frustrating cultural aspect of communication. Americans told you too much, the English prevaricated, the Japanese never admitted ignorance, and, from what she had already observed in this city, people in Budapest rarely gave straight answers.

The previous day when she had complained to Jancsi about Imre's response, he'd shrugged. 'Maybe is different in Australia, but here people are closed tight, like this,' he said, clenching his fists for emphasis.

'In past hundred years we have war with Romania, two world wars, and Holocaust. We lose territory to Romania, we are invaded, occupied and oppressed, first Nazis then Communists, and when we rebel, they crush us. Always we are defeated, always on wrong side of history, always afraid of informers, always in danger. So we learn important lesson. Is safer to keep thoughts to ourselves. If you don't speak, you don't suffer.'

Confronted by his impassioned recitation of Hungary's long and blood-filled history, she was embarrassed once again by her ignorance. 'But Hungary is free now, so there's no risk in speaking out,' she argued.

He didn't say she sounded naive, but his expression said it. 'It becomes habit not to trust. You suck in suspicion with mother's milk. You are lucky you don't understand this, Annika.'

Thinking about their conversation as she walks towards the Holocaust museum, she knows she will never understand this way of life or his way of thinking. The chasm of history is too deep for her to cross.

As soon as she enters the museum's foyer, she recognises the chilling soundtrack of marching boots coming from the exhibit on other side of the wall, and Jancsi's words come back to her. Perhaps he was right, and Imre's evasive reply was the result of wariness learnt from past disasters, but just the same she hopes that when he realises that she is genuinely interested and has no ulterior motives, he will be more forthcoming.

The foyer is empty except for a cleaner in a wraparound lozenge-patterned apron and headscarf twisted around her head, swishing a grey mop that forms arabesques of soapy water on the tiled floor. No sign of Imre. Behind the ticket counter a stout woman with long scarlet nails bustles around importantly, opening a register, checking the credit-card machine, and stacking a pile of brochures on the counter with a tapping sound.

'Do you know if Mr Imre is coming today?' Annika asks.

The woman looks up. 'Mr Imre?' she repeats, then laughs, showing a gap between her front teeth. She checks her watch. 'Orban Imre will come in twenty minutes,' she says, and points to the grey leather settee near the door. 'Sit, please.'

Annika is confused. Is Imre the man's first or last name? Then she remembers that in Hungary surnames are placed before given names. Another cultural difference. The enforced wait gives her time to think about her dilemma. She has already stayed in Budapest longer than she intended, and she wonders when she should leave. This is a beautiful city, but she knows that the attraction isn't the city but Jancsi. It is a long time since her last relationship. That had been so coruscating she hadn't wanted to risk embarking on a new one. In her experience, the flames of love invariably ended in a heap of ashes.

She knows she is fighting the attraction she feels for Jancsi. There's no future in this relationship, and I'm too old for a casual fling, she thinks. But her sensual side argues, So what? Nothing comes with a lifetime guarantee. Then she remembers Ella and the risk of having an affair in another country when you are alone and there is no-one to give you a reality check and stop you from making a fool of yourself.

She always comes back to Ella and her Cairo guide. But perhaps it is time to grasp life with both hands and take a gamble? The museum door swings open, and she swivels around expecting to see the guide, but it's a group of lively American women, some of whom she recognises from the concert at Rákoczy Castle. One of them rushes towards her, and enfolds her in a suffocating hug. 'Why, it's the Australian gal! Fancy seeing you here! How long you stayin' in Budapest, honey?' Over the woman's shoulder, Annika notices the buxom ticket seller watching them with unconcealed amusement. It's a relief when the rest of the group calls the woman to join their tour and they all disappear behind the door leading to the exhibition.

With all the commotion in the foyer, she doesn't hear the door swing open again, and almost misses Imre as he walks soundlessly across the foyer in scuffed brown suede shoes. Perhaps he recognised her and tried to get past before she saw him. When she jumps up and moves towards him, he gives a reluctant nod, but continues walking.

She falls in step beside him.

'I was hoping you'd have time to talk to me this morning. When I was here a couple of days ago, it was closing time and you were going home.'

He turns and studies her with his unhappy gaze. The pouches under his eyes seem more swollen than before, and the hair that hangs over his white collar looks greyer. From his deep sigh she realises that he had hoped she wouldn't return with her tiresome questions.

'I have fifteen minutes, then work,' he says. He opens the door to the guides' room at the far right of the foyer, and stands aside to usher her in. The room is neatly fitted out with furniture of minimalist Swedish design. There's an oak hat-stand, three wooden chairs arranged around a square table, and a settee upholstered in striped grey and white fabric.

'So, Australian lady, you came back,' he says, and drops into one of the chairs. 'Nagy Miklós is very important to you. Why?'

Put on the spot, she finds it difficult to come to the point. Should she begin with her grandmother, or her Hungarian heritage, or just admit to a crazy impulse? Then she remembers something her first editor had told her: *If you can't sum up your story in one sentence, you haven't got a story.* It was a sound principle, one she had often repeated to young reporters when she became an editor herself.

As Imre watches her with his heavy-lidded eyes, waiting for her to answer, she knows that the outcome of this encounter depends on her reply.

'I believe my grandmother was on the train that Miklós Nagy organised in 1944, and I want to find out more about him,' she begins. 'I've heard so many contradictory and tantalising things about this man that I'm fascinated, and I want to find out the truth.'

'The truth.' He considers the words as if they were some exotic delicacy to be turned over on the tongue and tasted, not swallowed whole. 'We all want truth, yes? But can you cut water with a knife?'

There he was again, with his mysterious pronouncements. This really was a waste of time. Picking up her handbag with an abrupt motion, she blurts out, 'You talk in riddles, but you never answer my questions.'

He doesn't seem to take offence at her comment. 'Not all questions have easy answers. This is long and complicated story. Who can know truth?' He raises his bushy eyebrows and spreads his hands in an eloquent gesture of doubt. 'Nagy Miklós is a puzzle in a puzzle inside another puzzle. There are many possible solutions but always pieces missing.'

Tell me something I don't know, she thinks. She is about to thank him for his time, hoping she will manage to sound polite, when she glances at him, and something in his demeanour makes her hesitate. As a reporter, she had often found that the most telling quote was the throwaway line uttered at the very end of the interview, when she was packing away her tape recorder and the person she was interviewing was off guard.

The lines on Imre's cheeks have deepened, and there is a haunted look in his eyes. She sits in silence and waits. Finally he says one word. 'Israel.' He says it in such a low voice that she sits forward to make sure she doesn't miss a single word, and he lapses into silence again.

'What's in Israel?'

He pauses and she holds her breath as if waiting for the pronouncement of the Delphic oracle, the one that the tragic characters of Sophocles and Aeschylus might have consulted.

He starts to cough, a tormenting rasp that makes him double up. His eyes bulge and tears run down his cheeks as his chest heaves with the effort of taking in air. Alarmed, she looks around for water and a glass, and spills half of it as she runs to give it to him. By the time he grasps the glass, the paroxysm is over. She is still waiting.

'If you want to know about Nagy Miklós, go to Israel,' he whispers, and adds, 'But truth? More than one. You will see.'

She sits very still on the edge of her chair, her eyes fixed on his face, and hopes he will say something else. But without another word, he rises and goes out of the room, closing the door quietly behind him.

CHAPTER THIRTEEN

2005

With Imre Orban's advice resounding in her head, Annika hurries from the museum. 'Israel,' she mutters to herself. 'Whatever next.' And yet she can't get the guide's words out of her mind, or the quiet conviction with which he uttered them. She recalls that back in Sydney, she read something on the internet about Miklós Nagy going to Israel. As soon as she finds a quiet doorway, she dials Jancsi's number. As she leans against the wall, her heart is racing. 'I've just had a conversation with the bloody Delphic oracle,' she says when he answers, but before she can explain what she means, he cuts in, and from his tone she realises he is probably escorting a tour.

'Can't talk now,' he whispers. 'Meet me outside Széchenyi Baths in one hour.' She is about to ask directions, but to her chagrin, he has already rung off.

She crosses the street to a kiosk. 'Széchenyi?' she asks the man, hoping she got the pronunciation right. He nods and starts giving voluble instructions in Hungarian, but she shakes her head and points to a copy of the *International Herald Tribune* tucked in below the Hungarian newspapers. 'Ah, English,' he says. From a shelf behind him he pulls out a map of Budapest and unfolds it, jabbing his index finger at a building in the middle of a large green area behind Hero Square. 'Széchenyi Baths, very nice. You like,' he says, and he mimics swimming strokes. 'City Park here,' he adds, pointing to the right.

As she strolls around the park, admiring its bright flower-beds, neat lawns, the hothouses with exotic plants, and the avenues of oaks, chestnuts and birches, she checks her watch every few minutes. Sitting on a wooden bench facing the rose garden, she breathes in their perfume and thinks about her impulse to share her news with Jancsi, her assumption that he would be as intrigued as she was, and her disappointment that he was too busy to talk to her.

A pretty young woman with a fresh, smiling face and long hair tied back in a ponytail sits on the bench beside her while her plump toddler chases a ball on the lawn. From time to time the ball lands at Annika's feet and she rolls it towards the delighted child, who rolls it back. Looking at the little girl's dress, Annika becomes nostalgic. It resembles the ones that Marika used to make for her when she was a child, all pintucks and frills. Marika continued making her dresses that were the envy of all her friends in primary school, but as she got older, she turned her back on dressy clothes in favour of casual pants and comfortable tops like the ones her friends wore.

Along the sun-dappled paths of the park, mothers wheel prams, cooing to their babies. As Annika watches them, she reflects on the choices that have shaped the course of her life, choices which have precluded having children. The facile self-help articles she used to publish in her magazine fed the insatiable hunger of readers in search of the key to happy, successful lives, not realising that they were churned out by writers who were no happier or more successful than they were, just more articulate.

The advice was often contradictory. For while some urged women not to feel pressured to have children, others pontificated that the things we regretted the most in life were the things we had failed to do. No-one ever seemed to pick up the contradiction of these two ideas. Neither had she, until now. But when she stopped to think about it, she realised that the things she regretted the most were the choices she had actually made in almost every area of her life: the Communications course she had studied at university that had stifled her creativity, the editorial job that had sapped her enthusiasm, and the lovers who had let her down.

But maybe she had let them down, too. Many years ago, when she had started work on a Sydney newspaper, she had dated one of the editors. Elliot wasn't like the other journos. He didn't grope the cadets, denigrate women, or come back staggering, swearing and leering at the girls after liquid lunches at the pub. He was old-fashioned with manners to match. He opened car doors for her, held her elbow when they were crossing the road, and bought her flowers, but his courtesy made her feel uncomfortable in a way she couldn't explain. He was the sort of guy that mothers and grandmothers approved of, she had told Cassie.

Looking back, she realises that he was the only guy who had genuinely cared about her, and she wonders why she had broken up with him. No-one had ever treated her with so much kindness and consideration, before or since. She'd said the chemistry wasn't right, but Cassie, brutally frank as always, said he was just too nice and too available. 'You're only attracted to the ones you can't have, so you can avoid making a commitment,' she said. But perhaps deep down she had felt she didn't deserve such considerate treatment. There was another problem with that relationship, she realises now: Marika, who always found something to criticise about her boyfriends, had approved of Elliott.

Then it strikes her that the most positive decision she had made in the past few years was to resign from her job. 'You've jumped off without a parachute,' Cassie said with admiration mixed with awe. It was true. Her mother and grandmother could only see that she had thrown away a high-status job with a good salary without having anything to replace it, but sitting here in City Park in Budapest, she realises that what she had done took strength of character. She had placed principles above prestige and pay packet.

She waves goodbye to the toddler, and, with a light step, follows a path crowded with people heading for the baths. The grandiose building with its colonnades, arcades and cupolas resembles an opulent palace rather than public baths, and she wonders whether she has come to the right place, then she sees Jancsi standing in front of the entrance, surrounded by a group of tourists, mostly women. He looks up, sees her, and makes a gesture of helplessness. She stands a short distance away and hears them firing questions at him, reluctant to let him go. Finally, too impatient to stand back and wait any longer, she comes over to greet him. The tourists look from her to him, thank him, and drift away.

'What happened? Did third world war start? Something must be very important, you are in so big hurry to tell me.' He is teasing her, and she laughs, pointing at the building in front of them. 'What is this place?'

'You must come inside, is marvel,' he says. They pass an enormous outdoor pool surrounded by Roman-style columns, where old men with bathing caps on their heads and huge round bellies protruding above their tiny swimsuits are sitting in the water, giving the pieces on the chess boards their thoughtful attention.

Swathed in the steam that rises from the baths, they resemble cartoon figures in a misty landscape. Inside, a series of smaller indoor pools are exquisitely decorated with mythical statues, turquoise mosaics and ornamental tiles.

'This looks like a scene from ancient Rome, or some Ottoman seraglio,' she says, amazed by the exuberant decor.

Jancsi nods. 'You are right. Romans built first spa baths here, then Turks, this is why you say Ottoman. Budapest is spa city, and Széchenyi is best spa. Has hottest thermal baths. You can have sauna, massage, medicine treatment. Hot springs cure many things,' he says, looking into her eyes. 'Maybe also cure women who don't know where they want to go.'

'Actually, I do know,' she retorts. 'I'm going to Israel.'

He stares at her. 'Israel? Annika, you are joking. Why?'

The words that just shot out of her mouth surprise her too, but as soon as she said it, she knows this is exactly what she wants to do. Instead of visiting Prague and Vienna, she will fly to Tel Aviv. They sit down near the trellised wall in the rose garden, and she tells him about her encounter with Imre.

'He told you what is in Israel?

She shakes her head. 'That's the frustrating part, he didn't. But he was adamant that that's where I'd find out what I wanted to know.'

'So you will go on a — what do you call it, a crazy duck race — just because old guy said that? Annika, that is crazy.'

'I suppose it could be a wild goose chase, but I believe him. I remember reading something on the internet about Miklós Nagy going to Israel after the war. I can't explain it, but there's something about him that won't let me rest until I find out the whole story. Besides, I've never been to Israel. It should be interesting.'

'I think you want to escape from Budapest,' he says, and this time she knows he isn't teasing. 'Nothing interesting here.'

'That's ridiculous,' she says, but before she can say any more, he spins her around and holds her so close that she can feel the hard contours of his body pressing against hers. Surprised, she stands very still at first, but wrapped in his strong embrace, she feels her bones softening.

'Annika, we go to my apartment, yes?' He is looking into her eyes, and his voice is husky with desire.

She pulls away and shakes her head.

'I think you want, but you don't think you want,' he says. 'Is true, no?'

'Jancsi, I'll be gone in a day or two, and we'll never see each other again, so what's the point?'

'Why everything must have point? Why you can't love and enjoy today without point? Yesterday is gone, tomorrow is not here. We only have today.'

He is pulling her closer and kissing her neck, and she breathes in the citrus scent of his aftershave as he murmurs, 'Annika, I want you.'

She can't remember the last time she had aroused such desire, the last time her blood was jumping like this. It is tempting to throw common sense to the winds, to surrender to this delicious moment, but she isn't in love with him, and a warning voice inside her head holds her back from giving in to an impulse that would end in her regret, and his pain.

'I think I'd better go back to the hotel,' she says.

He takes her arm. 'Don't go yet, Annika. You like music. Come, I will play for you.'

Half an hour later they reach Király Street behind the Dohány Synagogue. He takes her hand as they enter an old building with a crumbling balcony, and climb the wooden staircase to his apartment on the third floor. It's an imposing building that she supposes dates from Hapsburg times, but the original spacious apartments with their high ceilings and large windows have been divided into smaller ones like his bachelor flat, a bedsitter with a kitchenette, white walls and white tiles. The only splash of colour is the woven cover over the divan with geometric patterns in royal blue and white, and the only decoration is a framed photograph of two laughing children, one of whom has his smile.

His violin case rests on the small wooden table beside a pile of books, newspapers and musical scores. While she sits on the divan, he looks through the scores and places one on the stand. Then he takes the violin from its case and tunes it. A few moments later, he begins to play. The melody that fills the room is almost unbearably exquisite, and as she listens, she is enchanted by its honeyed sweetness. Transported to an almost unearthly level of existence, she sits in a dreamlike trance when the music ends, and doesn't move, not to disturb the magic of that moment.

Then she says, 'That's the most beautiful music I've ever heard. What was it?'

'"Romance" by Beethoven. I play this for you, Annika, because Beethoven says how I feel inside. Better than words.'

She nods, too moved to speak.

'But you go from Budapest soon, yes? You are hit and run woman.' She knows he is attempting to make light of a painful situation but the bruised look around his eyes betrays his emotion.

He puts his arm around her shoulders and they sit in silence until she turns to look at him. 'I'll never forget you, Jancsi. I'll always remember this moment,' she says softly.

That evening, back in her hotel room, she replays every note, every word of that interlude. She relives the beauty of the music that says so much more than words ever could, and remembers the tenderness of his gaze. She looks at herself in the mirror for a long time, without flinching or turning away as she usually does, but with a new recognition. She feels reborn inside her skin and smiles at her reflection. Jancsi would never know the magnitude of the gift he has given her.

CHAPTER FOURTEEN

October 1944

Miklós Nagy is walking towards the Gellert Hotel. He glances behind him, and often ducks into side streets to avoid the Arrow Cross gangs who roam the streets at night, searching for Jews whom they bash, torture and kill. Now that men of military age have been conscripted, any able-bodied man on the streets of Budapest is suspect, and he knows that if stopped and searched, he wouldn't have time to explain that he was on his way to meet a leading Nazi. The fascist thugs would kill before asking any questions.

The thick wad of notes in his inside pocket makes him more cautious than ever. So much hinges on this meeting with Kurt Becher that he needs to consider the best way to broach the subject. As he walks, he weighs up options, possibilities and probabilities. Everything depends on the right approach. Except that in this case, it isn't only his life, it's the lives of all those still being detained in Bergen-Belsen that hang in the balance. And among them are his lover and his wife.

*

Initially, Ilonka resisted his entreaties to join the group on the train. 'If I leave Budapest and Eichmann finds out I've gone, you'll be in danger,' she said. There was another reason. She and Miklós had agreed to divorce their spouses as soon as they reached Palestine so that they could get married, but knowing Judit would be on the train, she said she would feel uncomfortable travelling with his wife, especially as people were already gossiping about their affair.

'There will be more than fifteen hundred people on that train, so you probably won't even see each other,' he reminded her. 'And you don't need to worry about me. Eichmann won't have me killed as long as we can keep stalling and let him think that the Allies are considering his proposal. I've told him that Gábor is making progress. But as we know, Eichmann can change his mind at any minute, especially when he finds out that the negotiations in Istanbul have stalled, so you have to take this opportunity and get out now. There may not be another chance.' He became so overwrought as he spoke that all the muscles in his neck stood out, and he grasped her shoulders in a vice-like grip.

Despite her misgivings, in the end she agreed. 'But I do worry about what will happen to you, and how it's all going to work out. Sometimes I feel my head is going to split open with all the things I worry about. I wish I knew what was happening to Gábor in Istanbul,' she said.

What she didn't know, and Miklós didn't tell her, was that Gábor was no longer in Istanbul. He was in Cairo, being interrogated by the British. According to the latest coded messages Miklós had received from Klein, Gábor had left Istanbul for Syria to meet the representative of the Jewish Agency, but even before he stepped off the train in Aleppo, he was arrested by the British, taken to Cairo, detained and interrogated.

In his cable, Klein reported that the British had made it clear to Gábor that although Churchill sympathised with the plight of the Jews in Hungary, he forbade his ministers from negotiating with the Nazis in any way, no matter what was at stake. Klein reminded Miklós that the British, who had the mandate in Palestine, had made their own deal with the Arabs, and it involved a commitment to prevent Jewish immigration. He mentioned that Gábor's overheated response was received with distaste by the British, who valued cool understatement more than red-hot emotion, and added that his outburst would only reinforce their belief that Jews were an unstable, overemotional lot. In any case, it seemed to Klein from what he'd overheard in the corridors of power that the British suspected the whole plan was some kind of devious Nazi ploy, perhaps to split the Allies.

Klein's presence at these supposedly clandestine meetings puzzled Miklós, but he didn't spend much time worrying over what he considered a side issue. The depressing news about Gábor made him even more determined to get Ilonka out of Budapest before Eichmann found out that at least one major western power had refused to go along with his scheme. As Eichmann regarded her as his hostage and wouldn't allow her to leave Budapest, Miklós arranged false papers for her. She would be travelling as the sister of one of the Neolog rabbis on the train. And if Eichmann demanded to see her, he would say that she was ill.

After raising the money that Eichmann had demanded for the journey, Becher demanded even more, and to cover the shortfall, some Jews from the affluent Budapest district of Lipotvaros had agreed to subsidise the passage of those who couldn't afford to pay the exorbitant cost of staying alive.

When Miklós and Ilonka made love on their last night together in Budapest, the intensity of their passion had brought tears to his eyes. He had a presentiment that he would never experience such rapture again, and it crossed his mind that if he died in her arms right now, he would have the best death possible.

They wept when they parted, she to set out on an uncertain journey, he to an unknown fate in what had become the murder capital of Europe.

'No matter what happens, we mustn't lose hope,' she said. 'This must end soon and then we'll never have to part again. I can't wait till we can be together for the rest of our lives.' He nodded, and cradled her head on his lap, relieved that she couldn't see the despair in his eyes.

*

Miklós is the first to arrive at the Gellert Hotel. He hands his overcoat and hat to the platinum-haired hat-check girl, who is a dead ringer for Jean Harlow, the Hollywood star, and looks around.

Beneath the crystal chandeliers, waiters in tails and starched shirtfronts scurry around holding aloft platters of chicken Kiev and skewers of grilled pork and *csabai* sausage.

The restaurant resounds with light-hearted conversation, laughter, the clinking of glasses and the lively sound of a three-piece band playing gypsy melodies. It's as if nothing has changed, as if the occupation had never happened, and he has the surreal feeling that he has stepped through an invisible mirror into a parallel existence in a city where there is no war, no terror, and no sudden death.

His reverie is interrupted when the maître d' comes towards him with a supercilious expression which changes to deference as soon as he asks for Obersturmbannführer Becher's table. He is ushered to a banquette upholstered in burgundy velvet, situated a discreet distance from the central section of the ornate dining room. Miklós supposes this is the table Becher usually reserves for trysts with his Hungarian mistress, a nightclub singer whose white throat and slender arms always glitter with diamonds. He has no illusions as to how the Nazi lieutenant colonel has come by this jewellery, and the irony of the situation isn't lost on him. Desperation created unlikely bedfellows, and he can't ignore the fact that he is now hoping to benefit from Becher's insatiable greed.

As he waits, he reflects on the extraordinary turn of events that has put this affable Nazi unexpectedly in charge of the negotiations about the train. Over the past few weeks, Eichmann has become increasingly volatile and erratic, breaking whatever promises he had previously made and threatening with a reptilian smile to send Miklós to Auschwitz along with the people on the train.

Determined not to appear cowed, Miklós unconsciously began to mirror Eichmann's behaviour. He would pace around the room, chain-smoke, and retort to the threats in a mocking manner. 'Yes, Obersturmbannführer, why don't you go ahead and kill me and the Jews you haven't managed to send off to Auschwitz yet? But if you do that, what will you have to offer the Western Allies in return for your trucks?'

At times during these macabre encounters, he felt as if Eichmann was treating him as an equal, but as soon as he left his headquarters, he realised the absurdity of this notion. He wondered whether his double life was causing him to become detached from reality.

Eichmann was a fanatic who made no secret of his determination to fulfil his mission in Hungary, and he couldn't be trusted to keep any promises. Miklós increasingly despaired of his ability to arrange for the train to leave Bergen-Belsen, and he suspected that even in the unlikely event that the Allies agreed to his preposterous scheme, Eichmann wouldn't keep his word.

'*Und wo ist die schöne Frau Weisz?*' Eichmann asked at their last meeting. Holding the Nazi's cold gaze without blinking, Miklós explained that Ilonka had pneumonia, could hardly breathe, and was too ill to get out of bed. Eichmann's expression indicated scepticism, but he didn't pursue the subject.

Just as he'd been about to leave, Eichmann put him off balance again. In scathing language he usually reserved for Miklós in particular and for the Jews in general, he began attacking Becher who, he said, was an upstart who had been promoted to equal rank with himself despite his inferior talent and lack of experience.

'Remember what I said, Nagy,' he said, thumping his fist on the walnut desk. 'The trucks deal is mine. If you want that train to leave Bergen-Belsen, you'd better keep Becher's nose out of my business.'

This was an unexpected turn of events, and Miklós was relieved to hear that somehow, behind Eichmann's back, Becher was up to his ears in this affair. How he had inveigled himself into these final stages was a mystery, but Miklós felt confident that dealing with the corrupt Becher would be far more straightforward than with the fanatical Eichmann.

With Eichmann in charge, the outcome was always in doubt. He was drinking more heavily, his outbursts becoming more volcanic, his language more vituperative. During their last encounter he leapt to his feet several times and pointed his pistol at Miklós.

He ignored the belated order of the Hungarian leader Admiral Horthy to stop the deportations, and every day so many Jews were being sent to Auschwitz its gas chambers were being stretched beyond their capacity for mass extermination.

So it was an enormous relief when Eichmann was unexpectedly recalled and Becher took over the whole operation. He was an opportunist, not an idealist, and Miklós knew that it was preferable to deal with a man who was motivated by greed rather than ideology. But who had put him in charge, and why, remained a mystery.

*

The mystery is solved over pâté de foie gras and roast duck at the Gellert Hotel. After the sommelier deftly opens a bottle of vintage Veuve Cliquot and fills their champagne flutes, Kurt Becher leans forward and says in a confidential tone, as though speaking to a trusted colleague, 'Did you know that

Eichmann was dead against releasing any Jews? If it was up to him, he would make sure every single Jew in Hungary — and that includes you, Herr Nagy, and that charming lady of yours — ended up on a train to Auschwitz. You have no idea how frustrated he was that his mission was being undermined.'

Before Miklós can ask the obvious question, Becher smiles, and Miklós is struck by his innocent, boyish expression as he says, 'It was my boss, Reichsführer Himmler, who suggested this deal from the start.'

So the rumours he had heard were true: Becher really was Himmler's man! For the next twenty minutes, Miklós listens in amazement as Becher extols the virtues of Himmler, whom he describes as the wisest, kindest and most intelligent man he has ever met. Miklós surmises that this admiration and affection must be mutual, as it was Himmler who had promoted him — ahead of time and talent, if Eichmann's jaundiced view was correct.

But as he listens to Becher's paean of praise for his boss, one question bothers him. Why did Himmler initiate this scheme? Why did he send a Jewish representative to negotiate with western powers on behalf of the Nazis for a deal that promised to release the Jews that Eichmann had been sent to annihilate?

It doesn't make sense. Himmler is Hitler's deputy, a ruthless killer and vicious anti-Semite. Moreover, he isn't a fool. He can't possibly imagine that the Allies would supply Germany with trucks. There has to be some underlying motive for this apparently crazy plan. Does he anticipate that his scheme won't work, which would later enable him to blame the West for refusing to save Jews?

Over their hazelnut and chocolate *palacsinta,* the conversation turns to music, art and literature. Becher's boyish face is flushed after three glasses of Château Margaux, his eyes are shining, and he enthuses about Bach cantatas and Mozart operas. It turns out that he is a connoisseur of Impressionist painters, and Miklós supposes that his appreciation of fine art has been a great advantage in plundering valuable paintings from Jewish homes. He loves poetry, too, especially the work of Goethe. 'Have you read *Faust?*' Becher asks. 'A fantastic story about a man who does a deal with the devil.'

They look at each other for a moment without speaking, as if struck by the same thought. Then Becher breaks the silence with a loud recitation of a poem and says he wished he had written it in honour of Magda, his Hungarian lover. His voice resounds through the restaurant, and some of the diners, many of them immaculately coiffed Budapest women in elegant gowns who are dining with German officers, turn in his direction, smiling indulgently. '*Du bist wie eine blume,*' he booms, quoting from Heine, and clicks his fingers for the sommelier to bring the finest French cognac and Havana cigars. Miklós smiles to himself. He wonders if Becher is aware that Heine was Jewish, and that his works, along with hundreds of thousands of other banned Jewish literary works, had been burned in the squares of Berlin.

After their brandy balloons are filled, Miklós takes a deep breath, clears his throat and leans forward. He has waited all evening for the right moment to say this, and now that Becher is sitting back, puffing his cigar in a haze of alcoholic bonhomie, he senses that the time has come.

'I have a problem, Herr Obersturmbannführer, and if you don't mind mixing business and pleasure, I'd like to tell you what it is,' he begins, trying to sound relaxed. 'It's about my train. It has been stuck in Bergen-Belsen for several months now, even though I've already paid the ransom. The trouble is, our people in the West are beginning to doubt the sincerity of your boss's offer. I wonder if it's in your power to do anything to expedite the train's journey to Switzerland.'

As he speaks, he reaches into the inside pocket of his jacket and pulls out a thick envelope whose contents the Rescue Committee had managed to raise, and slips it under Becher's starched linen napkin.

Without saying a word, Becher nods, and with one smooth motion of his beautifully manicured hand he slides the envelope into his pocket with a smile. He knows that the envelope contains twenty thousand American dollars.

'You know I am doing this to help the Jews,' he says. 'I never had anything against Jews, not like some of my colleagues. One day you will remember that I helped to save them?'

His easy smile and jovial manner have disappeared and he holds Miklós's gaze with a compelling expression. Miklós understands what he means. The war was drawing to a close, and Germany was facing inevitable defeat. When it was all over, judgements would be made, and retribution would follow. Nazis like Becher would need all the friends they could get.

'I won't forget what you have done.'

Becher is smiling again. 'So, we shake hands?'

Miklós takes the hand extended across the table. He is aware that Becher will continue to exploit him and milk the situation for financial advantage as ruthlessly as possible, but he believes the Nazi officer will keep his side of the bargain. Whatever his motive, he is an invaluable ally.

Becher raises his brandy balloon in a toast. 'To the train!' he says.

As they clink glasses, Miklós knows that a promise has been sealed.

CHAPTER FIFTEEN

December 1944

Despite the handshake and the $20,000, several weeks pass without any progress. The passengers are still detained in Bergen-Belsen. For Miklós, the feeling of bonhomie that his dinner with Kurt Becher at the Gellert Hotel had engendered, with its seductive sense of being treated as an equal, seems an illusion. It is already December, and the days are cold, bleak and dark. The ground at night glitters with frost, and early snow cushions the branches of the spruce trees. Miklós thinks about the group at Bergen-Belsen, and imagines them oscillating between hope and despair. They have already spent four months in the camp, not knowing when they would be permitted to continue their journey, or if they would ever be released.

His frustration and helplessness make him so restless he can hardly sit still, as if ceaseless motion might distract him from his anxiety. Whenever it seemed that he had finally reached an agreement with the Nazis, new conditions were imposed and new demands were made. Becher's latest excuse is that unexpected impediments have arisen, but Miklós recognises this as a brazen attempt to extort even more money.

He knows the money isn't there, that it will never be there. For one thing, Szymon Goldberg, the representative of the American Joint Distribution Committee in Switzerland, is expressly forbidden from dealing with the Nazis, and for another, even if the AJDC lifted their ban, the outrageous amount the Nazis demand — 20 million Swiss francs — simply isn't available. Nonetheless, Miklós is willing to continue this exhausting game, to bluff and make promises he knows he can never keep, just to keep the negotiations going.

To add to his frustration, Goldberg is a stickler for rules and considers bluffing dishonest, so the meetings Miklós arranges for him with Becher and some of Becher's Nazi cronies on the border of Austria and Switzerland come to nothing.

And what is worse, these episodes put everything in jeopardy, because Becher and his offsider stalk out fuming that they have been tricked into a meeting that wasted their time. Exhausted and on the point of despair, Miklós tries to convince Goldberg to prevaricate and promise the Nazis something, anything, but it is useless. In normal times, Goldberg would be an ethical, honest businessman but these are not ordinary times. They are dealing with avaricious killers who have no qualms about extorting money, and Miklós has no qualms about lying to them. The lives of over a thousand people are worth a few lies and false promises.

He admits he has set himself an impossible task, but having reached this point, so close to a success that had once seemed improbable, he can't bear the possibility that it might all come to nothing. But as he paces around his room, smoking one cigarette after another, he knows that no matter how many times he has to keep arranging meetings between the Nazis and Goldberg, or what lies he has to invent to keep them believing that the money will be deposited into whatever bank account they nominate, the passengers have to be released as soon as possible to travel to Switzerland.

The reason for the renewed urgency lies in a letter Judit has managed to send him from Bergen-Belsen. It is brief, but he knows her well enough to sense the excitement pulsing behind her understated words: *I have wonderful news. The three of us will be so happy.* He reads it over and over, incredulous at first, then delighted, and finally panic-stricken. He feels he is being ripped apart.

The irony of it. From the day they were married he longed to have children, but she had refused. That was before the war, at a time when having a baby would have been a joy. But Judit had been adamant. Her musical career was flourishing, with invitations pouring in for her to give concerts and join prominent chamber groups. 'You married a pianist, not a *hausfrau*,' she used to remind him whenever he broached the subject. That had been the beginning of their rift. Afraid of an unwanted pregnancy, she had discouraged intimacy and never initiated or responded to his efforts to excite her. Hurt by her rejection, he had turned to women whose sexual appetites matched his, and whose desire for him nourished his ego.

Ever since Eichmann arrived in Budapest and ever-increasing anti-Jewish laws were imposed, the concert invitations had dried up, and Judit had to restrict herself to playing at home. It lifted his spirits to watch her play, her eager face leaning towards the score as her slender white fingers caressed the keys. He often wondered if she ever regretted her decision, now that music no longer occupied all her time and her career had come to a sudden halt, but their emotional distance precluded intimate discussions. She had become increasingly withdrawn, and now for the first time it occurs to him that she has probably been depressed, and perhaps he is the cause.

Was that why she had come into his bed? For he knew now without any doubt that it was Judit to whom he'd made love with such urgency that night. He often reflects on it. He had gone to bed alone, as usual, and had fallen into a deep sleep. How had he become so aroused? Had it been a dream, or had Judit stimulated him until his body responded with a pitch of excitement that could only find relief in the accepting warmth of a woman's body?

From her oblique comment about Ilonka, he realises that Judit is aware of their relationship. At the time, she hadn't voiced any distress or even concern about it, but she has always kept her thoughts and feelings to herself.

Was it desire that had led her to his bed, or just the longing for physical connection? Or was it simply her determination to reassert her status as his wife that had impelled her to make love to him, something she hadn't done since the early days of their marriage?

Judit's behaviour, so out of character, intrigues him, and the idea that she deliberately set out to seduce him is unexpectedly exciting, although at the same time he is angry at being tricked. He doesn't know whether she had wanted to become pregnant, but she must have realised that he wouldn't use a condom or withdraw in time to prevent filling her with his semen.

But a baby, now! He remembers an old Chinese proverb about being careful what you wish for. His anxiety for the passengers now intensifies as he thinks of his fragile wife with his child in her belly, suffering the privations of a concentration camp. Judit was so delicate, so spiritual. How would she cope in such harsh conditions, in the winter frost, surrounded by brutal guards? The food rations would be meagre, the bunks would be hard, and the blankets paper thin.

And what would happen to the baby, deprived of the nourishment babies need? Until that moment, his mission has been to save other people. Now he realises with a shock that he is also saving a part of himself.

In the middle of the night he sits up, wide awake. Ilonka! What is he going to do? He loves her, he still aches for her every morning, and he misses her smile, her warmth and her bright mind. They promised each other that when they reached Palestine, he would divorce Judit and she would divorce Gábor and they would marry. It had all been so clear to them then, but now everything has changed and nothing is clear anymore. He covers his face with his hands.

The memory of Ilonka's fingertips caressing the most sensitive parts of his body arouses him, and he tries not to think of her moans of pleasure as he unfolded her, petal by petal. How can he live without her? Without the pleasure whose intensity sometimes made him sob with joy? Without sharing everything with her, discussing every plan with her, and listening to her wise ideas? How can he betray the promise they made to each other?

But how can he leave Judit now that she is expecting his child? He makes a swift calculation. She must be almost five months pregnant now. He wonders if her slim figure has filled out, and whether she can feel the baby — their baby — kicking. As his feeling for her rekindles, she is in his thoughts day and night, and he is tortured by the dilemma that is tearing him apart.

But did he have to give either of them up? Perhaps he could explain everything to Ilonka, and they could continue their affair just as before. As soon as that comforting thought occurs to him, he dismisses it. Ilonka would never agree. He must make a choice that will crush one of the women in his life, and crush him as well. Whoever he chooses, he will be tormented by the loss of the other for the rest of his life.

The negotiations for the train have stalled once again, and with no agreement reached about the funds, the situation appears bleaker than ever. So when Szymon Goldberg cables that he will raise four million Swiss francs after all, despite orders forbidding him to do so, Miklós is ecstatic.

When he rushes to Becher's hotel with the good news, Becher demands proof that the money has been deposited. Without pausing to weigh up the wisdom of his words, Miklós blurts out, 'Tell me, Obersturmbannführer, what will you do with all this money when the war is over?'

Becher bursts out laughing. 'Who knows? Perhaps I will become a businessman and do business with you Jews.'

He surveys Miklós. 'And you, Herr Nagy. Why do you wear yourself out and risk your life with this mission of yours?'

Becher's question surprises him. It's a personal question, one a colleague might ask, and he wonders if, for the first time since their association began, this Nazi sees him as a human being, not just a means for further aggrandizement. A glib reply rises to his lips, but he reconsiders. Becher's question deserves a sincere response.

'For many years, I used to wonder if my life had any meaning. But if I can save this group of Jews, I'll feel I haven't lived in vain.'

'Ah so. *Naturlich*. You want to be a saviour, *nicht war*? And those Jews, they will be grateful to you? For how long? People have short memories. Jesus Christ also sacrificed himself, but the people he saved didn't appreciate him. They betrayed him.'

Miklós can't help chuckling at the comparison. 'Even if they don't thank me, at least they won't crucify me.'

Becher walks to the liquor cabinet, removes two glasses, fills them to the brim with schnapps, and holds one out to Miklós. This gesture surprises him. They have drunk together in bars, nightclubs and restaurants, but this is the first time Becher has offered him a drink in his office.

'I have news for you,' Becher is saying as he sprawls in his armchair. 'I want you to know that I've been doing my best to have your passengers released. I am also trying to send thirty thousand Jews to labour camps in Austria to keep them there instead of deporting them to Auschwitz, but Eichmann has been blocking my efforts. He wants them all dead. The Reichsführer is willing to stop the deportations and close the concentration camps, but Eichmann undermines his plans.'

Miklós shifts to the edge of his chair, every muscle taut with anticipation. He is still waiting to hear Becher's news.

'I can tell you that thanks to my efforts, your people will leave Bergen-Belsen tomorrow, and their train will reach

Switzerland in two days' time,' Becher says. 'I am sure you will want to meet it.' Leaning forward he clinks glasses, says '*Prost!*' and downs his schnapps in one gulp.

For the first time in many months, the burden that has been weighing Miklós down finally slips off his back, and he walks home with a lighter step. Just a few more days, and he will finally triumph after all these terrifying meetings, dangerous discussions and failed negotiations. Thanks to his determination, over fifteen hundred Jews will have been saved from a horrible death, and Judit and Ilonka will be free. He's the one who has achieved this, but he knows he couldn't have done it without Becher's help.

*

Three days later, on a frosty December day, the train from Bergen-Belsen pulls in at the station at St Margarethen on the border of Austria and Switzerland, brakes screeching, thick steam blowing across the railway track. Over a thousand faces are pressed to the slits in the walls of the wagons, anxious to catch their first sight of Switzerland. Some of the passengers are sobbing, overcome with emotion. Some are laughing, delirious with joy. Others are silent, trying to grasp the significance of a moment they have dreamed of for so long. Reporters are running along the platform and photographers have cameras poised to take their first shots of the liberated Hungarian Jews for international newspapers.

Pushing his way past the photographers, Swiss soldiers and Red Cross personnel, Miklós scans the passengers pouring from the wagons, impatient to place their feet on Swiss soil. Suddenly he hears someone shout his name. He turns, and Judit falls into his arms.

Resting her small head on his shoulder, she sobs, 'Miki, you did it! I can't believe I'm really in Switzerland. I can't believe you're here and we're safe. Tell me this isn't a dream.'

He closes his eyes and as he holds her against him, he feels an unfamiliar roundness. 'Oh my darling,' he says, and strokes her belly. The platform is crowded with passengers, porters and Red Cross officials, but they stand motionless in their embrace. Once again he caresses the hard swell of her belly with wonder, and knows his choice has been made.

He looks up. Standing apart from the crowd, Ilonka is staring at them. His heart is hammering. He longs to rush to her, to sweep her up in his arms and hold her, but he manages to control himself. Several moments later, he pulls away from Judit and starts to move towards Ilonka. But before he can reach her, she holds up her arm in a gesture that warns him to keep his distance. He wants to speak to her, to say something, but the words freeze on his lips as he hears her say, 'Don't come near me. I never want to see you again as long as I live.' Then she turns her back on him and walks away.

His face is the colour of the whitewashed station building, and he leans against it as he watches her retreating figure. Just then a cameraman asks her to join the group he is about to photograph near the St Margarethen sign and she forces a smile as the flash goes off.

It should have been the most triumphant moment of his life, but he knows he will never forget the words Ilonka spat at him. He has lost the only thing that made his life worth living. As he walks slowly from the station with his arm around Judit, he wants to weep. Everything in life comes at a price, but this time the price was too high.

ISRAEL

CHAPTER SIXTEEN

Tel Aviv, 2005

Annika flings her suitcase onto the hotel bed and opens the door to her tiny balcony. Squinting against the dazzling light, she gazes at the scene below and catches her breath. Nothing she has seen since arriving in Tel Aviv has prepared her for this sight.

As soon as the plane touched down at Ben Gurion Airport, hundreds of travellers jostled each other at the luggage carousel and then, pushing trolleys loaded up with trunks, cases, boxes and cabin bags, they'd rushed to the taxi stand like greyhounds released from their cages at the start of a race. They pushed past her, men in long black coats with beards and wide-brimmed hats, and women in long skirts with lots of children in tow, shouting addresses at the drivers even before they reached the cabs. 'Why don't you wait your turn?' she snapped at the woman who had shoved her out of the way and was already pushing her two small children into the back of a taxi.

Eventually she was able to secure a taxi, and as it made its way along streets jammed with cars whose drivers sounded their horns in frustration at the slow-moving traffic, she looked at the nondescript buildings and dusty palm trees and felt she wouldn't want to stay in Tel Aviv a minute longer than necessary.

But now she sees the view from her balcony, hears the boom of waves breaking on the shore and breathes in the familiar salty smell of the sea, and her muscles begin to unknot.

Coming from Sydney, she is rarely impressed by beaches in other countries, but spread before her is one of the most beautiful beaches she has ever seen. Stretching into the distance is a succession of scalloped bays, and spread out on sand the colour of icing sugar are rows of crimson, royal blue and sunflower yellow deckchairs under striped umbrellas. Young people leap up and toss balls across volleyball nets.

She rummages through her suitcase for her leggings and runners, changes her clothes, leaves the mess on the bed, and hurries downstairs. She doesn't want to waste a minute of this perfect afternoon. The promenade is wide and attractively paved and as she dodges dozens of cyclists speeding along it, she passes cafés, kiosks and juice bars, whose vendors chat up passers-by to lure them inside.

'Hi, come in, have a coffee! Madonna said we have the best coffee in Tel Aviv,' one of them calls out to her. He has olive skin and eyes as bright as polished obsidian, and she likes his cheeky smile.

'Go on, Madonna didn't even come to Israel, she cancelled her tour,' she counters.

Without missing a beat, he shoots back, 'But if she did come, she would have said that.'

Annika bursts out laughing. 'Is this what you call chutzpah?'

'Here we call it good business. I'm Ari. Come in, try my coffee, you will see.'

She sits on a bamboo stool and gazes at the beach. It's Saturday, and whole families are strolling along the promenade, groups of cyclists chain their bicycles to the rail and take off their helmets to admire the view, and girls with long tanned legs and brief shorts shoot flirtatious glances at the guys and walk on, whispering and giggling. If not for the occasional group of young khaki-clad soldiers of both sexes with semi-automatic rifles slung on their shoulders, it could have been a beach in any holiday resort in the world; a scene she did not expect to see in Tel Aviv.

She doesn't really know what she expected. There was ancient Israel, the so-called Promised Land, whose mystique encompassed thousands of years of history from biblical times, but she had seen no indication of that exotic past on the drive into this modern city.

Tel Aviv was often in the news, usually with a negative slant that focused on occupation, oppression and conflict. Especially since the second Intifada had broken out, with suicide attacks on Israeli buses and crowded markets.

The reports filed by foreign correspondents gave the impression that Israel was a dangerous country, yet here in the middle of its largest city, locals were enjoying a laid-back beach culture like carefree sun-lovers everywhere.

Ari is watching her as she sips the espresso, eager for confirmation of his claim.

'Madonna said she liked the coffee in Sydney much better,' Annika says with a straight face, and he shakes his finger at her playfully.

She points at the beach. 'I had no idea there was such a gorgeous beach right in the centre of town.'

'If you come here at night, you will see something that will surprise you even more. Our nightclubs and discos stay open until dawn, and people dance all night. You should see the action! Tel Aviv is the rave capital of the world.'

'You should be writing their travel ads,' she says.

'No, really. You like music? You dance? You should come. With your friend.'

She ignores his clumsy attempt to find out if she is alone. 'I don't understand,' she says slowly. 'How can there be such a light-hearted atmosphere here? Aren't people depressed about the Intifada and the suicide bombers?'

He shrugs. 'The rest of Israel calls us "The Bubble City". They think we close our eyes to the real world. But we think, who knows what will happen tomorrow? So we must live for today.'

It reminds her of something Jancsi said, and she feels a stab of nostalgia, but Ari is still talking to her, pointing to a sign hanging crookedly above the counter: *Yesterday's history, tomorrow's a mystery, but today's a gift, that's why we call it the present.*

'It's true, no? An American friend sent it to me from Los Angeles.'

That figures, Annika thinks.

A noisy group of locals has come into the café and someone orders a bottle of Yarden sparkling wine. The guy they are toasting has tightly curled hair that's lightly speckled with grey, and when he turns to look at her and smiles, she can't resist smiling back. But it's his mouth that makes her linger on his face, especially the sensual lower lip which is bisected by a cleft. He is wearing board shorts and a floral Hawaiian shirt and seems to have a personality to match, a beach bum perhaps, but a convivial one, judging by the laughter that comes from his table whenever he speaks.

She would prefer to observe him and his friends from a distance, but to her dismay, the bon vivant is beckoning to her. 'Come, sit with us, don't be by yourself,' he calls, and gives her that enticing smile. He holds out a glass of wine. 'Have a glass with us. It's my birthday.'

While she hesitates, Ari cuts in. 'Yes, do what he says, or he might write about you. That's Dov Erlich, the journalist.'

As soon as she hears that, the man at the next table stops being a jovial beach bum she would prefer to avoid and becomes an interesting colleague who might be able to help her. Okay, so I make snobbish assumptions and I use people, she thinks as she moves to his table, but what journalist doesn't?

Dov makes room for her and fills her glass. '*L'Chaim*,' he says, raising his glass to touch hers. 'That means "to life". Being alive is a major preoccupation in this country, but staying alive here is an even bigger challenge.'

Ari is already refilling their glasses. One of Dov's companions raises his glass and says, 'Happy birthday, Dov, may you live to one hundred and twenty.'

'Better make that one-twenty and a day,' Dov says.

'Why "and one day"?' Annika asks.

'You want I should die on my birthday?' Dov asks, and they all burst out laughing. So does Annika.

As soon as Dov finds out that she is also a journalist, he surveys her with an interested gaze. 'So are you here on an assignment for your paper?'

She shakes her head. 'I'm on holiday.' She is tempted to tell him about her quest but holds back. This isn't the place or the time.

Dov leans towards her and when he speaks, she finds herself looking at his sensual lips. 'I'm with the *Tel Aviv Post*. At least I think I am, but if you ask my editor, he mightn't agree. He has a reference ready for when I resign. It says, *Dov Erlich tells me he's been working for me for the past ten years. If you can get him to work for you, you'll be lucky.*'

When the laughter dies down, he adds, 'But seriously, if you need anything while you're here, you can call me.'

*

On her way back to the hotel, Annika feels light-hearted. Once again she is a stranger alone in a foreign city, but despite the threat of danger, she feels comfortable here in a way she didn't feel in Budapest. And although she misses Jancsi, she has no regrets.

Back in her room, she starts to unpack, but a spear of sunlight pierces the room through the gap in the curtains, and she sinks onto the bed and closes her eyes. As she lies there, her eyelids warmed by the sun, something that the guide in the Sydney Jewish Museum said comes back to her. *No good deed goes unpunished.* What did he mean? And how did that relate to Miklós Nagy?

She opens her eyes, alert now. That's what she has to find out. Not knowing Hebrew will make it difficult for her to search old newspapers and archives. She might need to hire a translator, but that will take time, and having overstayed her time in Budapest, she only has a week left before her return flight to Sydney. She closes her eyes again. She is too tired to sort anything out, and it's almost dinnertime.

The hotel terrace is already full of diners when she arrives, and above the buzz of conversation she hears Americans enthusing about their visit to Masada. At the table next to hers, an Israeli couple are speaking Hebrew which sounds guttural to her ears. The Israeli woman, a plump middle-aged blonde with hair that is too blonde and lipstick that is too red, looks up from her plate as Annika walks past, and gives her a friendly smile. 'Try the chicken, it's good,' she says in English.

Instead, Annika orders veal with mushrooms, which is dry. The sauce could have done with some cream, but as the waiter explains, the restaurant adheres to kosher rules, and doesn't mix dairy products with meat.

Suddenly, above the rhythmic sound of the waves pounding on the shore, she hears the shocking shriek of ambulances and police cars tearing through the streets. The restaurant grows silent. The diners stop eating, the waiters stop serving, and everyone seems to freeze. Some people pick up their mobile phones and dial with frantic fingers.

The couple behind her push back their chairs so violently that one crashes to the floor, and they rush towards the door.

An American woman keeps moaning, *Oh my God, oh my God. Shoshi's not answering. What if she's there?* Her knees are buckling as she clings to her husband who is trying to support and reassure her although his face is as anguished as hers.

Annika turns to the table behind her where another American couple are speaking in hushed tones. 'What happened?' she asks a man who wears a black leather *kippah* on his reddish hair.

'Another suicide bomber, this time here in Tel Aviv. At a falafel restaurant near the market. The bastards know it's a favourite meeting place for the young ones, and it's always crowded on Saturday nights. They stuff the bombs with nails and bolts to make sure they inflict as much injury as possible. And those are the people our government has given the Gaza Strip to. From the pinnacle of their delusional idealism, they decided to give the land to the Palestinians so they can breed more suicide bombers on our doorstep. And this is only the beginning.'

In the intimate atmosphere that tragedy creates among strangers, he explains that he and his wife made *aliyah* from New York some years before, but they have become disillusioned with the politics of Ariel Sharon and his government who forcibly evacuated the Jews from the Gaza Strip and returned it to the Palestinians without any assurances of peace.

'After years of hard work, those Jewish settlers had to walk out of there leaving everything they'd built up. They left hothouses full of tomatoes and strawberries that we exported all over Europe. And you know what the Palestinians did? They shattered the glass, wrecked the hothouses, and trashed the plants. That's how they value peace and prosperity. All they value is violence and hatred.'

In his bitterness, she recognises the disillusionment of expats who have left their homeland to settle in a country they have idealised, only to find it no more perfect than the one they left behind. She saw this phenomenon with English journalists she worked with, who were constantly criticising every aspect of life in Australia, forgetting why they had left Britain.

Annika's mind is on the victims of the bombing, and as soon as she returns to her room, she switches on CNN. *Breaking News: Carnage in Tel Aviv*, the scarlet headline screams. It turns out that twelve people were killed at the scene, but over thirty others have terrible injuries caused by the metal filings in the bombs. The carnage is captured on film which shows pools of blood on the ground, and bags and high-heeled shoes flung all around the marketplace. The camera zooms in on a dainty Chanel bag with a broken strap. Paramedics bend over bloodied youngsters, and rabbis are collecting body parts and placing them in special bags, while the wounded moan and bystanders scream. Annika shudders and her mouth is dry but she can't stop watching. She hopes that Shoshi wasn't there.

Too distressed to sleep, she wanders down to the beach and follows the insistent beat of disco music with its pounding rhythm until she reaches a nightclub near the café where she met Dov Erlich that afternoon. Young people are streaming in, lively girls in short, tight dresses that cling to their bums, and guys in blue jeans and short-sleeved shirts, surveying the talent with eager eyes.

Ari is in the doorway of his café, talking to a customer.

'Annika. You go dancing now?'

She shakes her head. 'How can people dance when such a terrible thing just happened?'

'Terrible things are always happening. If you are alive, you have to live, or they have killed you too.'

It's midnight when she returns to the hotel but she is too restless to sleep. Instead of going to her room, she goes to the business centre and opens the computer. As Miklós Nagy saved a number of Hungarian Jews, she supposes that the Holocaust Museum in Jerusalem must have some information about him online.

She clicks on various headings on the site, searching first by name, then by country, and later by rescuers, but doesn't find a single mention of him. It's as though he never existed. She switches off the computer and continues to sit in the empty office staring at the wall. Has she made this trip for nothing?

*

When she wakes the next morning, sunlight is streaming into her room, and from her balcony she sees that the beach is already crowded. Children are skylarking on the sand and running into the sea, and bronzed middle-aged women with disciplined bodies are lounging on the deckchairs. Vendors are circulating among them with trays of sliced mango and pineapple, iced drinks, falafels and ice cream. Her despondent mood of the previous evening has lifted, and she hurries down to breakfast.

In one corner of the restaurant, which overlooks the beach, a chef is cooking egg dishes. In another, a waiter is squeezing oranges, pomegranates and grapefruit. The long buffet table displays a mouth-watering assortment of cheeses, herrings and vegetables that have been pickled, chopped, roasted, grilled or marinated, as well as breads, cakes and pastries of every description. Breakfast over, she decides to call Dov. He will know where she should look for information. It is Sunday, but she knows that Sunday is an ordinary working day in Israel. As she waits for the operator to put her through, she hopes she won't be switched to voicemail.

But a moment later she hears his voice. This time he sounds brisk and businesslike, not like the jovial bon vivant she'd met in Ari's café.

'I'm calling to take you up on your offer of help. I said I was here on holidays but that isn't quite true. I've come to find out something about a Hungarian called Miklós Nagy, who saved some Hungarian Jews during the Holocaust and arrived in Israel some time after the war. Do you know where I can find some information about him?'

After a pause, he says, 'You're asking me if I know anything about the man who brought down the government of Israel!'

CHAPTER SEVENTEEN

Jaffa, 2005

Annika is strolling along the promenade that skirts the beach. It's already her third day in Tel Aviv and she still hasn't made any progress with her search. After she'd spoken with Dov the previous day, she'd tried to contact the city library for information, but the research librarian was on leave and there was no-one else there to help her. Rather than waste the day, she'd taken a trip to Masada. Her thoughts turn to that ancient clifftop fortress where, over two thousand years before, a community of Jewish rebels were besieged by Romans, and all had chosen to die rather than be taken captive.

She is wondering what it would take to choose death in such a situation when she notices a stone obelisk on the edge of the promenade. It isn't particularly attractive, a squat rhomboid with a pointed apex, but what catches her eye is the image of a cargo ship carved into the stone, which gleams in the sunlight. According to the English translation, this is a memorial to the *Altalena,* an arms ship carrying 930 passengers that had anchored off shore in June 1948. It had come to fight in the War of Independence but had been shelled on orders of the provisional government.

She reads the inscription several times and looks out to sea, past the bright beach umbrellas and rows of deck chairs, trying to visualise the dramatic event, wondering why it had happened and why it was being commemorated. It sounded a sombre note, incongruous with the vibrant beach scene and the carefree atmosphere. As she stands in front of the monument, a few tourists stop beside her, curious to see what she is looking at, but after a cursory glance, they shrug and walk on.

For the third time in the past few minutes she checks the time. She doesn't want to be late for her meeting with Dov. He'd said, 'I can't talk to you now,' when she asked him to explain his comment about Miklós Nagy, but he suggested meeting for coffee in Jaffa on Monday.

The concierge at the hotel told her that Jaffa was about four kilometres from Tel Aviv, and suggested taking a cab, but she has enjoyed the beachside walk and, determined not to be late, she has overestimated the time she needed to get there on foot. While she waits, she wanders around the area's narrow alleys until she comes to the flea market, and is delighted by the enormous Aladdin's cave of second-hand junk that occupies several blocks, and spills from the stalls and shops onto the narrow footpaths.

The goods on offer cover every kind of item imaginable: antiquated TV sets, coils of rope, spades, stand mixers from the 1950s, rusty trumpets, shaggy wigs, yellowed wedding dresses, faded shawls, metal pots, chipped plates and dolls with grimy porcelain faces, interspersed with antique clocks, Moroccan tagines, Persian rugs and pretty English tea sets, all heaped on shelves, piled on the floor, or suspended from the walls, with hardly any space in between.

The intoxicating mosaic of textures and colours displayed in the stalls reflects the crowded market itself: Arabs in *keffiyehs* smoking *narghilehs*, Ethiopian women in brilliant headdresses and colourful robes, sunburnt European tourists in skimpy tops, and Israelis in shorts having coffee and baklava at rickety little tables on the narrow footpaths. This was the Israel she had imagined, exotic, oriental and exciting.

Leaving the market behind, she climbs a steep street, and past the Ottoman clocktower she comes to a plaza of art galleries, silversmiths' studios, antique shops and jewellery boutiques. She lingers outside the shop windows, and admires the unusual designs within. Drawn to an interesting silver pendant on a fine chain, she enters the shop to have a closer look.

'You like the *chai*?' the saleswoman asks as she clasps it around Annika's neck. 'You have good taste. I designed this one myself.'

'*Chai*,' Annika repeats. From the conversation at Ari's café the day she arrived, she recalls that the word means life. The woman nods approvingly. 'It suits you.'

Annika has always disdained souvenirs in general, and religious symbols in particular. She has always dismissed Stars of David, crosses or saints' medals hung around someone's neck as displays of tribal membership. She has certainly never wanted to own such a symbol, let alone hang it around her neck to advertise her religion.

She had chosen this pendant on impulse, but apart from its eye-catching modern design, it was also meaningful.

Too hot to keep walking, she heads for the café beside the old sea wall where she and Dov have arranged to meet. From her table under a large umbrella, she looks down at five fishermen sitting on the wall wearing caps or woollen beanies, casting their lines into the sea, and past them to the trawlers, fishing boats and cruisers inside the breakwater of the lively port.

Beyond the sea wall a cluster of sinister-looking black rocks floats in the water. She takes her travel guide from her bag and looks up Jaffa. The paragraph about the rocks tells her that the largest outcrop is called Andromeda. It is a long time since she has thought about the Greek tragedies, and now, gazing at this rock, she realises that this port had been part of the Hellenistic world at a time when Aeschylus and Sophocles wrote the plays she loved so much.

According to one of the legends, Andromeda had been chained to this rock as a sacrifice, but at the very last moment, she was rescued by Perseus on his winged horse. She smiles at this ancient version of bringing in the cavalry. Past the harbour, she gazes at the wide sweep of beach that curves from Jaffa to Tel Aviv, and thinks about the ship that was shelled in these waters back in 1948.

'Do you realise you're looking at one of the oldest ports in the world?'

She swivels around and sees Dov mopping his face with a handkerchief as he takes the chair facing her. No longer a beach bum in board shorts, he looks trim and businesslike in grey trousers, an open-necked shirt with short sleeves, and rimless glasses that often slip down the bridge of his nose.

'Jaffa is unique,' he says. 'Right under our feet lie thousands of years of history.' Waving his arm in the direction of the visitors' centre behind them, he adds, 'If you're interested in ancient history, you should spend a bit of time in there — there's an amazing Hellenistic and Roman excavation site underneath.'

'As a matter of fact, I am interested,' she says. 'I've been reading some of the plays that were written during Hellenistic times.' She can't resist saying this, and knows she is trying to impress him.

Not taking his eyes from her face, he gives her that magical smile. 'What an interesting woman you are,' he says.

She is pleased at the compliment but changes the subject. 'I can see you love this place. Tell more about it.'

He doesn't need any urging. 'Jaffa was a hot spot for Jews, Muslims and Christians for four thousand years. An early example of what real estate agents call position, position, position.'

He rests his gaze on her neck, and when he takes off his glasses to wipe them, she notices that his eyes are as clear and green as the water below. 'So you bought a *chai*,' he says. 'Is that symbolic, religious, ethnic or talismanic?'

'Maybe just because I liked it.'

It is too early for wine and too hot for tea, so she orders an iced coffee, which arrives in a chilled glass topped with a scoop of ice cream, while he orders beer. Aware that his time is limited, she is reluctant to spend it discussing ancient history, intriguing as it is. Draining most of her coffee in one gulp, she places the glass on the table, wipes the cream off her mouth, and sits forward.

'You said Miklós Nagy brought down the government. Were you serious?'

His glasses slip again, and he pushes them back up with the flat of his hand.

'It was an exaggerated version of the truth. Journalistic licence, which I'm sure you're familiar with. It's a very complicated topic, and involves all kinds of political issues which will leave you confused without answering your question.'

He pushes his glasses up again, and she realises this is a habit that gives him time to organise his thoughts. 'This man, Nagy. Tell me why you're so interested in him.'

'I could give you the same answer that you gave me. It's complicated. Travelling all this way to find out something about the man who saved my grandmother's life doesn't even make sense to me.'

'It must make sense at some level, Annika,' he observes. His lips are twitching as if he is suppressing a smile, probably at her confusion.

She stares out to sea. A breeze has sprung up and waves are crashing into the Andromeda rock and splashing the anglers on the seawall.

He listens attentively while she tells him about her grandmother's strange reaction to Miklós Nagy's name and how it aroused her curiosity; about the comment of the guide at the Sydney Jewish Museum, about Jancsi's father's memoir, and the cryptic comments of the guide at the Holocaust museum in Budapest.

When she stops talking, he leans forward and looks straight into her eyes. 'You really don't understand why you're doing this, do you?'

'I just told you.'

He shakes his head. 'You've told me about a series of encounters linked with Miklós Nagy. But do I believe that this is really what motivated you to travel around the world? I don't buy it. No way.'

Annoyed by his arrogance, she is about to make a glib retort, but perhaps he can discern something that has eluded her, something that might help her understand her impulsive behaviour. So she waits for him to continue.

'I think your search for this man is a search for something about yourself and your own past. But only you can figure out what that is, and why it's so important to you.'

She shifts in her chair and grips her glass more firmly. Dov was obviously an opinionated journalist who felt entitled to make judgments about people he didn't know.

'Now that you've psychoanalysed me, can we go back to Miklós Nagy?'

Dov laughs and drains the rest of his beer. 'Touché. So, back to Mr Nagy. You need to understand that all this happened long before my time — I was born in the States, and didn't make *aliyah* until I was in my twenties. That was during the Yom Kippur war in 1973, but I know that the fallout from the Nagy case was toxic, and some people believe its legacy still haunts Israeli politics to this day. From what I've heard, even if Nagy wasn't personally responsible for what happened later, he was a catalyst. Perhaps he was in the wrong place at the wrong time or, to be more exact, through no fault of his own, he got tangled up with the wrong people.'

Annika is listening intently, trying to imagine the complex legal and political issues in Israel during the 1950s, when his mobile rings. He turns away to take the call, and from his tone she can tell he is talking to his editor, and is grateful for the interruption. This conversation wasn't answering any of her questions. Perhaps she should rephrase them.

But Dov is already standing up and motioning for the bill. 'Sorry, I have to go. There's been an incident in Ramallah and an Israeli soldier has been injured. Walk me to my car so we can keep talking.'

'I still don't understand it. Why is Miklós Nagy so controversial?'

'This story is a quagmire, and if you pursue it, you'll drown in political quicksand, and even then, I don't know if you'll get at the truth. But if you're determined to keep digging, and I figure you are, then you should start with a lawyer called Amos Alon who practised here in the fifties and sixties. I don't imagine he is still alive, but the Law Association will have some records. If you call my office later, I'll ask our secretary to look up the number for you. But you should be aware that not everyone will be enthusiastic about the subject of your search.'

He rifles in his pocket for the car keys, and as he opens the door of his dusty Ford Falcon, she suddenly remembers the strange memorial she saw on the promenade on Tel Aviv beach. 'It said something about a ship called the *Altalena*. Do you know what that was about?'

He turns to face her. 'So you noticed the *Altalena* monument. That's amazing. You seem to have a knack for ferreting out information.'

Now it's her turn to look surprised. 'What do you mean?'

'That inscription is actually one of the keys to unlocking the Nagy saga. You know I just mentioned a solicitor called Amos Alon? Well, he was directly affected by the *Altalena* incident. He was also the defence attorney in the lawsuit that involved Miklós Nagy.'

*

Later that afternoon, the secretary of the Law Association puts her through to the officer in charge of their archives. He sounds friendly when she says she is Australian, but his tone cools noticeably when she explains she is searching for information about Amos Alon. He would have to find the files, he isn't sure where they are, it will take a great deal of time as some of the old files aren't digitised, she'll have to fill in a requisition form ... Annika realises he is making excuses to put her off and, remembering Dov's warning, she tries to get him on side.

'I can imagine how busy you are,' she says. 'The last thing you need is some woman from Australia bugging you to dig out files about someone who practised so long ago. But if you could possibly find them, I'd really appreciate it because I have to fly back home in a few days.'

Mollified, he tells her that his grandfather fought alongside the Aussies at Beersheba in 1915. 'He told us they were amazing, those Australian horsemen, brave and fearless, and they looked after their comrades. Said they called each other "mate".'

He rouses himself from his reverie. 'The Alon-Nagy lawsuit happened a long time ago, and I don't think that file has been digitised yet. I'm out of the office tomorrow, but come back on Thursday morning and I should have it for you by then.'

Irritated at the delay, she goes to the hotel lobby and scans the tourist leaflets on the concierge's desk. With two extra days to fill in, she decides to take the tour north to Haifa, stopping on the way at the vineyards of Zichron Yaakov, the Roman ruins in Caesarea, and the crusader castle in Acre. The day after that, she books a trip to the Dead Sea and the Negev desert. She is looking forward to these excursions, but she can't wait to get to the law library so that she can finally find out what happened to Miklos Nagy, why there was a lawsuit, and how a lawyer called Amos Alon came to be involved in it.

CHAPTER EIGHTEEN

Tel Aviv, 1953

Isaiah Fleischmann is about to knock on Amos Alon's office door, racking his brains in an effort to recall the sequence of events that put an end to his reclusive existence and led him here. Someone must have suggested it, but he has no friends, and his neighbours in the rundown part of Tel Aviv were too preoccupied with their daily struggles to be concerned with his problems. Perhaps it was just chance that led him to this legal maverick. He muses that luck requires two disparate events to coincide, just as a hammer needs a nail to unleash its power, and he hopes that this encounter will prove to be a stroke of luck. He reckons he needs it.

The lawsuit fell out of the sky like a block of cement hurtling from a building site onto his unsuspecting head. One minute he was sitting inside his room in Neve Tzedek, in a street of crumbling, grimy flat-roofed buildings in one of the oldest parts of Tel Aviv, his pen flying furiously over sheets of paper as he composed his pamphlets, and the next that letter arrived. An unusual event for a start, because who would bother writing to him? Who would even want to?

This was an official letter, with the government letterhead embossed on the envelope. His fingers shook as he picked it up, and he stared at it for a long time without opening it, turning it this way and that, as if the contents might reveal themselves through the envelope. Perhaps, after all this time, someone from his family had survived after all, and they were writing to let him know.

People did turn up. Just the other day, he read that a man from some Polish city had surprised his relatives by turning up in Tel Aviv years after everyone thought he was dead. He had escaped the Nazis, joined General Anders's Polish army, been imprisoned with the Polish soldiers in Russia, and then, in one of those unaccountable turnarounds that history constantly produced, he had been released, because overnight Poland stopped being Russia's enemy and became its ally when Hitler invaded the Soviet Union.

The man had spent the rest of the war in Tashkent and Iran, and then returned to Poland in search of his family, but not one of them had survived the murderous efficiency of the Germans. They had perished in the camps or been betrayed to the Gestapo by Christian neighbours whose malice outweighed their mercy; on his return they made it clear they weren't overjoyed to see survivors coming back to claim their homes and property. Grief-stricken and depressed, he was unexpectedly traced by two cousins in Israel, who had long given him up for dead. Isaiah had carefully cut out the article and reread it several times, trembling with vicarious pleasure every time he came to the part where the cousins were reunited.

So miraculous reunions did happen. There wasn't a day when he didn't think about his mother and his sister Malka and their terrible deaths, all because that *mamser* Nagy had refused to save them. His blood boiled whenever he thought about that collaborator, especially now that he'd become a *maeven* in the Department of Rationing and Supply. He was glad he'd written that pamphlet to expose him even if no-one had so far been willing to act on it, or even acknowledge its significance. Exposing the traitor was the least he could do to avenge their deaths.

He recalls looking at the letter again, and, like a student on tenterhooks anticipating but dreading the results of an examination, he placed the envelope on the table, filled his saucepan with water, and set it on his primus stove to delay the moment of discovery. Only after he had sat down at his small formica table, poured himself a glass of black tea and started sucking a cube of sugar, did he reach for a knife and carefully slit open the flap of the envelope.

He unfolded the letter and started reading. In his anxiety, he scanned it so fast that at first the words appeared jumbled, and he couldn't make sense of them. It came from the Ministry of Justice, a department he often referred to in his pamphlets as the Ministry of Injustice. Was that why they were writing to him? Were they offended by his lack of respect? They certainly didn't deserve any. They prosecuted, or rather, persecuted, the small people, but allowed politicians and businessmen to get away with fraudulent deals, rotten tricks and dishonest schemes.

He forced himself to read the letter slowly, his nicotine-stained finger moving along each line, word by word, and when he had finished, he leaped to his feet and started pacing the small room, muttering to himself. Then he read it again from start to finish, to make sure he understood it. It appeared that the government of Israel was suing him.

Not on their own behalf, but on behalf of Miklós Nagy, of all people. He was shaking so violently that he spilled some of his tea but he hardly noticed his scalded hand. He didn't expect gratitude for exposing the man as a Nazi collaborator, but the government should have understood the significance of his accusations and acted on them. They should at least have looked into the actions of the man they had taken at his word and hailed as a hero.

His breath came in short gasps and he dropped into his chair, too dizzy to stand. He wanted to crush the letter and tear it into a thousand fragments. The bastards. Instead of investigating the matter, they were charging him with defamation and ordering him to appear in court.

'You can represent yourself if you like, but we advise you to appoint a lawyer,' the officious young woman in the Ministry of Justice informed him a few days later when his rage had subsided sufficiently to contact someone about the lawsuit. She was one of those modern Israeli girls, very sure of herself with her flint-edged voice and condescending manner. Nothing like the Hungarian girls back home with their flirtatious charm and seductive voices. *Sabras* they called these native Israelis, after the cactus fruit that grew in the desert. Prickly on the outside, sweet inside. The first description he concurred with, the second was debateable. Their arrogance infuriated him. They made it clear they considered themselves superior to Holocaust survivors like him. They saw themselves as victors because they'd fought for their country, whereas they regarded people like him as merely having been victims, obedient sheep who had allowed themselves to be herded into camps like dumb animals. He could feel his blood pressure mounting again just thinking about this insult to the memory of the dead.

'I'd like to see how heroic they'd be if they were unarmed and surrounded by guards with machine guns.' He didn't realise he was muttering to himself until he looked up and saw that the woman in the office was drumming her stubby fingers on the desk, waiting for his response with an impatience she didn't bother to conceal.

He had almost forgotten her question. 'A lawyer?' he repeated in a dazed voice.

'*Tov*,' she said briskly. 'Fine.' As he watched her making a note in the file, he realised too late that she had taken his absent-minded repetition as assent.

She slid the file into a pigeon-hole above her desk, sat forward, raised her thinly pencilled eyebrows and spread her hands to signify that there was nothing more to say and he was wasting her time.

Until then, it hadn't occurred to him to engage a lawyer. He had assumed he would represent himself. After all, he was telling the truth so he had nothing to hide and nothing to fear, as the charge was bound to be dismissed. In the course of venting his spleen in his pamphlets, he had found out that if it's a fact, it isn't libel. And what he had written about Nagy was the sacred truth. Besides, everyone knew that solicitors were *ganevs*, scoundrels who twisted facts, bandied long words, and bled their clients dry. And even if he wanted a lawyer to represent him, he couldn't afford to pay one.

All this is churning through his mind as he knocks on the door of Amos Alon's office. By now he has worked himself up to such a pitch of anxiety that he is gabbling incoherently about the injustice of his predicament even before he sits down. Now that he has cranked himself up, he can't stop. Hardly pausing to take a breath, he fills the poky office with indignation that bounces off the walls and threatens to dislodge the flakes of loose paint and crumbling plaster from the ceiling. The wooden chair digs into his thin buttocks, and its slats make his back ache, but he is in full flight and hardly notices the discomfort.

'It's outrageous!' he shouts. 'What is this country coming to when an honest man, a poor man like me, who fights corruption with the only weapon I possess, my pen, is being sued for telling the truth? I've devoted my life to pointing out wrongs and exposing evil-doers, and what do I get in return? Litigation. By the government, no less. Is that fair? Is it right?'

Like a car engine that runs out of fuel, he finally comes to a dead stop and looks at Amos for the first time. He is startled to see that the lawyer is probably younger than him, with the straight back and muscular build of a man of action, not one who spends his days in courtrooms and offices, bent over law books. A coiled spring, Isaiah thinks as he looks at the bald head shaped like a bullet. He can feel energy emanating from him. The deep scar that runs from the corner of his right eye to the edge of his square jaw suggests a past incongruous with a sedentary profession.

Amos leans back in his chair, tilting it so it rests on its two back legs, and fixes his gaze on Isaiah, not interrupting his diatribe. The word that comes into Isaiah's mind when he looks at Amos is steel. Unbending, unyielding and uncompromising.

Having ground to a halt, Isaiah suddenly feels panic-stricken. There is no expression on the lawyer's face, and he has no idea how Amos has reacted to his story. Perhaps like everyone else he regards him as a crank, and will refuse to compromise his good name by representing him. On the other hand, looking around the office, which was in dire need of a coat of paint and an energetic plasterer, it doesn't look as if Amos is overburdened with work. Either way, he probably couldn't afford to reduce his fee even if he wanted to take on his case, and Isaiah regrets his own *chutzpah*. How did he have the cheek to bother the lawyer with his problem? And even if Alon did agree to take on his case, he couldn't afford his fee. He is mortified at his own audacity, and embarrassed by his penury. He fidgets in his chair, looks at the floor, and curses his own stupidity in coming.

He is stammering his apologies for wasting the lawyer's time and has started backing out of the office when, to his astonishment, Amos tells him to sit down. He speaks in a tone used to giving orders, a military commander rather than a lawyer.

He expects to hear Amos say that he is too busy to represent him, that this isn't the kind of case he usually takes on, or that it isn't his area of expertise, but he doesn't say any of those things. When Isaiah starts apologising that he can't afford to pay, Amos dismisses his comment about fees with a deprecatory wave of his large hand, indicating that this is irrelevant and has no bearing on the situation.

What he does say is, 'I will take on your case, Mr Fleischmann.'

Isaiah can hardly believe what he has just heard. He asks him to repeat it, and when he does, he knows he will never forget the lawyer's next words.

'I will represent you, Mr Fleishmann, and you don't have to worry about the fee. I will do it *pro bono*. But I want you to give me a free hand in the way I conduct the case.'

Isaiah walks out of Amos Alon's office in a daze. He knows he has found his hammer.

CHAPTER NINETEEN

Tel Aviv, 1953

Amos Alon strolls along the sand in bare feet as he always does at daybreak. It's the time of day he likes the most, the hour before the city wakes. Tel Aviv is a city of loud sounds and bright colours, and he enjoys this interlude of peace when the sun tints the sky in streaks of peach, rose and apricot, and the streets are still empty and quiet. He walks close to the shore's edge, breathing in the clean, salty air and listening to the lapping of the waves as his feet sink into the sand, leaving deep imprints that are quickly filled by the inrushing tide. These early walks feed his spirit and refresh his mind, and he often finds that by the time he is ready to lace up his shoes and head back to the office, the stroll has worked its magic and provided the solution to a problem that has been exercising his mind.

On this particular morning, he is thinking about his new client. It's a strange case, and the more he thinks about it, the stranger it seems. He reflects on his own split-second decision to accept the brief, something none of his colleagues would have done in this situation, but his ability to trust his instincts and make swift decisions was honed during the War of Independence. As he recalls the war, his hand traces the ridge of the deep scar on his cheek, a souvenir of one of the skirmishes he led against the British while their Mandate was still in force.

His thoughts turn to the case he has taken on. If Isaiah Fleischmann has defamed Miklós Nagy, how come it's the government, and not Nagy himself, that has sued the pamphleteer? And this man Nagy. Amos doesn't know much about him apart from the article he read recently in *Ha'aretz*. According to the report, Nagy saved over a thousand Jews in Hungary during the war, and the government is grooming him for a ministry in the next elections.

Now that's something to conjure with: a government figure who was a wartime hero now being accused of collaborating with the Nazis, the most serious crime in Israel and the only one that incurs the death penalty. It sounds far-fetched, but Amos knows that in life the most unimaginable scenarios often turn out to be true. Besides, he believes he's a good judge of men. Isaiah might be a pompous crank with a bee in his bonnet, but he strikes him as sincere.

The more he thinks about this case, the more tantalising it becomes. He has a bloodhound's sense for the hidden secrets that men in power seek to conceal, and he doesn't trust the men running the country, especially the one with the bushy white hair who leads the government. To say he doesn't trust Ben-Gurion is an understatement: he loathes him and would do everything in his power to expose his duplicity. And now in this unlikely case, with its even more unlikely defendant, he glimpses a sliver of light shining through the apparently solid wall of government impregnability through which he might finally wreak revenge.

It's been a long-simmering hatred and, standing on the promenade, looking out to sea with seagulls wheeling and screeching overhead, the waves foaming the shore with lace-like patterns and the taste of the sea in his mouth, it all comes back to him as if it happened yesterday: the betrayal and the crime. And that memory ruins the serenity of his dawn stroll.

His thoughts turn to Eli, and the pain is as sharp and bitter as it was the day it happened, five years and one long lifetime ago. It was Eli who had joined the Irgun first and, as usual, Amos had been quick to follow in his older brother's footsteps. Eli was a firebrand searching for a cause, and this time the cause was just, and he couldn't wait to join. They would be part of the underground army, the Irgun, that would drive the British out of Palestine and set up an independent state of Israel.

Like their leader Menachem Begin, they believed that the provisional government had no vision and no courage. As long as those gutless men of the Jewish Agency were in power, they would go on negotiating and kowtowing to the British, and nothing would ever change. Two thousand years was too long to wait for the restoration of your homeland, but their land would never be free because their leaders were too pusillanimous to risk antagonising their British masters.

According to Eli, who knew much more about politics than Amos did, the British White Paper had swindled the Jews out of their homeland. What neither of them could forgive was that the British had made a pact with the Arabs to prevent Jewish survivors from migrating to Palestine, and they turned away ships bringing Jews who had managed to escape Nazi death camps. Prevented from landing, they perished at sea or were slaughtered when they returned to Nazi-occupied countries.

You can't blame the British, Eli used to say in his cynical way. After all, fifty million Arabs with oil wells were a better deal than a few Jews with nothing to offer but orange groves, patriotism, and an irritating sense of historical entitlement. But, he often added, our provisional government should have done more to expel the British and establish an independent Jewish state, instead of treating us as a Jewish outpost of Westminster.

Although he and Eli didn't join the Stern Gang, the extreme paramilitary group who sabotaged British military installations and blew up their military depots, they admired their audacious raids which succeeded against all odds. They were outraged that instead of siding with the young Jews fighting for independence and freedom, the provisional government denounced them as terrorists, and, like the loyal lackeys they were, they helped the British to capture, imprison and hang the ringleaders. The way Eli saw it, their leaders were actually collaborating with their oppressors.

When the British finally left Palestine, and the United Nations declared the independent state of Israel, Amos and his brother were overjoyed. They had been part of the group whose daring actions had helped to push the British out and that resulted in their nation's independence. To add to their triumph, Winston Churchill validated their struggle by acknowledging that it was really thanks to the actions of Irgun that the British were kicked out of Palestine. They had fought and won. After thousands of years, they had brought a Jewish nation into existence once more. They were on the right side of history, allied to the winning cause. No feeling in the world could equal that. He could still hear Eli's triumphant voice and feel the pressure of his fingers on his shoulder as he said, 'We did it, little brother!'

His brother's words still ringing in his ears, Amos gazes at the far horizon. Spotlit in the morning sun, a cargo ship is sailing along the Mediterranean coast towards Jaffa, and for a moment he imagines it's the vessel he watched that June day in 1948, the one his brother was on, bringing weapons and ammunition from France to help fight the War of Independence after the British left and to relieve the Irgun men in the siege of Jerusalem.

*

The *Altalena* was carrying around 900 young Jews from Europe, mostly Holocaust survivors, eager to defend the new nation from its neighbours — Lebanon, Trans-Jordan, Syria and Egypt — whose armies had attacked it the day after the United Nations voted it into existence. At that point, the fate of Jerusalem hung in the balance, and Irgun had arranged the purchase of the ship and obtained the weapons and ammunition to equip its men, who were facing annihilation.

Before he sailed for Marseille to help load the *Altalena*, Eli had scoffed at Amos's praise for the French who had agreed to supply the ship. 'Don't imagine for a minute they did it because they love the Jews,' he said. 'It's politics. France is furious that Britain usurped their colonial power in Syria and Lebanon, and sided with the Arabs against them, so they decided to help us as a slap in the face for Britain. See, where there's power there's always a hidden motive, something concealed or not revealed, an evasion, prevarication, or a downright lie. And behind everything, you'll find the ugly face of politics lurking in the shadows.' And Amos had listened, his eyes wide with admiration. How smart Eli was.

Amos remembers his excitement that hot June night when the *Altalena* came into view near the Tel Aviv shore. He rushed to the beach in the morning and found an eager crowd already gathered to watch the unloading of the vessel. Eli had told him that Menachem Begin, the head of Irgun, had made an agreement with Ben-Gurion, the head of the new government of Israel, that twenty per cent of the weapons and ammunition were to be allocated to the fighters of Irgun so that Jerusalem could be saved.

As he stood watching the cargo being unloaded, he noticed two corvettes moving towards the *Altalena*. They stopped a short distance away and he wondered why vessels from the Israeli navy had suddenly appeared on the scene. He supposed they'd come to protect the *Altalena*. Suddenly he heard a burst of fire. It seemed to come from somewhere on the beach. He turned, trying to figure out where the explosion had come from, then he heard a blast of heavy machine-gun fire. It was unbelievable, but there was no doubting its target: it was aimed at the *Altalena*.

If he hadn't seen it with his own eyes, he wouldn't have believed it. The gunfire came from the corvettes. There were shouts and screams from the crowd. People turned to each other in confusion at what they had just witnessed, debating what it could possibly mean. What was going on? Who could be responsible for such an outrageous action? Who had made such a shocking mistake? Heads would surely roll. But whose?

Amos stood there, frozen with shock. He watched as the *Altalena* started sailing towards the shore, but to his horror it was fired on again, and this time it returned fire. Boats crammed with passengers from the vessel were coming ashore, but suddenly gunfire exploded once again, and he heard himself yelling 'Stop! Can't you see, boats are coming ashore, the captain is on the bridge waving a white flag!' Everyone was shouting, cursing, protesting, lightbulbs were exploding as newspaper cameramen took photographs, and a reporter who had appeared on the scene was scribbling notes in shorthand to his right. But the firing from the shore continued. Amos couldn't swallow. His knuckles were white as he clutched the railing on the shore's edge. A rumour went around the crowd that it was Palmach, the military wing of the government, that was firing on the *Altalena*. A fellow standing beside him said he thought the commander was someone called Yitzak Rabin. It was unthinkable, incomprehensible, but it was happening before his eyes. He only had one thought: Eli. He wasn't on the boats that had landed on the Tel Aviv beach. Was he still on board?

But worse was to come. Smoke rose from the stricken ship, and someone shouted that a direct hit had caused a fire to break out in the cargo hold containing explosives. He could see men jumping off the vessel and starting to swim for the shore, but the firing continued as explosions erupted on board. Knowing Eli as he did, Amos was certain that he'd be one of the last to abandon ship, and he scanned the sea, squinting to catch sight of his brother, his eyes darting from one small figure in the water to another, searching for some familiar feature.

Eli was a good swimmer, he would definitely make it to shore. Any moment now he would emerge from the water. He could imagine how outraged his brother would be at the loss of the cargo that had been purchased at such great cost in the hope of relieving Jerusalem. Now the cargo that would have brought them victory was lost, and the holy city's fate was sealed.

As he stood there, flames rose from the stricken vessel, and he heard more explosions. There would be no-one left on board now. But where was Eli? Panic-stricken, he ran from one group to another, asking about him. Had he made it to shore further away? Had Amos missed him? He brushed past the reporter who wanted to know who he was looking for. A young woman with springy reddish hair and a white nurse's apron spattered with blood sat on the sand, her head in her hands, sobbing. 'The bastards,' she kept repeating. 'The bastards. Our own people and they fired on us.'

A cold dread took hold of him. She had come ashore on one of the boats. He had to know. 'Do you know Eli Alon? Do you know if he came on one of the boats or swam to shore?'

She looked at him as if she didn't understand what he was saying, and he had to restrain himself from shaking her, to make her understand. 'Eli,' he began, 'Eli Alon,' but before he could say any more, the look in her eyes silenced him.

She stared at him with tears flowing down her cheeks, and shook her head. He knew then he would never see his brother again.

He also knew that he would never forgive the treachery of those who had fired on the *Altalena*. Most of all, he would never forgive Ben-Gurion, with his bushy white hair and deceptively avuncular manner, the leader of the newly established Jewish nation, who had made the decision to fire on his fellow Jews. That day on the beach in Tel Aviv, Amos made a promise to his brother that no matter how long it took, one day he would avenge him.

*

The warmth of the risen sun has dissolved the delicate wisps of colour, and the sky is its usual cloudless blue. The blessed silence of dawn is shattered by car horns, shouts and arguments. Somewhere from the direction of Jaffa, a muezzin calls the faithful to prayer. It was going to be another hot and noisy day.

Walking back to his office, Amos quickens his pace. He senses that the strange case that has so fortuitously come his way will finally provide him with the opportunity for revenge that he has been waiting for.

CHAPTER TWENTY

Tel Aviv, 2005

Annika is studying the woman in front of her, trying to imagine this diminutive grey-haired grandmother as a teenage terrorist.

'But that's what I was, according to the British and our Haganah leaders,' Shula Stein says and laughs, throwing her head back so far that the wrinkles on her neck disappear. 'You should have seen me in those days. I was seventeen when I joined Irgun, and I couldn't wait to kick the British out of Palestine so we could set up our own homeland. Of course the boys in Irgun thought I was too young and too small to be any use, besides which I was just a girl, but when they saw that I could handle a gun, they started to take notice of me.' She pauses and her eyes soften with nostalgia. 'I remember it was a German Luger.'

Inside Shula's cramped little apartment, every surface is covered with photographs, sketches, piles of china plates, heaps of newspapers, silver ornaments, and tiny pots of cactus. Annika listens enthralled as the past comes to life in this woman's surprising story.

It was Dov who put her in touch with Shula. He called her the day after she had started reading the file on Amos Alon and the Miklós Nagy case in the Law Library. But before she could find out the lawyer's connection to Miklós Nagy, the librarian told her that as it was Friday afternoon, they were about to close and would remain closed the following day, so she would have to wait until Sunday to continue reading.

Frustrated at another delay, she decided to spend the day strolling around Neve Tzedek, which the guidebook described as a charming part of old Tel Aviv that had been gentrified in recent years. Charm was not a word she would have associated with this noisy beachside city with its modern buildings and busy thoroughfares, which struck her as functional rather than aesthetic, so she was curious to explore an area that retained its original character.

She strolled along shady tree-lined streets, past studios and boutiques where artists, jewellers and fashion designers displayed quirky designs, and little galleries exhibited avant-garde paintings, statues and installations. The forecourt of the building that housed the dance company was decorated with brightly coloured parasols hanging upside down, and its walls were covered in murals depicting Israel's history. The whole area had a bohemian atmosphere. A touch of Paddington in Tel Aviv.

At Ronit's café on Shabhazi Street, she ordered stuffed zucchini and minced lamb with dried figs and apricots, and chatted with the owner, who wanted to know where she came from, how long she planned to stay, and what she thought of Tel Aviv. From her table on the upstairs verandah she looked down at a busker in torn jeans strumming Spanish tunes on his guitar; a large tabby draped over one shoulder like a striped shawl challenged passers-by with its unblinking green gaze.

Lunch over, Annika stopped beside the unusual duo, patted the cat and asked its name. 'Shnorer,' the busker said. She flicked through her Hebrew-English dictionary and burst out laughing. It meant bludger.

'That's an amazing cat,' she said, and put a few shekels into the cap on the pavement.

'That's nothing. You should hear him play the guitar,' the busker retorted.

Still smiling, Annika strolled along the street, peering into the boutiques and galleries. Looking up, she saw a woman with hair the colour of fairy-floss tied with a big green bow arranging six rag dolls in various ballet poses on the railing of her tiny wrought-iron balcony. Catching Annika's eye, the woman waved. 'Come up! I won't bite! Just have a look!'

At the top of a steep, narrow staircase, Annika stood in an atelier covered from floor to ceiling with rag dolls in tutus, caftans and angel wings, dolls lying on tables, propped against walls, and sitting on shelves. 'I sell them to toy shops and puppet and marionette shows,' the woman said. 'Sometimes people walking past buy them for their kids. You got kids? No? So maybe you want to buy one for someone else's children?'

'I might buy one for myself,' Annika said, and selected a miniature doll in a meringue-like Cinderella ball gown. 'That's me, waiting for Prince Charming.'

The woman tilted her head to one side, so that the bow brushed her shoulder, and gave her a slow, penetrating look. 'Maybe you met him already and you don't know it. It happens.'

Annika looked up and read the sign on the wall advertising 'Tamar's Tarot readings'. So the doll-maker was also a clairvoyant, but this time her prediction was way off the mark. 'I don't think so,' she laughed. 'No Prince Charming in my life.'

From the way Tamar was studying her, it looked as if she was keen to probe further into her love life, so Annika decided to change the subject.

'This area is very different from the rest of Tel Aviv,' she said.

'You should have seen Neve Tzedek years ago, before they tore the old buildings down or fixed them up. My God, what a dump. Back then, no-one wanted to live here, and now no-one can afford to.'

It was while she was waiting for Tamar to wrap the doll, that Dov called. 'You wanted to know about the *Altalena*,' he said. 'Would you like to meet an activist who was on board?'

That's why at four o'clock that afternoon she is sitting inside Shula Stein's apartment in Ben Yehuda Boulevard. Before she can sit down, Shula bustles around clearing away piles of magazines and books from the settee, apologising for the mess. 'Housekeeping isn't my forte,' she says. 'Life's too short to dust furniture.'

Although Annika protests that she isn't hungry, Shula insists on cutting her a slab of honey cake, demurring that she isn't good at baking either. Having swallowed a mouthful, Annika suspects that Shula forgot to add the honey.

After a polite attempt to eat it, she turns it into crumbs and pushes them around on the plate.

Shula isn't offended. 'I told you I couldn't bake,' she says cheerfully. Despite her age, which Annika calculates must be around seventy-six, she moves with the energy of a much younger woman. 'I want to show you something,' she says and, jumping up, takes a framed black-and-white photograph from the walnut sideboard.

It's a photo of a young girl with springy hair and a wide smile, dressed in white. 'That's me at seventeen,' Shula says proudly. 'In my nurse's uniform.'

Annika looks puzzled. 'I thought you were a fighter.'

Shula laughs again, clearly relishing this opportunity to talk about her past. 'I was nurse and fighter. Have you heard about the bombing of the King David Hotel in Jerusalem?'

Annika nods. She remembers reading about a gang of terrorists who blew up the hotel, killing British officers. Now that she thinks about it, perhaps she saw it in an old movie with Paul Newman.

'I took part in that bombing,' Shula says. Her tone is matter-of-fact, but she can't suppress a note of pride.

Annika stares. So she really was a terrorist. What a story this would make for one of the Australian newspapers, an encounter with a former terrorist. She wishes she had her tape recorder. 'I'd love to hear about it,' she says.

Shula doesn't need persuading. Sitting on the edge of her chair, she says, 'It happened on July 22, in 1946. Irgun, the group I joined, made an incredibly daring plan to destroy the records the British kept in their headquarters in the hotel. They used those records to round our people up, but the trouble was, the hotel was practically impregnable.'

'You were very young,' Annika breaks in. 'What did your parents think of you joining an underground military group?'

'My parents practically disowned me as soon as they heard I'd joined Irgun. They were horrified, they threatened and cajoled, but nothing they said made me change my mind.' She pauses. 'What's the word to describe something you know you have to do in life?'

'A mission?'

'That's it, a mission. I felt it was my mission to do whatever I could to kick the British out. Anyway, this is what we did: ten of our men disguised as African servants carried big milk cans on their shoulders into the kitchen, but there wasn't any milk inside, only explosives with a time fuse. I was the one that brought the bombs and ammunition and transferred the TNT into those milk churns. Anyway, when the British soldiers saw them, they got suspicious but luckily our guys managed to escape. Of course the milk churns got left behind with the explosives inside them.

'Now, here's something you probably never heard. Our leaders phoned British headquarters three times to warn them ahead about the explosion. The first warning said, *Your hotel is mined and will be blown up in twenty minutes. Evacuate the building.* There were three warning calls. I bet you never heard about that. Hardly anyone did.'

'Why not?'

'Because the Chief Colonial Secretary got on his high horse when he heard about the warning calls. He said: "I'm here to give the bloody Jews orders, not to take them." He ordered his men to stay inside British headquarters and forbade anyone to leave, but luckily some officers did slip out. At exactly 12.30, twenty minutes after the first warning, the hotel blew apart like a house of cards. Ninety people were killed and dozens were injured, but we succeeded: those records were destroyed. Naturally the British condemned us as ruthless terrorists, but their Colonial Secretary never reported our warnings, or his arrogant response which caused the unnecessary deaths of all those officers.'

She falls silent and Annika's mind is in too much turmoil to speak. It's impossible to blot out the fact that this likeable old woman took part in a terrorist act, warnings or no warnings.

'How did you feel when you found out that so many British officers had died because of what you did?' she asks.

'How did I feel? We were all elated. Listen, we were like David when he overcame Goliath. Of course I was sorry for the men who died, we never meant that to happen, that's why we warned them ahead, but don't forget, this was a struggle for independence. The British were against us, they oppressed us, sided with the Arabs and caused the deaths of so many of our people when they turned away our boats during the Holocaust.'

Shula sighs and looks down at her hands, which are veined and covered in brown spots, and Annika notices that her nails are short and unpainted. So different from her grandmother's beautifully manicured and scarlet-polished nails.

This woman's turbulent and idealistic youth, and her lack of concern with appearances, were such a contrast with Marika's superficial values. She can imagine her grandmother shuddering at Shula's messy apartment, her lipstick-free face, and terrorist past.

'Have you heard the proverb about winning the battle and losing the war?' Shula asks. 'Well, even though Irgun won a victory in the King David Hotel, we lost the support of the other Israeli group, Haganah. They repudiated us, and treated us like enemies even though we succeeded where they had failed. They even turned our fighters over to the British. But what happened two years later was even worse. It was horrible. Unimaginable.'

Annika looks up. 'The *Altalena*. How did you come to be involved in that?'

'I'll tell you all about it but first let's have some tea.' Shula bustles about in her tiny kitchen and Annika hears dishes clattering, pots banging, a series of drawers slamming, and a kettle whistling. A few minutes later Shula comes back with unmatched mugs of steaming black tea. She sits back, both hands around her mug.

'It feels as if it happened yesterday, but at the same time, it's as if it happened in another lifetime, to someone else. Did you know that the *Altalena* was a troop and cargo carrier that had taken part in the D-Day invasion? It was due to arrive in Tel Aviv but it anchored off the coast of Kfar Vitkin instead. At the time, we couldn't understand why its destination had changed, but it turned out that Ben-Gurion had given that order.'

She pauses for dramatic effect. 'Later we discovered that it was a trap. Anyway, the passengers disembarked, and I boarded the ship, along with other Irgun members, to help with the unloading. But we'd only unloaded part of the weapons and ammunition when we were fired on without any warning. The captain decided to sail out to the open sea but before he could get very far, two navy corvettes fired on the *Altalena* with heavy machine guns.

'You can't imagine the confusion and shock we felt. No-one could understand what was going on, why Israeli guns were firing on a ship that was bringing guns and ammunition to supply the army at a time of war. But I didn't have time to think about it. I had my hands full trying to help the wounded. Beside me, one of our guys fell onto the deck. Blood was spurting from an artery in his neck, and the poor fellow died before I could stop the bleeding. I was running from one injured fighter to another trying to give them first aid, but five of our comrades died.

'After I got off the ship with the wounded men, the captain managed to get the ship to Tel Aviv but here's something you won't believe. In the morning, the commander, who later became our prime minister, shelled the *Altalena* even though the captain had hoisted a white flag on the bridge. But when a fire broke out on board, knowing how flammable the cargo was, he ordered everyone to abandon ship.

'Our commander, Menachem Begin, was the last to leave. I read a report by the captain a few years later saying that Begin had refused to leave and that he'd had to physically throw him overboard, but I think that might have been an exaggeration.'

Annika is breathless, enthralled by Shula's vivid recollection. She can practically see the events unfolding as she speaks.

'I'll never forget standing on the shore, watching men jumping off the ship and swimming to shore while the firing continued. Suddenly flames leaped up from the *Altalena* and a few seconds later, we heard a series of explosions and the ship blew up and sank, leaving thick black smoke hanging over the sea. I just stood there, tears pouring down my face, not just for the men, the ship and its precious cargo, but for all of us.

'All my illusions about Jewish solidarity and Israeli ideals sank with the *Altalena*. How could Jews fire on fellow-Jews, especially after all that happened during the Holocaust?'

Shula stops talking and stares into the distance, and her eyes swell with tears.

Annika is shaking her head. 'Why did they do that? It doesn't make sense.'

'Ben-Gurion and his cronies were paranoid. They were afraid that with those weapons Irgun would have too much power, so he chose to destroy our ship and blow it up, together with all the arms and ammunition, rather than risk a threat to his government.'

Annika sighs. 'That's terrible. What a traumatic experience. And you were so young.'

Shula is smiling. 'Well, one good thing came out of it. Because of this tragedy, I met the man I married.'

Annika sits forward, eager to hear a love story with a happy ending.

'I was sitting on the sand still in my white nurse's apron, crying my eyes out, when this guy came over and asked if I knew his brother. That was the man I tried to save when he bled to death on board the *Altalena*.'

'Are you still married?'

Shula shakes her head. 'We divorced a long time ago. After the shelling of the *Altalena*, we were all bitter and angry, but my husband became so obsessed with the incident and his brother's death that he couldn't talk about anything else.

It was eating him up, and poisoning our life together. And when he took on that case, he was like a man possessed. That's when I knew I couldn't spend the rest of my life with him. He won the court case but he lost me.'

'The court case?'

'It happened a very long time ago. Amos took on the libel suit against the guy who accused Miklós Nagy of collaboration.'

CHAPTER TWENTY-ONE

Tel Aviv, 2005

Back at the hotel that evening, Annika stands on her balcony and looks forlornly at the beach. The sun has begun to set, and the fiery brilliance of its rays casts a blood-red glow over the sand. A moment later it drops behind the sea and the beach is plunged into darkness. Inside the room, she flops down on the armchair, flicks through a magazine, then gets up again. She is unsettled by Shula's story of betrayal, but most of all she is shocked by her statement that Miklós Nagy was accused of collaboration. How could that be possible? That a man who saved so many people could have been called a collaborator seemed improbable. It was absurd. She is so deep in thought that she starts when her phone rings. It's Jancsi.

'Annika. I miss you. Tell me about Israel. Did you find something about Nagy Miklós?'

For a few moments, the affection in his voice, and the seductive way he says her name, reels her back into the warmth of their last day together, but when she tries to sum up her time in Tel Aviv, Budapest seems very far away, and the distance between them can no longer be measured in kilometres.

'All I know so far is that in some way he was responsible for the fall of the government here. The incredible thing is that some people even regarded him as a collaborator. Anyway I'm going to read a document that might clarify that. If I find anything interesting, I'll let you know.'

'I'm sure you will,' he says. 'You are good journalist but hit and run woman.'

She is still smiling as she hangs up and flops into an armchair. It's time to figure out how much longer she will stay in Israel. Shula's story has aroused her interest in Amos Alon and she plans to return to the Law Library when it reopens on Sunday to read the file, but after that, there is nothing to keep her here, and that realisation unsettles her. The goal she has been seeking has eluded her. Something is missing, something doesn't feel complete, but she is at a loss to know what it is.

It's going to be a long evening, and she doesn't want to spend it alone. She thinks about going for an espresso and some light-hearted banter at Ari's café, but on the spur of the moment, she decides to call Dov instead. Even though he often challenges her, she feels drawn to him. As she dials his number, she hopes he has time for a quick drink.

An hour later, she is sitting in the hotel bar, sipping a Yarden chardonnay and repeatedly glancing at her watch because Dov is late. Typical journo. No sense of time. It occurs to her that she has no idea whether he is single or married, or in a relationship with a man or a woman, but if she disturbed some domestic arrangement when she called him, he didn't mention it. In fact, now that she thinks about it, he sounded eager to join her.

The bar is brightly lit, and bottles of brandy, whisky and multicoloured liqueurs are displayed on shelves behind the marble counter. It is crowded with guests from many nations, and in the conversations all around her, she can make out French, German, Russian and Hungarian.

At the counter, a red-faced English guy keeps insisting in a slurred voice that he only wants the double malt whisky that he drank in Tobermory, and the exasperated bartender throws up his hands and asks if he is expected to fly to Scotland to get it for him. The English tourist pulls back his fist and it looks as if a fight will ensue before his two companions drag him away.

Annika has just ordered another white wine when she sees Dov's curly salt-and-pepper hair above the crowd. She had forgotten how tall he is. As soon as he drops into the chair facing her, he orders a Campari and soda. 'In a short glass, with a twist of orange,' he tells the waiter.

'You're obviously a man who knows what he wants,' she says, and knows she sounds provocative.

He studies her and hesitates, but if he meant to respond to her flirtatious comment he changes his mind, and after a moment he says, 'Sorry I'm late, I had to interview some politicians about a corruption scandal.'

The waiter brings his Campari, and he takes a few sips before asking, 'What did you think of Shula Stein?'

'Amazing woman. I really liked her. What a story. How do you know her?'

'We interviewed her a few years ago, on the fiftieth anniversary of the *Altalena* incident.' He chuckles. 'You should have seen the mountains of hate mail we got after we ran that story. Someone even sent me a piece of dogshit in an envelope. You'd think we were glorifying Hitler, even though we tried to balance her story with an interview with one of the IDF soldiers who fired on the ship.'

Annika thinks back to Shula's emotional account of the incident and her tear-stained face. 'That was shocking,' she says. 'Why did they fire on their own people and destroy that ship? After all, those Irgun people were bringing weapons for the Israeli soldiers, weren't they?'

Dov lets out a long sigh. 'We could be here for days discussing this and still not come to any conclusion, like hundreds of thousands of people before us. This is a tiny country with huge issues, and this one is bigger, more complex, and more contentious than most. If you're an Israeli, how you look at it depends on your political affiliation, whether you are Zionist, socialist, communist, capitalist or anarchist, left-wing pacifist, right-wing chauvinist, atheist or ultra-orthodox.'

'And if you're a moderate outsider like me who just wants the facts?'

He shrugs. 'Have you heard Pontius Pilate's response when he was asked for the truth? He washed his hands of it, and he was right. By the time you hear both versions of the facts, you will end up completely confused and feel like tearing your hair out trying to figure out who's right and who's wrong. But okay, here we go. You've heard Shula's side of things, so in the interests of fair play, I'll be the devil's advocate and give you the other version.'

He drains his Campari and orders another one. 'Another glass of wine?' he asks.

'From what you just said, I think I'd better keep a clear head.'

'You have to understand that this was a new nation, barely a month old, in fact, and it was already fighting for its survival...'

'But isn't that exactly why it needed the weapons?'

This time when he holds his hand up, she looks at it attentively, and is pleased that there's no wedding ring.

'Wait, it's not so simple. I'll try to explain. The new nation had a new prime minister, Ben-Gurion, who was the head of the new government of Israel. His army, the Israel Defence Force, was formed from the Haganah, the paramilitary organisation formed during the British Mandate. Are you with me so far?'

Annika nods. 'I think so.'

'So we have a new government and a new prime minister, and a national army, the Israel Defence Force, fighting the combined Arab armies of several neighbouring countries that have attacked Israel as soon as it declared its independence. Fighting alongside the IDF at this point is a splinter group, Irgun. Now, as you probably know from Shula, the methods of this group are very different from the methods of Haganah. Before independence, Irgun was a violent underground militia whose activities were denounced by the moderates. But they joined forces with the national army, the IDF, to fight their common enemy. So far so good, right?'

He glances at her to make sure she is following.

'But here's where things start going pear-shaped. The United Nations in its wisdom hasn't included Jerusalem in the map of the new nation, and Jerusalem is besieged by Arab armies. It's being defended by Irgun fighters who are desperate to save it, and are desperately short of weapons and ammunition. So their leader, an individual called Menachem Begin, organises the purchase of a ship in France, loads it up with all sorts of weapons and ammunition, fills it with about a thousand young Holocaust survivors keen to fight for the new Jewish state, and heads for Israel.

'Now here comes the controversial part. Watching this with worried eyes is the new prime minister, Ben-Gurion. He can see trouble brewing. For himself, for his government, for Israel's army and for the country's future. For one thing, a truce has just been announced, so bringing in weapons will be a violation. Not only that, if he allows this ship to land with its cargo, it will arm the Irgun and that will threaten his government, his position, and form another army. Can any nation countenance the existence of two rival armed forces?

'He is convinced that Irgun will start a mutiny against the government and he regards the *Altalena* as an attempt to kill the new state. I've read a report where he said that the moment our army and our state surrender to another armed force, we are finished. He foresees that if Irgun keep the weapons, Israel will become an unstable country of rival militias, like some of our neighbours are today. Whatever happens, no matter what the cost, he cannot permit this vessel to land and arm his rival and destabilise the new nation. So, with a heavy heart, he makes the most difficult decision of his life, one that will split families and will see him vilified to this day by those who opposed his action.'

There's a crash behind them and they turn to see what has happened. One of the English guys has fallen off his stool, erupting in a blast of four-letter words, then riotous laughter. Dov waits until things calm down. 'Well? Now you know both sides. Who was right?'

'What do you think?' she asks.

'You're avoiding my question. It's not so clear-cut now, is it? Personally, I think it was the wrong decision, but I can understand why he took it. In the end, it not only split families and friends, it split the entire country and left many people bitter and disillusioned with politics and politicians. I suppose it showed that we're like other countries with our share of power-hungry politicians and cynical voters. You could even say that the ghost of the *Altalena* still haunts Israel to this day.'

He leans forward and is looking at Annika so intently she feels the blood rushing to her cheeks and almost loses the thread of the conversation. 'What makes you say that?' she asks.

'In a way it was responsible for the case that Amos Alon took on, which ended in disaster for the government, and tragedy for Miklós Nagy. And even now — have you heard that Ariel Sharon, our present prime minister, has removed Jewish settlers forcibly from Gaza and left it to the Palestinians? Well, both his supporters and his opponents have used the *Altalena* incident to either justify or condemn what he did. That's the impact Ben-Gurion's decision has had. But if he hadn't prevailed, Israel might have splintered into ungovernable militias and descended into civil war.'

'He and Begin must have hated each other's guts,' Annika says.

Dov smiles. 'You'd think so, but Begin eventually gave his support to Ben-Gurion, and later he himself became our prime minister. So now you've heard the simplified version of this complex and controversial issue.'

He is still looking at her, and she feels confused, wondering if she is misreading his gaze. He checks his watch, wipes his mouth, places his empty glass on the table, and asks the waitress for the check.

'I have to go and pick up my daughter from a party. Yael is fifteen and thinks it's not cool for her father to collect her, so the controversy over the *Altalena* is nothing compared to the conflict in my home.'

Annika laughs. She watches him walk away, sorry to see him go. The way he looked at her was tantalising and she would have liked to continue the conversation to see if he would reveal what was behind that gaze. She is never sure whether he is mocking or challenging her, but she would have liked to spend more time with him. Although it's past midnight, her mind is too active to sleep.

Standing by the window in her room, she hears the relentless beat of disco music emanating from the nightclubs, its pulsating rhythm carrying across the water. The full moon is silvering the tips of the white-foamed waves that roll onto the darkened beach, and she thinks about the *Altalena*. People, not politics, are where her interest usually lies, but she is fascinated by the connections that she has uncovered between the small memorial she noticed on the promenade, the history of Israel, and, indirectly, the Miklós Nagy saga.

What intrigues her most, however, is the surprising frisson she feels whenever Dov's eyes meet hers.

*

After spending Saturday at the beach, Annika is impatient to get on with her research and on Sunday morning she is already at the Law Library. When she asks for the Amos Alon file, the archivist gives her a puzzled look.

'So you are writing a book about him?' he asks. Before she has time to reply, he adds, 'Because if you are, you should read the transcript of the Nagy trial. My father once told me that in the fifties the trial was the best show in town.'

He returns several minutes later, hands her a disk, and points to a computer on a small wooden desk by the window. 'You are lucky, we have just digitised it. You wouldn't believe it, but the original was handwritten by the judge.'

Her hands are shaking as she inserts the disc. Perhaps this will finally give her the answers she has been looking for.

CHAPTER TWENTY-TWO

Tel Aviv, 1953

As Miklós Nagy begins to read the mimeographed pamphlet that Ora, the minister's secretary, has placed on his desk, he wonders why she is still standing there, waiting for his reaction. The day is coming to an end and, eager to leave the office and get home to see the boys, his eye skims over the page, but after the first few sentences, he goes back to the beginning, frowning and shaking his head as he reads. *I have waited a long time to expose this so-called hero who is really a Nazi collaborator*, the pamphlet says. *He rescued his own relatives at the cost of hundreds of thousands of Jewish lives, and saved one of his Nazi cronies from being charged with war crimes in Nuremberg.*

A Nazi collaborator. Who is the writer referring to? A moment later he realises that he is the target of this diatribe. It would be laughable if it wasn't so outrageous. Everyone in the government knows how he achieved an almost impossible feat during the Holocaust in Hungary when he risked his life to save over fifteen hundred Jews. So why is the minister wasting his time showing him scurrilous rubbish written by some crank with a mental problem? He scrunches up the sheet, and tosses it into the wastepaper basket under his desk. As an official spokesman for the Ministry of Rationing and Supply, he is used to receiving letters from angry constituents complaining about the cost of living, the shortage of accommodation, or the venality of some clerk or other, and he isn't going to waste time on the rantings of some lunatic.

'You must be furious,' Ora says. 'Everyone in our office is jumping up and down. How dare he write such outrageous stuff after all you've done? The minister is shocked that anyone would write such garbage.' She is still waiting for his response.

He shrugs. 'That's exactly what it is, garbage. So why are they bothering with it?'

'The minister said he'd like to see you in his office tomorrow morning,' she says, side-stepping the question. She's stout, with heavy legs, but she's pretty, with the smooth, unlined face he has observed in many plump women.

She's single, and he can tell by her lingering glances and the excuses she makes to come into his office that if he suggested a rendezvous, she would jump at the chance of an affair, but his philandering days are long over. He is a family man now, with a loyal wife and two high-spirited little boys he adores.

He glances at his watch. Judit is giving a concert this evening, and he doesn't want to be late. As he walks briskly from the office, he passes the white Bauhaus buildings that are a remnant of Tel Aviv's pre-war architecture, and crosses the road in front of the town hall where the country's independence was proclaimed only five years before.

As he walks, he reflects on his own life during the past few years. Everything has fallen into place in ways he never expected. In 1946, a few months after their arrival in Tel Aviv, Judit gave birth to a boy they called Binyomin after her father, and a year later, they had another son, Gil. The ruling Mapai party, which had evolved from the Jewish Agency, knew all about his rescue of a trainload of Hungarian Jews, and his reputation smoothed the path for them both. It helped him secure a small but well-located flat near Dizengoff Street, and an administrative position in the Ministry. He had bought a piano for Judit from a family whose daughter had given up playing, and she had found a childless neighbour who was happy to help with the children, so she could resume her musical career in a city whose newly arrived European survivors were hungry for the culture they had enjoyed in their homelands.

Since then, his career has advanced as well. He has just been promoted to spokesman in the Ministry, and he has heard rumours that Moshe Sharett, the prime minister, has his eye on him, that he is destined for the Foreign Ministry in the parliament of a country with which he feels an almost biblical bond. During his teenage years in Hungary he had come under the spell of Zionism, and the fulfilment of his dream of settling in the Promised Land hasn't disappointed him. From the first moment he felt at home here, despite the stifling summer heat of the parching Hamsin that blew in from the desert, despite the war, the tension and the conflicts. Or, he admitted to himself as he turned into their street, perhaps it was on account of these factors.

After surviving on a knife edge in Hungary, living by his wits, an uneventful existence in a peaceful country would probably have been an anticlimax.

So far, everything in his life has worked out better than he expected, and his decisions have been vindicated. With one exception: Ilonka. Whenever her name comes into his mind, his triumphs turn to ashes. He tries to avoid thinking about her, tries to suppress the memories, but now that she has invaded his thoughts again, the ache returns. He sighs and quickens his step, but no matter how fast he strides, the memory of that last reproachful expression in her dark eyes, and the terrible words she uttered at the railway station in St Margarethen claw at his mind. They are words he will never forget. He still longs for her caresses, for the feel of her yielding body pressed against him, and for her strength and her love. He knows this longing will last for the rest of his life.

For the past five years he has tried to find her, to explain why he couldn't bring himself to abandon Judit, who was unexpectedly pregnant with his child. But Ilonka disappeared, and his efforts to trace her have been futile. Desperate to find out what had become of her, he approached various Jewish agencies in Europe and the United States, but drew a blank each time. It was as though she had vanished off the face of the earth so that he would never find her.

He felt bitter at the way she had erased him from her life without giving him the opportunity to explain. But even if he had the chance, how could he possibly explain Judit's pregnancy in a way she could understand? He had been motivated by honour and responsibility, but she had placed hurt pride before love. Gábor, too, had vanished, and he supposed that, wherever they were, they had resumed married life.

Judit's recital that evening consists of Hungarian melodies by Kodály and Bartók, and a sonata by Liszt. The crowded hall bursts into enthusiastic applause as the tiny pianist walks onto the stage, and he feels a surge of pride looking at his wife's dreamy expression as her agile fingers run up and down the keyboard almost too fast for his eyes to follow.

In the pause between the pieces, his mind turns to the pamphlet that Ora brought him. He would like to dismiss it as mischievous nonsense, but it nags at him like an aching tooth, impossible to ignore. He would like to confront the malicious writer and demand to be told how he dared to publish such malicious accusations, but he knows that these rantings on smudged bits of paper don't merit his attention. Still, his pride is injured. Why did that man, whoever he is, attack him like this, even if his accusations are lies that no-one in their right mind would believe?

The concert is over, the applause finally dies down, and he wraps a warm coat around Judit's thin shoulders as they walk home along Dizengoff Street, discussing her performance. There are plans to build a large modern concert hall, and she is looking forward to playing there when it opens. She is on a high, as she usually is after a performance, and as she slips her hand into his, he marvels that these small hands have the strength to play such powerful music, and the sensitivity to evoke such nuances of feeling.

From the moment he held her on the train station and stroked her swelling belly, he noticed that she looked at him more tenderly, more attentively, than before. Perhaps it was due to her pregnancy, but sometimes he wonders if it was on account of his affair with Ilonka. Although it had never been mentioned by either of them, he suspected that she knew everything and was relieved that he had given up Ilonka for her. Some things don't need to be articulated to be understood.

The boys are asleep when they come home, and as they creep into their room to cover them up and kiss their flushed little faces, Miklós knows that, all things considered, he is a very fortunate man.

That night, he dreams he is trudging up a mountainside. Even in his sleep, he knows he is dreaming. He recognises this dream. It's the one that tormented him for so many nights in Budapest in 1944 when he was weighed down by the responsibility he had assumed for saving those lives. In his dream, he has almost reached the summit, but when he looks up, there's a man standing there, and he's wearing an SS uniform. It's Adolf Eichmann, and his mocking laughter resounds all over the mountain.

Miklós wakes with a start, and although it's a cold night, he is drenched with sweat. It's a long time since he has thought about his terrifying encounters with Eichmann in his headquarters on Swabian Hill. Thank God those times are over, he thinks. From the pale light that shines through the thin curtain, he can see that day is breaking. It's too early to rise, but he knows he is too churned up to sleep. For a long time he stands at the door of the room that the boys share. They are still asleep, and he tiptoes out, dresses quietly not to wake Judit, brews some coffee, and reads the morning paper until it's time to go to the office.

Later that morning, Ora ushers him into the minister's rooms, which are sparsely furnished, but decorated with black-and-white photographs of old Tel Aviv. Miklós knows that they were taken by the minister's son, who was killed during the War of Independence.

Shlomo Segal is a snappy dresser who distinguishes himself by wearing a tweed jacket and a tie twisted into a Windsor knot to work, while everyone else wears open-neck short-sleeved shirts, even the prime minister. He knows he is laughed at behind his back for his formal English sartorial style, and that he is sarcastically referred to as Sir Shlomo. He is an expansive character who usually greets Miklós with a joke or an amusing anecdote, but this time he has an unusually sombre expression, and launches into the subject of their meeting without any preamble.

'You read that pamphlet?' he asks.

Miklós makes a deprecatory movement with his hands. 'Ridiculous stuff written by some deranged crank.'

The minister doesn't reply and the silence that follows unnerves him. 'Surely you're not taking it seriously?'

'*He* doesn't like it.' Shlomo inclines his head upwards, to indicate that he is referring to the head of the Department of Justice on the next floor.

'He can't possibly read every scurrilous note that someone writes. How come he's bothering with this one?'

'He thinks this one can't go unchallenged.'

Miklós looks at the minister. He can't find the words to express the emotions that are whirling around his head. 'So what does our attorney-general want to do?' he asks finally. 'Take some *nebisch* loser to court for writing nonsense?' He is joking, but Shlomo isn't laughing.

'As a matter of fact, that's exactly what he intends to do.'

'You can't be serious! No-one takes any notice of what this scribbler writes. People throw his pamphlets in the rubbish bin. I don't think anyone apart from this office has even bothered reading this one, but suing him implies that what he writes has some validity. We should just ignore it.'

Shlomo lets him finish. 'You're probably right,' he says, 'but that's not going to happen.'

'Do you have any idea why on earth he wants to sue him?'

'He is convinced that we have to fight back. He says a slur on you is a slur on the government because you are involved with the government, and the accusation is so serious. As you know, wartime collaboration is the only crime in Israel that merits the death sentence.'

'Well, I'm certainly not going to bother suing him,' Miklós says.

'You don't have to. The government of Israel is going to do that on your behalf.'

Miklós returns to his office in such turmoil that he can't settle down. He paces up and down the small room, seething. He is convinced of the folly of this decision, and feels frustrated by his powerlessness to prevent legal action in a matter that concerns him. There's no question that the government will win the case, because this diatribe is just malicious fiction, but won't people wonder why they took the trouble to pursue it? Can't the attorney-general see that taking this guy to court will only give him a legitimacy he doesn't deserve? Until now no-one has taken him seriously. Even though the scribbler will lose the case, Miklós feels insulted at the implication that there is something in this accusation against him that needs to be proved wrong, that he needs to be defended.

He is shuffling papers on his desk, brooding, when Ora knocks on his door. 'The minister wants to let you know that the attorney-general's associate will be the prosecutor in the Isaiah Fleischmann case.'

Miklós quails at the prospect of the publicity the case will attract, and wonders if the pamphleteer will manage to find anyone to defend him.

CHAPTER TWENTY-THREE

Jerusalem, January 1954

When Miklós Nagy arrives at the Jerusalem District Court, he is surprised at the size of the crowd clamouring to enter the nondescript sandstone building in the city's Christian Quarter. As soon as he sees the courtroom, however, it becomes obvious that most of the people won't be admitted; the chamber is far too small to accommodate more than half of them. He supposes that the prosecution chose this unimpressive venue anticipating that the trial would not last long. He takes his seat at the front, beside the prosecutor, and turns to look at the long wooden benches where people are trying to get comfortable on the hard seats with the narrow timber slats across the back. Unlike most courtrooms he has seen, this one has no jury box. It appears there will be no jury in this case, only a judge.

It's morning, and shafts of Jerusalem's golden light slant into the courtroom from the tall French windows on the left. If he were religious, he'd be tempted to assume that these beams came straight from God. The windows are the only attractive feature in an otherwise austere room. The two large ceiling fans are still: it's a cold winter's day. As they wait for the judge to enter, he hears the evocative tinkling of bells from the nearby monastery, calling the Russian Orthodox monks to prayer, and he realises that they are not far from the Church of the Holy Sepulchre which contains the tomb where Christ was buried and the site where he was crucified.

They all rise as the judge enters, a distinguished presence in a black robe that accentuates the whiteness of his smoothly combed hair and the pinkness of his complexion. With precise movements, Judge Yaron Lazar places a sheaf of writing paper and a bottle of ink in front of him. Miklós turns to Noah Elman, the attorney-general's associate, to ask where the stenographer is.

'Hebrew is a new language for court procedure and they're having trouble finding stenographers who know it well enough to take down legal proceedings accurately,' Elman whispers back. 'That's why the judge will have to take down the questions and answers himself. That won't sweeten his temper, but at least he won't have to do it for long.'

Miklós nods. Everyone knows that this trial will be over in a couple of days. He supposes that's why the Justice Department has appointed Noah Elman, a junior member of the attorney-general's office, to conduct the case for the prosecution.

As Elman begins to read out the charge against Isaiah Fleischmann, Miklós looks at the short, skinny man in a shabby jacket and a limp white shirt with a worn collar, who stands very straight as he hears the charge against him. He expects the defendant to look nervous or worried, but Isaiah Fleischmann seems composed, almost defiant, and surprisingly self-assured.

The way he's looking straight at the judge, you'd think he was here to receive a reward, not suffer the legal consequences of his malice. His attitude irritates Miklós but he is determined not to let this *nudnik* get under his skin.

The defendant whispers something to his lawyer and Miklós takes his first look at the man who has the unenviable task of trying to defend the pamphleteer. It's Amos Alon's stillness that strikes him most forcibly, his air of alert watchfulness, and the incisiveness of his gaze. He doesn't look like a man who has taken on a hopeless case. But as Miklós knows, a courtroom is really theatre, and he supposes that over the years the lawyer has become adept at playing a starring role in the drama. Whether he believes in it or not is irrelevant.

The young prosecutor, whose voice wavers as he reads out the basis on which the State of Israel is suing Isaiah Fleischmann, seems overcome by the occasion. He alleges that the defendant criminally libelled Miklós Nagy by falsely claiming that during the Holocaust in Hungary in the year 1944, he collaborated with Nazis, caused the deaths of hundreds of thousands of Hungarian Jews, and was responsible for the acquittal of a Nazi war criminal. Having stated the case for the prosecution, Elman breathes out as he sits down. Miklós notices that his hands are shaking.

Although Miklós has read a copy of Fleischmann's pamphlet, hearing his accusations read out in public shocks him. They make it sound as if, instead of rescuing over fifteen hundred Jews, he was personally responsible for the murder of half a million. He clenches his fists and feels his heart pounding. Take a deep breath, stay calm, he tells himself.

He is relieved when he is the first to be called to the witness stand. He has brought his worn leather briefcase which is bulging with reports, letters, documents, memos, cables and press clippings to support his statements. After each exhibit has been entered and labelled, the questioning begins.

Prompted by Elman's deferential tone, he details his activities in Hungary, before the German occupation. He describes how he became prominent in the Jewish community in Budapest, and organised help for the refugees from Slovakia, Poland and Ukraine. He explains the secret operation that involved smuggling the refugees across the border, bribing Hungarian officials, and providing the refugees with food, shelter and forged documents, all at enormous risk to himself.

The next part of his story concerns his efforts to save some of the Jews after the Nazis invaded Hungary and started deporting twelve thousand Jews a day. He tells it with quiet pride and knows that his pride is justified. No other Jew succeeded in rescuing so many fellow Jews who would otherwise have died a terrible death. He hears people in the courtroom gasp when he talks about his encounters with Adolf Eichmann, who offered him a deal to exchange Jews for trucks, and how, by cleverly playing for time, and expanding the number on his list, he managed to rescue over fifteen hundred Jews who were sent out of Hungary on a train which arrived in Switzerland.

There is dead silence when he finishes speaking, and he can't help casting a triumphant glance in the direction of the defendant and his lawyer. Despite his indignation at the outrageous accusations levelled against him, he feels almost sorry for them. Now that Fleischmann's accusations have been refuted, he supposes that the case will be dismissed. Amos Alon can't possibly have any grounds on which to defend his client's slanderous lies.

But Amos Alon doesn't look defeated. With his muscular build and aura of self-assurance, he might have been a champion stepping into the ring to reclaim his title. As he begins to cross-examine Miklós, he speaks quietly, and goes over his story patiently.

'How did you come to be in charge of aiding the refugees?' he asks.

'There was no effective central organisation of the Jewish community in Budapest because the Jews regarded themselves primarily as Hungarians, and didn't see the need to protect themselves. The refugees who had escaped from Poland, Slovakia and Ukraine were destitute. They had no papers, nowhere to go, and were in constant danger of being deported or killed. Someone had to take responsibility for them.'

'Were there any other members of this committee of yours?' Amos asks. 'Because so far we've only heard about you.'

'Of course there were other members. That's why it was a committee.' He knows he shouldn't retort but he can't control his irritation. Something in Amos's tone riles Miklós. Perhaps this is part of the role he is playing, to assume an air of mistrust and to plant doubts in the judge's mind. If that's his ploy, Miklós thinks, the facts will make him look foolish.

Two hours have already passed, and court is adjourned for lunch. The prosecutor is drumming his fingers on the table. 'Alon is dragging this out. He knows his client hasn't a leg to stand on.'

But Miklós feels anxious, and his mind drifts to something that happened the previous week when a policeman stopped him and asked for his driving licence. He knew he hadn't committed any infraction, but just the same, he wondered nervously if he had broken some rule, and, irrational though it was, he felt guilty. He senses something insidious lurking behind Amos Alon's tone. Part of the act, he supposes, and reminds himself that he has nothing to fear. He will emerge triumphant with his reputation reinstated. In fact, by the time this case is over, even those who didn't know anything about his daring rescue will find out about it. Fleischmann is the one on trial here. He's the one who should be quaking in his shoes.

The questioning continues in a similar vein during the afternoon, and by the time the day is over, Miklós is feeling more relaxed. Amos Alon's manner has become less accusatory. While he is giving evidence, the judge occasionally looks up from his notes, and Miklós detects a flicker of what resembles sympathy in his usually impassive face.

He is almost looking forward to the next day when he will have the opportunity of describing how, against all odds, he managed to wrest so many Jews from Eichmann's murderous grasp.

The following day, in answer to Amos's questions about his encounters with Adolf Eichmann, Miklós begins to describe the meetings at the Majestic Hotel on Swabian Hill but Amos Alon interrupts him.

'Why were you meeting with Eichmann?'

'Because he was the man in charge. No-one else had the power to release Jews.'

'Let me get this straight,' Amos says smoothly. 'You were visiting this luxury hotel to negotiate with the man who organised the murder of millions of European Jews as dispassionately as if he was disposing of waste products from some manufacturing business.'

Miklós is seething. 'You make it sound like a tea party, Mr Alon, but it was terrifying. You call it negotiating. Can a convicted man be said to negotiate with the hangman?'

The prosecutor leans forward and whispers, 'Don't react, Mr Nagy, he's just baiting you.'

'And why was Eichmann bothering to have these negotiations or whatever they were, with you? Did he need your help to exterminate Jews more efficiently?'

The prosecutor springs up to object to his comment, and the judge upholds the objection. He cautions Amos Alon to refrain from editorialising.

'Mr Nagy, you said you found these encounters terrifying. So why did you persist with them?'

Miklós is relieved to have the opportunity to describe his reaction to the situation of the Jews of Hungary. 'If you were a Jew in Budapest in 1944, you were doomed. Rather than being resigned to die, I knew I had to find the courage to assume responsibility. Ours was the last surviving Jewish community in Europe. In spite of the danger, I felt it was up to me to do whatever I could to keep at least some of the Jews alive.'

'That's very commendable,' the defence lawyer says, and Miklós cringes at the condescension in his words. He raises his eyebrows at the prosecutor who shrugs.

When Miklós has stepped down from the witness box for the day, the prosecutor says, 'Don't take it personally. Alon is a right-wing bastard. I think he was a member of Irgun at one stage, and he has it in for the Mapai government and anyone who is part of it. But his political agenda has no bearing on this case.'

The long day's questioning finally comes to an end, and as Miklós drives back to Tel Aviv, he feels frustrated. He had imagined that just telling his story would be all that was needed to convince the judge of the mendacity of Fleischmann's accusations, but he wonders if he has succeeded in conveying the audacity of his confrontations with Eichmann. The words seemed to die in his mouth, dry and colourless as dust. They were just words, they had no power to evoke the terror or the danger. What's worse, he suspects that he sounded boastful.

As he turns into his driveway, he wonders how to make Israelis in 1954 understand what it was like to live in Hungary in 1944, knowing that of the entire Jewish population of Europe, only the Hungarian Jews remained, and that if he didn't make a superhuman attempt to rescue some of them, not one would survive.

He is shocked how little the Israelis know about what happened in Hungary, how little they understand about the power of the Nazis and the powerlessness of the Jews. He has been outraged whenever he heard Israelis talk about European Jews going like lambs to the slaughter, how they identified as victors, and dissociated themselves from those they regarded as victims.

'It makes my blood boil, ' he says to Judit when they sit down to dinner. She has prepared chicken *paprikás*, his favourite dish, no doubt to help him relax after the day in court, but he can't eat, and pushes his plate away. 'I look at the people in the courtroom, and I can see they don't really grasp what I'm saying. I suppose I'm expecting them to imagine the unimaginable. There are times when even I can't believe what I did.'

She puts her slim arm around his shoulders. It's a friendly rather than a sensual touch, but he squeezes her hand, grateful for her support.

'Don't worry about it, Miki. The judge will understand, and that's all that matters. Anyway, don't forget, you're not the one who's on trial.'

CHAPTER TWENTY-FOUR

Jerusalem, January 1954

Three days pass, and by the end of each exhausting day Miklós hopes that Amos has come to the end of his cross-examination, but the relentless quizzing continues.

'In May 1944 you travelled to your hometown, Kolostór, did you not?'

Miklós assents.

'How did you get there?'

'By car.'

'How was this possible? My understanding is that Jews were not allowed to travel around the country.'

Relieved to have the opportunity to enlarge on his usually brief answers, Miklós explains that Eichmann gave him permission to visit his home town. He goes on to describe how he had managed to organise for six hundred Jews — which he had expanded to six hundred families — to leave

Hungary by train. 'Eichmann agreed that I could go to Kolostór so I could let the people on my list know about their impending release.'

'Ah, the people on your list.' Amos Alon pauses for effect. 'You mean your family and friends.'

The implication is unmistakeable. 'That's not true!' Miklós exclaims. 'For one thing, I wasn't the only one drawing up a list. The other members of the committee were also involved. And as far as my list is concerned, most of the people I selected had no connection with me whatsoever. I chose a cross-section of the Jewish community — rabbis, teachers, scholars, craftsmen, tradesmen and orphans. Even a few lawyers,' he adds, and a titter goes around the courtroom.

'So, no relatives and associates?'

Miklós tries to suppress his exasperation. 'Of course I included some relatives and friends. Wouldn't you?'

'What I would do isn't the issue here, Mr Nagy.'

'Well, I'd like to make it clear to the court that my relatives and friends formed a very small percentage of the people on the total list. And as I've already said…'

Here Judge Lazar breaks in and asks him to confine himself to answering the questions.

Miklós looks around at the people in the courtroom and his eye rests on a striking brunette with thick black locks, and his heart leaps. Ilonka! She was there after all! But a moment later he realises that his longing had created the resemblance. Ilonka had gone from his life forever, and the emptiness in his heart would never be filled. With an effort, he tries to focus on the defence lawyer's words.

Amos Alon continues his cross-examination. 'When you got to Kolostór to let your family and friends know that you were about to rescue them —'

This time, the prosecutor leaps to his feet. 'Objection, your honour. The defence counsel continues to imply that my client was only rescuing people who were close to him, which as Mr Nagy has already pointed out, was certainly not the case.'

The judge upholds the objection.

'I will rephrase my question,' Amos says. 'Did you know the fate that awaited the Jewish residents of your town?'

'Of course. That's why I tried so hard to save as many as I could.'

'And what was the fate that awaited them?'

Miklós is frowning. Why was Amos Alon going down this path when he knew the answer? 'They would be deported.'

'And where would they be deported to?'

'To Nazi concentration camps outside Hungary.'

'And what would happen to them in those camps?'

'They would be murdered.'

Amos is nodding. For some reason he looks pleased with himself, when all he has done is to elicit facts that are only too well known. He steps closer to Miklós. 'So, after you had informed the lucky few of their imminent rescue, did you then warn the less fortunate majority of the fate that awaited them?'

Miklós stares at him. So that's where these apparently ingenuous questions have been heading.

'Please answer the question. Did you warn them what was about to befall them unless they took action?'

'Yes, I did warn the Jewish Council,' he says.

'How did you try to warn them? Did you explain exactly what the Nazis had in store for them? I believe two men who escaped from Auschwitz had written a detailed report about the death camp. Was that available in Kolostór?'

Miklós frowns. 'It was, but most people hadn't read it,' he says. 'And those that had, didn't believe it.' He knows his voice sounds unsteady. He senses that he is being accused of something.

'But you read it. So did I. Those men described in chilling detail how, within a few minutes of arriving at Auschwitz, the women with their children and babies were sent straight to the gas chambers and soon all that remained of them was a handful of ashes and nauseating black smoke pouring from the chimneys.'

The judge is leaning forward, and, sensing that he is about to be told to come to the point, Amos Alon asks, 'So did you tell them that? Did you urge them to tell the rest of the community? Romania was not far away. Did you suggest they should escape over the border?'

'Escape? With German and Hungarian soldiers guarding them with machine guns?'

'According to my research, there weren't many German soldiers guarding Kolostór. The Jews could easily have over-powered the guards if only they had known the danger they were in.'

Miklós now understands the scenario the defence counsel is constructing. According to this vision of events, terrified women, children, babies and old people could have risen up against their captors, overpowered guards with machine guns, and run to safety if only he had warned them of their impending doom. The trouble was that in this distant country ten years after the event, to people accustomed to the heroics of Hollywood movies, this fantasy scenario probably sounded plausible.

'Can you please tell the court how you tried to warn them?'

Miklos thinks back to the scene at the Jewish Council, and tries to recall his exact words. 'The Jewish leaders I met mentioned the report that gave a detailed account of what went on in what they called the Nazi death factory, but they didn't believe a word of it. They said things like that couldn't happen in 1944. I told them not to trust German promises that they were being relocated to another town where they would be looked after. I warned them not to board those trains.'

'Did you say why?'

'I said the trains were going to concentration camps.'

'But you didn't tell them what would happen to them in those camps.'

Miklós sighs. 'Not in so many words. In any case, they already had the information but they didn't believe it. They wouldn't have believed me either.'

Amos Alon's penetrating eyes are boring into his face. 'So in 1944, when they were among the last surviving Jews of Europe, you took it upon yourself to decide that there was no point saving them because they couldn't escape from the few Germans who were guarding them, because there was nowhere for them to go even though the Romanian border was not far away, and in any case, you wanted to spare yourself the discomfort of being disbelieved.'

'I risked my life to save people, I didn't condemn them to death!' Miklós shouts, unable to control his fury at the implication that he was somehow responsible for the deaths of the people of his home town.

Amos Alon comes close to the witness stand and says in a low voice, 'Tell me, Mr Nagy, what do you think was the real reason Eichmann sent you to Kolostór?'

Miklós knows that this question is hinting at something, but he can't imagine what it could be. 'I've already told the court that it was on account of the arrangement we had made, that he would release a certain number of Jews as a goodwill gesture.'

If a crocodile about to pounce on his prey could be said to smile, that was the expression on Amos Alon's face. 'A goodwill gesture from the man responsible for carrying out the worst genocide in history.' He says it slowly, enunciating every word with great deliberation, for maximum impact, and turns to the courtroom with a knowing look as if to include them in his revelation.

Miklós sees that people are raising their eyebrows, shaking their heads, nudging each other, whispering. He feels like screaming at them not to be taken in by Amos Alon's innuendoes and insinuations.

'This idea obviously amuses you, but it happens to be the truth,' he says when he can regain control of his voice. 'Eichmann was hoping to show the Allies his offer was genuine so they would supply him with trucks.'

'Mr Nagy, I'm not a historian but even with my limited knowledge of the Second World War, I'm well aware that Eichmann wasn't a fool. He couldn't possibly have believed that the Allies would supply him with essential equipment during the war. I suggest that Eichmann allowed you to rescue six hundred Jews as a reward for not alarming the rest, so he could proceed with his planned extermination.'

'That's outrageous!' Miklós shouts. 'You're talking utter nonsense. Eichmann didn't need me to continue his genocidal plan.' He turns to the judge. 'Perhaps defence counsel isn't aware that by then the Nazis had managed to murder five million Jews without any help from me.'

The taut faces in the courtroom indicate that his sarcasm hasn't met with approval, and he changes his tone.

In a quieter voice, he says, 'Whether you believe it or not, Mr Alon, I have told you the truth. Eichmann was prepared to release one million Jews in return for ten thousand trucks. That's why he sent my colleague Gábor Weisz to Istanbul, to negotiate with Allied leaders for the trucks.'

'Ah, your colleague Mr Weisz.' Another long pause, another knowing look. Miklós is wondering what lies behind this enigmatic comment when Amos Alon says, 'I suggest to you that Adolf Eichmann sent you to Kolostór because he knew the Jews there would trust you. He didn't want a repetition of what happened in the Warsaw Ghetto the year before, and he used you to put the Jews' minds at rest so that they would obey orders and get into those wretched trains without making any trouble for the Germans. And that was the quid pro quo that enabled you to save your personal group.'

A hush has fallen over the courtroom. No-one is whispering now or unwrapping sweets. It feels as if everyone is holding their breath in shock, anticipating his response. Every eye is on Miklós, whose face is white as death. His hands are trembling. 'How dare you accuse me of making such a preposterous deal! I'm here to defend a case of libel, but you're the one slandering me with your lies.'

'Control yourself, Mr Nagy,' the judge warns him. 'You are here to answer questions not to bandy words with the defence counsel. I won't have outbursts like this in court.'

Finally the long day ends. Amos Alon has asked for a long adjournment to give himself time to research matters he considers pertinent to the trial, but instead of being relieved at having a long break, Miklós is too worn out to feel anything but apprehension. No longer confident of a quick vindication, he is dreading what new absurdity the defence counsel will come up with next.

He can hardly speak when he enters his home, and when he glances in the bathroom mirror, he sees his father in old age. When Judit asks about the cross-examination, he waves his arm wearily to indicate he doesn't want to talk about it, and sinks into an armchair. He can't comprehend the crooked path by which rescuing a trainload of people has led to a preposterous accusation of mass murder. Because that's what Amos Alon is implying, that by failing to forewarn the Jews of Kolostór about their imminent fate, he is somehow responsible for their deaths.

But his last allegation was the most scurrilous, the suggestion that he had been a willing tool of the Germans to engender a false sense of security among the Jews so that they would go quietly to their deaths. He can't stop shaking. How can Amos Alon get away with such slander?

For a long time he sits staring into space, then pours himself a glass of whisky, empties it, and braces himself to give Judit an account of the day's events. From the way she is looking at him, it's obvious that she expects to hear something distressing.

When he has finished, she says, 'That's his job, to vindicate his client. It really has nothing to do with you.'

He shakes his head impatiently. 'You didn't hear his tone or see his self-satisfied smile. He was doing his best to provoke and vilify me. Can you imagine, he accused me of going to Kolostór on Eichmann's errand? To facilitate mass murder? It would be laughable if it wasn't so outrageous. And I have to sit there and take it. What he's doing is unethical. It should be illegal.'

She takes his hand. 'Miki, don't take it so hard. You'll make yourself sick. Don't forget, the judge has heard these kinds of manipulations by lawyers before, so he won't be fooled by what this one says in defence of his client.'

But Miklós can't stop brooding. 'I should be able to sue this smart-arse for damaging my reputation.'

'Your reputation is safe. Everyone knows what you did, you're a hero. No-one else did what you managed to do, and there are over fifteen hundred people who can attest to that. As for accusing you of being responsible for the deaths of the other Jews, that's just ridiculous. It wasn't in your power to save them. You're not God, and even God didn't bother saving them.'

'That's what the prosecutor told him. But I looked at the people in court, and I had the feeling they believed what Amos Alon said, that I deliberately withheld information that could have saved them.'

'Then they're as ignorant as he is. Anyway, it doesn't matter what they think.'

Something else is nagging at him, but he doesn't mention this to Judit. It's the insinuating tone with which the lawyer mentioned Gábor Weisz's name. Miklós hasn't seen Gábor since the day he left for Istanbul. He doesn't know where he is, or whether he and Ilonka have reunited, but just hearing his name evokes memories that he has tried to suppress since that dreadful day at the station in St Margarethen, the worst day in his life.

CHAPTER TWENTY-FIVE

Tel Aviv, 2005

Annika's mobile rings, shattering the quiet of the Law Library, and she is startled when she hears Dov's voice. Absorbed in the drama of the trial, and indignant at Amos Alon's vicious questioning of Miklós Nagy, she has lost track of time. Glancing at her watch, she is astonished to see that she hasn't moved for two hours.

'This is an incredible story,' she tells him. 'I'm only a little way into the trial but if I read it in a novel I wouldn't believe it.'

'Well, you know what they say about fact and fiction. But maybe you've had enough facts for one day. Have you been to Jerusalem yet? I'm free for the rest of the day, we could go there for lunch.'

'Jerusalem and back? In one afternoon?

He bursts out laughing. 'Don't forget this is Israel, not Australia. The whole country is about one third the size of your Tasmania. If you leave Tel Aviv with a cup of hot coffee, it will probably still be warm by the time you reach the West Bank. You've probably heard the joke about the size of Israel? A tourist is talking to an Israeli, and he lists all the places he's going to visit while he's here — Masada, Haifa, Akko, Jerusalem, the Dead Sea, Beersheva, Eilat. And when he's finished, the Israeli says, "And what will you do in the afternoon?"'

She's laughing, as she often does when she talks to him. She hadn't noticed that reading about the court case seemed to have knotted all her muscles, and while listening to Dov she feels them loosening up. His amusing comments and anecdotes always have a relaxing effect on her.

She hesitates. She is eager to go to Jerusalem but the trial is as compelling as any detective story. While reading the transcript, she feels she's right there in the courtroom listening to Amos Alon sparring with Miklós Nagy, and she shares Miklós's indignation at the lawyer's accusations. She can't wait to find out what happens next. But does she really want to turn down Dov's offer?

*

Dov's car is just as grimy as it was the day they met in Jaffa, and before she can get in, he's redistributing the dirt on the windshield with a dusty rag, while she shifts piles of newspapers, books and CDs off the front seat. He switches on the sound system and a moment later they hear an Israeli pop tune at full blast. With an apologetic shrug he turns it off. 'Yaeli's favourite CD,' he says, and she wonders if Yael's mother is still in the picture.

The winding road to Jerusalem passes vineyards, citrus groves, pine forests and, to Annika's surprise, stands of gum trees whose feathery leaves and slender trunks cast dappled shadows on the ground in contrast with the tall pine trees whose dark, dense foliage lets in no light. She breathes in the warm smell of sundried grasses and the scent of the eucalypts.

Dov follows her gaze. 'You see, a bit of Australia, to make you feel at home.'

High on a hill above the road, terraced fields, lemon trees and olive groves surround a cluster of farmhouses. 'That's Samaria, a Palestinian village,' Dov says. A little further along, they pass the red-tiled roofs of a recent Jewish settlement.

'Have you heard of the prophet Samuel?' he asks, and points. 'His tomb is just over there.'

She shakes her head in wonder. Ancient and modern history, past, present and future in one tiny patch of land. Further on, they come to several overturned trucks lying by the side of the road. Annika leans forward, and sees a bunch of wilting flowers lying beside one of the trucks. She looks questioningly at Dov, and he pulls up, switches off the ignition, and turns towards her.

'In 1948, when Jerusalem was besieged, food and water had to be brought along this road, which was dangerous because Arabs from the villages on the hilltops would descend on the convoys and ambush them. The commander of this truck was under heavy fire for twenty-four hours. He was ordered to fall back but he refused. When a Molotov cocktail exploded and set his truck on fire, he ordered the others to get out but he stayed in the truck until the last moment and got blown up with his vehicle. The trucks have been left here as a memorial.'

Dov's account of the siege of Jerusalem reminds her of Shula's story about the *Altalena*, and as they drive on, she struggles to recall the details. Shula had said something about Amos Alon's brother who was aboard the Irgun ship which was bringing weapons and ammunition to relieve the siege. When the government shelled the *Altalena*, his brother was killed, and from that day, Amos had become obsessed by the idea of wreaking revenge on the government. Like a man possessed, he couldn't talk about anything else. Unable to cope with his single-minded obsession, Shula had left him. Now that Annika has connected up the pieces of this mosaic of vengeance and obsession that led from the siege of Jerusalem to the *Altalena*, and then to the trial, she thinks about Alon's misdirected rage that made him target Miklós Nagy as a collaborator.

To her surprise, forty-five minutes after leaving Tel Aviv, they are standing on the Mount of Olives, gazing at the fabled panorama of Jerusalem that she has only ever seen in news clips. The luminous limestone of the buildings spread out below them glows in the afternoon light, and the golden cupola of the Dome of the Rock sparkles under the cloudless sky.

Dov is pointing to the graves that cover the slope of the mountain. 'Orthodox Jews believe that when the Messiah comes, the first souls to be resurrected will be the ones who are buried here, and that's why Russian oligarchs are rushing to buy up these plots. They want to make sure of getting to heaven before anyone else.'

Overwhelmed by the view, she nods absently. 'There's something different about the light here,' she says. 'It seems to pour out of the sky in white-hot flames. It's like a painter's representation of the breath of God. It's almost ethereal.'

'Ethereal,' he repeats. 'That's what my wife used to say.'

She turns towards him and waits.

He is looking straight ahead but she knows he doesn't see the view. 'Nurit was a plastic surgeon, she was dedicated to patching up people who were mutilated by fire, bombs, and every kind of disaster you can imagine. She and her team reconstructed shattered and charred bodies, they looked after everyone who needed help regardless of nationality and religion, and that included Palestinians, Syrians and Lebanese who swore to destroy us.

'One day while she was in the operating theatre, trying to give a deformed baby a new face, a bomb went off and she was killed together with her colleagues and some of the patients, Jews and Muslims alike.'

Annika knows that any comment she might make, any commiseration she might offer, would sound trite. Instead, she asks, 'When did that happen?'

'About twelve years ago, during the first Intifada. Yael was nearly four. Nurit was pregnant with our second child.'

Her mouth is dry. She wonders how he can carry on a normal life and not be consumed by hatred and grief.

'You must hate them,' she says.

He sighs. 'I hate the ones who detonated those bombs, but Palestinians are fine people who are unfortunate to have corrupt, power-hungry leaders. I always remember what Golda Meir once said: if the Palestinians loved their children as much as they hate us, we'd have peace in this land. I think hatred is a poison that destroys everything good in humanity. Nurit was a positive force for healing in every sense of the word, and I want Yaeli to feel the power of that.'

She is looking at Dov with admiration. She never would have suspected that beneath the humour and high spirits he had experienced such tragedy, and she marvels that despite what happened, he has tried to raise his daughter without hate or bitterness. A breeze ruffles his curly hair and she feels an impulse to stretch out her hand to stroke it, but at the last moment she lowers her hand. She looks away, confused and embarrassed.

He turns towards her. 'Is there someone waiting for you in Sydney?'

'No, but I met a lovely guy in Budapest.'

He is looking straight into her eyes. 'So tell me about your guy in Budapest.'

She doesn't feel like going into details in this iconic place, with the ghost of his dead wife hovering around them. 'There's nothing to tell. Have you heard of the tyranny of distance?'

He raises his eyebrows. 'Do you think it's really impossible to overcome that?'

She wonders if there's anything behind his question and changes the subject. 'Tell me what made you decide to live here.'

'I'll give you the short version. I came from a close-knit Jewish family in Manhattan. I was educated in the best schools, and I was studying to be a lawyer like my dad, but I was bored. I hated the course I was doing, and the people I knew seemed pretentious and superficial. My future stretched in front of me like an unbroken grey line. Today they'd probably say I was depressed, but I reckon I was frustrated, living my parents' life, not mine.'

Annika has been listening intently. 'I can relate to that, it's such an empty feeling. And parents just don't get it. So what changed?'

'One day in 1973, I read that the armies of Jordan, Egypt, Syria and Lebanon had attacked Israel, and I suddenly came to life. Israel was in danger of being wiped out, and I knew I had to do something. To my parents' horror, I threw away my privileged life, left college without finishing my degree, made *aliyah,* and joined the army.'

'So you found a purpose in life.'

He gives a short laugh. 'You could say that. Back in 1973, everyone was swept away on a wave of patriotism, but after the war, the recriminations started. Whose fault was it that we were caught unprepared? The army's? Golda Meir's? Mossad's? I soon discovered that the idea of Israel is very different from the reality, and the political and religious divisions here are bitter and intractable. But imperfect though it is, it's home, and as you probably know, home for most people is the biggest battleground of all, with the most hurtful conflicts but also the fiercest love.'

Annika nods, and is about to say that she shares his sentiments about families, but he has already embarked on an explanation of the Israeli political system. 'It's impossible for any single party here to have an outright majority, so they have to compromise with minor parties which represent hawks, settlers, peaceniks, Ethiopians, Russians, Druze, Israeli Arabs, Orthodox Jews who think we have a God-given right to the whole West Bank, and Peace Now people who demonstrate on behalf of Palestinian rights. There's even a party that wants to legalise marijuana — but maybe they have a point: if Israeli and

Palestinian leaders got high together, maybe they'd solve all our problems!'

'So what's the good news?'

Dov pushes his glasses higher on the bridge of his nose with the flat of his hand and his gaze rests for a moment on two young women in army fatigues with rifles slung across their shoulders, who are chatting in animated Hebrew as they point at the view.

'Life here is chaotic, unpredictable, infuriating, volatile and dangerous, but people are committed and passionate. Everyone has an opinion about everything. Everyone cares deeply about something. I'm working on an investigative piece about corruption in the government. The politicians won't like it, and they'll complain, but it will be published, and I won't be imprisoned, flogged or beheaded for writing it.'

He pauses for a moment, and she can see that he's struggling to express the intensity he feels. 'It's like living inside a kaleidoscope — noisy, colourful, multifaceted, changeable, disorienting, incomprehensible, but also beguiling. Do I love living here? Yes. Do I loathe it at times? Yes. But would I live anywhere else? Not on your life.'

'You're talking about patriotism, aren't you?' she says. 'That's a dirty word in Australia these days. People accuse you of being a chauvinist if you sound patriotic.'

'Maybe that's because they never had to fight for their existence or their freedom. Having to keep fighting for your survival probably sharpens your patriotism.'

He clears his throat. 'Anyway, that's enough about politics and problems. Let's walk down to the Christian Quarter. I think you'll find it interesting.'

Interesting is an understatement, Annika thinks as they follow the steep road down from the Mount of Olives to the Garden of Gethsemane. Having been educated at a Christian school where other faiths were acknowledged with condescending tolerance, she feels a surge of religious nostalgia when they enter this sacred site. As they stroll along a path lined with rose bushes, she comes to a gnarled olive tree which, according to a sign nearby, was two thousand years old. She stands very still, overcome by the thought that she is walking along the paths where a tormented Christ walked before his crucifixion, where Judas planted a traitorous kiss on his cheek. Dov watches her but doesn't comment, and they walk on in silence.

Back on the road, they pass pilgrims from Poland, grey-robed monks from France and white-clad nuns from Spain, all coming to pray in the churches, chapels, convents and monasteries that line this historic road. They stand in the doorway of the sombre Grotto Gethsemane chapel, and listen while an African priest in a scarlet cassock conducts Mass in lilting English for his rapt international congregation.

The Via Dolorosa is jammed with priests, nuns and pilgrims as they follow the Stations of the Cross, and she is shocked by the profusion of tourist shops and stalls selling tawdry souvenirs. A young man in a long white robe dragging a heavy wooden cross stops right in front of her, barring her way. He wears leather sandals, his hair is long and tangled, and there's something compelling in his beatific smile as he leans on the cross and wipes his sweating brow. 'God bless you,' he says, picks up the cross, and continues trudging along the ancient cobbled street. A few metres further on, two grey-haired women in biblical garb hold up placards warning passers-by to repent as the apocalypse is nigh.

Annika turns to Dov. 'What's going on?'

'Jerusalem can make you crazy. Every year hundreds of visitors channel biblical characters, convinced that they're the reincarnation of Jesus, John the Baptist, Moses or the Virgin Mary. Some years ago, one of your compatriots, a sheep-shearer I think he was, set fire to the Al-Aksa mosque, believing he was on a mission from God to clear the Temple Mount of its non-Christian buildings. Biblical delusion has become so prevalent here that psychiatrists call it Jerusalem Syndrome.'

'It's amazing that a city can have such a powerful impact,' she says.

'In the Middle Ages, they believed Jerusalem was the centre of the world, and in a way it probably still is. You never know what effect it's going to have on you, so you'd better watch out,' he says as they push their way through a huge crowd approaching the Church of the Holy Sepulchre and fall in behind a procession of Ethiopian priests, vivid in their hot pink cassocks and elaborate black hats.

Inside the church which stands on the site where Christ was crucified and buried, the candle smoke and the aroma of incense add to the stifling atmosphere, which reaches fever pitch as hundreds of worshippers, gripped by religious frenzy, surge forward to kiss the rock where the cross once stood. Some have tears streaming down their cheeks, while others sob loudly. 'Mass hysteria,' Annika mutters, but in spite of herself, she can't help feeling moved by the powerful aura of this church and the pilgrims' heartfelt outpouring of emotion.

It's a relief to emerge into the fresh air again. 'Sadly, the teachings of the Prince of Peace haven't created harmony among the Christian sects which are the guardians of this holy site,' Dov says. 'In fact, the Greek Orthodox, Roman Catholic, Coptic and Armenian churches have fought so bitterly over control of the keys to the church that today it's a Muslim family that opens and closes the church!'

They are on their way towards the Muslim Quarter, where shopkeepers in the crowded bazaar try to lure them to buy woven rugs, brightly patterned pottery, or religious souvenirs. 'Are you hungry? I know a great place for lunch near here,' Dov says.

Inside the Bashura Café, the owner greets him with a hug. 'I am happy to see you again, my friend,' he says. 'I will cook special dishes for you.'

He notices Annika gazing at the vaulted ceiling and stone columns of the restaurant. 'Dear lady, can you believe, this place was built in Roman times when this part of the city was part of the Cardo, the main street of ancient Jerusalem, in the days of Christ and Herod.'

After they finish their lamb shashlik and roast eggplant, Dov says, 'If you're not too tired, I'd like to show you one of the best-kept secrets in Jerusalem.'

From the rooftop of the Austrian Hospice, they seem to be looking at the Old City through a close-up lens, and the golden dome of the mosque seems close enough to touch. As they gaze at the view, bells peal from the Russian Orthodox monastery, and the sound of male voices singing Gregorian chants floats in the air. The beauty of their voices makes Annika's eyes prickle, and she wipes them in embarrassment. 'I'm beginning to see why this city has such a profound effect on visitors,' she says.

Dov rests his large hand lightly on her shoulder and she leans into his firm, warm touch. 'Be careful!' he says. 'This is how it starts. I can just see you in a long white robe blessing passers-by.'

As they drive back to Tel Aviv, they pass the overturned trucks, and Annika thinks again about Amos Alon and Miklós Nagy.

'Next time we go to Jerusalem, I'll take you to the Jewish Quarter so you can see what goes on at the Wall, but we have to go on a Friday,' Dov says when he pulls up outside her hotel. 'That's if you'd like to.'

Annika hesitates. She was planning to leave in two days' time, on Thursday, and spending a few days in Budapest before flying home. While she is wondering what to do, he leans over and presses his lips against her cheek, and as she sees the searching look in his eyes and feels the warmth and affection of that kiss, she realises that his interest in her goes beyond friendship. She had assumed that their relationship was platonic and professional, but now she senses exciting possibilities.

'You never know, I might still be here on Friday,' she says.

CHAPTER TWENTY-SIX

Jerusalem, March 1954

Winter has been bitterly cold this year, and in March, when the trial resumes, large soft flakes of snow float down from the sky like feathers from a slashed eiderdown. They melt on Miklós's hat as he walks towards the courtroom, head down, hunched against the cold. The trial is no longer being held in the small room of the District Court where it began two months before. All over the country, in cafés, kitchens, homes and offices, people are buzzing with gossip. Isaiah Fleischmann's supporters are gloating, reporters are analysing the proceedings, and everyone is arguing over what is now referred to as the Nagy case. Because of the interest the trial has aroused and the ever-growing crowds surrounding the court to hear the latest revelations, it has been relocated to a larger courtroom.

Like the venue, Miklós has also undergone a change. The trial, which he thought would last only a few days, is now in its third month, and it has taken its toll on him. As he enters, those in the courtroom who have been observing him since the trial began nudge each other and comment that he walks more slowly, his face has become more lined, and he appears more weary. They note that a miasma of disillusion now clings to him like a second skin.

As he takes his place in the witness box, he is relieved that there is now more space between him and his legal nemesis, so Amos Alon will no longer be able to bully him by standing so close that he feels the unsettling force of his unforgiving eyes. Everyone rises as the judge enters, and Miklós notes that the judge now has two stenographers to record the proceedings, but, as before, he has placed his black fountain pen and sheaf of white paper in front of him. It could be that he doesn't trust the women's accuracy, or perhaps he just needs to make his own notes.

As Amos Alon approaches the witness stand, it seems to Miklós that his eyes look more dangerous than ever. In fact everything about him looks sharper and more threatening. For a few moments he stands in front of Miklós without speaking, no doubt for dramatic effect, and Miklós struggles to suppress the antagonism that threatens to overwhelm him whenever he looks at the man who, for reasons he can't fathom, regards him with unconcealed contempt.

That morning before he left, Judit said, 'He's just doing his job, Miki,' trying to reassure him, but he knows human nature well enough to sense that some personal agenda is driving Amos Alon, something darker and more powerful than simply a lawyer's professional desire to win a case.

As he waits for the onslaught to begin, Judit's advice runs through his head. *I know it's hard, but don't be sarcastic or clever, don't lose your temper or raise your voice, and be patient. Be polite, brief, and to the point. Don't forget that these people weren't in Hungary in 1944, so they can't really understand. Getting irritated will just antagonise them. You're right to feel proud of what you did, but don't sound too proud.*

She was in court last time he testified, and he knows she's right, but he's not sure he will be able to control himself. He keeps coming back to that last comment of hers which chafes like an uncomfortable truth. What did she mean by *don't sound too proud*? He straightens his shoulders. After all, he has nothing to fear. He's not the one on trial, he's the one who achieved something unique, a feat that should not have been possible.

'Mr Nagy,' Amos Alon begins, 'how friendly were you with the top Nazis in Budapest in 1944?'

Miklós takes a deep breath. He resists making an indignant retort to this provocative question. 'I wouldn't say I was friendly with them at all.' He speaks calmly and deliberately, and sees that Judit, who is sitting in the second row, is nodding approval.

'But you were seen at least three times having convivial dinners with Kurt Becher in Budapest restaurants, and nightclubs, and gambling with him at the casino. Wouldn't you describe that as being friendly?'

'It was a necessity. I had to cultivate his —' Miklos was about to say *friendship* but stops himself in time and says 'company' instead. 'But to call it convivial is to misconstrue the nature of our relationship.'

'And yet you were sharing jokes, laughing, smoking Havana cigars, eating Beluga caviar, and drinking French cognac together.'

At this point, the judge takes off his horn-rimmed glasses and leans forward. 'Mr Alon, where are you going with this? Are brands of cognac, caviar and cigars relevant to your case?'

'Your honour, I'm trying to establish the relationship Mr Nagy had with a top-ranking Nazi whose guest he was on numerous occasions at Budapest's most expensive restaurants, which were frequented by the SS but were off-limits to Jews.'

With a resigned gesture of his manicured hand, the judge indicates that he can continue but adds, 'Just spare us the epicurean details.'

'Mr Nagy, did you ever wonder why the Nazis favoured you and accorded you special privileges? Not being Jew-loving philanthropists, they must have expected something in return. Were they doing it in exchange for your co-operation in keeping their murderous plans a secret from the Jews of Kolostór, perhaps?'

This time Miklós can't modulate his voice. 'You keep harping on about me deliberately deceiving the Jews of Kolostór, and keeping the Nazis' plans a secret from them,' he snaps. 'There were many other provinces where Jews were living, and the Nazis didn't send me to any of those, so how come they weren't worried about enlisting my help to deceive all the other Jews of Hungary?'

The judge leans forward again and addresses Miklós, but his tone is sympathetic. 'Mr Nagy, confine yourself to answering the questions, don't ask them.'

Miklós continues in a calmer tone. 'They accorded me special privileges because, as I've already said, Eichmann was waiting to hear from Istanbul about the trucks, and I was part of the chain of negotiations for them.'

'Nevertheless, from what I've read, he still hadn't stopped deporting twelve thousand Jewish men, women and children from the provinces to Auschwitz every single day. How could you possibly believe that he would keep his word?'

Miklós suspects the lawyer is mistaken about the date of the deportations, but he can't be certain. 'I had to believe it,' he says finally, but he can't resist a note of sarcasm. 'For some reason Eichmann didn't take me into his confidence about everything he did.'

Amos Alon consults his notes. 'Let's move on,' he says. 'From August 1944 to May 1945 you were travelling with Becher and some of his Nazi cronies to Switzerland and Berlin, is that right?'

Miklós nods. 'That's correct.' He can still recall the perverse satisfaction he felt that despite his powerlessness, these high-ranking Nazis were treating him as an equal. It's a contrast with the helplessness he feels in this courtroom whenever he hears Alon's scathing tone.

'We had to travel to Switzerland to meet the head of the American Joint Distribution Committee because we hoped that he'd provide the funds to ransom the passengers who were still stuck in Bergen-Belsen.'

'And the trip to Berlin?'

'Becher wanted me to meet his boss Heinrich Himmler. But that never eventuated,' he adds quickly.

Before this trial, no-one had heard of Kurt Becher, but at the mention of Himmler, a ripple goes through the courtroom, and people turn to each other, eyebrows raised, wondering if they had heard correctly.

'So you didn't get to meet Himmler, Hitler's Reichsführer,' Alon elucidates, obviously making the point in case someone wasn't aware of Himmler's exalted role in the Nazi hierarchy. 'And I suppose that on these trips you were eating and drinking with Becher and his cronies, all nice and cosy, like one of the gang.'

The disparagement is insulting. Miklós looks around and catches Judit's eye. She is nodding encouragement, but he feels at a loss. He realises how all this sounds, but the vital context is missing. No-one in this court can possibly comprehend the situation he was in, no-one can appreciate his determination to do whatever it took to rescue at least some of the Jews, despite the personal risk and the imbalance of power between him and these men.

The one person who really understood, who had shared the anguish and the terror with him, was Ilonka, and, suddenly overwhelmed by his yearning for her, he feels such an intense pain that he pales, totters, and clutches his chest. It strikes him that this is what being eviscerated must feel like. The judge asks if he'd like a glass of water but he takes a deep breath, collects himself, and shakes his head. Water won't take away the ache and the regret.

'Thanks to my association with Becher, Himmler eventually issued the order to stop all deportations.' He says this quietly, remembering not to sound too proud.

Amos Alon smiles to himself. It's a calculating smile that indicates he is withholding something, and Miklós holds his breath, bracing himself for the next question.

'So those two exemplary humanitarians Becher and Himmler helped you to save some Jews. But you also met other top-ranking Nazis, did you not?'

'Possibly. I can't remember everyone I met.'

'But I'm sure you remember Hoess.'

Miklós swallows. This is one encounter he would have liked to keep out of the trial but he supposes that Alon ferreted it out during the long adjournment. Lost in thought about the best way to deal with this awkward subject, he hasn't heard the lawyer's last question.

'I asked where you met Hoess,' Alon repeats.

'In Budapest. In Becher's office.'

The judge, who hasn't shown much interest in the foregoing exchange, now takes off his glasses and leans towards Miklós. 'What did you talk about?'

'About the forced death march of Jews from Hungary to Austria. I told him about the inhuman conditions on the march. People were being herded along the road without food or drink, and were dropping dead from hunger or exhaustion, or being shot by the guards. He was shocked by what I told him, and agreed that it was dreadful. He promised he'd have it stopped.'

'Who was this Nazi you're talking about? What was his position?' the judge asks.

'Hoess was the Commandant of Auschwitz.'

There is a gasp in the courtroom and Judge Lazar repeats in an incredulous tone, 'The Commandant of Auschwitz? Are you telling us you had this conversation with the Commandant of Auschwitz who had over a million Jewish men, women and children murdered in his gas chambers?'

There's a terrible silence as the two men stare at each other in the courtroom. All eyes are fixed on Miklós, waiting for his reply.

'Yes.' He whispers so softly that the judge asks him to repeat his answer. Now, ten years later and in another continent, in a world that has the advantage of being able to pass judgment in hindsight, this sounds unbelievable even to him.

'Yes, he was shocked. I know it sounds strange, but it's true.'

The journalists scramble from the courtroom and Miklós knows they are racing to file their sensational scoop of the day, which will undoubtedly make the front page. He can imagine their report, that the man who is part of the present government of Israel, who has been lauded as a hero, drank champagne with top Nazis and discussed death marches with the Commandant of Auschwitz.

Outside, the temperature has dropped, and the snow has turned to sleet which stings his face as he walks shivering from the courtroom, arm in arm with Judit. Some of the reporters crowd around him shouting provocative questions about Hoess until a friend bundles them into a waiting car which skids on the icy road as it speeds away from the court.

Back home, he slumps into his armchair without a word, and Judit pours him a tumbler of whisky. He downs it in one gulp, and she takes his hand without speaking. A heavy silence weighs on them until they hear the front door slam shut. The boys are home from school but when they poke their heads around the door to greet him, Judit shakes her head and leads them away. 'Abba is very tired,' she tells them. 'Go and play.'

'Can you see what's happening?' he says when she returns. 'Alon has turned me into the defendant. I used to feel that the judge was sympathetic, but today, when Hoess was mentioned, I saw a change in the way he looked at me. Alon has got to him.'

For once she doesn't offer any solace, and her acquiescence disturbs him just as much as her reassurance would have irritated him. 'Judges aren't that impressionable, but I don't think the prosecutor is experienced enough,' she says. 'He lets Alon get away with too much. Can you ask for him to be replaced?'

Miklós shrugs. 'It could send the wrong message at this stage.'

'The only wrong message we have to worry about is for Fleischmann to win this case.'

They look at each other and look away. They both know the implication of that.

In the adjacent room, they hear the boys scuffling and shouting. When Judit opens the door, they see Ben, the eight-year-old, grabbing Gil's arm and twisting it so hard that his brother's eyes are watering.

'Stop it at once,' Miklós says, pulling him away. 'What's going on?'

'He called me a Nazi,' Ben says.

The pent-up emotions of the day erupt, and Miklós shouts, 'Don't you ever let me hear you say that again to your brother. Ever.'

Gil shrugs. 'That's what the kids at school call me,' he says in an aggrieved tone. 'They've made up a ditty about us, that we're Nazis because our dad's a Nazi. What's a Nazi anyway?'

Miklós glances at Judit. She sighs but he senses that she isn't as shaken by this revelation as he is, and he wonders if she has heard this before but has kept it from him.

That night when he falls asleep, he dreams that a man with a bald head and piercing eyes is digging into stony ground, deeper and deeper, until his spade strikes a body. Suddenly the corpse sits up and Miklós wakes with a start as he recognises his own face. Despite the cold, he is drenched in sweat. Judit stirs, mumbles, 'Miki, are you all right?', turns over, and goes back to sleep before he can reply.

Too shaken to sleep, he gets up and paces around the apartment. He thinks about Ilonka, and the memory of her enchanting smile as she raised her arms to remove her silk camisole evokes such an exquisite erotic ache that he closes his eyes and buries his face in his hands. She had shared this ordeal with him, she alone could explain what they went through. If only he could talk to her about this trial, she would advise him what to say to make them understand, to stop them crucifying him. If only he could touch her again, if only he could discuss this with her, perhaps this terrible ache would go away. But he knows it never will.

CHAPTER TWENTY-SEVEN

Jerusalem, March 1954

Like a starving dog that has clamped its fangs around a juicy bone, Amos Alon continues to interrogate Miklós about his association with the Nazis, especially with Kurt Becher.

'What did you know about Kurt Becher's career in the Nazi party?' he asks.

Miklós shrugs. 'I think he was the head of the Economic Department. Later I found out that he was Himmler's protégé. That's why he was able to influence Himmler to stop the deportations.' He can't resist adding that, though he knows it's an attempt to paint Becher in a good light.

Alon nods several times as though considering this information. 'I have heard that earlier in the war Becher served as an SS major in Poland, and there were rumours that he was a member of the Death Corps that murdered thousands of Jews. Were you aware of that?'

Miklós wants to believe that Alon is fabricating all this. 'How could I know that? I never heard that rumour, and even if it ever happened, it took place before I met him, before he arrived in Budapest.'

Alon is now in full flight. 'It was also before they invented gas chambers, Mr Nagy. It was a time of the *Einsatzgruppen*, when murder was up close, personal, and horrific, when the brains of murdered Jews spattered the immaculate uniforms of the killers, and the screams of desperate mothers and dying children echoed in their heads for weeks.'

The judge is shaking his head. 'Mr Alon, please stop editorialising. Just keep to the relevant facts.'

'I'm coming to them, your honour, if you'll just bear with me,' Alon replies, and turns back to face Miklós. 'I believe that this is where Becher performed with such distinction that he became the liaison between Hitler and his hero Himmler, who then made him chief of the Economic Department of the SS in Hungary.'

He fixes his rapier gaze on Miklós. 'You just mentioned the Economic Department as if it was a harmless office in some insignificant plumbing firm. Were you aware that its real function was removing gold fillings from the dead, shipping bales of human hair to Germany's mattress factories, converting fat into soap and inventing hideous tortures to make Jewish women and their children reveal where they'd concealed their jewels, their money and their last possessions?'

Miklós is so shaken by Alon's words that his tongue is paralysed. He thinks back. All he knew was that Becher was chief of the Economic Department, nothing more. From what he had observed about the man, that role suited his avaricious nature and enabled him to enrich himself by appropriating jewellery and works of art from Jewish owners. But he didn't suspect Becher's dark past, or the fact that the name of his department was a euphemism, concealing the fact that it was responsible for divesting Jews of everything they possessed, even their fillings, their fat, and their hair, which were transformed into valuable commodities for the Reich.

He had no idea that Becher might have played a major role in this horrifying process, and he doubts if he did. He can't reconcile the genial bon vivant who loved money, Beethoven and Goethe, with the ruthless cog in the Nazi machine that Amos Alon has described. But even as he considers that the lawyer is ruthless enough to exaggerate and fabricate, a reluctant corner of his mind suspects he might be telling the truth.

The courtroom is so silent now that when a woman drops a newspaper, it makes a loud slap against the wooden floor, making someone gasp and startling people around her. Miklós is so shocked by what he has heard that it takes him a while to gather his thoughts. When he speaks, his voice is unsteady.

'I did not know the true function of the Economic Department, and I wasn't aware of the ranks and promotions within the Nazi party. I did not know what Kurt Becher did before coming to Budapest, or if what you've heard about him is true. My only interest in him was getting his help in releasing the train from Bergen-Belsen. Without his help, I would never have been able to rescue that trainload of people, over fifteen hundred of them. Otherwise they would have been deported and murdered along with the rest of the Hungarian Jews.'

'As you have reminded us several times. So naturally you were very grateful to him.' Alon sounds affable but

Miklós mistrusts his tone. 'Was there anything you weren't prepared to do for him in return?'

It's another insidious question, and Miklós doesn't know how to answer it without falling into his trap. He looks questioningly at the judge who advises the lawyer to rephrase it.

'I'll come to the point. Were you prepared to write an affidavit for Becher after the war so that he would avoid imprisonment?'

People in the courtroom are craning forward to hear the reply to this new revelation.

His reply is loud, clear and unequivocal. 'I did not.'

People now sit back and breathe out, relieved that the tension is over. Miklós sees them nodding to one another and smiling. Their faith in him is restored.

'Are you quite sure about that?' There's something in the way Amos Alon says this that makes Miklós uneasy, but he says, as firmly as he can manage, 'Quite sure.'

Amos Alon nods, and his dark eyes linger on Miklós a few moments longer. Miklós hopes that he will accept his answer and let the matter rest, but the lawyer's next question fills him with dread.

'Mr Nagy, did you give favourable testimony for Becher to the German Denazification court?'

Miklós gives a sigh that seems to rise from the depths of his soul, and he tries to conceal it by coughing. This is a trick question, and there is no way of answering it truthfully without incriminating himself. It's a question that assumes that actions can be judged in black or white, but he knows that the truth always lies inside a narrow crack in between. He longs to explain this but knows that isn't possible.

In a strong voice he says, 'I did not. The German Court of Denazification invited me to give testimony about Becher when I was in Nuremberg in 1947. This was at the invitation of General Taylor, who was the chief prosecutor for the International Court. I was in Switzerland at the time, and I was about to migrate to Israel, when Taylor asked me to assist him on matters pertaining to the Holocaust in Hungary. Ben-Gurion agreed that I should go, and the Jewish Agency provided money for the trip. I didn't appear in person in that court, but I gave a sworn affidavit instead. But it wasn't, as you mistakenly put it, testimony given in Becher's favour.'

He notices that at the mention of Ben-Gurion, Amos Alon's face twists into a sneer but he doesn't have time to dwell on this because the lawyer steps closer, and asks, 'Do you have a copy of that affidavit?'

Miklós shakes his head.

'Why didn't you keep a copy?'

Furious at being baited, Miklós risks a rebuke from the judge by retorting, 'Why should I? Do you keep every piece of paper you write?'

The courtroom titters and he senses that people are pleased that he has defended himself in what has become a compelling duel.

'It wasn't just a scrap of paper,' Alon says. 'It was a document of historical significance. Can you at least recall whether you wrote it in favour of Becher or not?'

Miklós pauses. In spite of the cold, perspiration beads his forehead. He clasps his hands to stop them from shaking. He scrutinises Alon's face for clues. Is he fishing, or does he know something?

'I didn't write for him or against him. I kept to the truth, that's all.'

'So you were careful to avoid saying anything derogatory about a leading Nazi SS officer,' Alon says, and lets the significance of his words sink in before he continues. 'Let me get this straight: you just wanted to tell the truth about Becher without giving your opinion about him.'

'That's right. As I said, that's what I was asked to do, and that's what I did.'

Amos Alon is looking thoughtful. 'So, in your opinion, did that affidavit have any effect on his release?'

'I don't see how. I doubt it.'

There's a pause, and Miklós breathes out, hoping that now his adversary will drop this line of questioning, but in a ringing voice Alon says, 'I suggest to you that in fact it was on account of your favourable testimony that Kurt Becher was released from prison in Nuremberg.'

All attempt at control and restraint gone, Miklós shouts, 'How dare you say that! It's a malicious lie!'

Unmoved by Miklós's outburst, Amos Alon takes a paper from the pile of documents that Miklós had brought to the court to disprove Fleischmann's allegations when the trial began. He holds it up and turns to the judge. 'Your honour, this is a letter that Mr Nagy sent to the Jewish Agency in 1948. I'd like to read two sentences from it, and I remind the court that these are Mr Nagy's own words: *Kurt Becher was an ex-SS colonel who served as liaison officer between me and Himmler during our rescue work. He was released from prison in Nuremberg by Allied occupation forces due to my intervention.*'

He enunciates the last four words with great emphasis, as if putting them in capital letters. People in the court are gasping, some are murmuring *Oh my God! Can you believe it?* Some women are shaking their heads while others turn to their neighbours to discuss this shocking revelation, and the volume in the courtroom rises to unprecedented levels. The judge bangs his gavel for silence, and threatens to eject anyone who causes a disturbance.

Miklós is clasping his hands so tightly his knuckles are white. Now that it's too late, he can't figure out why he submitted that damning document to the court. Was it carelessness, boasting, or sheer stupidity? He knows he must think quickly to minimise the damage that he has brought upon himself, but a sense of panic overtakes him, and in his confusion he can't think clearly.

Meanwhile, Alon is still firing questions. 'You said before that you didn't do anything to help Becher. So is that true?'

'Yes.'

'But in your letter, you claim the exact opposite. You say that it was thanks to your intervention that he was released. So was that the truth?'

'Yes,' Miklós says, and adds, 'but it's not so simple.'

'I'm afraid I'm a bit confused, Mr Nagy. You see, your two statements contradict each other. Simple or not, they can't both be true. So can you explain to us, which one is actually the truth?'

There's a long pause while Miklós racks his brains for a way out of the quagmire that his hubris has landed him in. Finally, in a low voice, he says, 'In making the claim that my intervention resulted in Becher's release I exaggerated the importance of my role. When I wrote to the Jewish Agency, I was anxious to prove to them that the money they had provided for the ransom had been worthwhile.'

It's a mortifying confession, but Amos Alon isn't buying it.

'But you had the effrontery to accuse me of telling malicious lies when it was your own words I was quoting!'

At this point, the prosecutor leaps up. 'Your honour, I object. Mr Alon is harassing the witness,' he says, but the judge overrules him. 'You can't interrupt the cross-examination just because your witness has been cornered.'

In the cold glint of the judge's eyes behind his horn-rimmed glasses, Miklós sees a new hostility and it chills him.

Alon continues, 'You claim you were merely boasting and exaggerating in your letter to the Jewish Agency, but I suggest that you not only saved Becher from the International Court in Nuremberg, but you also gave a sworn affidavit to the Denazification Court of the Germans, and that affidavit saved him from being punished as he should have been, along with the other top Nazis.'

In a strangled voice, Miklós shouts, 'You're lying!'

The prosecutor breaks in again. 'Your honour, how is this relevant? Mr Fleischmann's allegations that form the basis of this libel suit don't mention any affidavit given to the German court.'

Miklós stares at the judge, willing him to agree, but the judge isn't looking at him. 'On the contrary,' Judge Lazar says briskly, 'it is totally relevant.'

'What would you say about someone who intervenes in favour of a prominent SS officer to bring about his release?' Alon asks.

'First I'd want to know the reason, all the details, and the historical context of that intervention,' Miklós retorts.

'Be that as it may, would you agree that such intervention is regarded as a criminal act in this country?' Alon asks.

Miklós bows his head. He is trapped and there's no escape. 'I suppose so, if you ignore the circumstances.'

Amos Alon opens a folder on his table and extracts a document from it. 'In your sworn affidavit to the International Military Tribunal, you wrote, and I quote, *Kurt Becher was one of the few SS leaders who had the courage to oppose the program of annihilating Jews, and tried to save Jewish lives. From what I observed based on my personal dealings with him, he did whatever he could to save them from the Nazi leaders. I never doubted his good intentions, and believe he deserves the court's fullest consideration. I make this statement not only in my name but also on behalf of the Jewish Agency and the Jewish World Congress.*'

Amos Alon says no more, and with a triumphant expression, sits down, allowing the devastating impact of the affidavit to hang over the courtroom. Desperate to defend himself, Miklós bursts out: 'As I stated, I wasn't writing a historical account or a biography. My testimony was solely based on what I observed and on my personal dealings with Becher. I didn't say he was a saint, or excuse anything he may have done. But testifying as I did was the honourable thing to do because without Becher's help, I wouldn't have been able to save all those people.'

But looking around the courtroom he realises that no-one is interested in his explanation. The damage has been done and can't be undone. He glances at Judit and sees that she is biting her lip. She stares down at her hands, avoiding the accusing looks, secret nudges, and shocked whispers of those sitting close to her. He looks at the judge and from his expression, he can see that the judge is shocked not only by the content of his affidavit, but by the fact that he lied about it while under oath.

The judge now takes over the questioning, and his voice is cold. 'Why did you think you had the right to make your statement in the name of the Jewish Agency and the World Jewish Congress? Who in the Jewish Agency authorised you to do this?'

Miklós stammers out the names of Moshe Sharett and Ben-Gurion, and again he notices the contempt on Amos Alon's face when he mentions the leaders of the Mapai party.

'I'd like to know, did they specifically give you permission to intervene on behalf of Kurt Becher, and recommend leniency for him?'

'At the time I believed they did.'

The judge looks sceptical and hands the cross-examination back to Amos Alon whose voice is deathly quiet. 'So when you told this court that you never gave any testimony or affidavit to the International Court in Nuremberg, you not only lied to the court, which means you committed perjury, but you intervened on behalf of a leading SS officer, which as you yourself admitted earlier, is regarded as a crime in Israel. So that makes you a criminal, doesn't it?'

Miklós shouts, 'I deny that! All I did was to acknowledge the assistance of a man without whom I couldn't have rescued all those people. Everyone knows I did the honourable thing. You're twisting the facts to suit your case.'

Amos Alon shrugs. 'I have one more document, your honour,' he says. 'It's an affidavit signed by Walter Rapp, who assisted Brigadier-General Telford Taylor during the Nuremberg trials.'

'How is this affidavit relevant?' the judge wants to know.

'It concerns Miklós Nagy's responsibility in the release of Kurt Becher, who was listed as a Nazi war criminal in the American war criminal file for his activities in Budapest and later in the concentration camp of Mauthausen in Austria.'

Amos Alon reads out Walter Rapp's affidavit. He reads it slowly and clearly, giving weight and significance to every single word.

'*To the best of my knowledge, Miklós Nagy arrived as a voluntary witness on behalf of SS Colonel Kurt Becher, and it seemed to me that the sole reason for his arrival was to help this man, as it was highly probable that he would be tried by us. This was the first and only time that anyone had come forward with proof that a high-ranking SS officer had been instrumental in saving thousands of Jewish lives at great risk to himself. Kurt Becher's release was solely the result of Mr Nagy's pleas on his behalf and the contents of his sworn testimony. His affidavit was the main, if not sole reason for our decision to release him.*'

No-one in the courtroom makes a sound, they sit motionless, mesmerised by Rapp's testimony, struggling to make sense of the extraordinary revelations they have just heard, and the contradictory statements made by Miklós Nagy. The prosecutor now rises, and turns to Miklós. 'If you had a chance to write that affidavit today, would you do it or not?'

Miklós struggles to find an answer to this loaded question. He knows that the prosecutor is trying to extricate him from the quicksand into which he is sinking, but although he knows what Elman wants him to say, he finds himself unable to say it. In any case, it seems to him that Walter Rapp's affidavit is a vindication, not an accusation.

Rapp has acknowledged that he spoke on behalf of the man whose help in the rescue was pivotal.

He thinks back to his last few meetings with Becher, not only to the companionable meals but to the conversations they had, and the connection that sprang up between them. He remembers the handshake that sealed the implicit promise which has led to his undoing. Was he now willing to betray that connection and break that promise to denounce the man whose help had been crucial to the rescue?

After a long pause, he raises his head and looks straight into the prosecutor's eyes. 'I would write it again today, because it's the truth, but I wouldn't say I acted on behalf of the Jewish Agency because that wasn't strictly true.'

The prosecutor still hasn't given up hope. 'Would you sign that affidavit in your own name?'

This time Miklós doesn't hesitate. 'Yes, I would. It's a matter of principle. Any honourable person would do the same.'

The court empties in deathly silence. Dazed, people attempt to process the unexpected admissions that they have heard that day which have turned everything upside down, challenging their moral compasses. How do you balance the merit of rescuing over fifteen hundred Jews against the crime of writing an affidavit to exonerate a Nazi? Can a man be a hero as well as a collaborator?

That evening, Judit tries to hide one of the newspaper articles from him but it's too late. He crumples it up and hurls it across the room in fury. The reporter asks why, instead of prosecuting Isaiah Fleischmann, the government of Israel isn't prosecuting the collaborator who helped a Nazi war criminal escape punishment.

*

The following evening, Judit has bought tickets for a performance of Gounod's opera *Faust*. It's a gala event in a city that's hungry for culture. A world-famous Italian diva is singing the role of the seduced Marguerite, and a Russian bass is to sing the role of Mephistopheles. Miklós is reluctant to appear in public, but Judit persuades him that he has to hold his head high and ignore the gossip and innuendo.

As he suspected, the evening is an unending torment. In the foyer, strangers who recognise him from newspaper photographs slide away and whisper. After a few awkward remarks about the singers, and the hope that the new Mann Auditorium will be an improvement on the present concert hall, acquaintances find an excuse to leave them to buy a program, a drink, or to meet friends.

He feels heartened when several people step forward to offer words of support, and one couple confide that thanks to him, they have survived. 'We'll never forget what you did,' the woman says. 'It's scandalous what that lawyer is doing in court. If there's anything we can do to help, we'll speak on your behalf.'

'Do you know who they are?' Judit asks. 'Ask the prosecutor to call them as witnesses.' He puts his arm around her shoulders. He's touched by her undimmed faith in him and her naivety but knows that no witnesses can undo the destructive impact of Amos Alon's campaign against him.

It's a relief when the lights are finally dimmed and Gounod's stirring music fills the concert hall as they witness the seduction and destruction of Marguerite, the pact that Faust makes with the devil, and the inexorable downfall of the hero.

CHAPTER TWENTY-EIGHT

Tel Aviv, 2005

As soon as Annika returns to the hotel from the Law Library, she changes into her leggings and sneakers and heads down to the promenade to clear her head. As she strides out, a brisk breeze is whipping up the waves and carving ridges in the sand, and the umbrellas above the striped banana chairs are flapping from side to side. The wind pushes her along and, for the first time in several years, she breaks into a slow jog. She wants to block out all the thoughts that toss inside her head. What would she have done in Miklós Nagy's place? Did making deals with Nazis amount to collaboration? Where did the truth lie? She was meant to leave Israel yesterday, but she has changed her flight, determined to get to the truth about Miklos Nagy.

But was that the sole reason? Her thoughts turn to Dov. Whenever her phone rings she hopes to hear his pleasant baritone voice, and whenever they meet, she feels as awkward as a smitten teenager and wants to impress him. She knows there's no future in this relationship but just the same she can't resist prolonging it.

Out of breath, she runs into Ari's café and orders an orange juice and a smoked salmon bagel. 'So, you jog now,' he says approvingly. 'You have problem, you jog, problem goes away.'

She sighs. 'I wish it was that simple.'

It's Friday, and she glances at her watch once again, wondering if Dov will call her about going to Jerusalem. She struggles to stifle the annoyance she feels at being left dangling, but as Cassie would say, no-one makes you dangle. It's a choice you make yourself. She pauses to listen to the interior monologue inside her head, and is astonished by what she hears: perhaps he has forgotten, or is caught up in his investigation. Perhaps he isn't as interested as she had imagined. *As she had hoped*, the little voice corrects her.

The irony is inescapable. Back in Sydney the men she had come across were a bunch of D-listers or self-absorbed wankers, but within a couple of weeks of leaving Australia, she has become attracted to two men with whom no lasting relationship was possible.

But perhaps it isn't really so strange after all, she thinks, watching the lean runners jog past, leaving snatches of laughter and conversation floating in the air behind them. As Cassie might say, she is being true to form, only wanting men who are not available.

Understanding herself has never been her forte, and she tries to figure out her feelings for Dov. She is aware that something inside her softens whenever she is with him, that he's a kindred spirit. She likes the way he looks at her, the way he smiles. He makes her feel attractive and interesting. But has the febrile atmosphere of Israel impaired her judgement? Perhaps when she saw him again she would realise that this attachment had evolved as a result of their shared interest in journalism, and his ability to stimulate her mind and make her laugh. But she knows that this is only part of the answer. The rest is shrouded in the mists of emotional confusion.

'Love problems?' asks Ari as he brings her juice and bagel.

'If I told you, you wouldn't believe it.' Her tone is light and teasing, but the prospect of confiding in a sympathetic stranger who lives on the other side of the world and whom she will never see again is hard to resist, and she is about to tell him about her quandary when her mobile rings.

Ari points to the phone. 'One of the problems is calling?' He gives her a knowing smile, moves away, and starts vigorously polishing glasses on the other side of the café.

'You remember I mentioned going to Jerusalem on a Friday?' Dov asks. She braces herself to hear that he can't make it when he says, 'If you're free, I can pick you up in about an hour. I want to make sure we get there before sunset. We're going to the *kotel* so don't wear anything revealing and don't bring your camera — once Shabbat comes in, they won't let you take photographs.'

*

In the car, he explains that usually he and Yael have Shabbat dinner at the home of Nurit's mother, but Yael is at a school camp this week. She looks at him with interest, envy almost.

Shabbat dinners with family sound like a close and warm ritual, an opportunity to share the events of the past week with people who care about each other, and once again she feels the loss of being disconnected from her Jewish roots.

She imagines candles being lit and prayers being said, like the display she saw at the Jewish Museum in Sydney. It's something she has never experienced, and she regrets that her mother hasn't passed on any Jewish traditions. She supposes it's because she didn't experience them herself while she was growing up, so the question, as always, comes back to Marika. Why did her grandmother sever the link with her ancestors? Annika is shocked to realise that in her absorption with the Nagy trial, she has almost forgotten that it was her grandmother's angry reaction to Miklós Nagy's name that has led her to make this journey.

'Our Shabbat dinner is more about sitting down together one night of the week than about prayers or religious ritual,' Dov says as he removes Yael's heavy metal CD from the audio system and inserts another. As she recognises the familiar notes and the hoarse voice, Annika sits forward and her eyes widen with astonishment. Of all the music in the world, Dov is playing her favourite CD.

'That's Leonard Cohen's London concert!' she exclaims. 'I play it all the time at home.'

'It's my favourite, too,' he smiles, and reaches for her hand. A moment later they both hum the chorus of 'I'm Your Man'. From time to time he glances at her, and she feels blood rushing to her cheeks.

The CD ends, and they sit in a comfortable silence. 'I can't get over that coincidence,' she says after a long pause.

'Maybe it's karma,' he says, but his mouth is twitching, and she doesn't know whether he is joking or serious. She is still trying to figure it out when he says, 'If you're still here next Friday, come and have dinner with us.'

She is touched that he wants to include her in his family dinner, and disappointed that she will miss it. She would like to meet his daughter, even though she thinks her taste in music, unlike her father's, is atrocious. She wonders how he would have introduced her. *My colleague from Sydney? The woman I'd like to share my life with?* The last thought startles her. Where did that bit of fantasy come from?

'Next Friday? No chance. But thanks anyway.'

'Never say never.'

He looks down at her sandalled feet. 'I'm glad you're not wearing high heels because we have quite a way to walk. Being Friday, I can't drive in the Jewish Quarter after sunset. If the ultra-Orthodox Jews see you driving on Shabbat, they throw stones at the car, so we'll come through the Damascus Gate and walk past the Muslim Quarter.'

Twenty minutes later, as Annika gazes at the elaborate crenellations on the ancient city wall, he says, 'This is the most beautiful of the seven city gates. It's been the main entrance to the city since the first century, and what you're looking at stands on top of a wall originally erected by Hadrian.'

'Why Damascus?' she asks.

'Believe it or not, once you could hop into a taxi and drive straight to Syria's capital.'

Inside the gate, they plunge into a narrow alleyway crowded with shoppers and push their way past barrows heaped with pita bread, stalls piled with oranges, dried apricots, olives and sesame cakes soaked in honey. In doorways, men squeeze pomegranates and they stop for a glass of the tangy red juice. They rub shoulders with Arab women in white headscarves and embroidered caftans carrying heavy bags, Bedouins in *keffiyehs* smoking water pipes outside their leather and brass shops, and schoolgirls eyeing bangles, earrings, and racks of dresses that hang in shops hardly bigger than closets.

Occasionally they pass young Israeli soldiers in green uniforms, confidently toting rifles over their shoulders. All the signs in the bazaar are in Arabic, and most of the shoppers are Muslims, the men carrying baskets, the women holding children by the hand, and it occurs to Annika that when you see people out shopping, you realise that what connects us all is stronger than what divides us. The twisting alleys pass through a succession of medieval stone archways, and she regrets not bringing her camera.

She is staring at an inscription in flowing Arabic script when Dov grabs her hand and pulls her to one side to avoid a handcart heaped with pita bread swerving among the shoppers on the narrow pathway. His hand is strong and warm, and she doesn't drop it as they walk on.

'It's so crowded!' she says.

'Wait till you get to the *kotel*.'

'*Kotel?*'

'That's the Hebrew for what you probably call the Western Wall.'

The alley widens, the signs are now in English and Hebrew, and a few minutes later they reach a large open plaza. She stares and catches her breath. 'My God, it's the Wall,' she whispers, suddenly overwhelmed. It's just a wall,

really, made up of huge slabs of weather-roughened sandstone, with spilling clumps of greenery that have taken root
in the inhospitable cracks, but it feels as if the prayers, long-
ings, tears and supplications of the past two thousand years
have soaked into the stone, drawing her towards it.

From somewhere in her past she recalls hearing a prayer
that included the words *next year in Jerusalem*, and she
realises that she is standing before the holiest site in Judaism, the longed-for destination for Jews all over the world
for thousands of years.

The plaza seems to be an open-air synagogue. On one
side, a group of Americans are celebrating a bar mitzvah,
and the bar mitzvah boy, a thin freckled kid with big ears
and a striped prayer shawl draped over his skinny shoulders,
is reciting his part in a tremulous sing-song voice while his
kippah keeps slipping off his head. Nearby, a group of old
men with wispy white beards, wrapped in prayer shawls,
sway back and forth as they lean over Torah scrolls.

From the languages she hears all around them, it's obvious that as well as the locals, visitors have come here from
all over the world — tourists, travellers and pilgrims, orthodox, reform and atheists alike. Some are praying, others are
gazing at the Wall in awe. In the centre of the plaza, young
soldiers have joined hands and are performing a *hora*, their
rifles bobbing on their backs as they dance in a circle. At the
Wall, men of all ages press their lips against the weathered
stones, praying with impassioned voices as they insert slips
of paper into crevices.

She turns to Dov. 'What are they doing?'

'Those bits of paper are called *kvitls*. They're messages to
God. People pray for themselves or for someone else, or to

ask for a blessing, and insert it in the wall. They believe that God will read it.'

Suddenly they hear singing, and look up. Coming down the concourse leading to the plaza, their arms around one another, are dozens of young men, all in wide-brimmed black hats and long black coats, their hair in curled side-locks, a vision from a seventeenth-century village in Poland. Although she can't understand the words, she is captivated by their joyous singing and the rapturous expressions on their faces. When they reach the plaza, they link arms, form a circle, and continue to sing, their coat-tails flying as they dance. Occasionally, carried away by their fervour, several dancers lift one of the men high in the air as they continue spinning around. There has never been a dance like this, she thinks, such a spontaneous expression of mystical ecstasy.

'I've never seen anything like this,' she murmurs.

'They're welcoming in the Sabbath like a bridegroom greeting his bride,' Dov says, and from the way his eyes linger on her face, she can tell that he is as delighted by her reaction as a parent who has arranged a special treat. 'To religious Jews, the beginning of the Sabbath is like the entrance of the bride, to be adored and celebrated.'

A man walks over to Dov, points at Annika, and says something in an angry voice. 'You have to go over there, to the other part of the plaza that's reserved for women,' Dov says. 'This part is for men only.'

A high fence divides the women's section from the rest of the plaza, and by their long skirts, long-sleeved tops, and the scarves covering their hair, she can tell that most of the women here belong to the Orthodox community. Some of them have formed a circle, and she is struck by their euphoric expressions. They are radiant, as though lit by an inner light.

They look as if they don't have a care in the world, as if rejoicing in the coming of the Sabbath is the highlight of their week. She can't help smiling back, and as she stands aside to watch them dancing, one young woman stretches out her hand to her. 'Come, dance with us,' she says in Israeli-accented English.

Without a moment's hesitation, Annika takes her hand and joins the circle. The last time she remembered dancing was with a guy she met at a party celebrating some journo's Walkley award. They had all had too much to drink, and as they stumbled around to loud music, he took the opportunity to hold her too tightly against his aroused body. She smiles now, delighted to be dancing in a circle with other women just for the joy of being alive and the innocent pleasure of connecting with others. Their movements are similar to the Zorba dance, and after a few trips and missteps, she is able follow the rhythm of the *hora*. They smile back, encouraging her, and as they dance together, hands linked, her problems melt away, and she can't remember the last time she had enjoyed taking part in a communal activity so much.

When the dance is over, she walks towards the Wall. Some of the women are holding prayer books as they press their lips against the sun-warmed stone. Others place their hands over their faces as they pray with expressions of aching devotion, as if their lives depended on conveying the intensity of their faith. Having prayed, they slip their *kvitl* into a crevice.

If I could insert a *kvitl,* what would I ask for? she wonders, and envies those who believe in an omnipotent being who answers prayers and grants wishes like a Santa Claus for adults. Just the same, she regrets her cynicism in the face of such overwhelming faith, and feels frustrated at not knowing what to wish for. Then it strikes her that if she has nothing to pray for, she already has all she needs.

*

As they drive back to Tel Aviv along the darkened highway, her mind goes back to the trial. 'From the transcript I can tell that Amos Alon really had it in for Miklós Nagy,' she says. 'I know he hated the Ben-Gurion government after the *Altalena* incident, and wanted to avenge himself, but how could he accuse Nagy of collaborating, knowing that he'd saved all those people? Did he think it would have been better to let them die?'

'For the people he rescued, it wouldn't have been better,' Dov replies, 'but for Miklós Nagy, unfortunately yes. Heroes don't always get the acknowledgement they deserve. How far have you got?'

'I've nearly finished. It's like reading a detective story. I can't wait to get to the part where the judge gives his verdict. I'll probably finish it on Sunday.'

'And then?'

They sit in the car in silence outside her hotel, and his question hangs in the air between them, heavy with unspoken feelings. He is playing the Leonard Cohen disc again. She turns to look at Dov, stirred by the sexy lyrics, and too restless to sit still.

She clears her throat. 'Would you like to come in and have a drink at the bar?'

He looks preoccupied, and instead of answering her question, he says, 'Annika, I'm wondering what you're going to do after you've finished reading that transcript of the trial. Have you figured out yet why it's so important to you? Or are you waiting for an epiphany?'

Her tongue feels heavy in her mouth as she replies, 'An epiphany would be good. No, I haven't figured it out. Maybe I'll never know. In the meantime I'm fascinated by the moral ambiguities of the story. That's something I'm sure you understand.'

'So it's just a story?'

She knows why he keeps probing, and feels annoyed, probably because he has articulated her own doubts.

'You were right about Shabbat in Jerusalem. I'll never forget it,' she says.

'Okay, I get it. Next subject,' he says. 'Shabbat in Jerusalem. So did the tribal collective unconscious get under your skin?'

She is still thinking about his question when he asks softly, 'Is that the only thing about your stay that you'll never forget?' She knows what he is really asking, and she teeters on the brink of honesty, but at the last moment she backs away.

'When I've figured that one out, I'll let you know,' she says lightly, and plants a light kiss on his cheek before getting out the car.

She closes the door to her balcony to shut out the synthetic blare of disco music from the beachfront that disturbs the lingering sense of peace she feels from the outpouring of impassioned faith and joy at the Western Wall.

Closing her eyes, she sits very still, replaying every moment of that scene, the unfathomable and eternal human quest for the divine. Something profound has stirred her soul in a way she doesn't comprehend and cannot put into words. She has read somewhere that sometimes the deepest emotions can only be expressed in silence, and she knows that words would merely trivialise what has been the first spiritual experience in her life.

CHAPTER TWENTY-NINE

Jerusalem, April 1954

The shafts of morning light shining in parallel columns through windows high on the courtroom walls distract Miklós from the drama about to unfold on yet another day of the trial. It's a soft light, softer than the pitiless rays that scorch Tel Aviv, and for the first time in months, he thinks of spring mornings in the Kolostór of his childhood, when the world was fresh and its possibilities unspooled before him as he jumped into the stream lined with tall reeds, and raced with friends in fields sprinkled with daisies and primroses. Sometimes, concealed among the tall grasses, he found clumps of his mother's favourite flower, lilies-of-the-valley, whose delicate white bells exuded a scent that touched his soul. That was why he had bought them for Ilonka that day, and handed them to her as awkwardly as a teenage suitor. That memory jolts him to the present, and he shifts as his bones grind against the hard timber bench.

When it's time for witnesses to be called, Miklós feels his muscles unclench. His breathing, which has recently become short and shallow, occasionally producing a dull pain in his chest, begins to deepen. As the shafts of light above him brighten, the courtroom, which has appeared a cold and threatening place, now seems neither wounding nor dangerous. The people he saved will tell their story, and the truth will emerge. He will be vindicated and he will triumph over the twisted minds that have tried to diminish his achievement and ruin his reputation.

As Judge Lazar enters, everyone rises, and Miklós studies his face, searching for signs of sympathy or at least acknowledgement, but without looking in his direction, the judge takes his seat, bangs his gavel, and the session begins.

The first witness that Amos Alon calls is not one of the men he rescued, but someone he has never heard of, who casts an angry glance in his direction as he identifies himself as Peter Bernsztein, a member of the Jewish community of Kolostór in 1944.

'Were you included among the Jews that Mr Nagy rescued?' Alon asks.

The witness gives a short laugh. 'No way. I wasn't fortunate enough to be part of his family.'

Miklós leans towards the prosecutor. 'That's outrageous. He can't be allowed to get away with that.'

'Objection. The witness is giving his opinion about something we know to be false,' the prosecutor says. 'It's a documented fact that only a small number of the people Mr Nagy rescued were relatives.'

Like an accomplished skater, Amos Alon glides to the next question. 'So when you returned to Kolostór after the war, what were people saying about Mr Nagy?'

Before the prosecutor has time to object, the witness replies. 'They said that if he dared to show his face here someone would bump him off for sure.'

'Your honour! This is inadmissible, it's asking for hearsay.'

But the judge overrules his objection, removes his glasses, and leans towards the witness, obviously fascinated. 'I want to know why you said that.'

'Because Miklós Nagy deliberately misled the Jews into believing German lies about being relocated to another town and getting jobs.'

The prosecutor raises his voice. 'The witness is repeating a lie, a spiteful rumour to discredit the defendant.'

He sees Miklós's stricken face and realises his blunder. It's Isaiah Fleischmann who is the defendant in this case, not Miklós, but Amos Alon has twisted this case so cleverly that his own lawyer has fallen into the trap.

Peter Bernsztein is dismissed, and the next few witnesses called to testify all appear to bear Miklós a grudge. One of them even refers to him as a quisling who colluded in the murder of Hungarian Jews.

Miklós feels that his head is about to explode. What have these people got against him? He knows that his professional success and social prominence aroused envy among the less successful members of the community in his home town, and that his impatience was sometimes mistaken for arrogance, but their spite shocks him.

He recalls being described as a wheeler-dealer, but that ability to manipulate became his strength in a tragic situation that required leadership and energy. Without nerves of steel, self-confidence, and the ability to bluff when he had nothing to offer in return, he wouldn't have been able to confront Eichmann or to rescue anyone. Did they hold those qualities against him now they were safe?

The next witness to be called is Ervin Szabo, one of the rescued Jews of Kolostór, but when he begins to praise Miklós, Amos Alon cuts him short.

'Just answer the question,' he says, and steers the cross-examination to what he describes as Miklós's duplicity in not informing the community of their imminent fate. 'You were one of the favoured few to be selected for the rescue train,' he says, 'but if you hadn't been, you would have been on one of the death trains, because Mr Nagy had made it his business not to let anyone know of their destination so they couldn't escape or rebel, wouldn't you?'

The prosecutor springs from his chair to object, but the judge surveys the witness with interest and directs his question to him. 'I'd like to know, Mr Szabo, what would you have done if you had found out that the Nazis were lying about the aim of the deportations and were deporting people to death camps instead?'

Ervin hesitates, and the judge waits for him to answer.

Finally he says, 'I can't possibly know today what I would have done back then.'

'You're being evasive,' the judge says. 'You mean to tell me you really don't know what you would have done in that situation?'

'I could tell you anything, but I'm trying to be honest. It's impossible for me to know today, in the safety of Israel in 1954, what I would have done in the hell that Hungary was ten years ago.'

Miklós sinks back in his chair, and closes his eyes. The judge hasn't understood that Ervin has given the only truthful answer possible, an answer that goes to the heart of this case, where people who weren't in that hell are sitting in judgement on those who were.

But even the people who are called by the prosecution to give favourable accounts of the man who saved their lives are disappointingly lukewarm about their rescue. Yes, they admit, Miklós Nagy did save them, but, when skilfully cross-examined by Amos Alon, they dwell on the hardships they experienced on the train to Switzerland, rather than the joy of being released from Nazi Occupation and rescued from certain death. They recall the primitive conditions during the journey, their distress at not knowing where they were being taken, the privations they endured during their months of detention in the camp, and the anguish they suffered not knowing when they would be released.

When one woman mentions her terror at the rumour that they were being taken to Auschwitz, Miklós leans towards the prosecutor to remind him that this was a vital point in his favour, because it showed that people did know about Auschwitz, whereas one of the most damaging accusations levelled against him was that he had deceived them by refusing to inform them about the extermination camp. But the prosecutor is too slow to capitalise on the advantage. From the corner of his eye, Miklós sees Judit closing her eyes and spreading her hands in a gesture of helplessness.

Miklós listens to their complaints with growing anger. He supposes that the sensational nature of recent newspaper reports with their screaming headlines about collaboration, together with Amos Alon's damaging accusations, have induced them to reassess their rescue in a less positive light.

Of all the accusations and insinuations made so far during the trial, it's their grudging acknowledgement of his role that has embittered him the most. An old Jewish saying of his mother's, that he never understood before, now comes into his mind: *no good deed goes unpunished.*

Then he recalls one of his father's stories. A man has a fishbone stuck in his throat and is about to choke to death when at the very last moment the doctor arrives and removes the obstruction. The man can breathe again. 'You saved my life, how much do I owe you?' the grateful patient asks. 'Just give me one-tenth of what you would have given me while that fishbone was stuck in your throat,' the doctor replies.

That story always made him smile, but now he understands its sad truth. Gratitude is conditional and memory is short. They have chosen to forget their plight and their relief at being rescued, and are now damning him with their faint praise. And these are the people for whom he negotiated with Eichmann and risked his life.

The prosecutor announces that his next witness is Yoel Maroz, a representative of the Jewish Agency who was based in Istanbul when Gábor Weisz arrived from Budapest. At the mention of Gábor's name, Miklós feels his muscles tightening.

'Mr Weisz arrived in May 1944,' Maroz testifies. 'He told us that Eichmann had offered to release a million Jews in exchange for ten thousand trucks. As proof of his intention, he said he'd allow a train carrying over fifteen hundred Jews to leave Hungary while we negotiated with the Allies for the trucks he wanted. Mr Weisz kept stressing that he had to return to Budapest with proof that the offer was being considered because the fate of the remaining Jews hung in the balance. He was also worried about his wife, who was Eichmann's hostage.'

At the mention of Ilonka, Miklós looks up sharply, flushes, then quickly bows his head and grasps his trembling hands to conceal his reaction from Judit's piercing gaze.

'How did you react when you heard this?' the prosecutor asks.

'We were speechless,' Yoel Maroz replies. 'Who ever heard of Eichmann doing a deal with a Jew to save Jews? And how did we know if this preposterous offer was genuine? But either way, we had to grab at the straw being offered. If we didn't do whatever we could, we would be haunted by guilt for the rest of our lives. So it looked as if we might manage to save the lives of the remaining Hungarian Jews.'

Hearing his story being corroborated, Miklós raises his head. The judge is engaged by the dramatic account, and the court is attentive.

The prosecutor turns to Amos Alon. 'Your witness.'

'Knowing how desperate the situation was, what did the Jewish Agency do to save these Jews?'

The witness appears confused and glances at the prosecutor for guidance but finds none. 'Our hands were tied. We weren't empowered to act until the leaders of the Jewish Agency in Palestine had time to study his proposal and make a decision. And they were in a bind. On one hand, their policy was dead against making any deals with the enemy, and anyway, how could they agree to furnish Hitler with trucks to help him win the war? In any case, they didn't have that kind of money at their disposal...'

Amos Alon cuts him short with a dismissive wave of his hand. 'The answer is nothing, isn't it? Given the opportunity to save Hungarian Jews, the Jewish Agency did nothing.' With expansive gestures and dramatic pauses, he launches into an impassioned account of the heroism of the Irgun members who fought to defend their colleagues in 1948, and defended the *Altalena* to the death in the face of attacks. Everyone listens enthralled, but Miklós is fuming. He can see through this performance, and knows that Alon is contrasting his fearless Irgun comrades with what he perceives as the cowardly attitude of the Jewish Agency. He stares at the judge, furious that he is allowing this self-serving, self-indulgent and totally irrelevant diatribe, whose only motive is to blacken the government, but even the prosecutor seems mesmerised by the defence lawyer's eloquence. Finally the judge snaps out of his trance and urges Amos to spare the court the history lesson, and confine himself to cross-examining the witness.

'You say that the Jewish Agency hadn't had time to study his proposal, but isn't it correct to say that shortly after Mr Weisz arrived in Istanbul, the Jewish Agency informed the British of his presence there, and told them about his mission? And isn't it a fact that the Jewish Agency colluded in the betrayal of Gábor Weisz because Ben-Gurion didn't want to do anything to upset his British bosses? Mr Weisz was persuaded to set out for Aleppo, even though they knew that the British would arrest him as soon as he got there. You all knew it was a British trap. Did you let Mr Weisz know that it was a trap?'

The audacity of that accusation shocks Miklós, and he wonders where this outrageous claim originated.

'I repudiate your melodramatic claim that we hatched some kind of conspiracy and deliberately sent him into a British trap,' Yoel Maroz retorts. 'We received assurances from the British consulate in Istanbul that Mr Weisz would not be arrested, so there is absolutely no truth in the accusation that the Jewish Agency trapped him or colluded with the British.'

'But if you received assurances, as you say, it must be because you suspected the possibility of him being arrested?'

'We knew it was a possibility, but we believed the British officials.'

Alon keeps hammering his question. 'So you knew he could be arrested. Did you let him know that he could be in danger, yes or no?'

'No,' Maroz concedes.

'And isn't that why the mission ultimately failed?'

The prosecutor is bristling. He knows how damaging this is for the Mapai party which evolved from the Jewish Agency when Israel became a nation. 'This line of questioning is irrelevant, your honour. The witness is in no position to make a judgement about decisions made by the Jewish Agency or by the Allies, or about possible reasons for the mission's failure. In any case, we're prosecuting a case of criminal libel here, not engaging in a political post-mortem. Besides, this has nothing to do with the case against Mr Fleischmann.'

But from the vulpine gleam in Amos Alon's eyes, Miklós knows that this is exactly what the defence lawyer is doing, and by allowing his questions and his editorialising, the judge appears to be encouraging this line of questioning.

He also knows that the prosecutor is hopelessly out of his depth, out foxed by Amos Alon's devious agenda, which is now blatantly clear.

Maroz steps down from the witness box, and from his dazed expression it's clear that he knows he has been used to sharpen the defence lawyer's political hatchet but has been helpless to prevent it.

People in the courtroom are becoming restless. They are frowning, whispering, asking questions. Only the politically savvy among them understand the significance of this twist in the questioning. The rest are bewildered by it and confer with their neighbours. 'Can't you see, he's dragging the government into this to incriminate it,' someone whispers loudly, attracting a glare and an order for silence from the bench. 'But what does that have to do with the case against Miklós Nagy?' someone asks in a voice loud enough to be heard.

Amos Alon's voice rings out in the courtroom. 'I would now like to call Gábor Weisz to the witness stand.'

Miklós swallows. He hasn't seen his old friend since their last meeting in Budapest just before Gábor left for Istanbul, and dreads coming face to face with him. But at least Gábor will be able to confirm his efforts on behalf of the condemned Jews of Hungary.

Meanwhile the prosecutor is strenuously objecting to Gábor being called. Miklós knows that the government is desperate to prevent him from giving evidence that could be damaging to them. In the heated altercation that ensues between the two lawyers, who step up the bench to argue their case, Miklós can hear Alon insisting that in the interests of justice Gábor must be allowed to testify.

'As my learned colleague didn't call Mr Weisz as a witness for the prosecution, I was within my rights to contact him. In fact I've been in touch with him several times because I am convinced that his evidence has a bearing on this case,' he states, and with a grandiose gesture, he adds, 'I refuse to be intimidated by the prosecution into abrogating my responsibility to the court.'

Miklós closes his eyes and suppresses a groan. But it's not Gábor's account of his mission that worries him, but the thought of any personal information the wily solicitor might have elicited during their private conversations.

Gábor's appearance shocks him. He has lost weight and his clothes hang loosely from his stooped shoulders. But the biggest change is in his face. His eyes look dull, and his cheeks have sagged and lost their buttery sheen. He has the hunted look of a gazelle on the savannah when, isolated from the herd, it feels the cheetah's hot breath on the back of its neck.

Miklós wonders if Gábor and Ilonka are still together, and where they are living. More precisely, he longs to know where she is, but he is forbidden from contacting a witness for the defence, and in any case, it's probably better not to know.

Gábor begins his testimony with a nervous account of his mission which Miklós remembers from the coded messages that the double agent Zoltán Klein sent back from Istanbul.

Looking around and clearing his throat, Gábor coughs frequently and pulls at his tie, which is loosely knotted around his scrawny neck. From the way his gaze skims over Miklós as if he doesn't exist, Miklós suspects that he probably knows about his affair with Ilonka.

With a tremulous voice his friend describes the tense flight to Istanbul on a diplomatic Luftwaffe plane, his difficulty in obtaining a Turkish visa, and his desperate efforts to arrange meetings with the representatives of the Allied governments and the Jewish Agency.

Time was running out, and messages from Budapest, where his wife was Eichmann's hostage, kept arriving with entreaties to return with a positive answer or the extermination would continue and the rest of the Jews would be killed, along with her. Miklós is uncomfortably aware that whenever Gábor mentions Ilonka, he shoots a baleful look in his direction.

'Knowing that the situation was so desperate, I suppose Moshe Sharett of the Jewish Agency rushed to Istanbul to talk to you about this vital matter?' Amos Alon asks innocently.

At the mention of the leader of the Mapai party, the atmosphere in the courtroom tenses, and people sit forward, not wanting to miss a single word of the answer now that the prime minister is in Alon's sights.

Gábor shakes his head. 'No. He didn't come to meet me in Istanbul. I was told he couldn't get a visa to Turkey, which seemed very odd. The Jewish Agency people in Istanbul suggested that I should go to Palestine instead, to report to him in person. They said I'd have to go through Syria. I didn't want to go to Palestine because it was still under British mandate, and I knew there was a risk that, as a Hungarian national, I could be arrested if I stepped on British soil, but they convinced me I'd be safe. Knowing what was at stake, I felt I had no alternative but to follow their advice.'

'And what happened when you reached Aleppo?' Amos asks.

'My worst fears were realised. I was arrested by the British. It turned out that Moshe Sharett was already in Syria, and he talked to me in the presence of a British intelligence officer, but the British refused to release me. First they detained me in Aleppo and then they drove me to Cairo where they kept me under house arrest for four months. They interrogated me for hours every day. The questions kept coming thick and fast, sometimes from several officers at the same time, all demanding to know every minute detail of our dealings with Eichmann.'

He looks around the courtroom and from his wild eyes it's evident that he is reliving the torment of those four months. 'After a few days I thought I was going insane. I kept talking but no-one was listening. Before my eyes I could see twelve thousand men, women and children being thrown into the gas chambers of Auschwitz every day, and I was powerless to make these people understand. I shouted, I begged, I wept, I was distraught. I went on a hunger strike for two weeks. In the end, I insisted to be allowed to return to Hungary so I could die with the rest of the Jews.'

'What was the reaction of the British officers when you said that the lives of almost a million Jews were at stake?' Amos asks.

'I'll never forget their words as long as I live,' Gábor replies. 'Lord Moyne, one of the interrogators, said, "What do you expect me to do with a million Jews? Where can I put them?"'

There's a shocked gasp from the courtroom. Gábor turns to the judge, and his body is as taut as a bow just before the arrow is fired. 'That was the worst time of my entire life. The fate of a million Jewish men, women and children depended on me, and I let them down. You know what a nightmare is? It's not a bad dream. It's a living hell from which you know you will never escape.'

No-one in the courtroom makes a sound, the tension is palpable, and every eye is fixed on him. Men clear their throats and women shake their heads. The journalists are scribbling furiously, their eyes shining with excitement. They know that they are about to report on the most sensational story of the entire trial.

To maximise the effect of Gábor's words, Amos Alon pauses before asking. 'And what was the result of your detention?'

Gábor's voice is almost inaudible. 'My mission collapsed. The remaining Jews of Hungary were doomed. And the British refused to allow me to return to Hungary so I couldn't find out what happened to my wife.'

Amos Alon drops his voice so everyone has to strain to hear his next question. 'And what did happen to your wife?'

This time Gábor allows his hostile gaze to linger over Miklós before answering. 'Eventually I found out that she was included on Miklós Nagy's list and ended up in Switzerland.'

Miklós is poking the prosecutor's arm. His hands are shaking. In an urgent whisper he says, 'You must stop this. It has nothing to do with Fleischmann and the libel suit,' but when the prosecutor objects to this line of questioning, the judge overrules him. He seems riveted by the unfolding personal drama of the couple who were separated as a result of Gábor's mission.

'I don't understand how a woman who was Eichmann's hostage managed to get away from under his nose,' Amos Alon is saying.

Miklós is holding his breath. He suspects that Alon already knows the answer.

'Miklós Nagy obtained false documents for her. She wasn't on the list as Ilonka Weisz but as…'

At this point the prosecutor shouts. 'Your honour! This is irrelevant and immaterial. It has no bearing on this criminal libel suit. I request that the defence attorney desist from wasting time on trivial issues for the titillation of the court.'

This time the judge sustains his objection and Miklós breathes out. He knows that some of the cynical older reporters, always alert for what is being left unsaid, have been watching him closely during this exchange, and probably sensed a tantalising whiff of scandal floating over the courtroom.

Amos Alon shrugs and turns back to Gábor. 'As a result of your experience, would you say that the Allies and the leaders of the Jewish Agency turned their backs on the doomed Jews of Hungary?'

Miklós is staring at Alon in disgust. The defence lawyer's machinations have widened the scope of this case from a libel trial into a political witch-hunt against the current government and its leaders past and present. He has managed to forge a spurious link between an incident that took place in Hungary in 1944 and the government of Israel ten years later, and he was destroying Miklós's reputation in the process.

'Your honour!' the prosecutor objects. 'Mr Alon is putting words in the witness's mouth!'

'No further questions,' Alon says quickly. He knows he doesn't need to say another word.

The prosecutor steps towards the witness box. 'Mr Weisz, did you believe that Eichmann's offer was genuine? That he really would release one million Jews if the British, Americans, and the Jewish Agency donated ten thousand trucks? Or that the Allies would provide those trucks knowing that the Nazis were losing the war, and that they would use them against them?'

Gábor coughs again and shifts in his chair as he considers his answer.

'I was bewildered by his offer, but when you are on death row, and at the last moment someone offers you a reprieve in return for a favour, wouldn't you jump at it, no matter how outrageous the request was? I didn't know what Eichmann had in mind, whether he was playing a cat and mouse game or not, but what did we have to lose? I knew I had to find a way to stall the murder machine he was operating.'

This isn't what the prosecutor is hoping to hear, so he rephrases the question.

'Since you didn't believe Eichmann, why would you imagine that the Allied leaders, or the leaders of the Jewish Agency, would believe him and provide the trucks, knowing that this would give the Germans an advantage in prosecuting the war?'

Now Amos Alon leaps up. 'Your honour should disallow that question. It asks for speculation about something the witness can't possibly know.'

Once more, the judge upholds his objection. Defeated again, the prosecutor concludes his examination of his witness with one final question. 'What happened after the British released you?'

Gábor speaks slowly and thoughtfully. 'I was forced to travel to Palestine, which as you know was still under British control. They didn't let me return to Hungary because it was occupied by the Germans.'

Suddenly his voice rings out over the courtroom. 'That's when I realised I'd been caught in a trap from the moment I arrived in Istanbul. Everyone knew it, the Allied leaders as well as the representatives of the Jewish Agency, and I had been too naive to suspect what was going on. They sold me out to the British. That betrayal will haunt me to my dying day.'

His words hang in the air like malevolent spirits and the courtroom erupts. In the ensuing uproar, it takes several bangs of the judge's gavel and threats to clear the court before order is restored, the atmosphere heavy with disturbing speculations. The judge breaks the silence by banging his gavel to adjourn for lunch.

Miklós is shaking his head at his friend's sensational outburst and as he watches him shuffle from the witness box, he wonders if this paranoid interpretation of events is a symptom of his depressed state or the result of brainwashing by Alon. But when he remembers Gábor's appearance and the hostile look he cast in his direction, and thinks of his flagrant affair with Ilonka, it strikes him that he is probably partly to blame for Gábor's depression.

The courtroom empties slowly and people file out, more subdued than usual. Not just the duplicity of international diplomacy but ingratitude and betrayal have been on display this morning. Human nature has been on trial and it has been found wanting.

Miklós feels wrung out by his friend's distress. He can see now that no-one had a chance of succeeding in that situation, and no-one could have fought harder than Gábor to convince the Allied representatives of the importance of the mission. Their ears and hearts were blocked by the exigencies of their own interests, not by humanitarian concerns.

He realises his own arrogance in assuming that a more skilful negotiator like himself could have succeeded. In 1944 Gábor was a pawn in the hands of the Germans and the Allies. He wonders if Gábor has realised that now he has been used again, this time as an axe to chop down the government of Israel.

Seeing him has reignited feelings he has tried for years to suppress: the terror of his confrontations with Eichmann, the ecstasy of his trysts with Ilonka, and the guilt and grief that gnaw at him in the dark hours of the night when he can't sleep. He betrayed his friend by his affair with Ilonka, and later, through no fault of his own, he betrayed Ilonka too.

But perhaps it was his fault. For the first time since the trial began, he puts aside his bitterness and sense of injustice and turns his attention inwards. He sees himself reflected in the cracked and pitted mirror of his ego, not as a heroic activist but an arrogant and egotistical lover of women, women whose love he probably didn't deserve.

He is relieved that Judit had had to hurry from the court to a meeting with a musical director about her forthcoming concert before the morning session was over, and doesn't know how close the defence attorney came to publicly exposing his relationship with Ilonka. He thinks about the impact of the trial on Judit, and how devotedly she has supported him and tried to shield him from the vitriol of his opponents. She knew of his affair in Budapest and said nothing, she has stood by his side throughout this Gehenna, but how would she react if his affair was publicly exposed in the press?

He comforts himself with the thought that Gábor won't reveal the affair and, with all the sensational revelations made in court that morning, it wasn't likely that the reporters would follow up something so nebulous. He makes himself a promise that when all this is over, he will make it up to Judit.

CHAPTER THIRTY

Jerusalem, April 1954

Miklós stays in the prosecutor's room during the lunch recess to avoid the reporters loitering around the court building in the hope of buttonholing him for a controversial quote. He picks up a newspaper and on the third page he sees a profile of Amos Alon. It depicts the lawyer in glowing terms as a typical *sabra*, the new breed of Jew, fearless, brave and uncompromising, a David fighting the power of the sinister government. Even as a child, the reporter writes, Alon was sensitive to the corrupt machinations of the government. He describes an incident when Alon, as a feisty ten year old, was about to hurl a rock at a government building out of a feeling of injustice, but his mother knocked it from his hand just in time.

Miklós pushes the paper away, infuriated by the journalist's fawning and by the implicit comparison between the stereotypical European Jews, who were so often insultingly portrayed as servile, passive sheep, and the image of the

Israeli Jew who never surrendered. He knows that Alon is holding a rock once again, but this time it's a much bigger rock, and it doesn't look as if anyone will manage to knock it from his hand.

'Why does Judge Lazar give Amos Alon so much latitude?' he asks the prosecutor. He takes a sip of black coffee that one of the court attendants has brought in, pulls a face, and pushes the waxed cup away. 'I can't understand why he allows Alon's irrelevant questions and upholds most of his objections, but overrules most of yours.'

Noah Elman looks up from his papers and shrugs. 'Who can understand judges? They all have a bee in their bonnet about something, if you ask me. Take a reasonable, competent solicitor and promote him to the bench, and suddenly he can see a halo around his head and thinks he's one of the archangels.'

He pushes his chair back and steeples his fingers as he looks up at the ceiling.

'Unfortunately for you, he and Alon share one crucial motive. They both hate the government.'

'Why's that?'

The prosecutor leans back, and from his expression Miklós can see that he is looking forward to sharing some gossip. 'In Alon's case, it's about the *Altalena*. You might remember this was in the early days of Israel's independence, and soldiers of the new provisional government shelled it, killing his brother. As for Judge Lazar, his resentment is more recent, but just as bitter. He was furious when he was passed over when they were appointing judges to the Supreme Court. He was sure he had it in the bag on account of his seniority, but they appointed his deputy instead. He hasn't made a secret of his disappointment. Or should I say *dis*-appointment.'

Miklós doesn't smile at the pun and struggles to refrain from voicing his own resentment that the judge and defence counsel sharing a common bias was bad enough, but having an incompetent prosecutor on his side was even more disastrous.

Back in the courtroom for the afternoon session, Miklós looks at the judge with new interest as Amos Alon announces his next witness.

'I'd like to call Zoltán Klein to the stand.'

Zolly Klein! Miklós is astonished. Most people regarded spies as ruthless people without moral fibre, but this one was a particularly duplicitous agent who probably acted for Germany, Hungary, Turkey and God knew who else, and was mistrusted by everyone. What could this disreputable spy possibly contribute to this case, and who would take him seriously?

While he waits for Klein to step into the witness box, Miklós recalls that, for some reason he had never understood, Eichmann had ordered Klein to accompany Gábor to Istanbul. He suspected that Klein's role was to spy on Gábor and report back about the progress of his negotiations. That was sheer speculation at the time, but his friend's evidence in court indicated that espionage must have played a major role in his arrest, most likely thanks to Klein. Either way, Klein wasn't likely to reveal his secrets.

Unlike Gábor, Klein looks sharp and confident. The years haven't ravaged him and neither, apparently, have his double dealings. In fact he looks less shifty than before, and he no longer dresses to blend into the background as he once did.

For his court appearance he wears expensive-looking beige slacks with turn-ups, and a crisp poplin shirt under a tweed jacket with leather buttons and large lapels, the kind that English tailors were renowned for. It's clear that Zolly Klein's shady deals have paid off.

Amos Alon begins his questioning. 'Can you tell us, what was your occupation in Hungary in 1944?'

Miklós is wondering how honestly Klein will answer when, with a self-satisfied smile, he says, 'I was an inter-government agent. I liaised between various agencies, ministries and organisations, and facilitated the exchange of important information.'

'And which agencies and governments made use of these special talents of yours?'

Klein is still smiling and shows no annoyance at the lawyer's sarcastic tone. 'Anyone who was smart enough to recognise my expertise.'

'So would it be correct to describe you as a gun for hire?'

Klein's thin lips twist into a condescending smile. 'You can describe me any way you like.'

The judge leans forward. 'Mr Klein, please stop equivocating. And Mr Alon, how much of the court's time do you propose to devote to this exchange? You don't appear to be making much progress.'

'Your honour, establishing the witness's credentials is crucial to this case,' Amos Alon replies. He turns to Klein. 'Why were you on a Luftwaffe flight to Istanbul in May 1944 with Mr Weisz, and who sent you?'

The question surprises Miklós. After all this time, Alon must know that it was Eichmann who sent Klein and Gábor to Istanbul to present his improbable offer of Jews for trucks.

But Klein is hesitating. He looks down at his hands, then up at the lawyer, and from his expression, it is clear that he is trying to decide how to answer. The judge props his elbows on the bench and looks as if he's about to direct him to reply, but Amos Alon beats him to it.

'I realise that you were in a delicate situation in 1944, but the war is long over, and I assume that past governments are no longer taking advantage of your expertise, so you can answer truthfully. I remind you that you are under oath. So I repeat my question: Why were you sent to Istanbul with Mr Weisz in May 1944, and at whose instigation?'

Klein holds the lawyer's gaze and when he speaks, his voice is loud and clear.

'At the instigation of Heinrich Himmler.'

The judge's eyes widen and he looks at Klein in disbelief. 'Heinrich Himmler? Hitler's right-hand man?' He doesn't say *You can't really expect me to believe this*, but his tone implies it.

'That's correct. Heinrich Himmler.' Klein lets his thunderbolt hit home without saying another word and looks around at the courtroom, clearly relishing the uproar he has caused.

The judge can't conceal a smile at the ludicrous notion. As if Heinrich Himmler would have sent this third-class spy on such an errand. The usually imperturbable Amos Alon is frowning. This wasn't the answer he was expecting and he is no longer in total control of the proceedings. As for Miklós, he can only stare at Klein, bewildered. He can't understand why the spy is fabricating such a bizarre version of events that can so easily be contradicted. He himself was present when Eichmann ordered Gábor to Istanbul. Is Klein saying this to make himself important, to create a sensation? Or does he have some other motive? He looks at Klein again, and, improbable as it seems, he begins to wonder if his statement could possibly be true.

Amos Alon continues his questioning, but he is thinking on his feet and sounds less self-assured than before. 'Mr Klein, up until now we have been told that Eichmann sent you and Mr Weisz to Istanbul to persuade the representatives of the Allies and the Jewish Agency to provide Germany with ten thousand trucks in return for releasing one million Jews. Are you now telling us that it was Himmler, the man in charge of implementing the atrocities of the Holocaust, the Nazi who was Hitler's right-hand man, that it was Himmler and not Eichmann who sent you on this errand?'

'Yes and no,' Klein replies.

'What do you mean by that?' The judge breaks in. 'You must stop talking in riddles, Mr Klein. The answer is yes or no, not yes and no.'

Klein shrugs. 'It's not so simple but I'll try to be exact. Yes, Himmler sent us, but no, it wasn't on the errand that you mentioned.'

'Another riddle. We are all ears, Mr Klein. Please enlighten us.'

'It was Himmler's idea from the start,' Klein says. He sounds relaxed, and takes his time explaining. 'Eichmann never wanted anything to do with it. The only mission he was interested in was killing Jews. Total extermination, that's what he was after, not trucks or money. And he hated Himmler. Professional rivalry, I suppose. He and Himmler were always at loggerheads. Not that Himmler loved Jews, but he had his own reasons for my mission, and being more powerful than Eichmann, he was able to overrule him. And he had Kurt Becher's support for his scheme.'

At the mention of Becher, Miklós tries to think back to their conversations. He recalls that Becher always lavished extravagant praise on Himmler's intellect and, what was even more extraordinary, on his humanity. But as he was Himmler's protégé, his admiration wasn't surprising. Miklós concedes that Klein's story is making sense, even though he had never suspected that this outlandish scheme had been foisted on an unwilling Eichmann.

'And what scheme was that?' Amos Alon is asking.

'Himmler was ready to make a separate peace with the Allies. That's why he concocted the trucks-for-Jews plan. It was a blind for his real purpose, and he didn't want Eichmann or Hitler to know about it.'

Everyone stares at the man in the witness box, transfixed by his words. Even the reporters have stopped writing as they try to comprehend the significance of what they have just heard. History has leaped from the pages of textbooks and punched them in the face.

'And you of course were privy to Himmler's secret thoughts.' Amos Alon can't keep the sarcasm out of his voice.

'As a matter of fact, I was,' Klein replies coolly.

Miklós feels dazed. His head is a spinning top, gathering speed with each gyration. Klein's bombshell turns everything he thought he knew upside down. Now he understands why Klein had been sent to Istanbul with Gábor. Not to convince the Allied leaders to give Germany trucks, not to facilitate the release of Jews, but to negotiate with the representatives of the Allies. Gábor's role was to provide a smokescreen for the real mission.

He thinks back to his conversations with Kurt Becher. All the time he was trying to persuade Kurt Becher to help him, Becher was in cahoots with Himmler, and they were both plotting against Hitler and Eichmann, and using Klein to further their aims. He marvels that Klein, the spy everyone despised and mistrusted, enjoyed such a prominent role in the corridors of power. He had underestimated Klein and overestimated himself. It was an unbelievable story but he believed it. No-one could have invented it.

'So will you share those thoughts with us?' Alon is asking.

'Himmler was a realist. In 1944, Hitler was still sending young German boys to die at the front, but Himmler knew it was hopeless. The Russians were advancing, and Germany was losing the war. So he decided to make overtures to the Allies and this trucks-for-Jews scheme was a ploy to let the West know that he was prepared to make a separate peace. Mr Weisz was his cover, and I was his instrument. Eichmann never intended to release a million Jews but he was forced to play along with Himmler's plan. It was a trick to induce the West into negotiating. But it didn't work, and the Jews of Hungary ended up in Auschwitz anyway.'

Klein has everyone on a knife edge. His testimony has provided the most explosive revelation of the entire trial, and the journalists, who thought that Gábor's testimony earlier that day would be the most sensational story of the trial, are so riveted by what they hear that from time to time they hold their pens in mid-air above their shorthand note-books and neglect to commit Klein's words to paper.

Amos Alon now addresses Klein in a more respectful tone. As for the judge, he is hanging on every word.

'How were you supposed to conduct those top-secret conversations?'

'Himmler knew that Germany's only hope was to split the Allies. From what he knew of communism and Stalin's plans for Eastern Europe, he didn't believe that England and America would stay allied with the Soviet Union for very long, so he cunningly proposed making a separate treaty with the Western Allies.'

Something about this sounds familiar, and Miklós recalls the conversation he had about trucks with Eichmann, in which the SS colonel had said that Germany wouldn't use the trucks against the Western Allies, only on the Eastern front. That statement had puzzled him at the time, but now it made sense.

'How did the Allies receive Himmler's overture?' Alon asks.

'It was ridiculed and dismissed. The massive German defeat at the battle of Stalingrad marked the turning point of the war thanks to the Red Army, and Churchill and Roosevelt knew that without the Russians, they risked losing the war. They mistrusted Stalin but they needed his continued help to defeat Hitler. Although they and their generals didn't trust Stalin, they didn't dare do anything that would make him suspicious or, what would have been far worse, push him into an alliance with Hitler. So nothing came of Himmler's scheme.'

Amos Alon frowns. 'So how did the idea of releasing a million Jews fit into this scenario?'

'It was Himmler's cunning attempt to whitewash the Nazi record for the future. He foresaw that when the Allies won the war, Germany would be held responsible for atrocities which he himself had orchestrated. So he thought he'd found a reason to mitigate Allied judgement about Germany after the war. It obviously didn't occur to him that it was a bit late in the day to seek absolution.'

Klein's lengthy testimony continued, and there was not a whisper or a rustle in the courtroom as he went on. 'There was also another aspect to his scheme. A cynical one. The war was coming to an end and Himmler was aware that Germany would be accused of unprecedented mass murder. Today we call the murder of six million Jews genocide, but that term hadn't been coined yet. He figured that if the West ignored his scheme to rescue the remaining Jews, as he expected they would, then the Nazis would later be able to point out that the West didn't do anything to save Jews when it had the chance.'

'Just the West?' Amos urges Klein on to the finish line.

'The Western Allies and, by implication, the Jewish Agency.'

There's an uneasy silence. People sigh and fidget. An accusing ghost has emerged from the shadows and stands in full view of the courtroom, no longer able to be ignored.

Miklós looks at Amos Alon and sees triumph in his eyes. This time his rock has found its target. Klein has articulated the calumny Alon has been working towards from the moment he took on Fleischmann's case. Not content with destroying me, Miklós thinks, he has tried to destroy the government by implicating the Jewish Agency in the inaction of the Allies during the Holocaust. The accusation shocks him with its lack of understanding of the realities of the war, but from the ashen faces in the courtroom, it seems to have hit its mark. It's unjust but justice seems irrelevant when the motive is vengeance.

'There's one thing that Himmler's scheme did achieve,' Klein is saying, and he turns his gaze on Miklós, 'and it's something that was never on the cards. I'm referring to the release of over fifteen hundred Hungarian Jews, and that happened thanks to Mr Nagy's tireless efforts.'

Miklós looks at Klein, grateful for his unexpected acknowledgement and struck by its irony. Of all people, it's not the ones he rescued, but the man he always denigrated, who has paid a tribute to his achievement.

He looks around the courtroom to make sure the comment hasn't gone unnoticed, but from the tense, pale faces he realises that it's not Klein's tribute but his political revelations that have had the most profound impact on everyone. History has just turned a double somersault in the Jerusalem District Court, and those present are dazed by its shocking spirals.

CHAPTER THIRTY-ONE

Jerusalem, May 1954

Miklós is watching Judit as she wriggles into her step-ins and pulls on her navy blue shantung suit. He notes her slim body and the wispy fair hair that frames her elfin face with the appreciation of an art connoisseur rather than the ardour of a lover. As she combs her hair back from her forehead, applies a slash of red lipstick and dabs rouge on her pale cheeks, he says with a lightness he doesn't feel, 'You look so young, they'll think you're my daughter.'

'I don't want to give them the satisfaction of saying I look old and haggard.'

He is already at the door, looking at his watch. 'It's time to go.'

As they drive towards the courthouse, she keeps up a cheerful conversation about the boys' last soccer game, the frustration of trying to learn a Rachmaninoff piano concerto, and the irrational nature of food rationing. His replies are curt and perfunctory, and she knows he isn't listening, but she keeps up the chatter just the same. They both know it's to avoid articulating what's on their minds.

The murmur of gossip greets them as they enter the District Court to hear the summations, and they take their seats towards the back of the courtroom without looking at anyone. Judit manages a smile that doesn't reach her eyes. Miklós sighs. He dreads having to hear it all rehashed, but he doesn't expect any surprises, especially not from the prosecutor. After his inept handling of the case, he isn't likely to display any belated brilliance that might sway the judge, unlike his opponent who is probably sharpening his claws for the kill.

They all stand as Judge Lazar enters, and Miklós wonders whether he has already made up his mind about the case, or if today's summations will affect his judgment. Either way, Miklós realises how naive he has been. This trial is a contest, not a search for truth, and the prize will be awarded to the side that tells the most compelling story.

The prosecutor speaks first. 'Isaiah Fleischmann's accusations against Miklós Nagy are preposterous. Preposterous is one word. Scandalous and libellous are others that describe his accusations. I will try to do justice to this brave man who has risked his life to save others in the darkest hours of our history. There is not one shred of evidence that Miklós Nagy was a collaborator. Quite the contrary. The defence attorney has tried to pull the wool over your eyes. He has tried to make you believe that it was in Mr Nagy's power to save every Jew in Hungary. Does my learned colleague live in some parallel universe? Is he totally ignorant of the situation in Hungary in 1944? He wants you to believe that the Jews of Kolostór could have resisted the Nazis. Without any weapons? He fantasises that they could have escaped. Where to?'

Judit breathes out. She is squeezing Miklós's arm. This is more like it, her gesture says. But a moment later, she groans.

'Even if Miklós Nagy forgot about his affidavit, that only proves that his memory let him down. That's not a crime. But no-one has the right to judge him and claim that he shouldn't have testified for a Nazi. He did what he thought was right at the time for a man who helped him rescue so many people. Claiming that his affidavit was instrumental in releasing Becher was boastful, but since when is boasting a crime? Does that prove he is a collaborator?'

The longer he speaks, the more he sounds as if he is pleading for the defence, not prosecuting the man charged with the offence. Isaiah Fleischmann becomes almost irrelevant in his summation, which is devoted to justifying Miklós's actions. The witness has been transformed into the defendant and the actual defendant has faded into the background and become an irrelevant shadow.

'You'd think I was the one on trial here,' Miklós whispers.

Judit squeezes his hand again. 'It doesn't matter,' she whispers. 'The judge knows you're not.'

But Miklós is fuming. He finds it so difficult to concentrate on the prosecutor's lengthy dissertation that he misses much of it. Refocusing with an effort, he hears the prosecutor's defence of the government during Gábor's failed mission to Istanbul.

'There was no shame in the Jewish Agency cooperating with the British who were fighting the Nazis,' he is saying.

'The defence has produced no evidence to show that the Jewish Agency was complicit in turning Mr Weisz over to the British.'

Towards the end of his summing up, he comes back to Isaiah's charge of collaboration. 'Sitting in this court, listening to my learned colleague, you would think that it was a crime to snatch so many Jews from the jaws of a terrible death. Wasn't he right to try and free a group of Jews when the majority were doomed to be murdered? The defence would like you to believe that Miklós Nagy deliberately sacrificed half a million Jews so that he could rescue a favoured few, but that's a travesty of the facts, a travesty of history, and an insult to the man who risked so much and fought so hard to rescue them. It wasn't in his power to save the half million, but he managed to save more than fifteen hundred souls who, without his heroic efforts, would have been murdered along with the rest.'

After a pause, he continues. 'The Talmud teaches us that whoever saves one life, saves the whole world. Well, Miklós Nagy saved over one thousand five hundred worlds, and for that he should be lauded to the skies, not accused of collaboration.'

Then, as if an afterthought, he adds, 'I ask your honour to convict the accused of the offense with which he is charged.'

There's a recess before Amos Alon begins his summing up. News of Alon's fiery delivery and sensational accusations have spread throughout the city, and at the entrance to the courtroom, people are standing three deep, pushing and shoving in the hope of getting inside for the fireworks they anticipate when it is the defence counsel's turn to speak. But the courtroom is already packed. No-one who has sat through the prosecutor's summation wants to risk leaving their seat for fear of losing it.

As he waits for Amos Alon to begin, Miklós sits in dejected silence. The defence counsel has the advantage of having the last word, and he expects that the impact of the prosecutor's low-key presentation will be forgotten the moment Amos Alon opens his mouth.

'This trial has been stacked against me from beginning to end,' Miklós whispers to Judit. 'Alon has a double advantage. He has the privileges of a defence counsel but he's virtually the prosecutor as well.'

Alon is even more ferocious than he expected. Just as the prosecutor has defended Miklós instead of attacking Isaiah Fleischmann, Alon proceeds to attack Miklós rather than defending Isaiah. And he rips into him without mercy. There are no doubts or ambiguities in his summation, no rhetorical questions or weak arguments. Just one continuous onslaught.

Alon's arguments electrify the courtroom. He sounds like an avenging angel sent to the Jerusalem District Court to identify evil-doers and put the world to rights. People are as still as marble obelisks, mesmerised by his thrilling words. He accuses Miklós of moral depravity, of ambition gone mad.

'He colluded with the Nazis' diabolical scheme to lull the remaining Jews of Hungary into believing the Nazis' lies, into passively acceding to their orders. His satanic alliance with Eichmann sealed the fate of the Jews of Kolostór. We hear about the collaborators of other nations — men like Quisling, Petain and Laval, but Miklós Nagy's actions surpass them all. It was his malevolence and collaboration that enabled him to select a favoured few to be saved, while he withheld information that might have saved the rest.'

Carried away by the admiring glances of the people assembled in the courtroom, Alon's oratory rises to even greater heights. 'We have erected memorials and forests in honour of the exterminated Jews of Europe. But those memorials don't silence the right of the voices of the slaughtered to be heard. These voices have now entered our courtroom and forced us to listen to what they are saying.

'The prosecutor accuses me of mud-slinging but the mud in this courtroom is in the facts that I have revealed. Miklós Nagy's soul was corrupted and his ideals were compromised when he became a trusted friend of the Nazis. In the last months of the war, Miklós Nagy became an agent for the Nazi gang — he was the most effective Jewish agent they had. He was their trusted ally and apologist. He sacrificed the remaining Jews of Kolostór, many of whom could have been saved, and he did it just so he could rescue his own friends and relatives and a few prominent people. He wanted to be a big shot, to hobnob with the top Nazis, and he did their bidding which resulted in the deaths of the Jews of Kolostór. And then he ran away and saved his own skin.'

Miklós springs to his feet. 'You're a dirty liar!' he shouts. 'You know I didn't run away. I could have stayed in Switzerland, but I returned to Budapest to try and save more Jews, even though I was risking my life.'

People turn around to stare at him, and Judit places a hand on his trembling arm to urge him to sit down. The judge bangs his gavel furiously. 'Silence! If you don't sit down at once and stop interrupting these proceedings, Mr Nagy,

I will have you charged with contempt and ejected from the court.'

Miklós slumps into his seat, still shaking.

Ignoring the disruption, Alon continues, 'But let us look at Miklós Nagy after the war. The terror and threat of deportation have gone, but two years later, he saved Kurt Becher, a war criminal, from judgement in Nuremberg. Then he lied about it, and perjured himself in this court. So I repeat: Miklos Nagy is a collaborator who should be put on trial in accordance with the law passed against Nazis and collaborators.'

Although ceiling fans are cooling the air in the courtroom, Miklós mops his face. He can feel sweat pooling down his neck and he shifts on the timber bench. Alon's words are a torturer's scalpel, flaying his skin down to bare bone, layer by layer. According to that law, which had recently been passed, death was the punishment for Nazi collaborators, the only crime for which the death penalty was imposed in Israel. How could Alon invoke that law against him when he was the victim of criminal libel?

He recalls the conversation he had with Kurt Becher in his office about gratitude, betrayal and crucifixion. Becher was right.

'Remember, it's just words,' Judit whispers, interlacing her fingers with his. 'He's talking utter nonsense. Anyone with half a brain can see that, especially the judge.'

Miklós is convinced that she is wrong but he doesn't reply. Nothing can convince him that Alon's diatribe is not having a powerful impact on the judge. From the rapt faces in the courtroom, he can see that whatever their opinions were before his summing up, this lawyer with the skills of a demagogue has now swept them along in his depiction of Miklós as a megalomaniac in the service of the enemy. He knows that a lie repeated often enough is eventually regarded as the truth.

Alon has already moved on to his next theme. In line with his conspiracy theory, he now attempts to link Miklós's actions with those of the Jewish Agency, which he accuses of co-operating with the British at the cost of rescuing the Jews of Hungary. He seems to be exhorting the judge to pass sentence on the Jewish Agency and, by implication, on its successor, the present government.

Judit leans towards Miklós until their heads touch. 'Isaiah Fleischmann didn't even mention the Jewish Agency or the Mapai party in his pamphlet. This tirade has absolutely nothing to do with the case.'

Miklós shrugs. He knows it may have nothing to do with the libel case but it has everything to do with Alon's political agenda and the outcome of the trial.

Perhaps aware that despite its sensational value, his attack on the government is irrelevant as the defendant didn't make that accusation, Alon moves back to his strongest weapon, the Becher affidavit. Miklós grits his teeth and tenses his muscles. He has the unsettling feeling that any moment now his body will snap apart, spraying tissue and blood over the entire court.

In conclusion, Amos Alon tells the court in a measured tone that he has been privileged to lift the curtain of lies and deceit from their eyes and rip it to shreds. Sounding like a humble David who has confronted Goliath, he says, 'I have revealed the honest truth without any agenda or axe to grind, but from a sacred duty to all those who didn't survive. The ancient Greeks believed that unpunished crimes brought plagues to the people who harboured criminals, and that punishing evil-doers purifies life. We don't face a literal plague, but we do risk losing our decency and humanity. Honour doesn't lie in forgetting mass murder or forgiving the perpetrators.'

'He sounds as if he's addressing a jury,' Judit whispers. 'This is all about him. I think he's forgotten about his client.'

Miklós doesn't reply. In full view of everyone present, Amos Alon has performed a sleight-of-hand that most conjurors would envy. He has turned a desperate man who managed to wrest over fifteen hundred Jews from the clutches of Eichmann into a vicious, calculating demon, and transformed the leaders of the Jewish Agency from overwhelmed, horrified men trying to deal with the extermination of the last of Europe's Jews into servile politicians who, instead of trying to save the Jews of Europe, collaborated with the British colonisers.

The summations over, the judge thanks the lawyers and leaves the bench, and there's a loud hubbub as people leave the court arguing heatedly about what they have heard. Miklós and Judit slip out of the courtroom to avoid the embarrassed glances of acquaintances and the accusing glares of strangers.

As they drive home, Judit looks anxiously at her husband, who hasn't uttered a word for the past hour. The lines on his face have become furrows, and his eyes seem to be covered with a dull grey film.

'The judge will see through Alon's political agenda,' she says. 'He won't fall for his manipulations.'

But Miklós doesn't reply.

At home, the boys want to hear about the day's events. In an enthusiastic voice, Judit expounds on the prosecutor's summation, telling them how he praised their father for his courage in saving so many people. While she speaks, Ben, their older son, doesn't take his eyes off his father's face.

'But what about the other one?' he asks. 'What did he say? He's the one the kids at school talk about. Even the teachers say how smart he is. Why don't you tell us what he said?'

There's a nervous, angry edge to his voice, and in the silence that ensues, Judit hesitates, wondering how to answer in a way that won't upset the boy.

But Miklós speaks first. 'He tried to make out I was a Nazi collaborator and a liar.'

Judit shakes her head, wanting him to stop, but he ignores her and continues, giving Ben the gist of Alon's speech, not sparing any painful details.

'Miki, don't,' she says. She can't bear to hear him inflict so much pain on himself, and on their son.

'They might as well know the truth,' he says brusquely. 'They'll hear all about it tomorrow when the newspapers come out. Anyway, the other kids will be talking about it at school.'

There is fury in Ben's eyes. 'How can he tell lies like that after you saved all those people?'

'He can say it because he doesn't care that I've saved people. All he wants to do is convince the judge that I've done those terrible things so he can get his client off.'

'That's not fair,' Ben says. 'It stinks.'

'Where's Gil?' Judit asks suddenly. Over the past few weeks she has been considering taking him out of the school; the children's name-calling has made him fearful and withdrawn. But Miklós disagreed. 'Running away isn't the answer. He should learn boxing so he can stand up for himself.'

None of them noticed that Gil left the room as soon as they began talking about the trial.

The following morning, Judit hides the newspaper from Miklós and the boys. On the front page the journalist reporting on the trial describes Amos Alon's summation as one of the most brilliant speeches ever heard in an Israeli court.

Just before setting off to school, Ben asks his father, 'So what happens now?'

Judit glances at Miklós, who is staring out of the window, but she can tell that he doesn't see the street or anything in it. She takes a deep breath and says, 'The verdict.'

CHAPTER THIRTY-TWO

Jerusalem, June 1956

Days stretch into weeks, and weeks drag into months, and still the judge hasn't handed down his verdict. Despite the delay, the Nagy trial, as it is universally referred to, is still a burning issue, and rumours are flying about why it is taking so long. An election campaign is underway, and there is friction inside the Mapai coalition. Some journalists have suggested that the government has deliberately delayed publishing the verdict because it fears its impact on the voters. Other commentators wonder if the judge has collapsed under the strain of trying to reach a decision in such a complex case. Whatever the cause, gamblers have already placed their bets on the outcome.

As Miklós awaits the verdict, his mind is full of recriminations, resentments and regrets. To add to his woes, he has been asked to relinquish his candidacy for a seat in the Knesset, and his job on the Hungarian-language radio program has been axed, ostensibly due to lack of funds. He isn't fooled by the excuse.

As he sits at home, waiting for the verdict and mulling over the events of the past year, he wonders if he should have taken his friends' advice and tried harder to persuade the government not to sue. Perhaps he should have refused to be the first witness, or not testified at all. Why didn't he push for a more competent prosecutor? Maybe he should have sounded less angry and self-righteous instead of unwittingly stepping into the minefield that Amos Alon had prepared for him. His friend Uri's warning before the trial began echoes in his head: *Don't let them pursue this libel suit. No matter what happens, you will never come out of this with clean hands.*

He vacillates between hope and dread but he reminds himself repeatedly that, after all, he wasn't the one charged with libel. He was only a witness, and the judge's sole task is to determine whether Isaiah Fleischmann is guilty or not. He reminds himself that despite the excruciating accusations of the defence attorney, he achieved something unique, which no-one can ignore. He has to trust that the judge will see the important issues, and distinguish between fact, innuendo and falsehood.

Just the same, he is restless, and sleep eludes him. Night after long night he paces up and down in their apartment. Like a sad lion locked inside a circus cage, Judit thinks whenever she wakes up and hears his slow footsteps. She slips out of bed to coax him back.

'Don't worry, Miki, it will be all right,' she says, taking his hand. 'The judge is experienced enough to see through Alon's diatribes. He's bound to find Fleischmann guilty.'

When Miklós hears that at last a date has been set for the judge to hand down his verdict, he is relieved that the anguish of reliving the trial, of wondering, surmising and dreading will finally end, but he can't bring himself to go to court. Going over the trial in his mind, he feels like a laboratory rat running endlessly back and forth along the same paths as he tries to find a way out of the maze. The pressure builds and sometimes he feels his head is about to blow off.

'I won't be able to sit through it,' he tells Judit. 'You can tell me what he said when you come home.'

*

Finally the appointed day dawns. It's a bright morning in early summer, the kind of God-given day that makes you glad to be alive, but joy isn't what Judit feels as she enters the courtroom.

She holds her head high but her stomach is flipping somersaults. The courtroom is packed and the atmosphere is charged. As she sits down she feels accusing eyes stabbing into her back. 'It's as if the whole country is holding its breath for this verdict,' a woman behind her comments, and her voice thrills with anticipation. Like bloodthirsty Romans assembling in the Colosseum to watch a fight to the death, Judit thinks bitterly.

Judge Lazar enters, holding a thick volume that he places in front of him. Everyone cranes forward to see his expression and assess his mood, but his stern face gives nothing away. If he feels any emotion, he conceals it beneath a mask of inscrutability.

'There must be at least two hundred pages in there,' a man near her whispers, pointing to the tome. 'We'll be here all day!'

After a brief glance around the court, the judge puts on his horn-rimmed glasses and begins reading in a voice so low that it demands absolute silence. Judit sits forward so as not to miss a single word.

Soon she is clenching her fists. For several hours, as he reads his interminable judgement, he upholds Isaiah Fleischmann's accusations, one by one. He pronounces that the Jews of Kolostór boarded the trains unaware of their fate because they were duped into believing the Nazis, who used Jewish agents to lull them into acquiescence. Because of that false information, they didn't try to overpower the guards in the ghetto, to escape, or to organise any resistance. And the person responsible for this deception was Miklós Nagy, whose silence the Nazis bought by allowing him to rescue a few friends, relatives and prominent members of the community.

Eichmann was afraid of another Warsaw Uprising, that's why he made the deal with Mr Nagy, but the cost was the murder of the remaining six hundred thousand Jews of Hungary. Sacrificing the majority of the Jews to rescue a few of the prominent ones was the basis of the agreement between the Nazis and Miklós Nagy, who was collaborating with Hitler's henchmen.

Judit buries her face in her hands, unable to maintain the pretence of equanimity any longer. Doesn't the judge know anything about Eichmann's proposed trucks-for-Jews scheme? Hasn't he listened to the evidence given by witnesses who explained that it was impossible for the Jews of Kolostór to escape or resist? Has he forgotten that they didn't believe the information they'd been given about the trains and Auschwitz? Isn't he aware that Miklós didn't have the power to save the remaining Jews? The judge is repeating Amos Alon's accusations as facts, and she is glad that Miklós isn't here to listen to his hateful words.

The judge pauses, pours water from a jug and takes his time sipping it. When he resumes reading, his voice is loud and emphatic. 'The Nazis bribed Miklós Nagy and their bait was the rescue train,' he says. 'He should have remembered the Trojans' warning: *Timeo Danaos et dona ferentes*. Beware of Greeks bearing gifts. By accepting the Nazis' gift, Miklós Nagy became a collaborator who sold his soul to the devil.'

If a bomb had exploded in the courtroom, it couldn't have created a greater shock. People gasp, they turn to each other in consternation, disbelief, and also a guilty sense of *schadenfreude* at this sensational statement.

They've forgotten that Miklós Nagy isn't the one on trial, and assume that they have just heard the judge pronounce a guilty verdict. Judit can no longer control her disgust. She jumps up, glares at the judge, and shouts, 'Shame on you!' Before he can have her evicted, she pushes her way through the courtroom and storms out, slamming the door behind her.

She hasn't waited to hear the judge speak about the Kurt Becher affair but she supposes that he will accuse Miklós of interceding on behalf of a Nazi war criminal to save him from being punished, and then of perjuring himself by lying about it in court. She doesn't need to wait for the verdict on the defendant, either. Having destroyed Miklós's reputation, maligned his motives, and accused him of collaboration, she has no doubt that the judge will acquit Isaiah Fleischmann.

She wanders the streets of Jerusalem in a daze, oblivious of crowds, cars, barrows and donkey carts. All she can see is the judge's accusing face as he utters his scurrilous words.

She dreads going home, and wonders how to break the news to Miklós that his worst nightmare has become reality. Bracing herself to face him, she starts the long drive to Tel Aviv, past a blur of olive groves, Arab villages and citrus orchards. By the time she swings into their street, she is relieved to see that friends who were in the courtroom are parking their cars outside their apartment block. At least she won't have to face Miklós alone.

He is at the door the instant he hears her key turn in the lock. He is pale and tense as he scans their faces.

'The judge had no right to say what he did,' Judit says.

'This will be remembered as a black day for Israeli jurisprudence,' says Uri, who is a lawyer.

'For God's sake,' Miklós shouts, 'will someone tell me what he said? What was the verdict?'

When Uri repeats the judge's words, Miklós sinks into the nearest chair, stares at the floor, and shakes his head, as though conducting a distressing inner conversation with himself. Finally he looks up. 'He actually said that I sold my soul to the devil?'

Judit nods. 'I walked out at that point. I couldn't sit there and listen to any more of his disgusting comments.'

Miklós shakes his head again. He realises that despite all the signs of bias during the trial, until that moment he has still been hoping that the judge would find Isaiah Fleischmann guilty.

'I can't believe it. It's unbelievable. Unbelievable. How could the judge say that about me?' He lights a cigarette but tamps it out a few moments later and lights another as if unaware of his actions. 'The injustice of it. Amos Alon must be celebrating. He wouldn't have expected such an outcome in his wildest dreams.'

'It is outrageous, a calumny, a travesty of justice,' Uri says. 'The judge should be censured for making such a comment. He sounded like a defence counsel addressing a jury, not a judge handing down a verdict.'

But Miklós isn't listening. The chaos in his head is threatening to overwhelm him. Judit goes into the kitchenette to make coffee, relieved to have something to do so she can escape from Miklós's distraught face. But when she returns, he waves away the coffee and cake, and with trembling hands lights another cigarette.

Alternating between anger and self-pity, he says, 'What sin did I commit in rescuing all those people? Should I have let them die with the rest? Would that have made the judge and Amos Alon happy? What wrong did I do to anyone? How dare he accuse me of selling my soul to Satan!'

White-faced, Judit sits beside him and takes his hand. She wants to comfort him but knows there are no words to take away this pain.

Miklós stares into space, unable to come to terms with what has just taken place in the Jerusalem District Court. If Fleischmann is innocent, then, by implication, he is guilty. Guilty of the crime his country regards as the most serious of all.

'You remember the Dreyfus case?' he says bitterly. 'He was cut down by a Hungarian anti-Semite and French anti-Semitism, but I've been destroyed by the political agenda of a fellow-Jew in Israel.'

*

For the next few weeks, Miklós sits slumped in his armchair, and the ashtray beside him overflows with cigarette butts. He hardly speaks, even to the boys; he refuses to go out of the apartment, can't be bothered shaving, and eats so little that Judit watches him anxiously.

'It's as if you're sitting *shiva*,' she says one day, referring to the Jewish custom of staying home and eschewing ordinary activities during the traditional period of mourning.

'I'm sitting *shiva* for myself,' he retorts. 'For the Miklós Nagy who died when he heard that he sold his soul to Satan.'

Unable to help him and terrified of what he might do, she never leaves him alone in the apartment and hides the newspapers from him. Some she crumples and stamps on. The trial has provided journalists with a rich seam of gold which they mine with the insatiable greed of prospectors lured by early success. Newspaper headlines blaze with the judge's words: *Miklós Nagy sold his soul to the devil.* Others present a jubilant Amos Alon as a hero, and quote him saying that the verdict was a triumph not only for Isaiah Fleischmann but for the country's soul.

Whenever she sees Alon's photograph in the newspaper, she rips it to shreds, cursing as she does so. Isaiah Fleischmann gloats that he has been vindicated, that he has proved the truth of his accusations. She rips up his photo too. One journalist writes in *Ha'aretz* that Miklós should be brought to trial as a Nazi collaborator, *or echoes of the trial will poison the air we breathe.* This theme is echoed by several reporters. She tosses them all into the garbage before Miklós can read their poisonous words.

She goes out as little as possible. She doesn't tell Miklós that some shopkeepers refuse to serve her, passers-by hiss insults at her, and one of their neighbours has emptied his stinking garbage bin outside their door. She tells the boys that if they have problems at school, they should come to her, not their father. The boys have become withdrawn, especially Gil. Instead of running around in the park or playing football after school as they once did, they now spend more time in their room. They tell her they're doing homework, but she knows they are avoiding schoolmates who taunt and bully them.

Whenever she reads an article favourable to Miklós, she shows it to him, so he will see that some influential people support him. At first he pushes the papers away. 'What difference does it make what they say?' he sighs. But eventually he picks them up, and for a short time he feels heartened by their comments, especially when they criticise the judge.

He rereads one article so often that he can recite it by heart, and sometimes quotes parts of it to friends who visit him.

'*This issue was far too complex and too huge for one person to decide, especially a man of limited understanding who sees the world only in black and white. How could he ignore the extraordinary situation in Hungary in 1944, and presume to pass judgement on how someone living in that black hell should have behaved? The judge's language was intemperate and inappropriate. It resembled a defence counsel's summation rather than a judge's considered opinion.*'

'That reporter got it right,' comments Uri, who drops in every evening to try and lift his friend's spirits. 'This case should have been heard by a panel of judges, not by a single one, and definitely not one with a grudge against the government.'

Always scouring the papers in search of articles to boost her husband's morale, Judit triumphantly places a newspaper in front of him one morning as he sips his black coffee. 'Read this. It's an interview with someone who was on your train.'

'He wasn't my friend and I didn't really like him,' the interview begins. *'Miklós Nagy was arrogant, patronising, and aggressive.'*

Miklós puts down his coffee cup and raises his eyebrows. 'This is supposed to make me feel better?'

'Just keep reading.'

'But it was precisely because of those qualities that he was capable of doing what he did during Nazi Occupation. To take any action in that situation, you had to have that kind of personality — lots of chutzpah and self-confidence. The verdict was a terrible injustice perpetrated by a judge who didn't understand the situation in Hungary. No-one living in safety and security today has the right to judge Miklós Nagy's actions or malign the reputation of a man who risked his life to save others.'

'So where was this guy during the trial?'

'He wasn't asked to testify,' Judit says. 'Look, it says here that he offered to testify but the prosecutor didn't call him. He probably never dreamed that the judge would arrive at such an unfair conclusion.'

'I was the victim of an underachieving prosecutor and an overachieving defence attorney.' His reply makes her smile. It's the first time he has referred to his situation with any humour, albeit black humour, and he realises it's a long time since he has seen her smile.

'You'd think the government would make some comment about the verdict, and support you,' she says.

'With the elections coming up, they can't say much or they'll be accused of attacking the judiciary for political advantage,' he argues. She is relieved that these days he is becoming a little more animated and engages in discussions instead of brooding in silence, and she no longer hides the newspapers from him.

'Did you see what Ben-Gurion wrote?' he says one morning. 'He doesn't mention the verdict or the judge, but it's obvious what he's referring to. Listen.' And he reads it aloud.

I would never have presumed to judge the actions of any Jew who was there while I was here. This should be left to the tribunal of history in the generation to come. Jews who were safe and secure during the Hitler era should not presume to judge their brethren who were burned and slaughtered, nor the few who survived. Those of us who did not experience this hell would do best, in my view, to remain silent in humility and grief.

But for every article or interview that supports Miklós, two condemn him and demand that he be tried for collaboration.

'Have you thought of leaving Israel?' Uri asks one afternoon. 'You should consider it. Life would be easier for you away from this toxic atmosphere. For the time being at least.'

'Leave Israel? Never. This is where I was vilified, and this is where I will be vindicated.'

'Then you should go and live in a kibbutz up north, perhaps, until things die down. Some kibbutzniks I know have suggested it.'

'I'm not going to hide in a kibbutz.'

'At least move to another apartment.'

Miklós tamps his cigarette in the ashtray and leans towards his friend. 'I'm not moving anywhere. I'm going to stay right here. I'll clear my name, just like Dreyfus did. But I don't need a Zola to vindicate me. I'm going to do it myself.'

CHAPTER THIRTY-THREE

Tel Aviv, 2005

Annika walks out of the Law Library archive dazed more by the insights into human nature revealed by the trial transcript than by the vagaries of history. She can't stop thinking about the testimony of the witnesses, the ones that Miklós Nagy saved. How can people be so ungrateful?

Preoccupied, she steps onto the road in HaMedina Square without looking and jumps back as a motorist pulls up with a screech of brakes, missing her by centimetres. He leans out of the window and yells something in Hebrew before gunning the engine and driving on. As she stands trembling on the edge of the footpath, a woman trying to control a frisky terrier stops to commiserate.

'You OK?' she asks in a New York voice while the dog strains at the leash towards a nearby palm. 'You're not from here, are you? Next time cross further up, at Arlozorov Street, it's safer. I've lived here for ten years and I still can't get used to the way they drive, they're like Fangio on steroids. And their language!'

'I didn't understand what he said.'

'Just as well,' the woman chuckles, and walks on.

A few minutes later, Annika is crossing Arlozorov Street when her mobile rings.

'Don't tell me you've spent this beautiful day in the Law Library again.' It's Dov, and her heart beats faster when she hears his voice. Ever since the day she discovered they were both fans of Leonard Cohen, her feelings for him have intensified. It seems to her that their shared love of the sensuality and raw honesty of his songs have transcended musical appreciation and created a powerful emotional connection between them. She wonders if he felt it too.

'I have to report on the opening of an art exhibition in Neve Tzedek this afternoon,' he says. 'Come with me. I think you'll find it interesting.'

*

'You don't usually write about art,' she comments when they meet outside the gallery in Shabhazi Street an hour later.

He smiles. 'This is no ordinary exhibition, Annika. You'll see.'

As soon as they enter the Liora Gallery, a tall woman with Frida Kahlo eyebrows and straight black hair severely parted in the centre and braided into one thick plait, rushes up to Dov.

She envelops him in a hug and kisses both cheeks while her eyes sweep over Annika, who feels she is being assessed, and not kindly.

'So glad you've come,' the woman murmurs, looking into his eyes. 'I'll catch up with you and your friend later. I want to hear what you think of the exhibition before I read about it in your paper.' And with that she rushes off to greet another new arrival.

'That whirlwind is Liora Bar-David. She owns the gallery,' Dov explains.

'Watch out, I think she fancies you,' Annika whispers.

'Me and anyone who can give her some publicity.' He takes her arm. 'Let's look around.'

In the first room of the gallery, Annika stands very still, staring at the paintings. She feels she has entered a deep cavern whose terrifying blackness offers no hope of light ever penetrating the gloom. Triangular faces with enormous black eyes stare at unimaginable horrors. The streets are deserted, with menacing shadows on the ground, and the dark branches of the trees seem to writhe in agony. Inside abandoned rooms, empty chairs, upturned tables and broken windows suggest shattered lives. The artist's sparing use of colour contributes to the effect of desolation and despair. The paintings are all in tones of grey, the dirty grey of overcast skies, and the emphatic darkness of charcoal, relieved only by daubs of startling vermillion slashed across each canvas.

Depressed by these paintings, Annika wants to share her reactions with Dov, but someone has buttonholed him, and she doesn't want to interrupt what appears to be an intense discussion. With a sigh, she moves on to the next room, bracing herself for more distressing images. She wonders how soon she can leave, and resolves never to trust Dov's taste in art again.

But as soon as she enters the next room, her head explodes with light, colour and movement. She feels as disoriented as Dorothy in the *Wizard of Oz* when she stepped from her monochrome life in Kansas into a dazzling world of fantasy. It doesn't seem possible that these paintings are the work of the same artist. Here the paint has been thickly applied with bold brush strokes in colours so vivid they glue her eyes to the canvases.

Mythical animals leap over gingerbread houses, naked couples fondle each other on emerald grass, and angels float above luscious plants that display erect stamens and soft fleshy petals that open like secret lips. There is no suffering here, no despairing faces confronting unimaginable horror, just a vision of life with all its pleasures, real and imagined.

These paintings are so engaging that she takes her time in front of each one, delighted by their innocence and sensuality, and increasingly curious about the artist. Dov is talking to a woman whose face she can't see, and when they turn in her direction, she recognises the American who stopped to help her in HaMedina Square. Dov beckons her to join them, but the small gallery is so crowded that she can't squeeze past the flustered waitress who is pushing her way through the throng with a tray of glasses of wine, orange juice and soda water jiggling precariously.

It's too difficult to get past, so she takes a glass of sauvignon blanc and waits for the crowd to thin out, amused to see that, unlike gallery guests in Sydney, most of these people opt for soda water. While sipping her wine, which she decides is no match for the Marlborough variety, she sees a woman bearing down on her wearing an Indian caftan with a mirror-encrusted skirt and a psychedelic scarf wound around her head. It's Tamar, the flamboyant tarot reader and doll-maker she met near this gallery soon after she arrived in Israel.

'So you are still in Tel Aviv,' Tamar says in her husky voice. 'I saw you come in with that guy over there.' She gives Annika a playful nudge. 'I was right, yes? You already found your man but you didn't know it.'

Annika thinks back. The fortune-teller was right. She had already met Dov.

'You made a good choice,' Tamar goes on. 'Dov Erlich is a very attractive guy.'

Annika laughs. 'So I'd better go and grab him before someone else does.'

She manages to push her way through the throng. By the time she reaches Dov, he is talking to a woman he introduces as Batya Barak, the art critic for the *Jerusalem Herald*. Batya nods briefly to acknowledge Annika's presence, and continues her analysis of the exhibition for Dov's benefit. She speaks with emphasis and authority, fixing her gaze somewhere in the middle distance, as if addressing an audience with opinions she expresses as incontrovertible truths. Irritated by her supercilious manner, Annika tunes out. She wants to find out something about the artist, but is reluctant to display her ignorance by asking. In any case, she can't get a word in.

Looking around the gallery, she notices a middle-aged man with a Salvador Dali moustache and a floral shirt unbuttoned to the waist, a thick gold chain resting on his hairy chest. He is surrounded by a large group of people all clamouring for his opinion, and she wonders if he's the artist. Just then there's a crackle followed by a low hum and some shrill sounds as Liora Bar-David fiddles with the microphone. When she has checked that everyone can hear her, she thanks them for coming, and says how privileged she is to present such a unique exhibition by such an extraordinary artist. Then she stands back and they all wait for the artist to appear.

Annika cranes her neck to see who it is. The man in the floral shirt is walking towards the dais but he is not alone. He is propelling a tiny woman by the elbow, and after depositing her in an armchair, he lowers the microphone so that she can reach it, and leaves the stage.

'That's Dora Zielinski, isn't she amazing,' the woman next to her says. 'Can you believe it, she's a hundred and one years old. A hundred and one! And she's still painting!'

Annika stares at the artist. The only centenarians she has ever seen were on television, white-haired, toothless, hunched people with faces like crumpled maps who lived in villages in Sardinia or Japan and answered reporters' predictable questions with monosyllables. Dora Zielinski has flamingo pink hair piled on top of her head, lips painted the same colour, and fingernails lacquered to match. She wears a purple velvet cape fastened with gold buttons, shoes with little heels and a strap across the instep, and she doesn't wear glasses.

The room falls silent as she begins to speak. The brown-speckled hand holding the microphone is shaking, but her voice is surprisingly strong. 'Maybe you heard of the American artist Grandma Moses?' she begins in a Polish-Israeli accent. 'Well, I'm Great-Grandma Moses.' While they laugh at her quip, Annika reflects that Dora has more in common with

Grandma Moses than just old age: she shares her innocent childlike vision of the world.

'This exhibition represents the two parts of my life. I was born in a Polish town called Oswiecim — you know it better as Auschwitz. I was one of ten children, and when it was over, they were all gone. Only I survived.'

There is total silence now, as if the entire room is united in a state of suspended animation, hardly breathing. Not even the clinking of a glass can be heard, only the voice of an artist whose urge to share her vision has impelled her to continue creating art long after most people have stopped communicating anything. Dov squeezes Annika's arm and she leans against him.

'So I don't need to explain what I painted in the first room,' Dora says. 'But here, in this room, I have come from the darkness into the light. And the light is shining on my second life, here in Israel, and I have painted the shapes and colours of hope and love, and all the wonderful things in life, including sex. I mention this in case some of you youngsters think I'm too old to remember such a thing.' She wags a mischievous finger at the crowd. 'You're never too old to remember that. Too old to find someone to do it with, maybe.'

They're still chuckling as she continues. 'There's a custom today of celebrating someone's life when they die. But I don't intend to die for many years, and I don't trust my colleagues. Who knows what they will say about me when I can't answer back? So I'm celebrating my life now, through my paintings.'

Dora takes a breath and in a more serious tone, she says, 'I am a very lucky woman and I want to say to you that

I am grateful for my long and wonderful life. Thank you all for being here and celebrating with me. Near the catalogue on the table, my dear friend Nella —' and she waves at the American woman Annika met in HaMedina Square, 'has left a pile of Peace Now leaflets.

'I know most of you are too mean to buy a painting, but if you want to do something good for our country, take a leaflet. It's free.'

With the help of the man in the floral shirt, who turns out to be her grandson, Dora steps down from the podium. Annika turns to Dov. 'What an incredible woman. I'm so glad I came.'

'What do you think of the paintings?' he asks.

'Marc Chagall meets Georgia O'Keeffe in the land of Oz.'

He smiles. 'I like that. Can I quote you?'

They push their way through the crowd towards Dora, who is surrounded by admirers, all talking at once. She glances up, sees Dov, and gives him a flirtatious smile.

'So, Mr Reporter, you going to write something nice about my paintings?'

'You never know your luck,' he retorts. 'What I want to know is, when's the next exhibition?'

'Probably in ten years' time,' she says tartly. 'I hope you're still around by then.'

Dora turns her gaze on Annika, who is enjoying their repartee. 'So you have a young lady. It's about time. You're no spring chicken, you know. Time you settled down.'

'The trouble is, she's Australian,' he says, looking at Annika with what she hopes is regret.

'Life is short. Make the most of it,' Dora Zielinski says, looking from him to her.

As they say their goodbyes, Annika says, 'I'll never forget you or your paintings, Mrs Zielinski.'

They are about to walk out of the gallery when Annika sees Tamar standing by the door, watching them. She gives an inscrutable smile, and Annika wonders if she can see into her future.

They walk several blocks along Shabhazi Street, past walls covered in dense graffiti. Further on, posters advertise the Batsheva Ballet and forthcoming rock concerts starring Mick Jagger and Celine Dion.

They enter Shoshi's Café, find a table in the shady courtyard, and order coffee and cheesecake.

'I can't stop thinking about Dora Zielinski,' Annika says. 'Those paintings are very powerful.'

'Not just the paintings. Her. After all she's been through, she sounds so positive. She said she was grateful. That made me think of the people Miklós Nagy saved. I can't understand why they weren't grateful.'

Dov puts a second spoon of sugar into his coffee and stirs it slowly. 'Gratitude can make you feel beholden,' he says eventually. 'It reminds you of a time you'd prefer to forget, when you were helpless, at the mercy of others, a victim who needed someone to extricate you from a dangerous or humiliating situation. I read a book by a psychologist who said that when people have been victimised over a long period of time, they begin to doubt their own worth. Then, after the danger is gone and they rebuild their lives, they feel ashamed of having been treated like that, of being so vulnerable. They want to believe they've been responsible for their own survival and success. They don't want to be reminded of the time when they had no control. I think he called it the shame of vulnerability.'

She looks at him with admiration. Then she thinks of her grandmother, and wonders if this is why Marika has shown no gratitude to the man who saved her, why she has tried to erase his memory from her life.

Dov is studying her. 'So how grateful are you?'

She frowns. 'What do you mean?'

'From what you've told me, you were given every opportunity. Your grandmother survived the Holocaust and migrated to Australia. Your mother sent you to the best school she could afford. She tried to turn you into a Christian so you'd be spared the persecution and pain her mother suffered. You were cossetted and sheltered and supported and sent to university so you could develop your intellect and have a good profession. How grateful are you for all that?'

She feels a rush of resentment. 'Are you trying to make me feel guilty?'

'Not at all. Just trying to point out how complicated gratitude can be.'

She doesn't reply and they sit in silence as she plays with the cake crumbs on her plate. To defuse the tension she can feel tightening her chest, Annika says, 'Dora mentioned something about Peace Now. What's that?'

'It's a protest movement that criticises our government's policy towards the Palestinians, and stands up for their rights,' Dov says. 'My daughter is a fervent supporter, and goes to their demonstrations. By the way, I love the neat way you skip to another subject whenever you don't want to answer a question or pursue an idea you find uncomfortable.'

She is about to retort when she looks up and sees that he is smiling at her, and her resentment melts away.

He rummages in his pocket, takes out a leaflet and hands it to her. 'My friend Nella, who you met, is involved with Peace Now. She publicises their protests. They're always looking for new members, so if you want to know more, I'm sure she'll be delighted to fill you in.'

He drains his coffee, pushes away the cup, leaves a few shekels on the table and stands up. 'I have to get back to the office. Can I give you a lift?'

She shakes her head. She needs time to think.

Alone at the table, she orders another coffee, and goes over their conversation. No-one has challenged her the way he does, and although she resents his words, she acknowledges that he has a point.

Who was she to criticise people for their lack of gratitude? She hasn't been grateful for anything. In fact she has rejected all the advantages she has been given and distanced herself from her mother and grandmother who provided them. Cassie would say she has been self-indulgent, self-pitying, and self-absorbed. And as usual, Cassie would be right.

The wicker chair has suddenly become hard and she shifts from side to side trying to find a comfortable spot. To distract herself from her confused thoughts about Dov, she thinks about Tamar and wonders what she was thinking when she saw them leaving. Then she takes out Nella's leaflet and scans it without absorbing the words. Until she comes to the last sentence. Then she reads it again to make sure she hasn't misread it. *For more information about our activities, call Eitan Nagy.*

CHAPTER THIRTY-FOUR

Tel Aviv, 2005

Cyclists whizz by on the promenade and hawkers offer fruit juice, falafels and ice cream to the sunbathers sprawled on banana chairs. Watching them from the hotel terrace, Annika dials Eitan Nagy's number. She is still figuring out what to say, and decides it's wiser not to mention she's a journalist. People don't trust reporters.

She's still mulling over this when a bright voice says, '*Shalom.*'

'I'm sorry to bother you,' she begins, 'but I was wondering if by any chance you are related to Miklós Nagy?'

Even as she says this, her toes curl in embarrassment. It sounds so gauche.

There's a pause. Then, in a voice ten degrees cooler than his greeting, he says, 'Who is this?'

'My name is Annika Barnett. I'm from Australia. I'm trying to find some information about a man called Miklós Nagy…'

He cuts her short. 'What is it that you want?'

She takes a deep breath. If she doesn't get this right, he will hang up, but from his reaction, she senses that he must be related. Otherwise he would have just said no. Perhaps she should tell the truth and hope for the best.

'I know this sounds odd, but I've come to Israel because of Miklós Nagy. My grandmother was one of the people he rescued.'

'So I suppose she travelled to Israel to testify on his behalf?'

From his biting tone, she realises she has to rearrange the sequence of events. Telling him that her grandmother had never mentioned her rescuer, and had refused to talk about him, would antagonise him even more, and ruin her chances of meeting him.

That would be unbearable now that she has finished reading the transcript, and she can't wait to speak to a relative who might be able to tell her what happened after the devastating verdict of the District Court.

'A guide in the Sydney Jewish Museum told me how extraordinary Mr Nagy was, and how he deserved more recognition for what he'd done, and, knowing that he had rescued my grandmother, I was intrigued. Then on my way here I stopped in Budapest where I met a man whose father was rescued on the train, so...'

'So you got more intrigued. OK, you'd better come over,' he says.

Half an hour later, she is standing outside a solid brick apartment block in Ben-Gurion Boulevard. Up and down the street walled balconies seem to be stuck onto the corners of buildings like architectural afterthoughts. She presses a buzzer and climbs two steep staircases to Eitan Nagy's apartment. He is already standing at the door, and surveys her with a searching gaze that makes her feel uncomfortable. There's an energy and restlessness about him that reminds her of an English rock star she once saw performing at the Sydney Super Dome, but Eitan's chosen stage is obviously a political one. The crushed T-shirt he wears over his faded denim jeans is emblazoned with the words: *Peace Now. If not now, when?*

He stands aside to usher her into a room piled with books, banners, posters, magazines and newsletters on every flat surface, including the timber floor. In the adjoining kitchen boxes and cartons are stacked on top of each other. She breathes in the familiar smell of paper and newsprint.

Eitan picks up bundles of newsletters off the casual table, and pushes away boxes to make room for her to sit on a chair whose wicker seat is unravelling. She looks around. There are no paintings on the walls, and no photographs, nothing that might reveal the owner's aesthetic taste. No memorabilia either. There was clearly only one thing in Eitan Nagy's life.

He sits on the edge of the only other chair in the room without speaking, and she doesn't break the silence. There's a question threatening to burst from her mouth, but she doesn't ask it. She waits. After several minutes, he goes into an adjoining room and emerges with an old-fashioned album.

As he flicks through it, she sees small black-and-white photographs with serrated edges stuck closely together on pages separated by sheets of crackly parchment. He turns a page towards her and points to an image of an unsmiling middle-aged man with dark-rimmed glasses. He looks like a man who is used to being in command, the kind of man who gets things done. Her heart is pounding. It's the man she saw in the group photo in the Sydney Jewish Museum, the one taken when the train arrived in Switzerland.

'That's my grandfather, Miklós Nagy,' Eitan is saying. 'The man who saved your grandmother. What did she tell you about him?'

Annika bites her lip. It's one of those tricky questions on which so much hinges. From the way he sits forward, waiting to hear what she can tell him, she realises that he is probably as hungry for information about his grandfather as she is. She doesn't want to lie, but telling the truth is risky.

'She doesn't like talking about the past,' she says, relieved to find an answer. 'That's not unusual for Holocaust survivors. And that's why I decided to come and find out about him for myself.'

He nods. 'So what do you do in Sydney, that you can afford the time and money to travel to the other side of the world to indulge your curiosity about a man you have never met?'

She shrugs. 'Not much at the moment. I'm actually out of work.'

And she tells him about resigning from a job she found unfulfilling, and from the intent way he listens and nods from time to time, she senses that he understands her, that perhaps he too was once in a similar situation. She thinks he is probably about her age, but with men you could never tell.

'A journalist, eh? Now I get it. Are you planning to write about my grandfather? There's plenty to write about, that's for sure. It's time the true story was written by someone without an axe to grind.'

'How come your English is so good? Is that an American accent?'

'I was born in Canada. But coming back to you, how much do you know about my grandfather's story?'

She explains that her interest in Miklós Nagy is personal, not professional, and tells him that for the past few days, she has been reading the transcript of the trial. 'I can't stop thinking about the judge's verdict. I can't get over it. I don't know how he could have arrived at such a preposterous judgment. It was bad enough that the defence attorney made those outrageous accusations, but then the judge just repeated them. And that shocking comment he made. The poor man saved all those people, and then he was accused of being a collaborator, of being responsible for the deaths of people he couldn't possibly have saved.'

She pours all this out in a torrent. The indignation pent up over several days pours out of her like water from a dam when the sluice has opened, threatening to submerge everything in its path. When she finally runs out of breath, she sits back. Obviously none of this is new to him, but he listens as if he has never heard it before.

He is looking at her with admiration. 'So you have actually read the entire transcript of the trial?'

'Every word. I've never read anything that felt so immediate and so suspenseful. It got under my skin. That's why I've stayed here longer than I meant to. But I just have to find out what happened next. Did Miklós Nagy manage to clear his name?'

'So you don't know what happened?'

'The transcript ended with the verdict.'

He pushes his chair away and gets up. 'This might take a long time. I'd better make us some tea.'

She hears him rustling packets, opening and closing cupboard doors, filling the kettle, and waits impatiently for him to come back. A few minutes later she is sipping green tea from a white mug patterned with maple leaves while she listens to his story.

'After the verdict was handed down, there was so much animosity towards my grandfather in the press, and so many threats made against him, that the government was worried about his safety and they appointed two armed bodyguards to keep a twenty-four-hour surveillance on him. Meanwhile, the Ministry of Justice lodged an appeal against the verdict in the Supreme Court. I believe they were keen to do it as soon as possible to prevent a charge of collaboration being brought against him. Apparently they couldn't charge him with that until his appeal was heard in the higher court.'

'What were the grounds for the appeal?'

'The points the judge made in his verdict, basically. The appeal said that the judge had acquitted Isaiah Fleischmann on false assumptions, and that his conclusions were based on faulty criteria. That he didn't take normal lapses of memory into account when assessing the reliability of witnesses, and as a result drew wrong conclusions about witnesses who contradicted themselves about events that happened ten years earlier. It criticised his inflexible interpretation of the situation, and ascribed that to his failure to understand the situation in Hungary in 1944.'

Eitan's voice becomes angrier as he continues. 'The appeal said there were no grounds for his conclusion that my grandfather's negotiations amounted to criminal collaboration with Nazis. As for his conclusion that he deliberately played along with the Nazis to help them exterminate the remaining Jews of Hungary, that was totally baseless. And in pronouncing that my grandfather had sold his soul to the devil, the judge was expressing his personal opinion, which he wasn't entitled to give.'

Annika is nodding. 'My blood was boiling when I read that. So what happened in the Supreme Court?'

'Before the appeal was heard, there was a heated debate about it in the press. Was the appeal motivated by a legitimate desire to correct injustice, or by a desperate effort to protect the ruling party? One newspaper — *Haaretz*, I think it was — claimed that the Supreme Court had to be given an opportunity to investigate the matter and arrive at a conclusion that was more rational and judicious than the one given by the District Court.

'Moshe Sharett's Mapai party maintained that the verdict was absurd and unjust. A man had been convicted in court without having the opportunity to defend himself, since he wasn't the defendant in the case. He didn't have a lawyer, so no-one could defend him. It was a miscarriage of justice, and the least the state could do was to launch an appeal. But then the right-wing *Herut* paper asked why Sharett's Mapai party, which they reckoned had blood on its hands, was covering up for a collaborator and defending him, despite a decision handed down by a respected judge.'

'Israeli politics is so confusing.'

'It's confusing for most of us. Parties here rarely have an outright majority, so to govern they have to form coalitions with parties that often don't share their values.'

'I'm amazed that you can remember all this,' Annika says when he rises and offers to refill her mug.

He gives an ironic laugh. 'If you knew how many thousand times we went over all this with my grandmother, father and uncle.'

'I wondered about that affidavit he gave for Kurt Becher while I was reading about the trial,' she says. 'Why do you think he wrote it?'

Eitan shrugs. 'I've wondered about that too. I've gone over it a thousand times, looking for an explanation. He himself said in court he was grateful to Becher for his help, so maybe it was as simple as that. Or maybe it was like Stockholm Syndrome, where the hostage becomes so dependent on his captor that he comes to identify with him. Maybe it was from some misguided sense of decency, or the result of a promise he made Becher in return for his help. He might even have come to see another side of the man and form a personal connection with him. If only I could have asked him, but maybe even he didn't understand his own motives. So we'll never know.'

'Don't keep me in suspense about the appeal. Tell me, was it successful?'

'First I have to tell you a bit more about the politics. Before the Supreme Court got to hear the appeal, there was a political crisis in the country. One of the coalition parties said that Sharett's party had been too hasty in deciding to lodge an appeal, which made it look as if they were covering up for him. There was a no-confidence motion in the government. My grandmother reckoned that they were exploiting the Nagy affair for their own political ends, but the upshot was that Moshe Sharett had no option but to resign. The government fell.'

Annika recalls Dov's comment the first time she mentioned Miklós Nagy.

'So you could say your grandfather was responsible for the fall of the government?'

Eitan nods. 'I suppose you could say that. The real issues in the election campaign were tangled up with the Nagy affair, which kept surfacing like scratches on an old record. The other parties were quick to try and capitalise on the Mapai party's misfortune, and the issue of Sharett's role in the arrest of Gábor Weisz came up all over again. Why didn't he appear in Istanbul? Why didn't he testify in court? Why did he remain silent?'

Annika has had enough of Israeli politics. 'Let's cut to the chase. What was the result of the appeal?'

'Fortunately the Supreme Court overturned the decision of the District Court. The majority of the judges on the appeal panel exonerated my grandfather of collaboration.'

But from the way Eitan is looking at her, she senses that there is more to the story. She raises her eyebrows. 'And?'

He is silent. Then he says, 'You really don't know, do you?'

CHAPTER THIRTY-FIVE

Tel Aviv, August 1957

News of the impending appeal invigorates Miklós Nagy. He spends hours discussing the possibilities with his friends as they wonder who will be appointed to the appeal panel at the Supreme Court, and how the five judges will assess the verdict of the District Court. He no longer spends his days indoors, withdrawn and brooding, and the insults of strangers no longer stop him from leaving the house. Even calls from various right-wing publications for him to be tried on charges of collaboration don't depress him as they once did. And, unlike Judit, he isn't concerned by occasional death threats.

'Don't take them seriously,' he tells her. 'It's just hot air. Who ever heard of a murderer announcing that he's going to kill someone? And don't forget I've got two bodyguards watching over me from morning till night.' He can't resist adding, 'Just as well I didn't listen to panic merchants like Uri who advised me to move from here.'

The Nagy appeal is now off the gossip agenda. These days everyone is discussing the current political crisis. Some of the coalition parties have moved a no-confidence motion in the Knesset and this pushes the ruling Mapai party to a knife edge. At the government office where Miklós still works, some of the clerks suspect that this motion is a cynical attempt by these groups to serve their political ambitions, while others maintain that it's caused by their hostility to the appeal that the government has launched on his behalf.

'I never thought I'd be at the centre of a political storm,' he says to Judit, and they both laugh at the absurdity of it, although her laughter is less spontaneous than his. He knows she would be even more apprehensive if he had told her that the bodyguards assigned to him have been removed. A few days ago he received a message from the head of Special Services that, as he was no longer in any immediate danger, they couldn't justify stretching their strained resources to guard him twenty-four hours a day.

Even though his appeal isn't due to be heard for another six months and he is still in legal limbo, he is optimistic. The majority decision of five judges is bound to overturn the verdict of one biased judge in the District Court. Sitting behind the wheel of his second-hand Ford, he whistles Bing Crosby's hit tune 'In the Cool, Cool, Cool of the Evening' while driving home from the office later than usual one evening. It's a dark, windy night, and as he watches the leaves blowing across the street, he thinks about the latest controversy over the government's recent Sinai campaign. He is looking forward to discussing it with Judit but remembers that she has gone to a teachers' meeting at the boys' school, and will be home late.

His thoughts turn to an article by Amos Alon which was published in *Herut* the previous week. Predictably Isaiah Fleischmann's defence attorney has condemned the appeal and accused the government of trying to defend a collaborator in its ranks.

He's like a dog with a bone, he just can't let go, Miklós thinks as he swings into Gavriel Avenue and parks under the palm trees outside his building. He notices that the street is unusually dark. When he looks up, he sees why: the street lamp outside his house isn't lit. He makes a mental note to tell the council to replace the light bulb.

He has just switched off the engine when he hears rustling. He assumes it's the wind whipping the palm fronds, but suddenly a young fellow dressed in a khaki jacket emerges from the bushes at the side of the house, flashes a torch in his face and asks, 'Miklós Nagy?'

'Yes,' Miklós replies, startled by the abrupt question and the sudden appearance of the questioner. He wants to ask the stranger who he is, and why he is lurking around his house, but he is struck dumb by what he sees. The man has a revolver in his hand, and he is aiming it at his head. Miklós ducks, jumps out of the car, pushes him aside, and starts running towards the entrance. Before he reaches the door, he hears a shot and then another one, and falls to the ground clutching his side. He hears footsteps running down the darkened street, and realises that his assailant is running away into the night.

His hand feels something wet and sticky pooling onto the ground beside him, and he smells the metallic odour of blood. He shouts for help but his voice is weak and there's no-one around on this dark night. He cries out several times in vain. He tries to drag himself back towards the car, to sound the horn, but he can't move. There are no lights on inside the building. Everyone must be asleep or listening to the radio. If only Judit was home. Perhaps one of the neighbours will wake up and hear him. 'Help!' he calls out. 'Help me! Police! I've been shot!'

Finally a wrinkled face on the top floor peers through the shutters of a window that faces the street, and looks down. Miklós thinks it's the old man who emptied his garbage on their doorstep several months ago, but he doesn't care who it is, just as long as he goes for help. After what seems like hours, the man hobbles towards him, and with a shocked expression murmurs, '*Oy gewalt*,' and says he'll go back up to call the police and Magen David Adom, the emergency ambulance.

Another neighbour emerges from the building and kneels beside him. 'They'll be here soon,' she says soothingly, placing a folded towel under his head, 'Don't worry, Mr Nagy, you'll be all right.'

He closes his eyes for a moment and when he opens them he is still lying in the street and Judit is holding his hand. Her face is the colour of chalk, and he wants to tell her that she doesn't look well, that she should look after herself, but no words come. By now a few onlookers have gathered, and everyone is talking at once, offering different suggestions.

'Please move back and give him room to breathe,' Judit is saying in a calm voice 'We're not going to move him until the ambulance officers arrive.' Then she asks one of the neighbours to bring a pillow and blanket, and asks another to stay with the boys for the rest of the night.

An insistent shriek begins vibrating inside his head, and a moment later the ambulance pulls up and two paramedics jump out. He hears one of them saying, 'We're taking him to Masada Hospital,' and as they place him on a stretcher, he sees Judit climbing into the back of the ambulance.

The high-pitched sound starts up again, and he supposes it's the shrilling of the siren. He is conscious but curiously detached from what is going on, as if he were an onlooker rather than a patient. When they bring him to the Emergency room, he explains to the doctor what happened, down to every detail, even the rustling of the leaves in the darkened street, as if he saw it all in a movie.

'We have to operate straightaway,' the surgeon tells him after he has been examined and X-rayed. 'The bullets have damaged some of your internal organs.'

Miklós listens to the surgeon's quiet voice with interest as though he were talking about someone else. It becomes difficult to concentrate as they wheel him into the operating theatre. Above him, blinding light scorches his eyelids, and the last thing he remembers is thinking that they must have already repaired the street light on Gavriel Avenue.

*

Miklós is lying in a private room, guarded by two policemen. The boys visit after school. Ben sits on a chair close to his father's bed and asks if he's feeling better, and whether he can bring him anything. Although he coughs from time to time, Miklós always says he's improving, and tries to smile. But Gil is like a coiled spring, unable to sit still or offer any words of comfort.

Every day Judit quizzes the nurses and doctors, and watches Miklós for signs of improvement. When he manages to swallow a few spoonfuls of soup, or says a few words, she pounces on them as a sign of recovery, and resents the doctors' measured optimism.

One morning, Miklós asks, 'Who shot me? Why?' His breathing sounds laboured, he coughs and closes his eyes, and for the first time, the chill of fear grips her heart.

In his hospital bed, Miklós hears that high-pitched sound again, but this time it isn't the siren, it's a black train, and it's shrieking into the darkness of eternal night. He is on that train, speeding through his own life. He hears Eichmann's frightening voice, he sees Becher's smiling face as he talks of redemption and crucifixion, and his head fills with the sweetness of lilies-of-the-valley while he gazes into Ilonka's lovely face and hears her husky voice comforting him. 'It will be all right, Miki,' she says. 'Hold on, please hold on. You will be all right.' Then he sees another train, it's his rescue train, and it's speeding from the darkness towards the light.

He opens his eyes and his expression startles Judit. He is muttering something she can't catch. He seems to be looking past her at something she can't see and talking to someone who isn't there. 'The dead can't save the living and the living can't save the dead,' he whispers. 'Is it wrong to use the devil to save them?'

She swallows and tightens her grip on his hand. There is so much she wants to say, to convince him that what he did wasn't merely right, it was noble. But before she can get the words out, he is whispering again.

'I'm sorry, Ilonka,' he says, and his eyes close for the last time.

CHAPTER THIRTY-SIX

Tel Aviv, 2005

It's a golden morning with just a hint of a breeze to ruffle the striped umbrellas on the beach, and the water glitters in the sunlight. A perfect day for a swim, Annika thinks as she heads to the dining room for breakfast. Then she stops walking. Why was she still in Israel? It was nearly a week since she'd spoken to Eitan Nagy. Surely she had found out all she could about his grandfather. But for some reason she couldn't bring herself to leave. So what was keeping her here? In her head, she hears Cassie laughing. *So you really don't know?*

It was thanks to Cassie that she had gone to Eilat. *When in doubt, stop making decisions and just relax,* Cassie used to say, and, deciding to take her friend's advice, she headed off to the south of Israel. After spending the last three days at the resort, she is feeling so relaxed that even her bones feel soft. She is reminiscing about the thrill of snorkelling with dolphins at Dolphin Reef, and the bliss of swimming in heated pools while listening to underwater music, when her phone rings and brings her back to earth. When she glances down and sees Jancsi's number, she lets it ring several times before picking up.

'How is story about Miklós Nagy? You are find interesting things?'

Aware of the discrepancy in their feelings for each other, she tries to be gentle. For her, he has been a transformative experience, a source of renewed confidence, but she knows that for him, she is the hit-run woman, a tantalising possibility unfulfilled. She has been so deeply immersed in the trial and its aftermath that she doesn't know where to start, but she knows she should tell him what she has found out about the man to whom they both owe their lives.

'It's an incredible story,' she begins, but the clatter of plates and the buzz of voices in the dining room drown out her voice and he asks her to repeat what she has said. Frustrated, she goes outside, and sums up what she has found out, aware that it must be difficult for him to follow such a complicated story. But he listens in silence, and when she has finished, he says, 'This is amazing story, Annika. Tragic. How they can say such terrible things about man who saved so many lives? Do they know who killed him?'

'I don't know yet, but I'm going to try and find out.'

'You are clever woman. I send my love,' he whispers, and hangs up.

Breakfast is usually her favourite meal of the day, but this morning the array of fresh rolls, wholemeal loaves, baguettes, cheeses, salads, marinated herrings, onion tarts, tomato frittatas, French toast, and walnut and custard pastries have lost their appeal as the sadness in his voice lingers like an unspoken reproach.

Relationships are like war, she thinks as she nibbles her eggplant and zucchini frittata: starting them is easy but extricating yourself is hard.

Ahmed, the Arabic waiter, breaks into her reverie. 'We have a special Shabbat dinner this evening, madame, you would like to book?'

Shabbat! She hadn't realised that it's Friday again. This time she isn't going to wait for Dov to call. She goes out onto the terrace, and dials his number.

He sounds happy to hear her voice. 'So you're still here after all. If you're not busy tonight, come and have Shabbat dinner with us. I can pick you up around six. You'll meet Yaeli.'

She counts the minutes until the familiar blue Ford pulls up outside the hotel.

*

On their way to his mother-in-law's home, Annika describes her experiences in Eilat, and then fills him in on what she has found out about Miklós Nagy since they last met. 'I can't believe what happened. Eitan told me all about it. Miklós Nagy was murdered before the Supreme Court handed down their decision, and he never found out he'd been exonerated!'

While she talks, he gives an occasional murmur of assent or sympathy. She's still talking about the injustice of it when he pulls up in a street of plain white-painted buildings with curved Art Deco facades.

'These were built in the German Bahaus style in the 1930s,' he explains. 'This area became a UNESCO world heritage site a couple of years ago because of those buildings.'

But Annika is too engrossed in the drama of Miklós Nagy's last days to pay attention to the architectural heritage of Tel Aviv. 'It's like a Greek tragedy,' she concludes.

'Life often is.'

It strikes her that while she was telling him about the appeal and the assassination, he didn't express any surprise.

'You knew all along, didn't you?' she says. 'Why didn't you tell me?'

'I thought you needed to discover it for yourself.'

She glances at him as they get out of the car. 'You're pretty perceptive for a journo.'

'Journo?'

She explains the Australianism. 'We abbreviate everything, sometimes it doesn't even make sense. If you were called Barry, for example, they'd call you Bazza.'

This time he isn't listening. He is looking at her. 'That top looks great on you.'

She blushes. She has taken more care with her clothes than usual this evening in order to make a good impression on her hostess. Instead of the baggy shirt she usually wears over her faded denim jeans, she is wearing her silky palazzo pants and the clingy black top with the revealing neckline, but as she sees Dov's admiring gaze, she knows that he was the one she was dressing for.

The woman who opens the door is short and plump with a Russian accent and an ebullient temperament. After ushering them inside, Nina Chaikin peals with laughter as she scoops up her grey tabby and cuddles it. 'Just before you came, Pussinka brought me a Shabbat present — a dead mouse!'

As soon as they sit down, she plies them with *piroshki* stuffed with cabbage, herrings in sour cream, cucumbers pickled with garlic and dill, gefilte fish, and slices of *challa* generously spread with chopped liver. 'All home made!' she says proudly. She fills small tumblers with vodka but shakes her head when she sees Annika taking a sip.

'Vodka you don't sip. Wine you sip. Vodka you pour down your throat. Like this. Watch.'

She throws her head back and when she tilts it forward again, the glass is empty and she is laughing again.

The vodka is aromatic, but it doesn't seem very strong, so while Nina claps her plump hands in encouragement, Annika downs another glass, and a moment later she is telling Dov and Nina about a cat she once taught to do a high five.

She knows that she is exaggerating because her cat never did succeed in learning this trick, but it's such a good story, and they are such an appreciative audience that she illustrates it with gestures and tries to enlist the co-operation of Pussinka, who gazes at her outstretched palm with startled eyes and bolts from the room. By the time she has finished her story, she is laughing so much that tears are running down her cheeks.

'I don't think you'd better have any more vodka,' Dov says, but he's laughing too.

The front door slams, and a girl with luxuriant black hair cascading down her back bounces into the room and throws her arms around her grandmother, who looks at her with delight. Watching them together, chatting like close friends, Annika feels envious.

She has never been as aware of the wall of coolness and restraint that Marika has erected around her as she is now, never been so conscious of what she has missed. For an instant she wonders if it's because Nina has lost her daughter that she is lavishing so much love on Yaeli, but she dismisses the thought. Nina is clearly a woman without boundaries where those she loves are concerned, and loss hasn't diminished her capacity for love or her zest for life.

They sit down at the table while Nina runs backwards and forwards bringing a tureen of beetroot borscht with mashed potatoes, chopped dill and a dollop of sour cream, followed by Georgian chicken, braised beef, roast potatoes and cucumber salad. It's hearty Russian food, and Annika is relishing the first home-cooked meal she has had since leaving Sydney. But more than the food, she is enjoying the closeness of the family atmosphere and their generosity in including her.

'I met an interesting guy yesterday called Eitan Nagy,' she says, and notices that Yael is listening attentively.

'You met Eitan Nagy?' From the astonishment in Yael's voice she might have said she'd just met Brad Pitt. 'Where?'

Annika explains how their meeting came about. 'Wow,' Yael says. 'That's awesome. He's so cool.'

'Eitan Nagy has been responsible for more young people joining the Peace Now movement than anyone else,' Dov says. 'It's a great example of sex appeal surpassing sense appeal.'

'*Abba!*' Yael rolls her dark eyes in exasperation. 'You don't understand.' She turns to Annika. 'So what did he say? Are you going to join? There's a protest meeting against the new settlements on Sunday. Want to come with me?'

'You've achieved something rare,' Dov says. 'My daughter's seal of approval. But you should go. You'd find it interesting, and learn something about one of the many divides in our society. There will be protesters protesting against the protest, and police surrounding them to keep the peace at the peace rally.'

'Do you belong?'

'It's like what George Bernard Shaw said about communism. If you're not a communist when you're young, you have no heart, but if you're still a communist when you're old, you have no brain.'

Yael rolls her eyes again and shakes her head. 'Abba, that's crap. There are loads of older people who believe in what Peace Now stands for. As old as you even. People who believe in peace.'

'Everyone believes in peace in theory,' he says quietly. 'It's the reality that's the problem. For peace to take place, both parties have to want it, not just one. Maybe one day it will happen, but I don't see it happening in the foreseeable future. Talk to the people of Sderot, ask them if they can envisage peace with the Palestinians who want peace so desperately that they keep firing rockets at Israeli kindergartens. If the Palestinians wanted peace as much as you do, they would have accepted Ehud Barak's offer five years ago when he proposed to give them ninety per cent of what they demanded, but Arafat rejected the offer without even trying to compromise or negotiate for the other ten per cent.'

Yael is shaking her head so emphatically that her hair swings from side to side and bounces against her cheeks. 'You're throwing statistics around as usual. We believe that if you wait for the other side to give in nothing will ever change. And if we let our government keep stealing Palestinian land and building more settlements, things will only get worse.'

Annika listens to Yael with interest. This girl was so passionate about Palestinian rights despite the fact that her mother was murdered by Palestinian terrorists. It amazes her that Dov, who suffered such a tragedy, is able to discuss the issue so dispassionately with his daughter.

Nina doesn't take part in their argument. Her lively eyes swivel from her granddaughter to her son-in-law as she carries in platters of sliced pineapple, cheesecake, and yeast cakes filled with poppy seeds and walnuts, and she refuses Annika's offers of help.

'Sit, sit, enjoy yourself,' she says. 'Dov says you don't have family in Israel. Where do your people come from?'

'Hungary.' Even as she says it, she feels no emotion, no connection with the country where her family originated. 'I stopped in Budapest on my way here,' she adds. 'It's a beautiful city but I don't have any relatives there either. I don't think I'll ever go back.' As she says this, she feels disloyal, as if she were erasing part of her life.

Yael and Nina pick up some plates and take them to the kitchen, leaving Annika and Dov alone at the table.

'Your daughter is a bright spark,' Annika says. Dov nods but she can tell that his mind is on something else.

He looks up and pushes his glasses further up the bridge of his nose with the palm of his hand. 'So what's next? Protest meetings with Eitan Nagy?'

'Maybe if I lived here I'd go. I agree with Yael. She certainly has a point.'

'So, you're not planning to return to Budapest?' He says it in a casual tone, playing with the pineapple slices on his plate. 'What about that poor guy you left behind?'

While she demurs, he moves closer and drops his voice. 'Annika, there's something…' But before he can say any more, Yael and Nina return, and he sits back, leaving his sentence hanging unfinished between them.

On the drive home, Yael is chattering about her school friends and the compulsory army service after high school and the trip to India many of them plan to make as soon as their military service is over.

'Most of them get so stressed out, they just want to lie on a beach in Goa or laze around in a village in Nepal and smoke pot. I don't want to walk around with an Uzi and make life tough for Palestinians at check points,' she says. 'They'll have to find me a job in an office or something, like they do for those ultra-orthodox Jews.'

Dov smiles indulgently. 'You're right. Stand up for what you believe in.'

He turns to Annika. 'Would you like to come in and see our place on the way to the hotel?'

It sounds like a casual invitation to check out the interior design of their apartment, but the air between them is charged, and she senses that if she accepts, everything between them will change.

*

On a small cedar table in the corner of their cosy loungeroom, she looks at framed photographs of a woman with Nina's smile holding a baby, and the same woman in a graduation cap and gown holding hands with a much younger, leaner Dov, whose crinkly hair was then light brown.

Yael has disappeared into her room, Dov excuses himself for a moment to check the messages on his answerphone, and Annika comes out onto the small balcony. Although it's late, it is still warm, and groups of people are strolling along the palm-lined avenue. Occasionally the sound of voices floats up from the street where young people are laughing and arguing under the lamp post. On the upstairs balcony of a nearby building, a man in a loose shirt leans over the rail and shouts at the revellers to take themselves and their noise somewhere else. One of the guys turns towards him and calls out, '*Shabbat shalom* to you too!' and they all burst out laughing.

A moment later she feels a hand resting on her shoulder, lightly at first, and then more firmly, and she likes its feel on her skin.

'I presume your peacenik is related to Miklós Nagy?' Dov says.

'His grandson.'

'Are you going to see him again?'

'I probably will, because there's a lot more I want to know before I leave.'

'And when will that be?'

'In a few days.'

His hand is still on her shoulder. It feels strong and warm, and she leans against him. When she turns, he is looking straight into her eyes. The tension between them is increasing, and her heart is racing.

'You started saying something at your mother-in-law's place but you didn't finish.'

'Let's go inside,' he says.

She sits close beside him on the leather sofa and waits.

He clears his throat. 'I was going to say that I fell in love with you that day at Ari's café on the waterfront, but I've always known it was hopeless because I'm much older than you, and I have a teenage daughter, and anyway you're going back to Sydney.'

She looks down at the sofa as her fingers trace the age-darkened creases in the leather and wonders if he can hear the beating of her heart. This is what she was hoping he would say but now that he has said it, she doesn't know how to respond. She has never thought of him as much older. From what he has told her about himself, she's worked out that he's fifty-three or fifty-four. Older, but not too old. His daughter isn't an issue either. Then she stops evaluating his comment. He has just made a declaration about his feelings for her, and he is waiting for her response.

She looks up. He's still waiting for her to say something and in that instant she longs to tell him that every moment she has spent with him has been exciting and stimulating, and that she waits impatiently for his calls, that she loves the feel of his hand on her shoulder, and the touch of his lips on her cheek. But she says none of these things. She knows she needs more time before she commits herself.

He has read her answer in her silence and doesn't press her to reply. He leans forward and gently kisses her lips. Then he says, 'It's getting late. I'll take you back to the hotel.'

CHAPTER THIRTY-SEVEN

Tel Aviv, 2005

Annika has come back to see. There are too many unanswered questions and time is running out. This time when he opens the door, she sees him through Yael's eyes, and understands why teenage girls think he's cool. It's the studied grunge look cultivated by male rock stars: unshaven face, messy hair, and an expression that hints at a mysterious past.

'Don't waste time thanking me or apologising,' he says. 'I have to go to a meeting soon, so just ask what you want to know.'

She takes a deep breath. 'Did they ever find the guy who shot your grandfather?'

'It wasn't very hard. They knew where to look: among the extremist right-wing groups. He'd migrated here from Poland, a loser in search of a cause, and found it when he joined a militant group that wanted to destabilise the government. They brainwashed him into believing that the Mapai party was corrupt and that my grandfather was a collaborator. The leaders of that group deified the Stern Gang and Irgun, and they had it in for the Mapai party, like that bastard of a defence attorney. The new recruit decided to prove his worth by assassinating my grandfather.'

'Is he still alive?'

'Probably. Moshe Binsztok was about nineteen or twenty at the time. He killed my grandfather, caused my grandmother's death, and traumatised my father, so he really destroyed our whole family, but he's probably still alive. As we know, there's no justice in the world.'

She looks around for a place to sit, and he takes a mountain of papers off the wicker chair and gestures for her to sit down. He remains standing, leaning against the wall, and keeps checking his watch to remind her that he hasn't much time.

'Did you know your grandfather?'

He shakes his head. 'I was born long after he died. But from the day he died, the family hardly stopped talking about him. All those unanswered questions, endless debates, and bitter regrets, the whys and what ifs. Apparently the funeral was huge. Thousands of people turned up. My grandmother told me that when she saw the coffin being lowered into the grave, she felt like throwing herself in there with him. She couldn't bear the thought of him lying there in the cold earth, alone. All the politicians were there, the ones who had stood by him, and the ones who didn't. My father used to say, "They didn't respect him when he was alive, so why did they come pretending to pay their respects now he was dead?" He was furious.'

She is relieved to see that he is consulting his watch less frequently. 'How did your father cope with what happened?'

Eitan is lost in thought for a few moments. 'He never got over it. He was consumed by anger all his life. It crippled him emotionally and ruined his marriage because my mother couldn't cope with his rage. He never told my grandmother that when he was about eleven he tried to kill himself because of the terrible bullying he and his brother suffered in and out of school. He couldn't bear living here anymore, so after he finished high school he migrated to Toronto and never came back. That's where I was born.'

'But you came back.'

He shrugs. 'The tribal pull of heritage and history, I suppose.'

As she reflects on that, he glances at his watch again and she returns to the subject of Miklós Nagy. 'What happened to your grandmother?'

'You could say she died of grief. She never came to terms with the loss. The injustice of it all.'

Without prompting he goes on to describe his grandmother's life after his grandfather's death. He tells her that even though Miklós was exonerated by the Supreme Court, the whiff of 'collaborator' clung to him like dogshit to a shoe, and, by association, to her as well. But even if she had been offered any musical engagements, she didn't have the patience to practise anymore. Music, which once had been her passion and her solace, now became irrelevant to her. Eventually she sold the piano; its presence in the apartment had become a constant reproach, and besides, as she didn't have any income, she needed the money.

'She started teaching music at a high school but her heart wasn't in it, and she kept apart from the other teachers, convinced they were talking about her behind her back. For some strange reason, she blamed herself for everything that happened, which didn't make sense to my father or my uncle, but I suppose when people are depressed, they don't think straight. In any case, her heart wasn't in teaching so she gave it up.

'My father used to send her money from Canada when he started working, and I think some of the people my grandfather rescued eventually got together and organised a small pension for her, but apart from that, she had no income.'

'That's terrible,' Annika says.

'The other thing that got her down was something my grandfather was supposed to have said just before he died. My father told me about it. Apparently on his deathbed my grandfather mentioned someone called Ilonka. None of us had any idea what that was about. My father suspected that my grandmother knew but she didn't want to say.' He shrugs. 'I suppose every family has its secrets.'

'So what happened to the killer?'

'He got the mandatory life sentence but somehow or other the bastard was released much earlier. Because of good behaviour, they said. He'd been rehabilitated and wasn't likely to reoffend. That's modern justice for you.'

'Your grandmother must have been bitter about that.'

'Of course she was, but in the end she said she didn't care whether they let him out in ten years or a hundred. It wouldn't bring her husband back.'

'And the defence attorney, Amos Alon? Did he ever change his opinion about your grandfather?'

'Until the end of his life he was obsessed with the idea that my grandfather was a collaborator, and he never passed up an opportunity to bring the matter up, never stopped writing letters and articles on the subject. It was a real *idée fixe*. I'll give you an example. A few years after my grandfather's assassination, Eichmann was brought to Israel and put on trial. You won't believe this, but Alon started writing articles to the newspapers and letters to the Justice Department demanding that they reopen the Nagy case. He said they now had the perfect opportunity to find out the truth because they had in custody the man who had taken part in negotiations with Miklós Nagy! He actually thought it was reasonable to turn Eichmann into a witness against my grandfather!'

'That's incredible.' Annika says. 'He really was obsessed.'

Eitan observes her with an appreciative glance. 'I'll tell you something even more bizarre,' he says. 'While Eichmann was here, a reporter asked him about Miklós Nagy. And you know what Eichmann said? He gave that insidious thin-lipped smile of his, and said, "I had great respect for Mr Nagy. He was an idealist like me!"'

Eitan sits forward, and she realises that he hasn't looked at his watch for the past ten minutes. 'You asked about Amos Alon. That story has an extraordinary postscript. Did you happen to hear about the three Israeli soldiers who were captured by terrorists about twenty years ago?'

She makes a quick calculation. That would have been in the 1980s, back in the days when she was an eager cadet at one of the Sydney newspapers, dreaming of becoming an investigative journalist like Oriana Fallaci, travelling around the world to interview powerful leaders and exposing the secrets they wanted to conceal. She can't remember why she betrayed her dream and ended up editing a magazine that relied on gossip and rumours about egotistical celebrities.

'Maybe it didn't make the news in Australia,' Eitan is saying, 'but it electrified us here because our government is committed to doing everything in its power to rescue any of our soldiers that are taken hostage. Well, the captors exacted an outrageous price: they demanded the release of over a thousand terrorists being held in Israeli jails. Many of them had the blood of Israeli civilians on their hands, so you can imagine the uproar that caused.'

Annika wonders if one of those terrorists had been responsible for the bomb attack which had killed Dov's wife Nurit and their unborn child.

'After a lot of soul-searching and bitter arguments for and against the deal, the government agreed to release all those prisoners in exchange for our three soldiers,' Eitan continues. 'And guess who played an important role in the negotiations for their release? Amos Alon. And to save them, he had to negotiate with the devil, just like my grandfather. I've always wondered if he saw the exquisite irony of that. But I don't suppose he ever did.'

Annika looks around the room at the papers and leaflets. 'It's interesting that you're so committed to working for peace, but you haven't found peace in your own life.'

She hadn't planned to say this, and she is taken aback by her own words. 'It seems to me that you take after your grandfather,' she continues. 'You're an activist like him. He was passionate about saving people's lives, and gave up everything to do that, and in your own way, you're trying to do the same. You're both men with a mission to rescue people. He was determined to rescue them from the Nazis, and you want to rescue them from themselves.'

Eitan is silent, obviously considering her words. Then he says, 'I've always admired him, but I never saw that connection before. Everyone says they want peace but hardly anyone is willing to do anything about it. Peace Now is accused of being naive, and some people even call us traitors because we're against our government's policies towards the Palestinians. The amount of hostility we encounter during our protests sometimes makes me wonder if we're achieving anything. But it's interesting that you think I take after my grandfather.'

'Speaking of peace, have you ever thought of forgiving that gunman?'

He stares at her as if he's just seen a serpent slither into the room. 'Forgive him? You can't be serious. Forgive the man who destroyed my family? Are you one of those people who think they can solve everybody's problems with New Age psychobabble?'

She manages to ignore the scathing tone and presses on. 'I read somewhere that you have to be very strong to forgive someone but forgiveness is liberating. It's the only way to regain power, overcome the destructive force of anger and bitterness, find peace, and move on.'

He is looking at his watch again and she can tell that he is having trouble controlling his anger. 'I don't know where you get this stuff, but I can assure you that there's no way I'd forgive that bastard, and even if I did, it wouldn't help me to find peace and move on, as you put it.'

Annika is as startled as he is by this unexpected turn in the conversation. She has no idea what has impelled her to talk about forgiveness, but despite his antagonism, she can't let it go. 'He was very young at the time. What if he told you that he regretted what he'd done and he was sorry?'

'That he was sorry?' He repeats her words with incredulity. 'Look, I have to go now. Perhaps you should take your helpful suggestions to someone who wants them.'

She is shocked by her own presumptuousness and can't comprehend how she came to offer unsolicited advice on such a personal matter. 'You're right. I'm very sorry, I shouldn't have said anything. It's not my business.'

He is studying her as if he still can't believe what she has said. 'I can't work you out. You came here to find out about my grandfather, and now you're telling me to forgive his killer.'

She squirms. 'Please believe me, I didn't mean to say any of this, it just came out, I don't even know why. I don't usually shoot my mouth off like this. It just came to me that it might help. I don't blame you for being angry.'

Mollified by her contrite tone, he calms down. 'Okay. Thirty seconds ago you thought you were being helpful but now you can see you weren't. Anything else you want to know?'

'That group Moshe Binsztok was involved with. Does it still exist?'

Eitan's mouth tightens again. 'I have no idea. I'm not interested in right-wing fanatics. Only ten years ago, one of them murdered our Prime Minister Rabin. I'm sure you heard about that even in Australia.'

Annika decides to change the subject. 'Last time I was here, you showed me an old photo album. You said you kept it in a box with your grandfather's papers. Did he leave any letters or documents?'

'Why?'

'Have you thought of donating them to a museum so they can be kept for posterity?'

Eitan sighs. 'There are some old papers, but I haven't gone through them in any detail. As for museums, you don't understand the situation here. Even now, after all these years, the name of Miklós Nagy evokes violent reactions, and for every one person who praises him for his courage, another one condemns him for collaboration. He isn't even mentioned in any museum. When we tried to persuade the curator of the Holocaust Museum to dedicate some space to him in the section devoted to those who saved Jews, she told us that she couldn't do it as it would upset too many people. She said he was too controversial.'

'But that can be said of anyone who ever achieved anything, from King David to David Ben-Gurion. Your grandfather did something extraordinarily courageous and he should be publicly acknowledged and commemorated.'

'I don't understand why you're so het up about this. Do you have some connection with my grandfather?'

She hesitates, wondering whether to tell him, and decides that having had the audacity to ask personal questions and give him advice on such a sensitive issue, she owes him the truth.

'It started with my grandmother, Marika Horvath,' she begins. 'She had never mentioned him to me before, but when I told her I saw a photo of her taken in Switzerland just after the rescue train arrived, and asked about him, she refused to tell me anything. Actually she said she never wanted to hear his name again.'

She glances at him, hoping that her grandmother's reaction hasn't upset him, and adds, 'I don't know why she said that. It sounds terribly ungrateful.'

'Don't talk to me about ingratitude,' Eitan says. 'There was an orthodox rabbi on that rescue train who migrated to

New York and formed his own congregation. When he was asked if he'd testify in the District Court that my grandfather saved him, he refused. And you know why? He said, "Miklós Nagy didn't save me. God saved me!" So, coming back to your grandmother, I suppose you asked her why she was so antagonistic towards the man who saved her?'

'You don't know my grandmother. She is silk on the outside but granite on the inside. She's a very private person with a high wall around her and an electrified fence. You trespass at your own risk.'

'Come on, you're not shy about asking personal questions. You must have tried to find out.'

'I did try but it was impossible to get anything out of her. I can't explain the power she has. Sometimes it's easier to talk to strangers than to relatives.'

'And your mother? Doesn't she know anything?'

'My mother is a very different kind of person. All her life she has protected my grandmother. She would never contradict her or say anything to upset her. Maybe it's a second-generation thing, a belief that they have to protect the survivors.'

'So by coming here you thought you'd clear up the mystery. And did you?'

'I don't suppose I ever will, but at least I've found out what an amazing man your grandfather was. And in the process I've found out a lot about human nature, and a bit about myself too. How I poke my nose into other people's business,' she adds with an attempt at lightness.

He rises. 'I do have to go. The government is planning to build new settlements and we're organising a protest rally for Sunday.'

At the door, she puts out her hand. 'No hard feelings?'

He smiles. 'No hard feelings. When do you leave?'

'On Tuesday.'

She wishes him success and he wishes her a safe journey.

*

The warm afternoon stretches lazily ahead of her and she turns off Allenby Street and loses herself in a labyrinth of narrow alleys, twisting lanes and dilapidated houses that seem to be relics from the past, so different from the world of quirky boutiques, shopping malls and pavement cafés that she has left behind. Past Nahalal Binyamin Street, she comes to a bustling outdoor market squeezed into a narrow passageway.

The sign on the corner says Shuk HaCarmel, and she realises that she has wandered into the Carmel Market, which Dov once recommended for a glimpse of old Tel Aviv and a tasty casual lunch. All around her people are shouting, spruiking, arguing, and bargaining over fake designer handbags and T-shirts, or selecting flowers. 'They're roses, not diamonds,' a stout florist snaps at a buyer who is examining the flowers petal by petal.

Past stalls heaped with St Peter's fish, red mullet, sardines, and barbouni, where fishmongers chop crimson tuna with murderous cleavers, she passes colourful displays of dried apricots, dates and figs, jars of olives, mounds of aromatic spices and baskets of the reddest tomatoes and the biggest cherries and strawberries she has ever seen.

Soon she breathes in the yeasty smell of fresh pita bread, and her mouth waters at the smell of lamb skewers being roasted on charcoal braziers. Unable to resist the smell of cooking food, she stops at one of the stalls, orders a falafel, and, perched on a rickety stool, she bites into a bun filled to bursting point with crunchy falafel balls, hummus, tahini, fried eggplant and pickled cucumbers.

Sitting there, jostled by the noisy crowd of shoppers, she gazes contentedly at the scene around her, and laughs as she tries to catch bits of the filling that escape from the bun. For the first time that day she isn't thinking about anything. She is enjoying the present moment.

And in that instant of complete relaxation, she suddenly understands why she has come to Israel. She dials Dov's number.

'You remember when we first met you asked me why I had embarked on this search, and when I told you it was on account of my grandmother, you didn't believe me? I think you said you didn't buy it. And another time, you asked me if I was grateful for everything I had received? Well, you were right on both counts. I've realised that I came to find out as much as I could about Miklós Nagy because it is personal. If not for him, I wouldn't be alive today.'

Dov is silent, and she is about to ask if he is still there, when he says, 'So you've made a pilgrimage of gratitude.'

She smiles. 'A pilgrimage of gratitude. I like that.'

'I like it too. When did you have that epiphany?'

'This morning. By the way, do you know how can I find out if the right-wing group that Miklós Nagy's assassin belonged to still exists?'

He laughs. 'You never give up, do you? I'll look into it and let you know if I come up with anything.'

In the silence that ensues, she is wondering how to say the words that she knows will change everything. But she has to say it face to face. Her heart is pounding as she says, 'Dov, I need to see you.'

Twenty minutes later she sees him coming towards her. It's obvious that he has been rushing, and he tries to catch his breath as he pulls up a stool.

'I had to make an excuse to leave the office,' he says, looking at her searchingly.

'Dov, it's about what you said the other night at your place,' she begins. 'I want you to know that the things you mentioned don't matter to me at all. I like your daughter, and I don't think you're too old.' She takes a deep breath. 'What I'm trying to say is, I feel we're right for each other.'

He leans across the table and takes her face between his hands so tenderly that, as they look into each other's eyes, she feels that their souls have touched.

He shakes his head, as though unable to believe what he has just heard her say. 'But you are still going back to Australia.'

'Yes, but not forever.'

This is the second thing she has said on impulse that day, but as they both rise, and hold each other in a wordless embrace, she knows that this is one statement she won't regret.

CHAPTER THIRTY-EIGHT

Tel Aviv, 2005

Standing in a windblown street in a seedy part of Tel Aviv, Annika tries to summon the courage to press the buzzer on an intercom sticky with spider webs. It takes her back to the time she was writing investigative pieces for a daily newspaper, trembling with equal degrees of apprehension and anticipation each time she stood in front of the door of someone who would not welcome her intrusion.

With only two days left before her departure, she was impatient to spend as much of the remaining time with Dov as possible, but the unexpected phone call from Eitan later that afternoon promised to provide another piece of the Nagy puzzle.

'After you left, I thought about what you said, and I came up with the name of an ultranationalist group that often tries to disrupt our meetings. They call themselves Israel First. They reckon we're Palestinian collaborators, and threaten us with divine vengeance because we're agitating for a two-state solution,' he said. 'They could be connected with the extremists who killed my grandfather, but even if they're not, they might know something about Moshe Binsztok. Just tread carefully. They're zealots with fundamentalist ideas and they don't take kindly to opposing views.'

An hour later, she arrived at the busy office of Israel First in a cul-de-sac off Dizengoff Street. One wall was covered with maps of the West Bank marking terrain labelled Samaria and Judea, while another was hung with posters demanding the integration of these territories into the state of Israel. There were banners denouncing the government's acceptance of a two-state solution as the betrayal of the Torah and God's gift to the Jews.

The word God, she noticed, was either spelled without the 'o', or written in Hebrew letters. She also noticed that most of the men milling around the office wore skullcaps, and the women covered their hair with wigs, scarves or floppy berets. Small groups were huddled together, fervently discussing something, while in the far corner of the room a bearded man of about fifty was banging his fist on a wooden desk as he argued with a younger guy who was jabbing his finger at what looked like a blueprint for a poster.

She was in unfamiliar territory, and remembered Eitan's warning.

A tall slim woman of about thirty in a long dress and a floral scarf twisted around her head, put down a book she was reading when she saw Annika. 'You are looking for someone here?' she asked in a tone that implied Annika must have wandered in by mistake.

'I'm an Australian journalist and I wondered if you had a public relations person I could talk to. Your group doesn't get a good press in our media. All we ever read are negative reports about you being extremists who ignore Palestinian rights, support settlements on Palestinian land, and fight with Israeli soldiers who are trying to evict settlers. So I'd like to write an article from your point of view, so that people back home can see you in a more balanced, sympathetic light.'

She doubted if the ethics section of the Journalists' Association would approve of this approach, but she knew that coming straight out and asking about Moshe Binsztok would be guaranteed to arouse mistrust. Besides, she rationalised, what she said wasn't altogether untrue. When she got back to Australia, she might write about their movement, though not, perhaps, in a way they would approve.

'I'm Rahel. You can talk to me,' the woman said curtly, and ushered Annika into a small room at the back of the office. 'So what do you want to know about us?'

Rahel wasted no time talking up her beliefs and discrediting the opposition. With messianic zeal she denounced the treacherous agenda of politicians who were about to sell out their country, and the dangerous naivety of groups like Peace Now and their followers whose efforts to create a Palestinian state from land that the Almighty had given to the Jews not only threatened their nation, but constituted a crime against God. Judea and Samaria must be reclaimed.

'Isn't peace worth a piece of land?' Annika asked.

'A piece of land? Is that what you call it?' Rahel's eyes flashed with anger, and Annika remembered Eitan's advice too late. She should have held her tongue.

Determined to convince Annika of her heresy, Rahel hardly stopped for breath for the next thirty minutes, speaking in an impassioned voice, and emphasising her arguments with sweeping gestures.

Occasionally members of the staff put their heads around the door to ask questions, and seeing Rahel glancing at her watch several times, Annika realised that their meeting would end before she had time to obtain the information she had come for.

'I've heard something about the courage of the Irgun fighters in the terrible incident of the *Altalena*, and the role that Begin played,' she said.

Her ploy worked. Clearly impressed by her appreciation of the Irgun position, Rahel became less didactic and condescending, and she recounted the story in a ringing voice, her eyes shining at the heroism of the Irgun fighters against the betrayal of the Jewish Agency leaders.

'Moshe Binsztok was one of the members back in the fifties, wasn't he?' Annika said innocently. 'Wasn't he involved in the assassination of that guy who was accused of being a collaborator?'

'Oh, yes, Binsztok. I believe he keeps to himself these days, but you should talk to him if you're interested in those times. He could tell you all about the corrupt Mapai government that tried to protect the collaborator.'

Annika tried to keep her voice steady and casual. 'That sounds like a great idea. Do you happen to know where I can find him?'

Rahel shakes her head. 'I hear his name mentioned from time to time but I've never met him and I have no idea whether he lives in Tel Aviv. The group he was part of doesn't exist anymore, and he never joined ours, but I can ask my colleagues. Someone might know where he lives.'

*

Now, as she presses the buzzer on the door of Moshe Binsztok's building, she is almost relieved when no-one answers. Talking to Rahel wasn't threatening, but how could she have the temerity to talk to the assassin himself? Why would he agree to answer her intrusive questions? She is about to give up and walk away when an unshaven old man in a loose singlet leans over a crumbling balcony on the second floor.

'*Shalom*. You look for someone?'

'Moshe Binsztok…'

'You friend?'

There's no simple answer to this question other than the one that will close Moshe's door to her. 'Yes,' she says. It seems that in her quest for truth, she has become enmeshed in a web of prevarications, half-truths and lies, but she comforts herself with the thought that truth is usually found in nuanced shadows, not in the dazzle of sunlight.

The man looks at his watch. 'He back ten minutes. You wait?'

Annika nods, thankful that this is a street where people seem to know their neighbours' movements.

As she strolls past buildings damaged by salt air, parching desert wind and unforgiving heat, a thin man with closely cropped iron-grey hair and a dark tracksuit casts her a quizzical glance as he limps past. She supposes that as this shabby neighbourhood doesn't attract tourists, a foreign woman in jeans must be an object of curiosity.

Then she stops walking. She has no idea what Moshe Binsztok looks like, but the man who just passed her is limping towards the building where she pressed the buzzer a few minutes ago. From Eitan's description, she visualises a skinny young bloke in a khaki jacket, but Moshe must be in his early seventies by now. Like the man who has just walked past.

She runs after him. 'Mr Binsztok?'

He turns around, startled, and eyes that seem to burn with a menacing inner fire scan her face. 'Who are you? What do you want?'

They're standing on the doorstep, and the unswept leaves that the wind has pushed against the door crackle under their shoes. His key is in his hand and she knows that any moment now he will open the door and slam it shut in her face.

Speaking quickly, she explains who she is and why she wants to talk to him.

With a threatening expression, he takes a step towards her but although her heart is racing, she stands her ground.

'You've got a nerve,' he says. 'You're a complete stranger, and you just walk up to me in the street and expect me to talk to you. Who do you think you are? Who sent you here? What are you really after?'

Put off balance by his onslaught, she is stammering a reply when he cuts in. 'How did you find me?'

She hesitates. Confessing the subterfuge by which she obtained his address will antagonise him even further and destroy any possibility of a conversation.

'I don't know what you want or why you're here,' he spits the words out, 'but whatever it is, I'm not interested. Get this through your head: whoever you are, I don't want to talk to you. Now go back wherever you came from and leave me alone.'

He is stepping away from her now, and she knows this is her last chance to change his mind. She speaks quickly.

'I realise you don't know anything about me, and I'm happy to tell you whatever you want to know. But please believe me, I don't have any ulterior motives. No-one sent me here. I'm sorry if I upset you appearing out of the blue like this, but I'm leaving Israel soon, and I just want to hear your story, that's all.'

'My story. And exactly what part of my story do you want to hear?'

He is mocking her, but he is still standing there, so she pushes on.

'I've read about the Nagy case and I just want to hear your side of it.'

'To satisfy your morbid curiosity.'

'No, my sense of fair play.'

He studies her in silence, and in that moment when the scales could tilt either way, she holds her breath. If she were superstitious she'd be crossing her fingers, but she holds his gaze instead. 'I'll give you five minutes,' he says, and with a resigned gesture, he opens the door and lets her inside.

Up a steep flight of stairs, he opens the door to a bedsitter where the smell of mould makes her eyes water, and when she peers into the tiny space that serves as a kitchen, she sees a primus stove, a chipped enamel sink with a gas heater above it, and a few wooden shelves stacked with tinned food.

Throwing his tracksuit jacket on the chair, he goes into the kitchenette. This is her only chance of finding out about the assassination, so while he is gone, she tries to organise her thoughts into questions that won't irritate him. Looking around, she flops onto a sofa with scratched wooden arms and brown upholstery that resembles the fur of a mangy dog. She realises that at night it probably opens up into his bed. A kettle whistles, and he emerges from the kitchen with two mugs of black coffee and drops into a folding canvas chair.

'I work as a night cleaner at the Menachem Begin Museum,' he says.

That name gives her an opening. 'Wasn't he a member of the Irgun, like some of the people in your group?'

He gives her an ironic look. 'So you've been doing your homework. You're not a journalist by any chance, are you?'

This time she decides to come clean. 'I am a journalist,' she begins, and he's already on his feet, like a wild animal about to spring. Her heart is pounding and she speaks very fast. 'Please believe me, this has nothing to do with my profession. As I told you, I'm here on a private visit, and my interest in this affair stems only from my grandmother's connection with Miklós Nagy. I've been reading about that case, and that's why I wanted to meet you.'

'So you've come here to look at the man who killed your hero.'

She shakes her head. 'No, I only want to hear your side of the story.'

He looks straight into her face for the first time. 'You know, you're the first person who has ever wanted to hear my side of the story,' he says slowly. 'Everyone always assumed I was a gun-happy extremist ready to commit any crime to ingratiate myself with my group.'

'But you weren't?'

He sinks back into his chair and shrugs. 'I don't know what I was. How do you put yourself back into the head of the person you were fifty years ago? That person doesn't exist anymore. I never talk about what happened that day but you said you wanted to hear my story, and that's what it is, a story about a stranger I now despise.'

'Despise? Why?'

'What I did that day has ruined my life, and that's why I don't want to talk about it. There hasn't been a day when I didn't wish I could turn back time.' He is staring into space now, and he seems to be musing aloud, as if he has forgotten she is there. 'You hear about people overcoming all kinds of disasters and tragedies, but how do you get over killing someone for the wrong reason?'

She is taken aback. She had expected him to give excuses on account of his youth or the political climate at the time, not to confess his guilt.

'I've heard that murderers often say they have no recollection of what they did, that their mind went blank or they lost consciousness, as if someone else pulled the trigger or wielded the knife,' he continues. 'But I remember every detail as if it happened yesterday, and when I close my eyes, I replay the whole scene, as if it's happening now. I often have nightmares about it. I dream I'm about to pull the trigger and I sit up in the middle of the night drenched in sweat, horrified by what I've done. That's my curse.'

Annika thought she would be repelled by the man who had killed Miklós Nagy, but she is moved by his remorse. This is a man haunted by his crime. Then she wonders if he is manipulating her, trying to work on her emotions with calculating words. She looks at his downcast face and decides to trust her instinct. Moshe has been paying for his crime for over fifty years, a far longer sentence than any judge could have imposed.

'You said you killed him for the wrong reason. What did you mean?'

He seems startled by the sound of her voice, and the anger flares up again. 'You're a leech, sucking my blood. You're trying to claw into my soul.'

His attack shocks her but she remains silent. It was no use giving excuses or apologies. The trust between them, flimsy as it was, had been rent. But a moment later he surprises her by saying, 'I'll start at the beginning. I was born in a *stetl* in Poland ...'

As he speaks, his life unspools before her. The terrified ten-year-old boy running into the forest in panic when his parents and young sisters are rounded up, living by his wits for the next few years, sometimes joining groups of partisans, always hoping that when the war was over, he would be reunited with his family. When the war finally comes to an end, and he goes back to his village, he discovers that his whole family has been murdered in Auschwitz, and his neighbours have moved into his home and appropriated all the possessions that had been left with them for safekeeping. He thought they'd be happy that he'd survived, but the way the men look at him with knives in their eyes makes him shiver. A neighbour warns him to leave as soon as possible and never come back. He is fourteen years old and he is alone in the world.

She can see him in Warsaw, a ragged, skinny kid knocking about among the ruins of the devastated city, scavenging for food and sleeping in doorways. He joins a gang of street kids living hand to mouth, stealing food from market stalls and selling contraband cigarettes. One day a black marke-teer he deals with offers him a glass of vodka, and from that moment he is hooked. Alcohol takes away his pain, his fear, and his grief, and brings blessed oblivion.

'I would have died drunk in a gutter if someone from a Zionist youth group hadn't picked me up,' he says. 'They were looking for orphaned Jewish kids and sending them to a scout camp. For the first time in years, I had discipline and purpose in my life. They weaned me off alcohol and steered me away from crime.'

They look at each other as he says that, both aware of the irony of that statement. Engrossed by his story, she has let her coffee grow cold, and he limps to the kitchen to refill her mug. He is talking even before he sits down, and she senses that now the floodgates of painful memories have opened, the story pours out in a torrent, unstoppable and uncontrol-lable. All she has to do now is let him talk.

'By the time I arrived in Israel at the end of 1948, I was like a pressure-cooker, with no outlet for the steam to escape,' he says. 'Israel had been held up to us as the prom-ised land where we would be among our own kind, and I couldn't wait to get there, but it wasn't like that. Far from it. No-one seemed to want to know what happened in Poland during the Holocaust.

'The survivors didn't want to talk about it and the locals didn't want to hear about it. They were busy congratulating themselves on their victory over the Arabs. They boasted they were Sabra Jews, not *stetl* Jews, victors, not victims, as if they were some kind of superior race to the rest of us. Some of them even talked disparagingly about European Jews going like sheep to slaughter.'

The recollection of that slur rekindles his anger and he stops talking. Annika doesn't take her eyes off him, and waits.

'I didn't know what to do with the rage I felt. I thought I'd explode,' he goes on. 'So I joined a militant right-wing group and as you already know, many of them had been Irgun members or sympathisers with a grudge against the government and everyone in it. For the first time I was among people who were as angry as I was. I was relieved that they shared my rage but I didn't realise they were using it as a weapon.'

Over the next few years, Moshe was indoctrinated with the subversive views of his leaders. According to them, all the problems of this country were caused by the Mapai party which, they claimed, had ignored the plight of Europe's Jews, and later betrayed the courageous fighters of Irgun over the *Altalena* affair. When the Nagy trial began, they found their target. They told him that Miklós Nagy was a quisling who was being protected by the treacherous Mapai party, that he had collaborated with the Nazis, hobnobbed with prominent SS officers, and done a dirty deal with them to rescue a few of his own relatives and friends in return for colluding with them on the deportation to Auschwitz of the remaining Jews of Hungary.

Moshe is clasping and unclasping his hands as he speaks. 'I believed them. They worked on me until I was obsessed with the idea that this man was a traitor to our nation, that he was responsible for the deaths of hundreds of thousands of Jews. I lost my whole family in Auschwitz, and I knew it was my sacred duty to avenge their deaths by killing this collaborator.'

As Annika listens, she feels a shift in her attitude. The preconceived ideas she had about the perpetrator and his unforgivable crime seem to blur and dissolve in a perplexing stew of moral ambiguity. She abhors his action but at the same time she is coming to understand it in the context of his experiences and his indoctrination. Perhaps no sin is unforgiveable if you can understand the sinner.

Moshe now comes to the fatal night, and he describes it as if it he is reliving it.

'I can still feel the heavy coldness of the revolver in my hand,' he says. 'When you hold a gun, the tension builds up and your finger itches to press the trigger. I can still see the palm branches swaying in the wind, and the leaves of the oleanders rustling while I waited in the bushes for his car to pull up. I had intended to say *This is for the murdered Jews of Europe,* but when the moment came and he got out of the car, I was too nervous to say anything. I just wanted to get it over with and get away before anyone saw me.

'I made sure it was him and pulled the trigger. He looked at me for an instant and saw the revolver, but he didn't look shocked, not even surprised. It was as if he expected this to happen. The revolver didn't feel cold anymore. I fired twice, but hearing the gunshots made me jump. I'd forgotten about the sound they would make, and I broke out in a cold sweat. I was sure everyone would hear it and come after me. I panicked and ran down the street as fast as I could, scared as hell, but proud that I'd obeyed the order and done my duty.'

Spellbound by his story, Annika feels as though she has witnessed the shooting herself. Recalling his earlier comment, she says, 'But now you say you shot him for the wrong reason. What did you mean?'

The irritation comes back into his voice. 'Don't rush me. I'm coming to that. Not long after they sent me to jail, one of the prisoners cornered me in the laundry and attacked me.' He points to his leg. 'You probably noticed my limp. He lunged at me with an iron bar, yelling that he was going to kill me because I'd killed his hero. He kept whacking me until I blacked out. I stayed in hospital for a couple of weeks. My leg was broken in two places, and I had some broken ribs. While they were healing, I brooded about paying him back. I decided I'd get my people to deal with him. But I had a lot of time to think in hospital, and I started thinking about the crazy thing he said, that I'd killed a hero. I couldn't work it out. He wasn't one of those violent inmates that everyone steered clear of, so why had he picked on me? In the end, I knew I had to confront him and sort it out one way or another. When they sent me back to jail, I looked for him, but he warned me to keep away or next time he'd kill me. Eventually he calmed down and talked to me. I think it was because I never told the screws he was the one who had attacked me.

'And this is more or less what he said: "Miklós Nagy saved my life, and you're a fucking moron to believe that right-wing garbage about him only rescuing friends and family. I wasn't friends or family and he rescued me, along with about a thousand other strangers, and put me on that train. And he had to deal with that monster Eichmann to do it. He did something no-one else had ever done, and only a pathetic half-wit like you could believe that he collaborated with the Nazis to send Hungarian Jews to Auschwitz."

'He got so worked up about it that his eyes bulged and his face went red, and I thought he was going to bash me again. He said what I'd done was worse than a crime because a judge could make you pay for your crime, but only God could forgive a sin.

'He was released a short time after that, and I didn't think I'd ever see him again, because they sentenced me to fifteen years, but to my surprise they released me earlier, for good behaviour. In or out of jail, it didn't make any difference to me. I've been living in my personal prison ever since. In my own hell.'

He looks down at his hands while she thinks about his words. 'Do you think you'll ever forgive yourself?'

He doesn't reply, and looking at him she realises the corrosive power of guilt. Perhaps it required even more strength to forgive yourself than to forgive others. She thanks him for talking to her, and she is almost at the door when she remembers something he said.

'You said that the guy in jail told you that Miklós Nagy rescued him, that he was on that train. Can you remember what he said about it? Did he mention anyone in particular?'

Moshe shrugs. 'What am I, a genius? How do you expect me to remember what he told me forty years ago? But if you want to know something about that train, ask Shmuel.'

'Shmuel?'

Moshe points to the ceiling. 'Upstairs. That's the guy I was in jail with.'

'The one who bashed you up?'

'When I got out, he helped me find this flat. Don't look so amazed. You know what they say, that when you rescue someone you become responsible for them for the rest of their life? Well, he reckons he saved me because I never went near that extremist group again. But part of him still hates me for what I did. He's got a shocking temper and it doesn't take much to get him worked up into a frenzy about it. He'll probably enjoy talking to you about his hero. Only don't tell him I said we met in jail. He's sensitive about his past.'

CHAPTER THIRTY-NINE

Tel Aviv, 2005

At the top of the stairs, she knocks, and recognises the man who opens the door. It's the one who leaned over the balcony earlier that day, and told her that Moshe would soon be home.

'You talking to Moshe, yes?' Shmuel booms, a cigarette stuck to his bottom lip. She can hear music playing inside his flat. It sounds ethnic, and reminds her of the rhythmic melodies the musicians played when she and Jancsi were in the café in Budapest. It's a pleasant memory, although it feels far away.

The stale smell of thousands of cigarettes smoked in this room over decades has seeped into the walls and ceilings, and left tea-coloured stains. Shmuel tamps his cigarette in a metal ashtray overflowing with butts, and scurries to a battered old radio in a walnut case. 'Bartók,' he says as he switches it off. 'Hungarian music. Very good.' He scans her face. 'Why you here?'

Using simple language and speaking slowly in the hope that he can understand what she is saying, she explains that she had heard that he was rescued by Miklós Nagy. 'I came so you could tell me whatever you can remember about that train journey,' she says.

Lighting another cigarette, he says, 'Long time ago. Too long. Old story.'

'But it's such an important story,' she says and looks straight into his eyes with a candid expression that she hopes will convince him. 'The whole world should know about it, especially as some people still regard him as a collaborator.'

As soon as he hears the word, he bristles. 'Collaborator? Fucking lie!' he shouts, and immediately apologises for his language. 'Nagy Miklós hero. Best man in Hungary. He save my mother and he save me. He save more than thousand Jewish peoples. This is collaborator?'

He has now worked himself up into a fury and occasionally sprays saliva as he talks. 'Judge, idiot. Say Mr Nagy collaborator. Never collaborator. Lawyer also liar. Says he will call me to talk in court for Mr Nagy, but he not call. Never.'

She tries to untangle the diatribe. 'So you offered to give evidence in court but they didn't call you?'

'Yes, I say this.'

'You must have been upset that you didn't have the chance to tell the District Court judge about your experience. That might have influenced his decision. That's why it's so important to tell the truth about him now, isn't it?'

He looks at her suspiciously. 'How you know about me?'

'From Moshe,' she says, and immediately realises her faux pas.

'Moshe say you about me?' he shouts, and leaps to his feet, looming over her, his face distorted with rage. 'Fucking *mamser.*'

Annika is in a panic. She knows why he is so furious, but it's too late. All she can do now is back-pedal.

'He said he was grateful to you because you made him understand that Miklós Nagy was a hero. He said that if I wanted to find out more about him, I should ask you, because you knew the truth,' she says quickly.

He sits down again and she heaves a sigh of relief. Having seen this demonstration of his erratic temperament and the ferocity with which he defends his rescuer, she can imagine him picking up a weapon to bash the man who killed Miklós Nagy.

To calm him down, she tells him that Miklós Nagy saved her grandmother.

'Why you not ask grandmother about Nagy Miklós?'

There's no way she will tell him that Marika refuses to talk about the man he venerates. 'She's old, she can't remember things,' she says, and to mollify him, she adds, 'Because it's such an important story, I want to find out as much as possible about him from people he rescued.'

Her approach works. He leans back in his large armchair and lights another cigarette from the stub of the one he's been smoking.

'Yes, we all old now. I old also. Soon no peoples left to tell stories.'

With an ease that surprises her, he starts reminiscing, and sixty years melt away as he describes life in his provincial town near the Romanian border when the Nazis invaded Hungary in 1944. 'Some peoples believe Germans that they go to other town for work, they go into German trains, but my father, he not trust Germans. Peoples going on trains. Never coming back. Then, miracle.' He claps his big hands. 'Nagy Miklós. He brave man. He argues with Nazi monster Eichmann — you know who is Eichmann? Nagy Miklós comes to Kolostór to save Jewish peoples.'

Shmuel stops talking and leans towards Annika, wagging his finger at her for emphasis. 'Look, we not family, we not friends, we not rabbis. We nothing. But Nagy Miklós sees mother sick, very poor. He saves us. We go on special train.' A beatific expression comes over his face as though he were speaking about a saint.

He describes the train journey that seemed to go on forever. 'Some peoples they think we to Auschwitz going, but my mother say, Nagy Miklós, he not sending us to Auschwitz. Then we in Bergen-Belsen, waiting. Terrible camp. Peoples angry, why we here? We die here? But mother always say, trust Mr Nagy. He doing what he promise. And one day he fixing everything and we to Switzerland going,' he says with a euphoric smile.

'Do you remember any of the people on the train?' she asks.

He spreads his hands. 'So long time ago. How I can remembering? You say grandmother was on train. Grandmother name?'

'Marika Horvath.'

He stares at her. 'Horvath Marika?'

With growing excitement, she says, 'So you remember her?'

His eyes light up. 'All people knowing Horvath Marika. Special woman.'

Annika smiles at the compliment. She has seen the photograph, and knows how lovely her grandmother was in 1945.

'What do you remember about her?' she asks.

He rubs his stubbled chin, muttering to himself as he tries to recall details. After a long pause, he says, 'Very kind lady, she with children playing. Also, she vomiting.'

'So she was ill on the journey?'

'Other womans talking about her. Not good things.'

'Talking about her? Why? Do you know what they said?'

He pauses again. Then he says, 'Horvath Marika not Horvath Marika.'

Was he having trouble expressing his thoughts, or was he being enigmatic? 'I don't understand what you mean.'

'Before, not Horvath. Horvath name for train.'

She wonders if he has become confused and mixed her up with someone else. After all these years, it wouldn't be surprising, but she can't dismiss the disquieting impression that he sounds very sure of his facts. So why did the other women say nasty things about her? Was it because she was ill, or because she had changed her name?

'Are you saying that she changed her name for the train journey?'

His eyes are boring into her face as if he is weighing something up, struggling with something, and even though she is still convinced that he has confused her with someone else, his silence unsettles her. 'Do you know why she did that?'

Before replying, Shmuel exhales a thick column of dark smoke which makes her cough. 'Sorry, I not speaking English good,' he says,

She supposes that he is about to admit that he has made a mistake, but he says, 'Nagy Miklós change Horvath Marika name for train.'

She knows that people often falsified details on documents during the war. He must have had a reason for changing her grandmother's name, although she can't imagine what it could have been. It was intriguing to discover that the grandmother she has always known as Marika Horvath might once have had a different name.

Shmuel is still looking at her with a peculiar expression, and in between puffs of his noxious cigarette, he is saying something that doesn't make sense. Even when he repeats it, she still can't grasp what he means. Perhaps it's his accent, or his limited English. Then he says it again, very slowly and this time she gets it, and her heart is thumping so fast she feels it will jump out of her chest.

'On train, Horvath Marika. In Budapest, Weisz Ilonka.'

CHAPTER FORTY

Tel Aviv, 2005

Weisz Ilonka.

Ilonka.

Where has she heard that name before?

Two blocks from Shmuel's building, Annika leans against a wall whose crumbling plaster is covered by layers of torn posters and caricatures of politicians. A toothless man in a torn T-shirt is sitting on the pavement with a blank expression, a scrawled cardboard sign in front of him and a rib-skinny mongrel stretched out beside him. Sunk in his own world, he doesn't look up when she bends down, places a few shekels in his empty bowl, and pats the dog.

Suddenly she straightens up. Eitan Nagy! That's where she heard the name.

Ilonka. That's the name Miklós Nagy uttered just before he died, according to Eitan. He said that had upset his grandmother. Ilonka. An unusual name. But could there have been two Ilonkas?

She stands still, struggling to figure this out. Shmuel insisted that Marika Horvath had once been Ilonka Weisz. So it was probably another Marika Horvath. But what if it wasn't? She dismisses that thought. There was no reason to suspect that her grandmother had changed her name. Then who was Ilonka Weisz?

The surname is familiar and Annika knows she has come across it before. It wasn't Eitan, and it wasn't Dov either, so who said it? Her heart is racing now as she sifts hurriedly through a tangle of memories. She hasn't discussed the Nagy case with anyone else.

She walks on, aware that she has been muttering to herself, but in this neighbourhood that probably wasn't unusual. Somewhere among the millions of neurons whirring inside her brain is the synapse that contains the vital connection but it eludes her. Where did she hear that name?

If she didn't hear it, how else could she have come across it? Could she have read it somewhere? There was only one possibility. Her mind scrolls through the names of the witnesses who testified during the trial, the names that were mentioned in connection with Miklós Nagy.

Then she stops walking again. Gábor Weisz. Miklós Nagy's colleague, the one who was sent on the doomed mission to Istanbul. Now it comes back to her. Didn't he mention in his testimony that his wife was on the rescue train under a different name? That Miklós Nagy had obtained false papers for her? But Weisz probably wasn't an unusual surname, so that didn't prove anything.

Without making a conscious decision, she wheels around and retraces her steps. The beggar on the pavement glances up as she hurries past, and his dog wags its tail in joyful recognition, but this time she doesn't stop to pat it.

Shmuel raises his bushy eyebrows when he sees her on his doorstep again. 'You forget something?'

She shakes her head, panting, and he asks her to come inside. The radio is blaring but this time she hardly registers the noise, the smell of stale nicotine that emanates from the walls and the threadbare carpet, or the loud ticking of the clock on the mantelpiece. She gulps down a glass of water and tries to catch her breath as he switches off the radio.

'I had to come back to ask you about this Ilonka Weisz because I don't understand something you said, so I'm hoping you can remember a few more details.'

'Again with the remembering. I say you I not remembering much.'

'But you remembered that Marika Horvath was Ilonka Weisz, so perhaps you'll remember other things too.' She sits on the edge of the wooden chair. 'I'm sorry to bother you about this, but it's very important to me.'

'So what thing you want to know?'

'Tell me something about Ilonka Weisz. Anything.'

He scratches his bald head and runs his hand along the stubble on his jaw. She waits expectantly but from the way he is looking down and shaking his head from time to time without speaking, she begins to lose hope.

Then he looks up. 'Ilonka Weisz wife of Gábor Weisz.'

From the little that Annika knows about Marika's life, she recalls being told that Marika arrived in Australia with her baby girl, Annika's mother Eva — and she had always assumed that they had migrated from Hungary. She was told that Marika was widowed soon after her arrival in Sydney. Marika never spoke about her husband, and Annika had assumed that the grief of losing him so soon after arriving in a new country must have been traumatic. But she had never said anything about being married before that, and she had never mentioned Gábor Weisz.

Ever since Annika was old enough to eavesdrop on adult conversations, she has overheard her mother gossiping with her friends about other women, their heads close together as they whispered about scandals involving lovers, affairs, mistresses and divorces. From these conversations, Annika gathered that men and women were often unfaithful to their spouses, and that affairs were common occurrences, whereas divorces were something to be ashamed of, as if having a lover was exciting but divorcing a husband was a sign of failure. Knowing how carefully Marika had reinvented herself in Australia, Annika supposes that this first marriage was probably an inconvenient fact that cast a shadow over her otherwise perfectly reconstructed life.

Annika thinks back to the transcript, and recalls Gábor Weisz saying that while he was in Istanbul, his wife remained in Budapest as Eichmann's hostage. Like a detective piecing clues together, she figures that this adds up: as Gábor was in Istanbul at the time Miklós Nagy was organising the departure of his train, it was natural to include his friend's wife among the people he rescued. And that was probably why he changed her name, to prevent Eichmann from finding out that she'd escaped.

'Now I understand.' Annika smiles at Shmuel, pleased that she has been able to make sense of this puzzling information. 'She was on the train under a different name because she was married to Gábor Weisz.'

He is looking at her with that strange expression again. 'But you not understanding.'

She taps her foot on the floor, and tries to speak calmly. 'Then please explain what it is I don't understand.'

He looks up at the ceiling, scratches his head again, and looks at his hands.

'Ilonka Weisz wife of Gábor Weisz, but Miklós Nagy's woman.'

A speeding train has just crashed inside her head, leaving smashed carriages and twisted metal in its wake. Is he saying that Marika was Nagy's mistress? It's not possible, surely it can't be true. He must be mistaken. Or has she misunderstood?

A long silence stretches between them. Speaking very slowly, she says, 'Do you mean that this Ilonka Weisz and Miklós Nagy were having an affair?'

He nods.

'But how can you possibly know that?'

'Everybody in Budapest knowing,' he says. 'Weisz Ilonka and Nagy Miklós lovers.'

She stares at him, too shocked to collect her thoughts. The clock on the mantelpiece seems to be ticking inside her head like a time bomb about to explode. Just a moment ago, she thought she had made sense of Marika's marriage and her changed name, but now the world has turned upside down again, and nothing makes sense. It is impossible to entertain the idea that her controlled, restrained, elegant grandmother who had such uncompromising views on morality, had an affair with her husband's closest friend and colleague. Not discreet tête-à-têtes and secret rendezvous, but a flagrant affair apparently conducted in the bright light of public scrutiny while her husband was on a tragic mission in Istanbul.

This Marika is a complete stranger. Not the cool paragon of virtue on a marble pedestal she has always known, the woman whose high standards always made her feel inadequate, but a fallible and impulsive woman who risked her reputation and her honour to surrender to a love that was so all-consuming that nothing else mattered. Annika is horrified, but at the same time she is intrigued, almost envious, of the passion that must have fuelled this illicit love affair. How astonishing — and how incredible — to learn that Miklós Nagy must have been the love of her life. This Marika is more human. Less perfect. More like her, really. How ironic, and how typical, that she has had to travel to the other side of the world to discover her grandmother's secret life.

But there are still too many loose ends, and Annika has a nagging feeling that there are parts of this puzzle that don't fit into her neat solution. If they really did have this reckless love affair, why did they separate? How come Miklós migrated to Israel while Marika ended up in Australia, adamant that she never wanted to hear his name again?

'Did they part because she decided to stay with her husband?' she asks.

Shmuel shakes his head. 'Miklós Nagy married.'

'Married when? In Israel?'

'In Budapest. Before Germans occupating Hungary.'

So Marika not only betrayed her own husband, she had an affair with a married man.

Then she remembers Eitan saying that his grandmother never got over hearing Miklós utter Ilonka's name on his deathbed, although she never told anyone why this upset her so much. She supposes that Eitan's grandmother had found out about her husband's past love affair, and had kept silent about it to avoid humiliation. So did Miklós divorce the woman he had married in Budapest, and did he remarry in Israel?

But Shmuel is shaking his head again. 'Not second wife. Same wife,' he says in a tone that leaves no room for doubt.

Once again the picture she has constructed is out of focus, like a photograph hurriedly snapped by a shaking hand. As she struggles to comprehend this information, she comforts herself with the thought that she doesn't have to believe what he says, it could all be the result of conjecture, supposition and gossip, typical of the web of unsubstantiated rumours that people often weave around a famous person who can't refute them.

But she can't ignore the fact that Shmuel, who initially claimed to remember nothing, obviously knows a great deal about this affair, and in his awkward way he has been trying to be diplomatic.

She recalls the rancour with which Marika reacted to the mention of Miklós Nagy sixty years later, and once again the picture blurs. What became of their passion that flouted all the rules? There's a question she needs to ask, but it takes her a few minutes to articulate it.

'It doesn't make sense to me that as soon as she had escaped from Hungary, and they could finally be together, they went their separate ways and settled on different continents. Do you know why they parted?'

Now it's his turn to remain silent, and she waits, aware that the clock on the mantelpiece is ticking more insistently than ever. From the way he avoids her eyes, she suspects he knows the answer. She takes deep breaths to slow the beating of her heart.

'In camp, Weisz Ilonka vomiting.'

'You said that before. So she was ill. That's not surprising given the conditions in the camp. But that doesn't explain why they separated.'

'Other womans saying baby coming.'

Annika tries to control her impatience. 'What baby?'

Shmuel is looking at her meaningfully as he pats his stomach.

'Are you saying she was pregnant, that she was expecting a baby?'

'Yes, baby.'

Now she knows he's just repeating rumours. Marika only had one child and that was her mother Eva. Either way, being pregnant was no reason to break up and run away to a country on the other end of the earth where she didn't know anyone.

He was obviously repeating malicious gossip that must have circulated around the camp, where boredom and close proximity would probably have provided a fertile ground for rumours.

'That doesn't make sense,' she says. 'Why would they have parted if she was pregnant?'

He ignores her comment. 'Nagy Miklós's wife, she also,' and he pats his stomach again. 'Two womans, two babies, one man.'

Once again, her carefully constructed scenario collapses. She is riding a rollercoaster that's out of control. If Miklós Nagy was in love with Ilonka, how come his wife was also pregnant?

'What happened to his wife?'

He looks puzzled. 'Nothing happening. She having baby, and she having husband also.'

Annika swallows. 'And Marika. What happened to her?'

This time he looks straight into her eyes. 'Train arriving in Switzerland. Nagy Miklós to station coming. He kissing wife. This I see. Madame Marika, she sees also. She saying something to Nagy, and she walking away. I not see her again, never.'

'Do you have any idea what she said?'

Shmuel spreads his hands. 'I not hearing, but she looking angry and he looking sad.'

*

That night Annika can't sleep. Shmuel's words keep running through her head like a continuous newsreel she can't switch off. She would like to believe that this is just a fantastic story created by rumour, malice and exaggeration, but she knows she is merely trying to avoid confronting the truth.

As she goes over the facts yet again, it reminds her of her attempts to solve maths equations at high school, where she was given all the necessary information but the correct solution always eluded her.

She is about to drop off to sleep when she sits bolt upright, her heart hammering in her ears. Before her is the scene at the railway station in Switzerland. She can see her grandmother climbing down from the train, looking eagerly for Miklós Nagy. She can feel Marika's excitement throbbing in her veins. Now she catches sight of him, and hurries towards him. She can't wait to tell him the news. But suddenly she sees something that makes her freeze. He is embracing his wife, who is obviously pregnant. She strides towards him and, with the implacable fury of a woman betrayed, spits out that she never wants to see him again as long as she lives.

Annika sinks back onto the bed, convinced of the truth of her vision. A feeling of sadness wraps itself around her. It feels as if she has lived through this herself. She can almost feel it in her bones. She feels it in her heart. And she is certain that Miklós Nagy never knew that Ilonka was pregnant. Perhaps after all, love wasn't enough.

Annika makes a rapid calculation. She doesn't know the exact date when her grandmother arrived in Sydney but she thinks it was some time in 1946 when her mother Eva was about a year old. Marika had told Eva that her father was a Hungarian called Sándor Horvath who had died when she was a baby. Annika knows now that there was no Sándor Horvath.

It's about three o'clock in the morning when Annika makes the connection that has been circling over her all day like a bird of prey, its flapping wings swooping ever closer until at last they brush her face and can no longer be ignored.

It catapults her out of bed and makes her pace up and down the hotel room, talking to herself, feverishly checking and rechecking dates to make sure she hasn't made a mistake. She can't keep still, and if she doesn't tell someone, her head will split open.

There's only one person she can call at this time of night who will forgive the intrusion and share her excitement at her revelation. Only one person she wants to confide in.

'Dov?' Her voice is trembling. 'Dov, there's something I have to tell you. I know it's the middle of the night, but can I come over?'

On the way to his apartment in a taxi, her brain is throbbing and every red light makes her groan. He is already standing downstairs waiting for her, and as soon as the taxi pulls up she rushes out, and falls into his arms. He holds her close, caressing her, and doesn't ask any questions. That's the moment, she later realises, that she felt the joy of being understood and accepted, and knew he was the man with whom she would always feel that unconditional love, and that she would never let him go.

He puts his arms around her, and she leans against him and feels his warmth as he leads her inside and waits for her to speak.

'It's so incredible, I can't believe it. You won't believe it either, you'll think I'm crazy, or that I've made this up. This is the most amazing thing that has ever happened to me. I had to come and tell you.'

He is still holding her, gently stroking her hair, waiting for her to explain.

She pulls away, takes a very deep breath, and with an unsteady voice, she says, 'It sounds so bizarre, I don't even know how to say it. Miklós Nagy was my grandfather.'

CHAPTER FORTY-ONE

Tel Aviv, 2005

The day she has dreaded has now arrived, and Dov is driving her to the airport, one hand on the wheel, the other clasping hers. Annika squeezes his hand and tries not to think of the moment when they will have to say goodbye.

He gives her a sidelong glance. 'Are you sure you're not going to stop over in Budapest to see that guy?'

He's jealous, and she likes that. 'Maybe I will,' she teases.

He leans towards her and presses a kiss on her cheek.

'That's like the chaste kiss you gave me the day you dropped me back at the hotel after we'd been to Jerusalem, remember?'

'After you went inside, I sat outside the hotel for half an hour, fighting with myself. I wanted to go after you, to kiss you the way I wanted to, and tell you how I felt, but I didn't want to scare you off.'

They look at each other and laugh, the knowing laugh of lovers who have just shared a night so tender and intimate that every cell in her body is still tingling at the memory. She marvels how naturally it happened that one minute she was in his arms, blurting out her improbable news, and the next she was in his bedroom, and they were making love. She can still hear his voice thick with desire, murmuring, 'After we met in Ari's café that day, I couldn't stop thinking about you. You were such a fascinating mixture of confusion, vulnerability and determination. I felt like putting my arms around you to make you feel safe.'

She can't resist teasing him. 'So why didn't you?'

'Because I knew it was hopeless. You were a tourist from the other side of the world. We were probably never going to see each other again.'

'You kept your feelings well hidden,' she said with a hint of reproach. 'I had no idea you felt that way right from the start.'

He held her against him and looked searchingly into her eyes. 'What about you? When did you feel that we might have a future together?'

'When you played that Leonard Cohen CD.'

Although she was teasing him, there was some truth in what she said. She started to explain why their connection with her favourite songwriter meant so much to her, but before she had a chance to say it, he was pressing those sensual lips against hers, exploring her mouth, whispering that he loved and wanted her, and gently undressing her. By then she felt no need to explain anything.

After making love, they talked until morning about their lives, their regrets, and their dreams, the things they had done that they were proud of, and the ones they felt guilty about, revealing themselves without embarrassment or inhibition. It seemed to Annika that they were looking into each other's souls. For the first time in her life, she knew that she had been truly seen and understood. This wasn't just sex, it was the connection she had always dreamed about but didn't believe she'd ever find, the ache for the other half that had always been missing, the soul mate she had always longed for, the loving partner who accepted her as she was without trying to change her, who cared as much about her pleasure as about his own.

'Do you realise,' she murmured, 'everything in our lives, every single thing, had to happen exactly the way it did so we could be together now?'

His eyes glistened, and he held her closer.

He pulls up outside the airport and they turn towards each other. Even if she could find the words, there is too much to say and too little time to say it. But she looks at him, and knows that after last night, there is no need to say anything. She has seen her future and it's flooded with light.

They step out of the car and he folds his arms around her. She looks up and sees that behind his glasses, his sea-green eyes are brighter than usual. He is holding her so tightly that she can hardly tell where she ends and he begins.

'I can't bear the thought of losing you now that we've found each other,' he says in a hoarse voice. 'I'll come to Sydney to meet your folks, but I'll wait for you to let me know that you still want me to come, in case you change your mind.'

She blinks a few times and strokes his hair. She knows that home is not a place, it's the person you love, that this is what she has been longing for all her life. This has been a gradual awakening that feels solid, deep and secure, and despite the distance and the difficulties ahead, she will try and make it work. Then she thinks about her grandmother and Miklós Nagy, and a thought chills her. What if love really wasn't enough?

Her voice is husky, and she has to clear her throat several times before speaking. 'I won't change my mind. I can't wait for my mother and grandmother to meet you. Then I'll come back to Tel Aviv so we can be together. And when I'm back, whether you like it or not, I'm going to join Peace Now.' She had never imagined that making a commitment could be so easy.

In reply he cradles her face in his hands and kisses her lips softly, tenderly, and then more passionately, and they cling together. With tears in her eyes, she pulls away, picks up her suitcase and walks into the airport building. Although she doesn't trust herself to look back, she knows that he is still there, watching her, as she knows he will always watch her, with love and solicitude.

CHAPTER FORTY-TWO

2005

As she boards the plane, Annika is in a daze, reliving her night with Dov, thinking about the life ahead of them, but unafraid of the challenges ahead. Love was worth fighting for. Her thoughts turn to Miklós Nagy and her grandmother, and to the secret that Marika has concealed all her life. Had she really stumbled on this revelation by chance? Was her obsession to uncover the truth about a total stranger whose only link with her was her grandmother's inexplicable reaction more than a journalist's curiosity to pursue a mysterious story? Is it possible that, in some hidden corner of her psyche, she has sensed all along that this was not just an intellectual quest, but a search for a personal connection that her unconscious mind had somehow divined?

It seemed as though everything had conspired to lead her to the unlikely door of the ex-prisoner who held the key to a mystery she didn't even know she needed to unravel. She recalls that it was Dov whose perceptive mind had intimated this the day they met in Jaffa. She had dismissed his idea then, but now she marvels at his insight. So soon after they met, he was already so attuned to her that he had intuited the meaning behind her search. Her love for him courses so strongly in her veins that she wonders if that radiance is visible to those around her.

It seems a lifetime since she arrived in Israel, and yet it also seems as if it was only yesterday, and she still can't believe what has happened in those few weeks. Her thoughts turn to Eitan, and the way fate had thrown him in her path. Before leaving the hotel she called him to explain why his grandfather had died with Ilonka's name on his lips, but she only told him part of the story. The part about the love affair. She couldn't bring herself to expose the secret shame that her grandmother had guarded all her life, even though it would have meant revealing that she and Eitan were cousins. One day, when she was back in Tel Aviv, she would tell him everything face to face.

She can't wait to see Cassie's face when she tells her that she has finally made a commitment and has decided to move in with Dov. She can almost hear her friend saying in her deadpan voice, 'And your perfect guy lives in Israel? That'd be right.'

This time she changes planes in Budapest without stopping over. She thinks about Jancsi with affection and gratitude. He made her feel desirable again, rekindled her capacity to love. Love was a leap into the unknown, a risk she had always avoided, but thanks to Jancsi she now had enough faith in herself to make a commitment to a man who lived on the other side of the world.

Now, on the flight home, window blinds are pulled down and passengers settle down for the night with eyeshades and blankets, but her tumultuous thoughts make sleep impossible. She thinks about Miklós Nagy, the man who was so unjustly maligned. It is still hard to think of him as her grandmother's lover, or as her grandfather. Not only had he never received the acclaim he deserved, but what was even more cruel, he had died never knowing that he'd been exonerated. Now she understands the cryptic comment of the guide at the Sydney Jewish Museum: *no good deed goes unpunished.*

The injustice of Miklós's fate, and her determination to do something to restore his reputation and his memory, makes her so restless that she tosses and turns in her seat, unable to find a comfortable spot.

In a somnolent zone between wakefulness and sleep, she sees herself back in Israel, no longer powerless, but full of energy and hope. She is arguing with the director of the museum in Tel Aviv that he should create a space for Miklós Nagy among the section devoted to the rescuers, and she succeeds in convincing him. Next, she contacts the survivors and their descendants and persuades them to contribute to a memorial to the man who saved them. She envisages thousands of them arriving from all over the world to honour him, the remaining survivors from the rescue train, and their children, grandchildren and even great-grandchildren. At the unveiling of the memorial, which consists of a marble obelisk with his name and a simple inscription on one side, and the names of those he rescued on the other, she can hear herself making an impassioned speech, a fitting tribute to her heroic grandfather. She looks around at the gathering, and there's her grandmother sitting in the front row...

Then she stops fantasising. There was no way her grandmother would ever honour the man who, in her eyes, had deceived and betrayed her. No way that she would ever forgive him, even after sixty years. Sixty years. Marika had disappeared from his life without another word, and wrapped herself in a lifelong cocoon of resentment and hurt pride that had fed on itself and become a second skin. She had succeeded in guarding her secret, but had lost herself in the process.

Marika had become a phantom in her own life, picking her way through it in her fine Italian leather shoes, her chic French suits, advising her clients in her silken way how to enhance their good features and make the most of their appearance. Because that was all her life was — appearances, images, and mirrors smudged with smoke.

Annika is suddenly overwhelmed by a wave of anger. She too had been compelled to live in the shadow of that deceit which precluded intimacy and honesty. Her grandmother was entitled to keep a secret if it affected only her and no-one else, but this one affected the whole family. She and her mother were entitled to know who their father and grandfather was. Her mother had accepted what she was told, but deep in her soul, Annika knew that she herself never had, and she wonders whether her lifelong resentment and rebellion is the result of sensing that her grandmother was hiding something, that what she was presenting to the world was a brightly fashioned mask concealing a darker reality.

What a heavy burden the fear of exposure must be. Unable to face the shame, Marika had created a new persona, and foregone the freedom of being herself and the relief of being truly known, even by her closest friends. But how close could those friendships be, when she had deleted her past, concealed her true self, and presented only an invention? Don't we all long to be accepted and loved for who we really are, regardless of our mistakes? Surely what we yearn for is the warmth and comfort of connectedness. What Annika has always perceived as Marika's strength and fortitude is merely pride fuelled by anger, revenge, and frozen disappointment.

Most of the other passengers are sleeping, but she sits up, wide awake, immersed in her thoughts. For the first time in her life, she understands her grandmother. She feels empathy for Marika, and no longer judges her. So what should she tell her? Should she presume to tell her anything at all? Did she have the right to strip away the image so carefully cultivated over a lifetime and reveal that she knew the truth?

Marika was in her eighties. How would she cope with the fact that her granddaughter knew her secret? Knew that she had lied to her own daughter about who her father really was? Perhaps she had wanted to shield Eva from discovering that she had had an affair, and to shield herself from gossip that she wasn't the paragon of virtue she set herself up to be. Perhaps she was desperate to keep Eva from discovering that she was illegitimate, and that her father was a man Marika hated, a man she had tried to erase from her memory and her life. But, as Annika now realises, her effort to erase him had only made the memories fester. She had probably wanted to protect herself from having to admit the most painful fact of all, that the man for whom she had given up everything had betrayed her love.

Annika's thoughts turn to her mother. She wonders how Eva will cope with the news that all her life Marika had lied to her, not only about her own life, but about the identity of her father. How painful would it be for her to discover that she has been deprived of knowing anything about the man she never had the chance to meet, a hero who had been vilified, crucified and vindicated, and was still a controversial figure after fifty years.

How would Eva feel knowing that she was illegitimate, and that Marika regarded her birth as a source of such shame that she had concealed the truth all her life? Would she ever forgive her mother for withholding that knowledge and cheating her of her true identity? And would Marika forgive her for divulging it?

Annika has always felt powerless in her grandmother's presence. Now that she knows the truth, she is the one with power, but the knowledge doesn't bring a sense of triumph.

What she feels is a heavy sense of responsibility to use this power carefully, compassionately, and with love. Her training as a reporter emphasised the importance of digging relentlessly for the truth and then revealing it, irrespective of its effect on anyone, especially those who most wished to conceal it, but now she wonders whether this is one story that should be suppressed.

Before deciding whether she would reveal all or any of it, she has to be sure that whatever she does is for her grandmother's benefit, not for the gratification of her own ego. Once the story was revealed, it could never be redacted, rescinded or deleted. It could bring destruction in its wake, to her grandmother's peace of mind, to her mother, and to their relationship.

Annika must have finally fallen asleep because she wakes with a start in the darkened cabin. And in that moment she knows exactly what she is going to say.

SYDNEY

CHAPTER FORTY-THREE

2005

When Annika steps into the crowded arrival hall of Sydney's Kingsford Smith Airport, she is astonished to see her mother waiting for her. She's even more surprised when Eva throws her arms around her and says, 'I've missed you, Annika. You were away for such a long time. I'm glad you're home at last.'

She picks up Annika's suitcase and as she rolls it towards the car park, she pats her daughter's arm and says, 'You must be tired after such a long flight.' And she repeats, 'It's good to have you back.'

Annika glances at her mother. Eva is not usually so demonstrative, and she decides this is a good omen. She can't wait to tell her about Dov, or to reveal that she has found out the secret that Marika has guarded all her life, but at the same time she feels nervous at the prospect of revealing both these things — particularly the latter. It is such explosive, potentially destructive information. What if she says too much, shakes her mother's confidence about her own identity, and destroys her relationship with Marika?

'Your hands are shaking, you look as pale as a ghost,' Eva says. 'I hope you didn't pick something up on your travels. You have to be so careful on flights these days.'

'I'm fine, don't fuss.'

'I can't wait to hear all about your trip,' Eva says as she hauls Annika's suitcase into the boot of her green Toyota. 'You didn't say much on the phone, I was worried about you. So tell me, what was Budapest like?'

'Let's wait till we get home. I'm tired, I couldn't sleep on the plane, and I'm dying for a cup of tea,' Annika mumbles, and closes her eyes while Eva drives.

From time to time she opens her eyes. Although it's early June, the weather is mild with the bright freshness of early winter. The bright blue bays of Sydney Harbour are dotted with white yachts, their spinnakers swelling in the nor'easter. In parks beside the road, Moreton Bay figs cast wide circles of shade on emerald lawns. Annika takes a deep breath. It was good to be back.

Inside her apartment, Eva bustles around the kitchen, taking out mugs and filling the kettle. Annika glances out of the window, and sees a flash of olive and scarlet, and hears the metallic twittering of lorikeets flying towards the umbrella tree. The bright red berries of the cotoneaster make a mess on the paving of the courtyard, and the narrow leaves of the stringybarks shiver in the breeze. The brightness of the light pouring from the sky makes her heart skip. She feels her resolve wavering. How can she leave this behind and move to Tel Aviv?

As they sit in the kitchen waiting for the tea to cool, Annika watches her mother unwrapping a packet of biscuits she has brought. In the shape of Eva's oval face she detects a resemblance to Eitan. The tragedy of Marika's secret strikes her with new force: her mother knows nothing about her real family.

Eva turns her searching gaze on her daughter. 'Come on, own up, you must have met someone over there, or you wouldn't have stayed away so long. Something about you is different. You don't look as uptight as usual, so there must have been a holiday romance.'

Annika had intended to wait a few days before telling her mother about Dov and her decision to move to Israel, but suddenly she can't hold back any longer, and in her excitement it all tumbles out.

Eva puts down her mug and stares at her in dismay. 'I can't believe what you're saying. I thought you were too smart to let a holiday romance turn your life upside down. You've done some crazy things in your life but this takes the cake. Tell me I've got it wrong — you can't possibly mean you're thinking of going to live in Israel.'

Annika represses the urge to retort that as usual her mother doesn't trust her judgement.

'I know this comes as a shock, and I understand how you feel,' she says carefully, 'but for the first time in my life I've met a man who is right for me. You said I looked different, and that's because I'm happy. For once I know I've made the right decision. I'm not going to let distance ruin my chance of happiness.'

'Distance? This isn't just a matter of kilometres. You're talking about living in a country on the other side of the world. And not just any country. You've never led a normal life or had normal relationships. Trust you to choose a man you've just met, and a country that's so dangerous.'

Determined to ignore the criticism, and avoid an argument that would only create rancour and solve nothing, Annika swallows an angry retort.

'Look, I know how crazy this sounds, sometimes I can't believe it myself, but when you meet Dov you'll understand. He's coming here next month because he wants you to meet him, and then you'll see for yourself what a wonderful man he is.'

Eva shakes her head. 'I was so glad you were back, and you're already talking about leaving. I don't know why you're rushing into this. It makes no sense to me. I just hope you know what you're doing. Your grandmother will be devastated.'

At the mention of Marika, Annika tightens her grip on the mug. She has to tread warily so as not to reveal too much. 'Mum, there's something else I have to tell you.'

Eva frowns as Annika begins to talk, and looks increasingly stunned as she continues talking. She tells her Marika's real name, her passionate affair with Miklós Nagy, the drama of the rescue train, and the tragedy of his death, but she doesn't mention that Marika was pregnant on the train. Perhaps she would tell her after some time had elapsed, but hopefully one day Marika herself would tell her daughter who her father really was.

Eva looks dazed, clearly struggling to comprehend what she has heard. Then she shakes her head. 'I can't believe the things you've just told me about my mother having a different name, and keeping it secret all her life. And the story about an affair with that fellow. It's like something you read in a novel. How do you know any of it is true?'

'I know it is,' Annika says, and tells her what she heard from Shmuel. 'Remember me telling you before I left that I saw her in the photo that was taken of the passengers who were rescued on that train? Well, Shmuel was on the train, and he remembered her. He told me the whole story. I heard it from Miklós Nagy's grandson as well. It's such a tragic story. He must have loved her all his life, because the last word he uttered on his deathbed was her name.'

'Marika?'

'Ilonka. That's her real name.'

Eva clutches her head as if to make sure it stays attached to her body. 'I can't make any sense of all this. It's too much to take in. I just don't understand. Why did Mother never mention any of this? And if they loved each other so much, why did they marry other people?' She pauses. 'I've just remembered something you told me — you said that when you mentioned that man — Miklós, was it? — she told you she never wanted to hear his name again. Do you know why she was so angry after all this time?'

Annika opens her mouth to reply, but thinks better of it. She doesn't want to risk an explanation that might reveal that Marika had been pregnant on the train. Instead, she says, 'You didn't want to upset her by raising the subject at the time, but maybe now you can ask her yourself. But tell me something. Did you ever suspect that Grandmamma lied about her past?'

Eva puts down her biscuit and pushes her mug away. She gazes out of the window at two Indian mynas pecking at grass seeds on the lawn next door for a few minutes before replying. 'Your grandmother was always secretive. When I was growing up, whenever I asked about my father, she was always curt and evasive, and I wasn't strong enough to push her. I assumed she was too upset to talk about him, and I stopped asking. These days people search documents and archives, and send DNA to a genetic laboratory, but it never occurred to me to do any of that back then, especially as any mention of my father upset her so much. Whenever I read anything about the Holocaust, I used to wonder what happened to her in Budapest, and how she managed to survive, but she always clammed up. She said it was too traumatic and she wanted to forget all about it. You know how forbidding she can be. She never even told me that this Miklós guy saved her life!'

Eva speaks in an unusually bitter tone, and Annika moves closer to her mother and strokes her shoulder. This is the first time the mask of filial loyalty has slipped and her mother has spoken openly of her resentment at her powerlessness in her relationship with Marika. Annika had always been contemptuous of her mother for living in Marika's shadow, but now she senses her pain at being excluded from major events in her mother's life, even the ones that affected her. She quails at the thought of what it will do to her mother, if she ever found out who her father really was.

'You were always so devoted to her, I was jealous,' Annika muses. 'All my life I felt I was on the outside. I never realised how hard it must have been for you.'

Eva swallows and looks gratefully at her daughter. They sit in silence, aware that sharing the story about Marika's secret past has created a new bond between them.

'I'll go and see Grandmamma in a day or so,' Annika says, and adds, 'Will you come with me?'

*

Annika's hand trembles and she has butterflies in her stomach as she stands outside her grandmother's apartment in Bellevue Hill, her finger poised to press the buzzer. In the days since she returned to Sydney, she has been gathering the courage to visit Marika, going over and over in her mind what she will say.

As Marika opens the door, Annika feels an unexpected rush of warmth. For the past few weeks, her grandmother has been a conflicting but abstract presence inside her mind, but now, face to face with her, she feels a surge of affection. The resentment and anger momentarily dissipate.

With a cry of delight, Marika embraces her. 'You have been away so long, Annika *édesem*, it's wonderful to see you again. Let me look at you.'

She looks at her grandmother, and for the first time she sees the sad depths of Marika's dark eyes. As they enter the lounge room, she becomes aware of the melancholy atmosphere that hangs over the apartment, the heaviness of secrets and suppressed feelings.

'You look good, I think you've lost weight,' Marika says approvingly.

Her grandmother's obsession with her weight has always been an irritant, but this time Annika smiles indulgently. 'Do you think so?'

'So come and tell me all about your trip,' Marika says as she places her culinary masterpiece on the walnut table in front of them. 'I've made your favourite, *dobos* torte.' She sits beside Annika on the brocade-covered sofa, and pats her hand.

'Budapest is a beautiful city.' As Annika says this, she and her mother exchange glances, and they both watch Marika for her reaction. Annika wonders if her grandmother will ask about the city where she was born and where she had the affair that has had such a catastrophic impact on her life, the city she last saw in 1944 and tried to block from her mind ever since. But Marika remains impassive, and waits for Annika to continue.

'You were born there, weren't you?'

Marika shrugs. 'Ancient history. Where did you go after that?'

But Annika refuses to change the subject. 'I went to that marvellous old synagogue on Dohány Street. It's such an unusual building with a rose window and an organ. Outside there's a touching Holocaust memorial in the shape of a tree with silver leaves. Survivors and their relatives have engraved the names of Holocaust victims on each leaf. Did you ever go there?'

Marika shifts in her seat. 'I never went to that synagogue.'

'Where did you live? I wish I'd asked you before I left, so I could have gone to see your street.'

'There's nothing to see there. It would have been a waste of time.' Marika's voice is crisp. It's a tone Annika knows well, a warning not to pursue this topic. But she presses on, describing the Danube, the Fishermen's Bastion, Hero Square, and the magical nightly illuminations on Chain Bridge, Parliament House and the Castle on Swabian Hill, hoping to evoke some pleasant memory.

'I never knew that Budapest was such a beautiful city,' Eva remarks to break the silence, but apart from an occasional nod that owes more to politeness than interest, Marika doesn't engage with Annika's enthusiastic description.

Annika perseveres with an account of the *dobos* torte at the Europa Café. 'The café was gorgeous, like something from the set of a Viennese operetta, but their *dobos* wasn't nearly as good as yours, Grandmamma,' she says, scraping up the last smidgin of chocolate and toffee from her plate. Encouraged by Marika's appreciative smile, she goes on to tell her about the chamber-music concert at Rákoczy Castle, and the elegance of the aristocratic owner.

'Budapest must have changed so much since you were there, Mama, you probably wouldn't recognise it today,' Eva says.

Marika remains impassive. 'Probably not.'

So Annika gives up and talks about her stay in Israel, another country Marika has no wish to visit. She describes the spiritual atmosphere at the Western Wall on Shabbat, the mesmerising view from the Mount of Olives and the cemetery where Russian oligarchs have bought plots in the hope of being the first to be resurrected. She talks about the exotic mix of people in Jerusalem's souk, the jewellery boutiques and lively markets of Jaffa, and the quirky galleries of Neve Tzedek where she bought each of them a silver bracelet.

This time she evokes a response, but it's not the one she had hoped for.

'First you didn't intend to go to Israel, and then you stayed longer than you told your mother you were going to. Israel is a very dangerous country with that Intifada going on and rockets exploding all over the place.' She turns to Eva. 'We were worried about her, weren't we?' Turning back to Annika, she adds, 'What on earth made you stay so long?'

'It didn't feel dangerous at all. I loved it. It's frenetic and fascinating. There's no other place like it, so full of life, with so much history. You can actually stand on the spot where David stood three thousand years ago, and where Christ was buried. Thousands of people still pray at the wall of the temple that Solomon built.'

Marika eyes her shrewdly. 'But that's not why you stayed.'

'Well, I met someone special. An Israeli journalist,' Annika says, exchanging a quick glance with her mother.

'A journalist?' Marika pulls a face. She studies her granddaughter with her penetrating gaze. 'So I suppose he's the reason you stayed on?'

In the past, Annika would have interpreted that as a criticism of her flighty nature and her lack of discrimination where men were concerned, but this time she takes the comment at face value. She knows she has to tread lightly. She doesn't want to antagonise her grandmother at this stage of the visit.

'You know how you've never approved of the men I've been involved with? You've always said you couldn't understand why I chose such unstable, unsuitable guys. You used to say you wished I'd find someone intelligent and reliable that I could settle down with. Well, that's exactly what Dov is like.'

This time it takes Marika a little longer for the significance of her words to sink in, and when it does, her eyes flash with anger. 'Settle down with? I hope you're not telling me that you're thinking of settling down with this journalist?'

Before Annika can reply, she continues, 'You've never had a good word to say about male journalists. You always said they were unreliable and drank too much.' She looks at Eva for support but Eva is studying her hands and doesn't meet her mother's glance.

'Dov is nothing like that.'

Marika stares at Eva. 'Did you know about this?'

Eva nods but doesn't comment. She steals a glance at Annika who feels encouraged by their unspoken complicity.

Marika's tone and her comments transport her back to the contentious past. She is a teenager again, her opinions trivialised and her feelings dismissed, being rebuked for her thoughtless behaviour. The most desperate battles are the ones fought with those you love, and the last thing she wants now is a fight with her grandmother, although her resentment is rising to dangerous levels.

Determined not to lose her cool, she speaks as calmly and patiently as she can, listing Dov's professional achievements and personal qualities as if she were applying for a job on his behalf.

'Anyway,' she concludes defiantly, 'all that matters is that I'm in love with him and he loves and understands me. We're going to live together in Tel Aviv. I've never been so sure of anything in my whole life. He's coming to Sydney to meet you next month so you'll be able to judge for yourself.'

Marika shakes her head. 'Don't you realise how ridiculous you sound? None of this makes any sense.' Once again she looks over at her daughter for support.

'It makes sense to Annika,' Eva points out.

'You hardly know him,' Marika continues. 'You can't just move to a different country because you've met a man you think you're in love with. Have you thought of all the problems involved in moving to a different country where the language is different? How good is your Hebrew?'

Annika is tempted to remind her that she did exactly the same, without the support of a man who loved her, but she bites her tongue in time. In the meantime, Marika is saying, 'And how will you earn your living?'

'I don't *think* I'm in love with him. I know I am. He's the man for me. Grandmamma, you make me sound like a thoughtless child, but I'm forty years old, and I know what I need. As for work, he told me I can get a job on his newspaper. They publish in English. I can't wait to work on a real newspaper again. And when his daughter finishes school and her army service, they might migrate here.'

Marika is obviously frustrated and puzzled by Eva's attitude which demonstrates an unusual absence of support. 'You're not saying much about your daughter's extraordinary plan. What do you think about this hare-brained idea?'

Eva looks at her daughter. 'Annika isn't a child. If she thinks that this will make her happy, she should do it, even if we don't like it. She hasn't been happy so far, so it's worth a try. After all, we want her to be happy, don't we?'

Annika regards her mother appreciatively. It's the first time she can remember that Eva has defied Marika and stood up for her.

Marika tightens her lips. 'You say you can't live without him, but how do you know you can live with him?' she asks.

It's the first comment that Marika has made that hasn't been critical, and Annika moves closer to her on the settee. Mollified by her grandmother's concerned tone, she looks into her face. 'I know Israel is far away, and you'll miss me, and I'll miss you too. Of course you're right, it is a risk and it mightn't work, but I know I have to give it a try. You've often said that I've never had a stable relationship because the guys were never right for me, or because I was afraid of compromise and commitment, but this time I know it's different. If I walk away from this, I'll regret it all my life.'

She notices a faint flicker in Marika's eyes and wonders if her words have finally struck a chord. 'You'll like Dov, I know you will. He's smart and caring, he's what you call a real *mensch*. He has a lovely daughter...'

'A daughter! So he's married?'

'He's widowed.' She is on the point of telling her grandmother how Nurit died, but decides against it. She doesn't want to remind her of the perils of life in Israel. 'I'll come back to see you as often as I can. And you never know, you might even come and visit me.'

Then she looks straight into Marika's eyes and says, 'I think when we come to the end of our life, we regret the things we failed to do even more than the things we did, and I don't want to live with regrets. That would be a very sad way to live, don't you think?'

Marika looks down at her hands and twists her filigree Florentine ring around her finger. When she raises her head, Annika is still looking at her.

Now that the argument is over and the tension has dissipated, Annika takes her grandmother's hand and takes a deep breath.

'Grandmamma, there's something I have to tell you. While I was in Israel I found out a lot about Miklós Nagy.'

Marika stiffens and pulls her hand away. 'Why are you telling me this? It's of no interest to me.'

Annika hadn't intended to start this conversation so soon or so bluntly. She had decided to broach it much later, and in a more subtle way, but she has crossed the forbidden Rubicon, and there's no going back. The question is how much she should divulge.

'I thought you might want to know what happened to the man who saved your life.' Now that the words are out, they sound sharper than she had intended.

She hears Eva clearing her throat and sees her tearing at her thumbnail, and knows that she is apprehensive about her mother's reaction.

Marika leans forward, and her eyes narrow with anger. 'Well, you were wrong. You shouldn't talk about things you don't know anything about. Especially when I've already told you I don't ever want to hear about that man.'

Annika's heart is pounding. It's hard to overcome the decades-long nervousness she feels at confronting her grandmother, especially about such a personal issue, but no matter what happens, she knows she has to forge ahead.

'I know this is painful for you, and you don't want me to talk about it, but there's something you have to know.'

Out of the corner of her eye, she sees Eva running her tongue along her lips to moisten them. Marika's face is averted. She looks as if she longs to run from this room and from Annika's persistent voice which threatens to tell her something she doesn't want to hear.

'Annika, don't meddle in things that don't concern you.'

'Grandmamma, this does concern me. Please listen.' Annika takes Marika's hand between her own hands, and looks into her eyes. 'The last thing Miklós Nagy said on his deathbed was your name.'

Marika stares at her. 'What's this nonsense you're telling me?'

'It isn't nonsense. Please listen to me.' She is gripping her grandmother's hand. 'You have to know this. When Miklós Nagy lay dying, his last words were *I'm sorry, Ilonka.*'

In a strangled voice, Marika whispers, 'It isn't possible. I don't believe you. Why are you telling me this?'

'Because it's true, Grandmamma. That's what he said in the hospital just before he died.'

Marika repeats Annika's words in a voice that's almost inaudible, as if she is talking to herself. *Sorry Ilonka. When he lay dying. In the hospital.* Then she turns to Annika and in an accusing voice, she says, 'You're making this up. How can you possibly know that?'

Not taking her eyes from her grandmother, and speaking as gently as she can, Annika tells her how she came to meet Miklós's grandson Eitan Nagy, who told her about Miklós's last words. Then she tells her about her conversation with Shmuel, who cleared up the mystery by telling her who Ilonka really was.

Marika's face is white. She grips the arms of the sofa. 'Miklós dead? He can't be. When? Was he ill? What happened?'

Annika tells her about the assassin who shot Miklós because he believed he was a collaborator.

Marika's hands fly to her mouth and her eyes widen in horror. 'Miklós a collaborator! After everything he did! He was a hero! That man must have been insane!'

Without going into the details of the trial, Annika sums up the accusations that were made against Miklós, and the verdict of the District Court judge.

Marika sits motionless as she hears the story unfold. She looks dazed, shakes her head in disbelief, and can't stop trembling. Her voice rises with indignation. 'How could the judge say such a terrible thing about the man who confronted Eichmann and risked his life to rescue all those people?' Then she whispers, 'After all we did, after all the risks we took!'

'We?' Annika asks, wondering if she heard correctly.

'We,' Marika repeats, and there's pride in her voice. 'That's something you should know. He and I planned the rescue together.'

Annika is stunned. Her grandmother's collaboration in the rescue wasn't mentioned at the trial, or recorded in the transcript. Marika is rocking backwards and forwards on the couch, arms folded tightly as if she is trying to hold her body together as she repeats, 'If I could have been there, I could have told them. If only I had been there…'

'That terrible verdict was later overturned by the Supreme Court,' Annika says, 'but unfortunately Miklós died before they announced their decision, so he never knew that he'd been exonerated.'

Annika scans her grandmother's face anxiously. There's no sound in the room, and she can hardly bear the suspense. Then she hears a sound she has never heard before, a frightening, visceral sound that seems wrenched from the depths of her grandmother's being. Marika is sobbing. The granite facade has crumbled, and a lifetime of sorrow and regret is pouring through the cracks.

Eva moves to the sofa, and puts her arms around her mother's shoulders.

'Oh Miklós,' Marika sobs. 'Dearest Miklós, my dearest Miklós. How could they do this to you? There was never anyone else but you. Only you.' She rocks backwards and forwards, her hands pressed against her face. 'What have I done? Miklós, forgive me.'

And now Annika does something she has never done before. She takes her grandmother in her arms and holds Ilonka's frail, trembling body, and they cry together for the man who died with her name on his lips, for the love that was lost and can never be regained, for the fragility of being human, and for the redemptive power of truth and forgiveness that might now set them all free.

AUTHOR'S NOTE

A shiver ran down my spine when I first heard about Rezsö Kasztner. I recognised this shiver: it meant that this incredible story in the footnotes of history had captured my imagination and I had to write it. I already knew it would be a novel.

I had never heard of this man nor the feat he had achieved against all odds in Budapest in 1944, during the Holocaust in Hungary. The proliferation of memoirs, history books and novels that deal with some aspect of the Holocaust has continued unabated, probably because they shine a light on our human condition in extreme situations.

But this was different from any story I'd ever come across. The first time I heard it was from a Hungarian Holocaust survivor I knew who mentioned a rescue train organised by a Jew in Budapest in 1944. It seemed that Kasztner had somehow managed to save over a thousand Jews from the death camps. But what intrigued me even more than Kasztner's astonishing feat was this survivor's ambivalent attitude towards him. Kasztner was clearly a controversial character, and this alerted me to the possibility that this could be more than a heroic rescue story with a happy ending. From that moment, I sensed that this might be a story spiced with moral ambiguity, but I had no idea at that stage just how extraordinary this story really was.

Surprising coincidences have occurred with every one of my books, and this was no exception. When I told my friend David that I had become interested in the story of a man called Rezsö Kasztner, he was astonished. 'That's the man who rescued my sister-in-law's parents. They were on that train,' he said. He lent me a non-fiction book about the rescue, a vivid piece of historical research by Anna Porter called *Kasztner's Train*. By the time I'd finished reading it, I was thoroughly hooked. Kasztner had had the audacity to confront Adolf Eichmann, the most dreaded Nazi in Hungary, and, risking his life, negotiated with him for the release of a trainload of Jews at a time when Eichmann had arrived in Budapest to send the last surviving Jewish community in Europe to the gas chambers of Auschwitz.

As I proceeded to research the story, I became increasingly intrigued by the contradictory assessments made about him by historians and survivors. There was Kasztner's own account of his activities and those of the Rescue Committee, naturally written from his point of view. Some writers deified him as a hero, while others vilified him as a collaborator. I have always been fascinated by the behaviour of ordinary people thrust into extraordinary situations, and the story of Rezsö Kasztner was an outstanding illustration of this.

The questions implicit in his story challenged me throughout my research. Was he a hero or a collaborator? Was it possible to be both? Was it a case of the proverb that no good deed goes unpunished? Can the end justify the means? Were human actions able to be judged in absolutes? Should a promise always be kept regardless of the circumstances in which it was made? What would I have done in his situation? Would I have remained a passive onlooker, or, trusting that even one person can make a difference, would I have found the courage to take action?

As I continued to read about Kasztner, I was shocked to discover that the rescue had consequences that no-one could have foreseen. This wasn't just a story about a daring rescue: it was a tale of vengeance and injustice ending in tragedy. And although it took place so long ago, to this day, Kasztner remains a controversial figure in Israel.

Absorbed as I was by the story of this extraordinary individual and his audacious feat, I discovered that the Kasztner affair had an unexpected historical background which blew me away with its revelations of behind-the-scenes machinations by top Nazi figures and the western powers. It seems that history, like personal relationships, is a complex tapestry interweaving infinite threads. Uncovering one leads to the discovery of unsuspected layers that lie beneath.

The Collaborator is based on true events. The *Altalena* incident took place in 1948, in the early days of Israel's independence. Eichmann did arrive in Budapest in 1944 to exterminate the last Jewish community in Europe, and Kurt Becher was a prominent Nazi. Rezsö Kasztner did confront Eichmann at the Majestic Hotel, and later negotiated with Kurt Becher, for whom he wrote an incriminating affidavit after the war. After migrating to Israel, Kasztner was groomed for a role in the government when he was accused of collaboration by a pamphleteer. The trial scenes and their aftermath are also based on proceedings in the Jerusalem courts, as is their tragic outcome. The historical bombshell that was dropped during the testimony of some characters actually took place and is based on fact.

Writing a novel that is based on real people and historical events poses considerable challenges for a novelist. Although my protagonist, Miklós Nagy, is based on Rezsö Kasztner, I have fictionalised many aspects of the story. I have invented conversations and characters, and I have ascribed thoughts and motives to real people that owe more to my imagination than to reality, although I have tried to be psychologically consistent. For instance, although I know why Kasztner met Eichmann and Becher, I have fictionalised their conversations. And although the pamphleteer's attorney did have a secret agenda, I have fictionalised him and his backstory.

While the character of Miklós Nagy is based on Rezsö Kasztner, I'd like to emphasise that the people in Miklós's life and his relationships with them are entirely fictional. I have invented the characters of Judit, Ilonka, Ben, Gil and Eitan.

All the characters in the Australian strand of the plot — Annika, her mother and grandmother — are fictional, as is that part of the plot.

In the course of researching this novel, I visited Budapest, Tel Aviv and Jerusalem, and read historical accounts of the history and politics of Israel and Hungary. I also read about the tragedies of Euripides and Sophocles which proved relevant in my exploration of what in many ways resembles a Greek tragedy.

ACKNOWLEDGEMENTS

First of all, I'd like to thank my publisher Jo Mackay. She had the foresight to see the possibilities of my manuscript right from the beginning, and her enthusiasm never wavered. I'm very lucky to have such a warm and understanding publisher, and such a supportive and enthusiastic team at HQ as the super-efficient Annabel Blay, Natika Palka and Adam van Rooijen.

It's been a joy to work with my editor Linda Funnell. Throughout the editing process, I've been awed by her intelligence, attention to detail, patience and impeccable literary taste. Her insightful suggestions have eliminated repetitions and strengthened the plot. Any mistakes are my own.

The day Selwa Anthony became my literary agent was a very lucky day for me. Selwa has always been indefatigable in her efforts on my behalf, and she has championed this novel from the very first moment. Her encouragement and belief in me throughout the years have been very nurturing.

My friend Dasia Gutman has been a valuable sounding board for the anxieties and frustrations I've had while writing, and I appreciate her wise counsel. Every book brings its own set of challenges, and it never gets any easier, but pointing out that I've moaned about exactly the same issues while writing my previous books has been revealing and helpful.

Thank you to my friends Susi B, Susie W, Peter, Gabby and Egon, for helping me with Hungarian names and accents.

The encouragement and interest shown by my children Justine and Jonathan, my daughter-in-law Adrianne, and my granddaughters Sarah, Maya and Allie, have been heart-warming. Allie, you told me you couldn't wait to read this novel, so finally here it is! Thanks also to Jonathan for his patience in taking the head shot.

I appreciate the work of Kate James, who did such a great job proofreading this manuscript.

Lastly, my deepest gratitude to Bert who shares my life. I handed you each chapter as soon as I'd written it, and I couldn't wait for your reaction. You stopped whatever you were doing to read them, and your comments were always thoughtful, positive and illuminating. Living with an author who is obsessed with her novel is an excellent test of a relationship, but thanks to your understanding, love and support we have passed with flying colours!

SELECTED READING

The Kasztner Report: the report of the Budapest Jewish Rescue Committee 1942–1945, by Rezső Kasztner; edited by László Karsai and Judit Molnár, Yad Vashem (The International Institute for Holocaust Research), 2014

The Man who was Murdered Twice: the life, trial and death of Israel Kasztner, by Yechiam Weitz (translated by Chaya Naor). Yad Vashem (The International Institute for Holocaust Research), 2012

The Making of Modern Israel 1948–1967, by Leslie Stein. Polity Press, 2009

Perfidy, by Ben Hecht. Messner Press, 1961 (reissued 1997)

Kasztner's Train: the true story of an unknown hero of the Holocaust, by Anna Porter, Scribe, 2008

Jews for Sale?: Nazi-Jewish Negotiations 1933–1945, by Yehuda Bauer. Yale University Press, 1994.

Reszso Kasztner: the daring rescue of Hungarian Jews, a survivor's account, by Ladislaus Löb. Pimlico (an imprint of Penguin Random House UK), 2009

Into the Darkroom, by Susan Faludi. Metropolitan Books (an imprint of Henry Holt, US), 2016

The Theatre of War: what ancient Greek tragedies can teach us today, by Bryan Doerries. Scribe, 2015

talk about it

Let's talk about books.

Join the conversation:

 facebook.com/harlequinaustralia

 @harlequinaus

 @harlequinaus

harpercollins.com.au/hq

If you love reading and want to know about our
authors and titles, then let's talk about it.